HARPAN'S WORL[D]S:

WORL

HARPAN'S WORLDS:
WORLDS APART

TERRY JACKMAN

Elsewhen Press

Harpan's Worlds: Worlds Apart
First published in Great Britain by Elsewhen Press, 2022
An imprint of Alnpete Limited

Elsewhen Press, PO Box 757, Dartford, Kent DA2 7TQ
www.elsewhen.press

British Library Cataloguing in Publication Data.
A catalogue record for this book is available from the British Library.

ISBN 978-1-915304-07-0 Print edition
ISBN 978-1-915304-17-9 eBook edition

Designed and formatted by Elsewhen Press

CONTENTS

FOREWORD

Dear Reader,

If you enjoy the read, please consider leaving a few words on the site of your choice; all writers really appreciate feedback.

My thanks go out:

To Elsewhen Press, who took on this book in the midst of covid, even though they weren't officially accepting new submissions. I hope I didn't cause you all too many nightmares, especially Pete and Sofia.

To the BFS and BSFA, whose volunteers work hard to bring SF readers and writers in from an often lonely sense of isolation.

To the Milford Conference, and its offshoot 'up north', NorthwriteSF, where those lucky enough to be published can escape the everyday world and access some awe-inspiring critiques. And stay human, occasionally.

Finally, to all the Clatterbridge teams, without whom it's quite possible nothing of mine, past or present, would have reached print at all.

Terry Jackman
29th September 2022

1

'So, you see how it is, son?' Old man Goss slumped back behind the homemade table.

'Yessir.' Now he knew why Missus hadn't cleared their evening meal before she disappeared, or looked him in the eye while they were eating. He was being moved around again to suit the govment's orphan-budget and to pay the Goss's land-bill; he was going to have to leave the only decent billet fostering had ever got him. So what if the Goss's 'boys' still sometimes picked on him to do their screen-chores cos it took them so much longer. Even, once, to sit their End-of-Education grade-tests. He'd done that, and welcome. Getting them a better wage rate helped their grandparents, and Mr Seth and Missus Destra had been good to him, way better than the prior fosters he'd been stuck with. But now the Gosses had to pay the tithe, and he was what they had to pay with cos he didn't have no planet-rights yet. Not their fault. Not his. But dammit. 'When, sir?'

'Militia cruiser comes collecting end of the month. They'll test you. If you suit...'

A test? So if he failed, which he could...

Then Mr Seth and Missus Destra might default and lose their ranch, and all their years of work was wasted, never mind it wasn't their fault. And they'd more than likely lose their old age privileges too. The govment out there on the bigger planet wasn't kind to failures, didn't seem to count the reasons.

The old man sighed. 'But you try real hard for them, Harp, hear me? You're not dumb, so you impress those townies all you can, and mebbe you'll do better there than here, see? Make yourself a proper future.'

'Yessir, I see.' There didn't seem much else to talk about. Harp got up from the battered table. 'Guess I'll get to bed then. Work tomorrow.'

'Yeah, g'night. And Harp, I'm real sorry, son.'

He looked it.
Didn't change anything, though.

+++

'Hey, Grik, you up there? What we collecting this time, meat, plant-stuff, or actual credit?'

Private Bays cast a jaundiced look across the barren-looking ground outside the cruiser's ramp. Their bloody captain couldn't land them near this homestead, friendly like. Oh no; the blasted Worlder always had to make folk ride for miles on those hulking rangers Bays would rather stay well clear of. *And* make him stand watch in all this heat for bloody hours. He could feel the burning air out there from here – and he didn't care what anybody said, being darker-skinned *didn't* make it more comfortable. How could it? Over half Moon's southern landmass looked like this now, grey and brown and dust-hazed when you looked from orbit, nothing like the climate even of his childhood. He'd heard someone saying if they didn't get some decent rain this year their whole damn planet would be bankrupt. Rumours going round on their new Orbital were claiming somebody on World cut corners on the terraforming of their smaller neighbour; said they even had "contingencies" to relocate Moon's settlers – mostly not-so-golden skins who'd been replanted here, once World began to fill, to work the mines and feed the bigger homeworld.

Bays shook his head. That last couldn't be right, cos if it *was* wouldn't *both* worlds starve? He shrugged away unease, a man who liked his life kept simple. Simple, like come rain or drought the militia still had to collect the tithes, though… 'How these farmers pay us these days is beyond me.'

'You didn't hear?' Corporal Grik, the nearest thing they had for medic, muttered in his earpiece. 'This one can't. We got ourselves a body-payment this time.'

'Crip, a conscript? Bet the Sarge is happy.'

'I'd be happier if people kept their minds on sentry

duty,' Mullah growled from right behind him.

'Yes, Sarge. But these bloody hills are blocking scan again, and nobody's in sight yet.' Which made these farmers late, if Sarge was here. Sarge wouldn't like that, 'specially if their stuck-up captain started griping. Only then a head appeared above the nearest hilltop to the east and grew into a single figure, pretty much an outline with the barely risen sun behind it, head protected by the locals' wide-brimmed hat. The silhouette came trudging down the distant slope toward the cruiser. Neither man said anything until the shape got close enough their wind-scraped goggles picked up details. Tallish, thin, a youth who'd maybe had a growing spurt, his clothes a size behind him.

As if he felt their gaze the youngster raised his head. They got a sight of knife-sharp, angled cheekbones then a flash of longish, red-gold hair that curled a bit beneath the hat brim, striking features none of them had ever thought to see out here. Bays whistled, glancing sideways at the taller sergeant. 'Oo-ee, you see that?'

'It doesn't matter what he looks like, private,' Mullah grated as the stranger's footsteps faltered for a moment, likely staring at the ugly cruiser that had razed the brittle growth into a blackened circle round them. Then the kid walked on, head down again, same plodding farmer pace, expression hidden by that hat brim.

'Not much of him,' Bays remarked, 'You think he'll pass, Sarge?'

'Let's hope so, otherwise we'll have to serve another penalty and then come back for the eviction.' Mullah started down the ramp, his boots a ringing impact on the pitted metal.

+++

Crossing from shade to sunlight meant stepping out of hot to oven-roasting. Mullah's goggles took a second to adjust as usual. No wonder farmboy didn't hurry. How far had he walked? Perhaps he wouldn't tear him off a strip for being late? He thumbed his wristcom. 'Mullah to bridge. Conscript's in sight, on foot and alone.' A long walk in this heat. Another back? Either someone was convinced he'd pass, or didn't like him.

The captain's oh-so-cultured voice came back. 'He's late. Proceed with the inspection. If he passes dock his pay.' And gone.

The sergeant grunted. Regis liked his bodies from Militia's sketchy basic training so, he said, at least they knew their left foot from their right. After a year here the man still seemed convinced all Mooners were stupid. Just cos most of them couldn't quote their ancestors back to Founding any more, nor didn't boast about it like Worlders... The captain also liked to suck up to the brass whenever they were docked, although the man was downright lazy when on board the *Mercy*. But this kid, he could draw attention, which likely wouldn't suit the captain. If, of course, he passed inspection.

By the time the youth reached Mullah, Bays falling in behind, the sergeant had hit ground so hard it jarred his boots and had re-read the meagre file on his wristcom. Farmboy stopped, glanced up then down again; stayed in the shadow of the hat but that was normal out here in the ranges. Mullah thought they made a fine set between them; Bays stunted, scarred and all-the-way dark; himself big-boned and washed-out pale, where he wasn't sunburned; and this kid, golden-shaded hair and skin and pretty-featured. Hell, he even had the Founder's slanted eyes, cept his were kind of caramel where Founder eyes in all the vids he'd seen looked darker. Skin more bronze than golden if you wanted to be picky, but Moon's climate could have made it darker.

Up close the kid was as tall as Mullah, just a hell of a lot thinner. Govment issue clothes, coarse pants, plain shirt, beneath a handmade leather vest and belt. The sergeant's gaze slid lower. The heeled boots for riding herd weren't new, the leather cracked in places. Nondescript. But for the colouring, the features...

'Goss, is it?' The name on file, taken from his current fosters.

'Yessir.' Farmboy stood and waited as if used to waiting; didn't drop the duffle.

'Right. You know you need to pass a medical, and ap-test?'

'Sir.' The head was down but Mullah saw the swallow.

'Private Bays?'

'Sarge.'

'Escort Mr Goss here to medical, then to the wardroom.'

'Sarge.' Bays turned. The farmboy followed him into the cruiser. Mullah wondered what would happen when their oh-so-well-bred captain saw the new kid was more golden-skin than he was.

+++

Harp kept his head down as he trailed the man with the scar through the metal passageways. He'd never been close to a militia ship before; it was a lot bigger than he'd thought, and seemed to house an awful lot of people. But maybe that was him being ignorant. Well, the only real crowds he knew these days had six flat feet and chomped on pasture. He stifled a sigh; he guessed he'd get used to change, again. Your life was what you got, as Missus Destra said. And his? Was clearly labelled "reject".

Most of the looks he got so far were at least neutral. One wasn't; he noted that too. He'd already figured he'd have nowhere here to run.

The man ahead ducked through a smaller, brighter doorway, the light inside striking the scar on his cheek. 'Conscrip for a medical, Corporal.' He waved Harp in. Harp bent, stepped through and straightened, then went still. The corporal, whatever that was, was a woman?

One who turned round from a fancy screen-desk, looked him up and down but only raised her eyebrows. 'Thanks, Bays.'

'Want me to stay, Corp?' Bays stood in the entry, grinning.

'No, I think I'll manage.' That sounded like there was some kind of joke, one Harp was missing, but then that wasn't new, nor the worst of it. Bad enough if she was old like Missus, but she wasn't. Nor bony like Missus but that wasn't important either. He'd handled medicals every childhood year since the first scare, but he hadn't had to strip in front of a woman since he was, what, ten? Hell, he'd barely seen one. Not that the space in here was that different. Desk, tilted-up exam couch, storage doors was about it. It looked like the usual combi anyway, blood and DNA in one. While he was dithering the woman tapped more buttons, glancing down at something. 'Goss, is it?'

'Yes, ma'am.' There was no escape; he'd heard the metal door clack shut behind him.

'You can take off the hat. Roll up your sleeve.'

That all? He sure hoped. He took a breath; he'd always managed before, hadn't he. The hypo looked more streamlined than the foster-medics carried but it surely worked the same. He concentrated, heard the hiss and felt the sting, and let himself relax again when she retreated without comment. It was stupid, wishing. He was all growed up now. But he couldn't shake the memory, the way that medic's face had altered...

Maybe cos that was the first day he could remember. There was a blank before, except a hazy sense of screaming noise, then silence, but he had been pretty young then. They had washed him off, then poked and prodded. Fed him. Weighed him. Measured him. Told him his parents' house name, though he hadn't kept it long as they replaced it with his Orphan House name two days after. But they'd taken blood; he hadn't liked that. DNA as well perhaps, he'd been too young to notice. He'd submitted to these bigger strangers and their reassurances, more interested in food and water than their ministrations. "Miracle" they'd called it when they found he wasn't injured, nothing worse than scratches. Only then there'd been the exclamations.

He hadn't known what the fuss was about, just it was

about him and a "possible malfunction". Strange how words he didn't even understand back then stayed with him. It was obviously something bad though, cos he saw the way they changed, the way they turned and looked. He hadn't liked the word "abnormal" either. He'd preferred it when they smiled.

So when they came again, to do more poking, he had *wished* with all his heart the things they'd frowned at would behave this time and not cause trouble. And their faces cleared. They talked about "a faulty run" and all was well. They smiled. And so all his life that he remembered he had *wished* that every medical would show him normal. And they had done. And now he guessed he was too scared to do without it cos he'd wished again in here, and likely would again in future.

If he'd been distracted, didn't look like she had noticed. 'Prints here.' No worries there. His fingerprints went on a clear plate as usual, turned red then black then disappeared into their log. Would that be it?

'Strip off, then step in there.'

"There" was a narrow cupboard in the corner behind her, not even a door, but he figured it wasn't a request. He shucked the vest, the boots. The shirt. Then hesitated. Luckily the woman was pushing buttons again. He flipped the seal on his pants then dropped them fast and took himself inside that cupboard, facing inward. Least the worst was hidden now, the way the cupboard curled around him made this almost decent. And surprise, his shoulders didn't have much play in here. He must have grown again. Although the rest of him would fit in twice and then some.

'Stand quite still, please.'

'Yes, ma'am.' See, she didn't need you to turn round. It's–

A grey glass door slid out and shut him in here. What the?

+++

7

Curious, Mullah patched in from the multipurpose space the captain called the 'wardroom' just as the corporal pushed the scan button. She'd slouched against the desk now the youngster couldn't see her; he was probably feeling relieved about that. Mullah's lips twitched. The poor kid had actually blushed. Judging from his face he hadn't been in a scan tube before either.

Then she straightened. The external exam had appeared on her screen, and Mullah's. Oo-oo-ee. The kid might be half starved but there was muscle on him, and with all that hair, that face as well, this one could pose for naughty pictures for a living. Mullah knew a few would buy one.

But the kid was also underweight, and nervous, and an orphan – and could do without *that* sort of attention, cos he was going to have enough on dealing with the captain.

The internal scan started; Mullah heard a muffled yelp as it checked a few things the guys didn't enjoy but yes, the scan said A-OK, prime livestock, and he'd take a bet the kid'd pass the rest. A quick ten cred on Mr. Goss looked good, get in before the others saw him and the usual odds receded.

Mullah was still reading the medical transcript when Bays brought the kid into the only space not filled with bunks or mech, which could convert to storage for the extra tithe goods they'd collected. That left scant room for this single table. This time he was slow to look up from the screen. The kid had had the worst kind of luck, including being orphaned at four when a pirate raid flattened his homestead and he was the sole survivor. No mention of… other connections? No, he'd gone into the system same as any other orphan. One oddity; there were no recent images on file, nothing since he left Nursery. It looked like someone, several someones in the years between, had chosen not to make the kid's record any more noticeable than it needed. Bribes or kindness; playing politics, or just avoiding extra work some high-up might have caused them? But now he was eighteen, and underweight – too many Mooners were these days – but otherwise in perfect health.

Hang on, *perfect* health? A foster got the bare essentials, health-wise, yet there were no prior illnesses, or injuries? He'd never fallen off a ranger or been stomped on by a steer?

But med scans didn't lie. Mullah scowled. Maybe healthy genes were fate's payback for the kid's bad luck being born at all. He rose and gestured to the screen he'd pulled up from the one remaining table. 'Sit. You done screen tests before, right?'

'Yessir.' Steadier, no nervous swallow this time. Good, cos Mullah had already laid down money on him passing. Crip, it wasn't as if their so-called ap-test was much challenge.

'Right. First part's asking you where you been and what you done. After that there's what they call a General Aptitude Assessment, see if you're suited here. Clear? You've got an hour. If you finish early you report to Private Bays here. He'll be stood outside.'

'Yessir.' Definitely calmer now; maybe the kid just didn't like medicals.

+++

It was a pretty standard coord/intel test, almost dangerously easy, so Harp paced himself. Even then he finished early. "Do you wish to review your answers?" appeared. He knew most people did that so he tapped a yes and ran through the thirty questions again. A sudden fit of annoyance, maybe at himself, made him alter a few answers and up his score. Mr Seth had reckoned decent scores could earn him better treatment and he might be shut in this tin can a while, with all these strangers. Fosters weren't supposed to be too smart, he'd learned that early on, especially ill-bred ones. He was no genius, but maybe scoring halfway decent might be useful this time?

2

In the quiet of his berth – Militia cruisers only got one captain and one sergeant so the tiny single cabin was his refuge – Mullah also watched the screentest, this time on his wallscreen; kid was quick, say that much. He jumped back to the foster-records. Kids the govment paid for got no extras; mostly what they got was chores disguised as pre-employment. But this kid could read and write and figure, had some screen skills too; someone had taught him that much.

Back to check the test. Good scores appearing, for a foster, yet they'd dropped him on a nowhere-ranch to train as herder? Maybe no one more respectable would take him, or whoever took those bribes had orders to conceal him as an adult. On Harpan's World and Harpan's Moon your bloodlines were a point of law, the Founding Family insisted. Even if most born-Mooners were more tongue in cheek about saying so. Yeah, that would account for the poor records. The officials the kid'd crossed paths with might have looked down on him, but they must have been paid to lose him in the system. Being Moon, there'd likely been some sympathy mixed in with the greed.

Back to those records, starting to feel like his head was rotating. There'd been a glitch then though, the first farm gave him back at the end of his initial year even though he'd have been worth a better allowance after. They said he'd been too small. The sergeant frowned. But then the Goss place took him and that lasted – looked like he had settled.

Back to the kid's answers. He'd learned to ride herd, sleep outdoors, and some basic animal stuff. Not much use to them, even if one ranch this year had paid partly in hides. But he had also learned to shoot, like many farmboys. That was better. Maybe. By the time the kid signed off the test Mullah had organised the makeshift try-out he'd used a few times before out in the sticks…

'You learned on projectiles, I guess?'

'Yessir.' They were out in the sun again. The kid had put his hat back on, was still toting that duffle, but slid it to the dirt when Bays held out the simple mech-rifle, a model a lot of ranchers still used. The HR4 had an actual wooden stock, was scratched to hell and had to be a hundred years old; as basic as it got, but still reliable. The captain claimed the R meant Regis, that it was his House's merch. It seemed unlikely anyone sent here would be that well connected, but it was a decent weapon. More than Mullah could say for the new HUR67 deck-mounted uni-cannon Regis had just blown their budget on. If that was his House's too, all Mullah could say was their standards had slipped all round.

Mullah thumbed his com, got back to business. 'Target up.' Watched the kid's face when the target flickered. 'Holo. You seen one before?'

'Yessir, once, but not outside.' The kid looked back at the cruiser, as if he thought he'd see where the thing came from, but then he took a stance. It was, after all, obvious what Mullah wanted.

'It's set to two hundred metres. You have three rounds. Shoot when ready.' If any of those found the target they'd –

The rifle came up, steadied as the kid felt out the weight and balance, then a single shot rang out. The old projectiles were loud, but being outdoors compensated – not to mention he and Bays had activated ear plugs in their helmets. Which he'd swear were getting hotter by the minute. His wristcom confirmed the flashing blue marker; middle ring. Not bad. 'You see the marker?'

'Yessir.'

'Try again then.'

Two more shots, this time in quick succession; one red: inner ring, one black: a bull, dead centre too. Bays whistled, then went quiet when Mullah scowled. 'Hm. Used anything else?'

'Hand gun, sir, couple times.'

Couple times. The sergeant took a breath. 'Let's see

what you can do with a pulse.' Bays unpacked it, Mullah gave the kid a rundown on the basics; kid paid due attention. A pulse was almost a handgun but it did have a kick, and needed the two-handed grip he demonstrated. He neither mentioned, nor activated, the targeting software.

The kid took a few shots to get the hang of it then scored more bulls, the last two dead-on. By the time Mullah was showing him their only larger, sniper version, liquid-loaded and a real beauty, word had spread. There was a huddle in the shade inside the ramp, an audience the kid was so far unaware of. Either Bays had talked, or someone on the bridge had. Mullah wondered how they were reacting to the close up.

By now the target had shifted to five hundred. Once the kid got his eye in again Mullah called for eight. Then a thousand. Then saw the kid's arms shaking. At his nod, Bays took the weapon back. 'Secure weapons, Private. Looks like you have a rookie to get settled.'

'Yes, Sarge.' Bays' grins made him evil, the scar on one cheek twisting his mouth some, but the kid didn't blink.

'Goss, Private Bays here will buddy you for now, get you set up, a meal. The captain might want to see you later, so make sure you look presentable.' A speaking look at Bays, who pulled a face, then Mullah strode back up the ramp into the blessed cool, the unofficial watchers scattering before him. Now all he'd got to do was tell the captain.

+++

Bays watched Mullah disappear then turned to Harp. 'You know how to stow the guns?' He jerked his head toward the weapon cases.

'I know that one.' Harp walked over to the old rifle, sitting on its carrycase.

'Prove it.' Done, in no time. 'Huh, OK, now watch and learn.' The kid watched then repacked, fast and fine. Bays began to think being nursemaid might not be so bad. 'Now we lug 'em back to lower deck twelve, that's L12 from now on.' That led to a quick rundown on reading the cruiser's signage. 'This cruiser's named *Mercy*, bless her. Only got two real decks to worry about, plus the hold, that's underneath, and upper deck's ops and officer territory. You don't go there less you're on duty, got it?'

'Yessir.'

'I'm not sir, I'm Bays. Sir's for sergeants and above, corporals get corporal, right?'

'Yes-' The hint of a frown.

Bays tried to recall what it was like being a rookie, new words, new rules, and for a foster… 'We walk on the right, left's for folk coming the other way. If somebody yells "Make a hole" we, like, flatten, or duck through the nearest hatch.'

'Make a hole.' A nod, face partly hidden. He ought to tell the kid to take that hat off but between the weapons cases and that duffle… aw, the sergeant wouldn't bawl him out, nor would the corporals, and the captain hardly ever came down here.

+++

"Armoury" meant a small hole in the metal wall, it seemed. A woman checked the guns back on a screen set in the metal. She was older than the medic woman, old enough to have grey hair, but was another corporal; Bays said so. The big sergeant, Mullah, had three curved stripes beneath the Harpan H on his coverall shoulders. Bays had none, this woman and the medic had two. More stripes was higher then? Harp filed that for later. This corporal gave him an up and down too, with the same pursed lips, but didn't comment. More polite so far than he had feared.

After that Bays took him "forward" to a "hatch" labelled L8, which Bays called "General Stores"; more names and numbers to remember. He came out of there with his arms full, his uniform and such, Bays said. No one had asked his size but maybe they already knew; he hoped so cos he certainly didn't. In his world, size had always meant what someone else thought looked right, held against you.

'Right, now we find you a bunk and get you pre-sentable, and then we eat.' They went "forward" some more till Bays pulled the clamps on another "hatch" marked L3, and ducked through into light, and chatter. It was a long room with bunks three high on one side and lockers on the other. And a sudden silence. 'Got us a rookie, here.' Bays waved at Harp. 'Sarge says keep him pre-sentable, and he'll take it out on me if he ain't. We clear?' Movement. Rude remarks from a half dozen bodies Harp assumed were currently off duty, but they pretty much stopped staring. Bays was protecting him? Why? What would he owe him? Playing dumb, Harp trailed Bays down the room. 'Here, this one's free.' A bottom bunk, so he'd have to put up with other folk sitting on it. 'Make it up later, you better get changed now before the chow bell sounds.'

There weren't any women in here, so he was fine with dropping everything on the bunk and letting Bays play teacher, shoving things at him and explaining them. There was shorts and tees; he hadn't had those for a while. New too. Stripping off around other males wasn't new, and he had to see how they reacted sometime, so he got right to it. He had the slick-feeling dark grey coverall they all wore up to his waist and was pulling the tee over his head when the hatch swung inward and two women entered, with another man behind them.

The women oohed, the man let out a rumbling yowl; someone burst out laughing. All three looked him up and down and Harp could feel his face grow hotter as he tugged the tee shirt down and turned away to seal the suit up. Not that that felt so much better; he hadn't noticed till he fastened it how… clingy… it became. Sitting down felt safer and he had to pull the boots on anyway – until they startled him by clicking shut around his ankles. How did he get them off again? He'd have to ask about that.

Later. Face it, he'd probably have to ask a lot.

The women slid past him to bunks at the inner end where they perched casually, one above the other, adding things to nifty pockets on the recessed walls, then looked at him again. The new man halted by the door – no, hatch – and leaned against a locker, watching him without expression. Not that Harp was obviously looking, but his sideways vision had always been good. Good enough to spot the double curves on this man's shoulders. Top dog here then? But Bays had stepped in front of him. 'Yeah, rookie, ladies – and my buddy, right? No hazing.'

The women smiled and shrugged. The big man grinned. 'You calling dibs, Private?' Something changed around them, more attentive.

'Figure that's up to him, Corporal Sanchez.'

'We'll see then.' Big man's gaze went back to Harp.

Harp sighed. 'He's here, listening.' From Nursery to farm, it never ended. He was really tired of being "pretty". He would hope that talking worked, cos talking his way out of trouble hurt less.

Sanchez chuckled. 'So he is then. Does he have a name?'

Harp spoke up first this time. '*He's* Goss, Corporal.'

A female voice above his head said, 'Nah, he can't be, captain's orders; no two names alike, an' being as we're both so pretty too we wouldn't want 'im to confuse us, would we?' When Harp looked it was clear the woman meant to joke. Not that she wasn't pretty, she was, but she was a lot shorter than him and every bit as dark as Bays. No way would anyone who looked confuse them.

Even so it was apparently important to this captain, judging from the shared reaction.

'Damn, I clean forgot you'd got your single name back, Goss.' Bays looked at Harp. 'You gotta first name, kid. A given?'

Blast it. 'Harpan,' adding quickly, 'but folk mostly call me Harp.'

The corporal straightened slowly. 'Harpan? Like the Founding Family?'

'There's no connection.' Saw the disbelief around him, yet again. 'It was the name they gave me in the Orphan House, OK? I didn't choose it.'

Sanchez shook his head, perhaps in disbelief. 'Crip, stupid move, we'll have nothing but trouble if you hit Orbital with that label. Harp, you said? Right, Harp it is, I'll set it up before the captain sees you.' Sanchez's hand went to his wrist. 'Harp, private third class, berth L-three, bunk… where are you, six, on record as of… now.' So he *was* the boss in here. He finished tapping as a muted whistle sounded. 'Right, show's over. Chow time, children.'

'Yes, Corp,' came a cheerful chorus. Bodies undulated through the hatchway. Sanchez looked him up and down again as Harp approached with Bays, who disappeared. Only the two of them left. 'Crip, curls as well. When you've eaten come back here, get squared away, get the name patches on and get your hair cut, Private.'

'Si– Yes, Corp.' Harp stood back to let the other man out first.

The man looked back. 'You do know who you look like, kid?'

'Yes, Corp.' How could he not. He saw the vids each Founder's Day. Officialdom might seem not to notice his existence, but he'd grown up being called a Founder bastard, and could hardly argue what his own reflection proved so clearly.

'Yeah, well, keep your head down, specially near our captain, right?'

'Yes, Corp.' More a friendly warning than an inquisition. Nothing like as bad as some new starts he'd weathered. Harp followed the rest to L5 where the "crew's mess" turned out another contradiction; it was very tidy, and the ship's canteen, at least for corporals and lower. Everybody queued, but everybody stopped what they were doing for the few minutes it took an odd-sounding voice on com to recite the Thanksgiving, thanking everybody for their contribution, others for their food and such, the Founding Family for giving them their planet. Here people stopped, listened, muttered the 'thankyous' then went back to whatever they'd been in the middle of. It felt wrong, but Mr Seth had warned Harp these folks had to work in shifts, so he supposed they couldn't really wait till everybody sat together. Noise swelled up again. It looked like talking was allowed here, but he kept his head down.

More crew behind another metal counter – only bigger – doled out shockingly large portions. It might be the largest meal he'd ever seen, bar a Settlement Day spread. He followed Bays to a long, narrow table bolted to the floor – no, deck – and tried to relax enough to eat the feast before him; one that several others griped at? Maybe this move wouldn't be so bad, if he could deal with all the scary women.

Mullah escorted him to the upper deck two days later. He'd inspected Harp first, nodded at the shorter hair courtesy of Other-Goss – who he now owed five cred out of some future payday. Pursed his lips at the packet-creases in the grey coverall.

'Right, stand straight, hands at your sides, head up. Don't look him in the eye, don't speak less you're spoken to. His House name's Regis, but you call him sir or captain. Got all that?'

'Yes, Sarge.'

'Right then.' Did Mullah take a breath before he hit the button flashing green beside the panel labelled 'Captain'?

'Yes.'

'Sergeant Mullah, sir. You wanted to see the new recruit.'

A pause then, 'Come.' Unlike the noisy hatches on the lower deck the entry opened sideways and without a murmur, and the room, office, beyond was the fanciest place he'd ever seen. There was a big, shiny-metal desk, and wall screens showing images he thought might be places on World, cos they had colours he'd never seen before. And the captain wore a fancy uniform, a jacket looked like it might reach his knees with bits of gold at neck and shoulders. The man didn't look up, didn't speak either. Mullah had stopped in front of the desk, planted his feet and just stood – so Harp did the same, eyes front as Mullah put it. The place wasn't so big he couldn't see everything anyways. This Regis guy had one hell of a chair – it reached up past the man's head and looked like a whole steer had gone into covering it. Harp had to figure it was meant to impress. Unfortunately, what it did was make its occupant look smaller.

Regis looked shorter than Mullah and him. Paler skinned too, like he didn't spend much time outdoors, with maybe a hint of golden there that Harp associated with important. He wasn't bad looking in a round-faced, boyish fashion, only what he made Harp think of most was vermin; sleeked back, very dark brown hair, a narrow nose and somehow kind of… slinky.

A drawer in the storage part of the desk wasn't quite closed – like maybe he'd shoved something in before he opened the door – and he was pretending to read the screen pulled up from his desk but his eyes weren't tracking across. He was just making them wait. Not a new experience for Harp, but telling cos the man was also being rude to Mullah, and he'd figured out by then that Mullah was respected.

Eventually the man signed off on something and raised his head, ignoring Mullah in favour of looking at Harp. Regis' dark eyes weren't as angled as Harp's but they almost looked it now the way the man was sneering. '*This* is the recruit?'

'Yes, sir. Private Harp.' Mullah sounded like the name wasn't important, but it clearly was to Regis.

'He actually calls himself Harp?'

Harp, used to being either bottom of the bucket or an embarrassment, forced his gaze onto one of the screens behind the captain, showing what he thought were flowers. New place, new name. But old disdain, like being branded. But he recognised the voice. It was a live version of the ship's Thanksgiving recording, the sharper, sing-song accent he'd eventually realised was Worlder. That was why it sounded out of place here. The Head of the House, as it were, so that hadn't changed. Except this 'father figure' didn't do the thanks in person.

Right now this Head of House didn't look at all thankful. Or sound it. 'Surely conscript-recruits are at our discretion, Sergeant, not mandatory?'

'Legitimate recruit procedure since last year, sir, as per revised regulations.'

'Legitimate.' The captain's sneer resurfaced. Harp tried not to wince.

'Yes, sir. In the regs, sir.' Mullah's voice stayed wooden.

'Oh, very well, but I really don't appreciate recruits foisted on us in the middle of our tour of duty. It will lower our performance levels.' The man stared up at Harp. 'No, Sergeant. Ap-test or not, if you can't drag this one up to somewhere near acceptable by my next crew inspection, he's out. I won't have anyone substandard.'

This guy meant to dump him, and it sounded like that'd be wherever the ship landed next. Without pay? Suddenly the cruiser looked a lot worse than he'd begun to believe.

This Regis wasn't finished. 'Yes, we have the good name of the ship to consider, Sergeant. We can't just take in any mongrel who strolls onboard. But I suppose we must give this one a chance. Very well, till next inspection. Dismissed.'

The final words sounded more reasonable but as Harp copied Mullah and turned to go he caught a glimpse of teeth. The mask had slipped, pure rage slipped through. This wasn't the common, casual disdain of many Mooners. This must be the real, World-bred, 'Family is all-important' version both the Harpan worlds were built on. This was trouble.

He could feel Mullah's eyes on him too, once they hit the corridor. 'Won't deny that was nasty, him being Worlder-bred, see, but with any luck he won't want to set eyes on you again for a while.'

That feeling was mutual. Harp's turn to draw breath. 'Not the first time, Sarge. I'll live.'

The sergeant's mouth curved upward. 'Yeah? Guess

we'd better get you up to scratch then.'

'Yes, Sarge.' Harp already had it figured; Regis aimed to get rid of him, leave him stranded somewhere with the clothes he stood in. Which would also ruin the Gosses cos their tithe would still be down as owing. But *he* owed the Gosses, and Mr Seth had reckoned he could do this. And he'd never been as easy to push around as strangers thought. And maybe Sarge would help, cos he sure looked as if he had a mind to.

Bring it on then.

3

Half a year later…

Mercy had landed, curls of smoke around her but no fire, yet. Harp quick-released his harness, saw his new, reluctant buddy copy. 'All set, Ludwiz?'

No response, again. No matter, do the job. 'Got a full canteen? Bandana? Deck gloves? Blisters get infected easy.'

Ludwiz, Harp's age but lankier, just looked insulted by the questions. Buddying a guy who took one look at him then turned his nose up wasn't fun; Ludwiz sussing out Harp never did the training course on Orbital hadn't helped any either. But Mullah wanted it so Harp kept trying. Ludwiz was a townie, maybe didn't really get the danger even if he'd heard some lectures. Hence the checklist. 'Pulse charged up? Spare clip? The steers, they can panic.' Ludwiz finally looked nervous. Good, cos a new coverall and a snappy salute were worth crip-all 'gainst sky-high flames or a stampede. Harp hid a sigh. Being a buddy was harder now than when Bays had buddied him, but at least *Mullah* thought he knew enough to be one.

He'd made it past that first crew inspection. OK, by the skin of his teeth, more thanks to Mullah than himself. And the fact Regis'd known even less. He'd spent a few weeks in orbit on Moon's half-built way-station – what they called its Orbital – but most of the rest on board ship. Even in that time things had changed. Suddenly official channels were talking about "civil unrest", and there'd been this rash of newbies filling out their crew lists. The little planet he inhabited – he'd learned Moon was a misnomer; yes, it was smaller than World but wrong sort of orbit – was barely a dot in the empty universe beyond, but right now it was an increasingly unhappy dot. The drought hadn't let up. Times were hard. But Militia ships were still sent round to gather tithes. Also, increasingly, to quell a population grown rebellious. A population now protesting that the Family on Harpan's World took everything they had and gave back very little.

Shipboard update called such rumours nonsense. Cited new govment emergency programmes instigated by the Founder himself, no less, a "personal response to their plight". Which seemed only fair, seeing as how the two worlds belonged to the Family. Further updates said the Family "had despatched relief cargoes" so maybe things would start to improve.

But unrest wasn't today's problem and at least Ludwiz wasn't one of Regis' new pets, or he'd never have allowed him to be paired with Harp. And unlike some of them, he did do his share of the chores. Right now the guy was checking his pulse, actually listening at last. 'Good.' Harp tried for encouraging. Apparently that was insulting too, but he told himself insulted was better than unprepared. 'Let's go then. Watch your six, keep your place in the line and you'll be fine.' He hoped so.

+++

Day Two: Smoke and embers fogged the scorching air, the fire was getting closer. Harp had talked Mullah into sending Ludwiz to the rear, on reloading duty rather than the firebreak; the poor guy looked ready to drop. Or weep. But Bays had come forward instead. Now Bays hopped from one foot to the other, cursing as he crossed the hard-baked ground. 'I think my boots are melting.' When Harp laughed, his smaller crewmate rolled his eyes above his own bandanna. 'How d'you always find a cooler patch?'

'I don't.' Harp paused to wipe his face with *his* bandanna. 'Ranch hand; used to heat.' He'd noticed he stood these temperatures better than most, certainly better than Bays. 'You want some water?' Bays' need was greater. His canteen was always empty, whereas Harp had been raised on lower water rations. When Bays nodded Harp unclipped his canteen.

Tugging the non-uniform bandanna – even Regis wore one these days when they landed – back across his nose and mouth, Harp played the heat gun over yet another swathe of scrub; it curled then blackened. They were fighting fire with fire. If he'd had the time he'd figure that was weird, but he'd stopped worrying about it. Bays tossed the canteen back, dropped in behind and started beating crumpled growth to even safer ashes.

Was the fire slowing, finally? Small hope unless this wind dropped. It'd ruined miles of the meagre pasture steers and ranchers needed and it clearly didn't want to die yet, but it was, once more, their job to kill it – theirs and *Faithful*'s this time. *Charity,* the third cruiser, was busy lifting someone's precious steers to safety. They'd be getting stomped on; *Mercy*'s crew were down here getting broiled. Regis, naturally, had stayed on *Mercy*, dumping tons of dirt to try to douse the fire. And had almost buried some of *Faithful*'s crew the day before by over-shooting. Other-Goss, on *Mercy*'s com, had happily repeated what the *Faithful*'s captain yelled at Regis. 'Words a lady wouldn't recognise, much less come out with.' She had chuckled. 'Good thing I'm no lady or I couldn't share them. Regis went bright red and stalked off to his cabin. Haven't seen him for an hour but Hobar said he had his feet up, drinking caffee.'

While Bays was coughing again, bent double, hand raised to his scarf. Harp had just replaced one worry with another. 'Need a break? You could go fetch another heat gun.' The more fires they fought, the more the other man had trouble breathing.

'Nah, I'm good.' Bays shook his head and went back to work. Harp tried to keep an eye on him. A decent captain might have kept him on board ship or signed him off to wear a breather, but Regis called his cough malingering and Bays was always ground crew. So was Harp, but he expected that from Regis and if truth be told he didn't mind it.

Harp would never admit it but he both hated and loved the prairie fires. Hated them for the hopes, and lives, they destroyed. Loved their awesome beauty. Even liked the choking air and furnace heat all round him, liked the way it filled his lungs and made him feel somehow lighter. Yep, riding herd had definitely made him tougher than these townies. A glance round told him the fire break was starting to look real at last; maybe this one would work and they could finally take a break.

The man next in line, another newbie, one of *Faithful*'s, had more bush than scrub to clear. Harp debated helping out. They had strict orders to stay in their lines, but if the guy was still behind next time he checked…

Right now most of *Mercy* were feeling obliging. *Faithful*'s crew hadn't blamed them for the deadly avalanche of dirt, the frantic digging out; their curses had been aimed exclusively at *Mercy's* distant captain. Harp contemplated that; if other crews knew where to point blame he figured at least some of their officers did too, yet Regis never acted anything but –

Someone shouted. Harp swung round. The wind had changed again, sparks flew, the fire was shifting, and as if it knew, a lick of flame was heading straight toward the next man's thinner stretch of firebreak. Within seconds it was at the beaten ashes, seemed to hover, hesitate, and he began to think – but then it hopped and skipped across the bushes, clean across the almost-cleared ground and pounced on better eating. Round him, others yelled and ran. The other fellow didn't, stood there gaping. Harp was close enough to see the terror in his eyes above a frayed bandanna as the fire spread. He pulled his own scarf down and shouted, 'This way, quick!' The fire was trying to trap him too, the stranger maybe hadn't heard him, missed him waving in the crackling, smoke-filled air between them. Now he was bent double. Time to go, and there was only one way out; the hard way. Pouring the last of his precious water over his bandanna Harp yanked it tight and ran toward the spot the other guy had been in, tripped over him and hefted him onto one shoulder, spun and raced the wind, part of the fire. The smoke got thicker, and the heat. He thought he heard the man he carried screaming, or perhaps it was the fire, but they were still moving, wind still at his back, the fire all around him. Fire, screaming. Smoke and ashes…

The wind, the smoke, still tried to steer him forward, but the crackling flames were gone and he could hear the other crewman retching.

A confusion of sounds replaced the roar. Hands tugged the weight off him, slapped at him. Somebody – his eyes were full of smoke – was bawling orders. Someone closer – Bays? – shouted "Run!" and pulled at him, uphill it felt like. He could hear engines growling, louder than the fire. 'Harp? Crip, someone – Here.' Water splashed his face. 'You see now?' Bays stopped talking to cough too. 'You're crazy, you know that, right?' Bays was still tugging him on.

Harp wiped at his eyes and tried to keep up. 'Guy… all right?'

'Move. *Faithful*'s got to lift.' Ah, that was the rush. Harp blinked water. Yep, the cruiser was hovering at the crest of the hill. Two crew were carrying their man onboard – and Bays was coughing, doubling over.

In the end Harp wasn't sure who helped who up the ramp. What was certain was the fire almost beat them to it, but hands grabbed onto them and *Faithful* lifted as the ramp came up behind them. The threat was over, for the moment.

Harp turned down the breather after a couple gulps. Truth to tell, he only took it to be polite, Bays needed it more than he did. But he wasn't saying no to the offer of a shower while they were airborne, or the hurried sit-down meal, another thing he hadn't had since all this started. So two hours later when they reached the rendezvous he walked off *Faithful* clean and fed and watered and in working order and he didn't care if Regis scowled. *Faithful*'s captain had come down to shake his hand, had said the man he'd saved should heal once they got him back to Orbital and borrowed navy's regen. And Harp himself was fine if he ignored the partly melted boot soles and some charring on his jacket. Well, maybe a bit redder than usual, but nothing worth mentioning. He was OK; no call for fussing.

Which was just as well cos Regis put him straight on cleanup, since he'd "obviously had it easy dodging work on Faithful". Yep, back to normal, till the next time. But he'd rather fight the fires than face another bankrupt settler.

Bays's feelings weren't that different, judging by his words next time they landed.

+++

'Crip! Damned if I wouldn't take firefighting over days like this.' The wind swirled again, picking up more dirt and dust, and Bays stopped bitching to cough up whatever had gone in his mouth. Mullah flashed him a look, then gave up. Corporal Sanchez had transferred out a while ago, but Mullah was still stuck here. Harp figured that was cos Regis realised he couldn't do the job without him.

The rest of them kept their mouths shut, pulled up bandanas and collars. They weren't wearing helmets today cos Regis had one of his new pets *polishing* the things; they were due back on the Orbital and Regis seemed to think they'd get inspected. So the Militia coveralls were about all that identified them, pretty normal these days; uniformity had given way to improvisation. Nobody looked exactly alike and nobody looked happy, but then nobody was looking forward to the coming confrontation. Farms were bad enough now, but a township meant they'd have to deal with a sight *more* angry people.

When Harp had joined, Militia's standing orders called these landings a "public relations opportunity". It was "Community Policing" in the manual – which he'd ended up renting with his own wages the first time he went up to the new Orbital, because Regis wouldn't clear him to read the bloody on-board version he was meant to learn from. Wouldn't let him access anything that went on record so "his presence wouldn't sully *Mercy's* reputation". If he believed Regis, the Militia brass must be as uptight about respectability as he was. It felt like how Old Man Goss always said; the best bred steers were more valuable. That was why he culled the runts for meat and hide. Yeah; Harp was the mongrel Regis still called him, something to be kept away from the thoroughbreds.

But these days standing orders talked about "a show of strength on landing" which pretty much said it all. As folk got poorer their anxiety too often turned to anger.

Anger simmered in their groundcar too right now. Regis's notion of a show of strength this time had been to land the cruiser on a hilltop two whole miles clear of this little township. Then their captain, rot his snivelling, vindictive hide, sent Mullah with a 'force' of only six and in their second, older groundcar, which he knew damn well had lost its canopy, half melted in the recent fire. So here they were, bouncing and lurching, other-Goss – clearly someone had blabbed about her sharing those insults – forced to drive even slower than she did normally and the town of Welcome barely visible down in this dustbowl. At this rate it would take them half an hour yet, maybe more, and by then they'd all be covered in a layer of dust and sweat. Oh yeah, impressive.

The worst of it was Harp knew why Regis had done this; cos Mullah had stepped in to keep Harp off a spurious report, again. Because the captain plain hated the sight of him, calling Harp "an embarrassment to the good name of our illustrious Founding Family" of which the captain claimed to be a part, though Bays reckoned any branch that Regis figured on must be extremely distant or he wouldn't be here. Regis also called Harp "a damned disgrace to have to see aboard my ship" and kept him scheduled on scut work. While Mullah, worth a hundred Regis, kept on trying to train him properly, and stop the captain finding reason to discharge him. This was the latest petty response, punishing Mullah, him, and anyone else close enough to get caught in the mess.

Because it was a mess. Regis might be the worst straw

he could have drawn, but Harp wasn't stupid enough to think the other captains might have welcomed him with open arms. The Harpan Founding Family was god-like here, all powerful, however distant. Crip, they owned Moon, like they did World. And they were pretty much fixated on genetics, bloodlines. Truth was, nobody with a career to lose would risk offending them, however hard Harp tried to earn a place here.

Look at it that way, it plain puzzled Harp how well his crew did treat him, but maybe it was the enemy of your enemy; anyone Regis hated so much qualified for backup. He'd also figured maybe he amused them – like, he was an oddity, but *their* oddity. Maybe that was even what belonging felt like. Not that everyone *liked* him – Ludwiz, here at his side, still didn't. But most were fair-to-neutral. He sometimes thought it'd be better if people stopped trying to protect him. He wasn't a kid any more, even if they still called him one, and it wasn't like he was hoping for promotion. Fat chance. Staying at the bottom of the bucket was a fulltime occupation.

The car hit another rock, lurched then slammed down again, bruising Harp's tailbone. He wasn't the only one cursing. Their present wasn't good, the near future no joke either. Nor was the continuing "dormancy" of Collar Mountain. Less infrequent smoke from the 'extinct' volcano had been headline news for weeks now.

Maybe Bays could mind read. 'You hear anything about Collar?'

'Nothin since the latest newsvid.' Which hadn't looked any worse than he'd seen for himself a month before, but the fact he'd seen the peak with his own eyes apparently made him their expert. Still, the way the prairie fires were growing he had to figure thought of Collar getting worse was lurking like some bogeyman in all their minds, a monster they pretended couldn't hurt them.

'Huh.' Bays dived back into that game he'd loaded on his wristcom – one he claimed improved intelligence and Mullah called a waste of power. No one else was talking. Harp allowed his mind to drift back to the better portions of his recent past instead; the things he'd seen, the things he'd learned now…

No, he didn't feel like a kid any more. Course, the ladies up on the brand new Orbital had helped there. Once he figured they might treat him better than the males he'd fought off in his childhood. Yep, he'd sure learned from the ladies. He hid a smile. Enough to know how to treat other ladies – when the captain let him off the cruiser.

Regis had no choice but let him off sometimes when *Mercy* flew off-planet, and oo-ee, that was something. The Orbital floated in what they called a high orbit. Turned out *Mercy* didn't have what Mullah called artificial gravity so he'd got to float too, in that zero-g Bays had tried to explain and he *thought* he understood now. And zero-g wasn't the only sort either; gravity *on* the Orbital was a mite stronger, made doing stuff more effort. Slowed the captain down as well, which Bays had called a bonus, but it meant the crew got tired quicker which, of course, the captain jumped on, saying they were lazy. Harp had taken time to check what exercise would best build extra muscle for the next time *Mercy* went there.

Mercy wasn't really much of a spaceship, as he'd stupidly thought at first. She was "an atmospheric shuttle"; couldn't go farther than Moon orbit. Traders – not a lot – and bigger navy ships from World went right out into space. As for the Orbital, everybody said that it would end up like a giant wheel in space, with docks, warehouses, bars, bunks, you name it. He supposed it was a floating city. He'd never got into the core section, cos that was brass and admin, but the outer rim sure was an eye opener even if it wasn't finished off yet. Bays said they'd already built a VIP dock with restricted access that was rumoured to be real special, more like World. He'd sure have liked to see that.

Course, the reasons behind building the Orbital weren't so nice. Mullah said World had always had one like it and he'd heard the aliens on their nearest-but-still-reachable neighbour planet, Kraic IV, had something smaller, so he figured other human worlds did too, if they existed. They were adding one for Moon cos the Kraic had warned them how the "pirate problem" was increasing. That was why they'd raised the tithes, to add these new defences. His old teachers had explained how there'd once been other, so-far-off-you-couldn't-see-them planets out there, talking distances their pupils gawked at, showing maps that made Moon seem a dot in space instead of something they all lived on, but apart from Kraic IV they'd never said which ones were lived on, alien or human. They'd never said anything about pirates either, but maybe nobody had wanted to scare little kids. Maybe ordinary folk knew all about them and it was just folk like him, orphans, who didn't. He guessed maybe the Orbital was worth the sacrifices folk were making if it scared off pirates.

But times *were* leaner, even on their cruiser; there was always something they were short of. Newscom cited new govment emergency programmes, warned everyone "not to be swayed by agitators and insurgents from outside the sector". That had them speculating if it meant some foreign power was interfering, though Mullah said that never happened – they were on the fringes, not "strategic". Harp had looked the word up and agreed the logic. Kraic IV, their so-called neighbour, was so far they hadn't reached it till the Worlder navy ships had somehow made it. Even World was far enough away he couldn't think it had much influence, let alone some other universe would interfere?

He hadn't really doubted the official messages, had probably ignored them till a ragged civ had thrust a leaflet at him in one township. He had wisely stuffed it in a pocket before someone told Regis he had it, but had maybe not-so-wisely read it later, real hardcopy reading being a rarity. It had claimed the folk down here were starving now in earnest and the govment *wasn't* helping. Nowadays, he had to wonder. Times had been thin enough when he'd lived on the surface. Even on a ranch, the Gosses hadn't made enough to pay their five-year tithe. And when he'd gone to visit…

4

He'd had 'home leave' one whole week; he'd never had so much freedom. He'd managed to get back to the Goss ranch, the nearest to a home he could think of. It was the first time he'd ever gone back anywhere. He'd taken gifts and Missus Destra cried, said how he'd grown, and Mr Seth had actually shook his hand and said how he was proud. Yeah, but he'd realised he'd changed. They hadn't, cept for looking older, wearier. He didn't fit there any longer.

But the rest of the crew made a big thing of the leave and he didn't want to look different. So after an awkward couple of days he'd hitched a ride to Riverbend and visited his Pre-Employment house, last place he'd lived before he'd been apprenticed, and in some ways that was better. His old principal had him talking to the kids about the farm, the ranch and then the cruiser; gushed a bit about how well he'd done, how hard he must have worked to earn it. Course, some of the kids gave him the eye about that, but some looked thoughtful. He remembered a kid called Mik somehow smuggled a little sister in from Nursery. She'd asked to touch his name tag and the *Mercy*'s patch stuck on his shoulder. And they'd all been happy with the store-bought sweets he brought. That memory was definitely worth a smile. And of course he'd seen a real live volcano where there'd always been an ordinary mountain. The newsvids were right, you could sometimes see sparks in the night sky. Pretty, but he'd wondered even then if it was safe as govment Newscom said, especially for nearby folks in Riverbend, a lot of whom were miners.

Talking of safe…

Goss had rounded a big outcrop, and this township was finally in direct sight. The groundcar hit some level ground at last and they sped up a little; looked a way to go yet, and it was hot as hell out here in the open – even though the air flowed round the forward screen and past them, tugging at his hair, which needed cutting. Harp allowed himself a single sip from his canteen, washing it around his mouth. Regis had cut the water ration again, so what Harp had left was it for the day if cook couldn't stretch to caffee come chow time. And, bad mood or not, Bays could be right about it being as hot out here as in that fire...

He'd never seen a prairie fire before the Militia, but his luck had sure changed since. Mullah said the land was "tinder dry" now; how the slightest spark was all it took, and flames would spread so fast – he'd seen one fire leap across a dried-up river bed, another swallow a stampeding herd in seconds. He still heard them screaming sometimes, so the thought of that volcano, all that hidden fire... he really hoped someone was watching.

At least the last prairie fire hadn't been that bad; they'd rescued all the livestock, and the farmers were so grateful. All the heat and dust and blisters had been worth it when you saw their faces. And Collar Mountain's smoke was no worse.

Grit blew in his face and jerked him back into the present. Mullah was standing up and holding on up front; the township's Main Street – half of what there was – was trundling closer. When Harp wiped his goggles he could see a bunch of locals stepping out their bar and off the roofed-in sidewalk they'd have built to keep folk clear of the muddy street, back when mud had been a problem. Now the dust made all of them wear scarves across their faces, same as he did.

Further off Harp saw a local hurrying her kids indoors, and with his eyesight – which the crew claimed was the best on board – he picked out faces peering out from distant windows, didn't need the goggles others would have. He quashed a sigh; the locals often hid now, beaten-down, and scared. He hated that they caused it. Mullah made a point these days to sit with folk a spell and ask them what they needed. It was always medicines or extra hands to till the rock-hard soil. And of course more water. But the crew still had to take the tithes, and he suspected Regis never passed on the reports cos

Mullah looked increasingly frustrated.

Not that that was evident in public. 'Right, lads and lasses, here we go again. Look friendly.' Everyone pulled down their scarves. Harp sat up straighter. Bays ditched his game and muttered, 'Ready to pour oil, kid?' Harp grunted. Bays insisted he was good at calming people, but it felt like folk were angry every time they landed these days. He could almost taste it. Harpan's Moon had turned into a powder keg, and Regis sent them here short-handed, in an open groundcar?

'Fellik, with me. Bays, Goss, Ludwiz and Harp hang back. Weapons live but holstered.'

'Sarge.' Mullah usually took Fellik, probably cos the woman smiled at folk. Harp checked his pulse – the cheapest version with an unpowered holster was the best Regis would sign him off on – was set to lo-power stun, and hoped to hell he wouldn't need it this time. It jammed, a lot, and didn't charge well – plus he hated seeing folk jerk helplessly and wet themselves, ending up dizzy and humiliated. He'd obeyed orders to fire though, cos what else could he do when crewmates were threatened?

The groundcar wheezed to a halt the regulation twenty paces from the four men and two women. Interesting. One more man hung back, and had a lot more stomach than the others. Maybe he should check if Mullah noticed, though they likely wouldn't be here long enough to find out how he'd managed extra rations.

Mullah landed two footed, stirring up more dust. It didn't make a difference, he was covered in the stuff already. 'Howdy. Sergeant Mullah. One of you the mayor?'

One of the women took a step. 'That's me, Ami Bell.' But she had glanced at Fatso.

If Mullah saw he didn't let it show. 'Pleased to meet you, Ma'am. You'll have taken over from Mr Gomek?'

'Yeah.' The woman swallowed. 'Died, a while back.' And hadn't been reported?

Mullah didn't argue the infringement, keeping the encounter friendly. 'Then I'm sorry for your loss, ma'am. Is there somewhere we can get this over with out of the dust?'

Bell eyed him for a moment, then nodded. 'Bar, I guess.'

She turned and led the way, her little deputation shuffling after; Mullah and then Fellik. Goss stayed at the controls, half hidden by the filthy windscreens. Ludwiz looked at Bays, who didn't move to join him, then he chose a bench outside the bar while Bays and Harp strolled casually down the boardwalk, peering in the one store window.

'Hey, they got soap, cheap too. Stores was out again last time I tried.' Bays stepped toward the door, Harp stayed where he was. 'You want some?'

Harp fumbled out a few credit chips, with the hand not near his holster. 'Yeah, and anything you think I like. Pay a bit over, if they'll take it?'

'Kid, you're too soft.' But Bays would do the same, Harp knew. The street stayed quiet. When Harp first joined folk would have come out, to say hi, to ask for news. Now shutters fell, on windows and on faces.

Harp's ears were a match for his eyes so it was easy to keep tabs on Bays inside. He could even pick up fainter voices from the bar – the woman's flatter vowels then Mullah's rumble. Talk back there got louder for a moment, not uncommon, then subsided. But he couldn't pick up Mullah's voice at all now.

Then Ludwiz rose and went inside as well. Harp got a bad feeling and tapped on the window beside him. 'Bays?'

The stilted talk inside cut off and Bays was at his side a second later, empty handed, right hand at his holster. 'What?'

'Ludwiz's gone inside.'

'Yeah, well…' Bays trailed off.

'I can't hear Mullah, and it's awful quiet.'

'Crip.' Bays tried to look both ways at once. 'You think we should go check?' Bays was a great guy, but not much for taking charge on missions.

'If there's trouble we don't know what we're walking into. If there isn't, charging in might spook some.'

While Bays cursed, Harp weighed their options. Goss was still in the car, in the middle of the street. He touched his earpiece, spoke into his tiny throat mike. 'Goss, can you see into the bar?'

A crackle from the cut-price gear. 'No, but I'm guessing you asking ain't good?' She was close enough he could hear her real voice as well as the one in his ear, hoped to hell nobody here had ears like his.

'Keep it down, eh? Can you put in a quiet call to *Mercy*, tell 'em to keep a channel open, in case?' Their suit mikes couldn't reach that far; the car-com was their only option.

'OK.' He saw Goss leaning forward; she'd sounded shaky, probably rethinking her position in the open. Would it be a good or bad idea to have her back off out of town? She would be safer but these folk might read it as a threat.

The way he read this silence?

Bays fidgeted. 'What d'you think?'

'I'm thinking trouble.' Harp took a breath. 'Stay here. I'm going to chat to Goss.'

'Out in the open?'

'I want a look at those upper floors. And Bays?'

'Yeah, kid?'

'You might want to put your back to something safer than a window?'

'Shit.' Bays scuttled sideways. Bays didn't, what was that word, *strategize* real well, until the action – then he went on sheer instinct. Wasn't the first time Harp had thought fostering and farming had been better training than they got in the militia. This captain of theirs only wanted them to salute, maintain what tech they had and follow orders. Harp's civilian life had taught him when to fight and when to run, or talk; to hide the fear. Goss and Bays were older hands but they would wait for orders, preferably Mullah's. Only right now something told Harp they didn't have that luxury.

He'd barely stepped onto the dirt below when the bar door opened and the sergeant stood there. Harp stopped walking. Mullah looked too stiff, his hands... his holster was empty! Harp reached for his gun, heard Bays's boots scrape, figured he had crouched and pulled his weapon. Bell's voice interrupted. 'You outside, throw down your guns or your sergeant's a goner.' Mullah jerked, Harp saw a barrel jammed against his head. Oh crip, that wasn't Mullah's weapon. The locals had projectiles; no option there to stun, only kill. Harp was probably near enough to break for the car and try to run, but that would leave the others; even Bays would never make it. And he made out movement in these upper windows, and a barrel sticking out a little. Rifle fire made them sitting targets.

'Goss?' he muttered, trying not to move his lips, 'You sent a distress, right?'

'Yeah.' This time Goss was whispering, and breathing fast. 'What now?'

He had to play for time and put his hope in *Mercy*. He took another step forward. 'Missus, we sure don't want any trouble here, or see anyone hurt, right?'

Slowly he pulled out his gun – wasn't much use anyway – and bent to lay it on the ground, deactivating it in the process. A curse and sounds behind him told him Bays had trusted him and copied. Goss sat rigid.

'You in the car too, throw out your gun and climb down.'

Goss's mouth had tightened but she moved, though she 'accidentally' kicked her gun under the car as she landed. Clever girl. Once she was down someone pulled Mullah back inside and locals emerged, from the bar and two other doors, all armed, converging on the three militia. Fatso, very much in charge out here now, waved the others off and zeroed in on Harp, a head to toe inspection ending with a sickly smile; different kind of trouble.

'Back up.' He waved a newer looking handgun, scooped up Harp's disabled pulse and shoved it in his belt then stepped in, grabbed at the back of Harp's neck and shoved him toward the bar. The locals herding Goss and Bays stayed out of reach but Fatso obviously relished getting closer – close enough that Harp could smell the liquor on him. Then the guy breathed in, real deep, and pulled him to a stop. 'Crip, boy, you sure do smell good. Pretty hair as well, ain't never seen that colour here before. Damned if you don't look like one of the Founding Family. You Family, boy?'

Maybe Bays heard; he turned his head. That made a local look back too. 'You all right, Izak?'

Izak laughed and pushed Harp forward, fingers gripping at his hair now. In the bar his other crewmates were sitting on the floor at the far end of the big room, disarmed but unhurt. Harp felt sticky fingers stroke his neck before the man pushed him to join them. Some of their attackers looked excited, others nervous. The nervous ones didn't have weapons. Fatso swaggered off to join the mayor, who also wasn't armed; more confirmation. Mullah was doing his job.

'Folks, let's not make this any worse, eh?' He'd have seen the empty bottles too. 'We're not your enemy. We get our orders same as you do, from the govment. How will taking us prisoner help you?'

Bell's voice quavered. 'That ship'll do as we want and go.' She didn't sound convinced though.

Harp blinked. Of all the lame brained... hadn't they ever dealt with govment? No, of course; they'd only ever met Militia's half-baked 'soldiers'. Harp had read a lot this last half year, or as much as he could sneak past Regis, plus he'd seen the real navy up on Orbital. He knew World's govment had their rules and stuck to them like glue, and govment didn't *care* like ordinary folk. Forget that Harpan slogan of "a world that cares, built on a strong foundation; righteous family values". Moon was very much the poor relation, not so different than he was. Hell, Regis typified the Harpan's World Harp knew about. Regis was the bottom rung of govment's ladder and he only cared for what was good for Regis.

Very likely he'd pass the buck to brass on Orbital, and that would probably take hours. Longer. Then? Small chance the Family would even hear about them. Would their brass, or navy, or some politician back on World care shit a paltry Moon Militia got themselves in trouble?

All they'd want to do was make examples of these stupid settlers. Harp huffed, then hooked his arms around his knees to draw attention from his sergeant. 'I sure do hope you're right, Missus. I was aiming to go see my fosters next stop.' Mullah had been making him tone down his farmboy accent cos he said it made him sound the idiot he wasn't. Now he brought it back, full measure. Hey there, farmboy, just like you folks.

Bell's head jerked his way. 'Your fosters?'

'Yes, ma'am, the Goss ranch up Deslin way, perhaps you know it? I was 'prenticed there until their tithe came due last year. Good people. Didn't want to send me off but...' Harp shrugged helplessly.

'They sent you in to work off their tithe?'

'Yes, Ma'am, five years. Had to, didn't they.' He looked down at his boots. 'I been savin' my pay, going to transfer some to 'em when I see 'em. Sarge is going to drop me near enough to walk it.'

The woman frowned, hesitated, glanced at Fatso. 'But you still come here to take what's ours.'

'Fraid so, yes, Ma'am.' Harp paused to let her see him thinking. 'See, word is these new pirates are real bad, and getting' closer, so we gotta be ready. Plus, the way I figure, if this drought don't ease up soon the Family could need to send in help anyways, mebbe even take some of us back to World awhile till Moon can feed us again. But if they don't get their tithes, well, it's all their's, ain't it? They're, like, our landlords. Who's to say what they'll do if they get angry? Cos there ain't no one else to help us, is there?' Harp spread his hands, a young man caught in things beyond him. Locals looked toward the mayor for her reaction. Good.

But Izak spoke up first. 'We listening to that? Anyone here ever see these pirates? He don't even look like a Mooner. I say he's a lackey out of World, come here to lie to us and steal from decent farmers!' Bell hesitated. Seemed like Izak took that as his cue to give out orders. 'Lock 'em up; easier that way while we talk to the ship.'

Turned out the place had a modest cellar, empty except

for a broken jug, a stack of small plas cylinders against one wall and a parcel hold tagged on one side where stuff folk ordered in stayed safe till they could come collect it. Unsurprisingly it was half underground, and windowless. More surprisingly, the place stood empty cept for dust. These days he knew a lot of folk slept underground where it was cooler. More importantly, he couldn't see a thing he could fight back with when the squad were herded down the wooden stairs and pushed inside. The door slammed shut, leaving them in stuffy darkness.

Harp slid down beside the door, as lookout – easy done cos Izak brought him last again, and leered at him till he pushed him in here, fat hand on his backside; definitely trouble coming. Count on it. Something more was definitely off though. 'Sarge? It don't add up for locals this time, how they had folk watching like they were expecting trouble. They must know even if *Mercy* leaves town for now she'll come back. And that Izak's too fat, and too calm about it all. I mean…'

Mullah nodded. 'Yeah, kid, it's worse. You missed the good part.' Bays and Goss just looked confused. The sergeant grimaced. 'Looks like we walked into a black merch nest.'

Harp caught up. '*That's* why the mayor wasn't armed. That Izak guy's taken over the town?'

'Looks like. I figure we were only supposed to see what he wanted, then go on our way.'

'But I messed up.' Fellik looked miserable. 'I slipped in a puddle near the cellar trapdoor, put my hand in it and realised it wasn't liquor, it was water. Spilt liquor would be bad enough, but water, left there? I should have kept my stupid mouth shut till we got away from here, but I blurted it out, didn't I?'

Mullah shook his head. 'Wasn't your fault, Fellik. The water by the cellar was just the sweet on the bun. They must have spilled some when they hid those canisters out there. No, they were too stupid or too complacent to hide those till the last minute, and as for the liquor bottles…, no way a place like this could afford to stock a bar – not with labelled bottles.'

Water smuggling. The worst crime on Moon next to murder, which it practically was. The worst kind of criminals. No wonder that mayor woman looked frazzled. Had they been passing through? No, more like they'd been here a while. Long enough to disarm the locals anyways. Long enough the old mayor was dead?

And now they'd been rumbled. The boss, Izak, wouldn't care about the town, but he and his gang couldn't make a run for it while *Mercy* sat up on the hill watching everything – maybe suspicious now. So, what, Izak meant to use them as hostages, to force *Mercy* to back off far enough he could escape, leave the town to take the resulting heat? A decent captain might oblige; no Mooner wanted to fire on other Mooners, if they didn't have to. Yeah, they'd back off a few miles, raise the alarm and figure the reinforcements would settle it. Only Regis wasn't a Mooner. And might not react like one.

And those down here could identify Izak, and at least some of his gang. Which didn't seem to worry Izak.

Fellik wrung her hands. 'You'd realised anyway, cos of the bottles…? Sarge, guys, I'm real sorry.'

No one answered this time, likely lost in similar conclusions. Silence wrapped them for a while till of course Bays broke it, voicing all their fears. 'Sarge, will *Mercy* come for us, before…?'

'They know by now something's wrong,' Mullah said firmly. 'Even if they don't know what.'

'Yeah, but will the bastard leave the ship to get us out of this, because, you know, I kinda doubt it.'

Others murmured, backing Bays' opinion. Mullah sighed. 'Whatever happens it won't be quick. There's procedures. Captain has to call it in. Orders come back. Maybe they send reinforcements. We're safe enough while the gang's still stuck here, we just have to wait it out and not make things worse, so settle down and do that.'

Dammit, they were vermin in a fire circle. There was no way out.

Waiting was it.

5

So they waited. Some muttered, some cursed Regis. Someone wondered if the ship would shoot into the township, saying they were safer in the cellar. Bays complained of being hungry. Harp sat quiet, head down, and listened. There'd been a clatter of boots above then quiet, so he thought most of their captors had left. Maybe gone to talk to *Mercy*, much good would it do them. Then he heard the clink of glass. A while later two or maybe three men's voices rose and there was even laughter, and one voice was Izak's, so Harp wasn't much surprised when boots stomped down again. 'Incoming, Sarge.'

The lock rattled then the door swung inward. Izak and another guy waved handguns. Izak's gaze found Harp. 'Get up. No, not the rest, just him.'

'Why him?' Bays' hands were fists.

'He's going to earn you supper.' Izak leered, his comrade snorted.

Harp stood slowly, signalling to Mullah with a hand behind him. 'Doing what?'

'Whatever we say. Your pals could be a long time down here. Might need a meal. Or a bucket?' Izak's grin showed crooked teeth. 'Right?'

Harp stared back, head tilted. Not dead yet, don't let him see you realise why he thinks he can do whatever he wants. 'Right.' Then he walked out, before Bays tried to interfere.

Izak pushed him up against the nearest wall before his pal even got the door locked again. The other man objected, not to the intention but the setting. 'Hold it, Izak, there's a bed upstairs, all comfy; got a big old headboard. And,' a twisted smile, 'I got some rope.'

The hands on Harp stopped moving then the fat man chuckled. 'Comfy, eh? You like it comfy, kid?'

Harp licked his lips. Then twitched a smile. 'Nope.' He looked his captor in the eye. 'But I sure do like it with ropes.'

There was a startled silence then the fat man grabbed at him again, this time to pull him to the ladder. 'Wilky, get that goddamn rope!' Wilky ran. Upstairs, he only had to cross the barroom to collect a coil of homemade rope left on a table. There was one more 'sentry', but the man was out of it, his head down on another table. Their arrival didn't wake him. Was that why these two had waited?

Wilky led the way round the bar, where a narrow door led to a steep stair. As Wilky's feet moved higher, Izak held Harp back. His tongue slurped up Harp's cheek. 'My turn first, boy.'

Harp turned his head, and maybe breathed a little faster. 'Yeah? How long can you last?'

Fat fingers stroked his jaw. 'Oh, you'll see.'

'Uh-uh.' Harp looked him up and down, then smiled. 'You like it willing or you want a fight?' The fat man's turn to lick his lips.

'Hey, Izak, where the hell are you? We don't want your old woman coming back, getting all righteous.'

'Coming. Oh, I'm coming.' Izak pushed Harp upward, gun against his spine, his free hand lower. 'If you're scared you can always keep watch.'

'Forget that.' The room above spread straight off the stair, open to the eaves, with a big bed one side and a cot the other; a family space, clothes hanging on a line across one corner, a wooden spaceship on the cot, a slingshot lying underneath it. Yes, these folk hadn't got to sleeping underground where it was cooler then, like many. Some of the later buildings he'd seen in his travels didn't even have an upper storey any longer. Though he'd noticed miner townships were often the last to live below – probably got enough of it at work. With Izak around, maybe these folk were more concerned about being robbed, or trapped?

Wilky, weaving a little, had a knife in one hand and the coiled rope in the other, cutting. Harp stepped up into the room, away from Izak, and held out a hand, palm upward, waiting. Both men gaped then Izak whistled, threw himself across the bed and raised up on one elbow, watching. While his other hand, the one without the gun, undid his belt then disappeared inside his grubby trousers. Harp ignored him this time, smiling at his crony. Wilky stepped in close enough to wrap the length he'd cut around Harp's wrist. He shoved the knife into his belt to do it. 'Tie it tight,' Harp purred, and felt the fingers tremble. Then the man's own knife sliced through his grubby shirt, and up his chest. The man's mouth gaped, a silent scream. His hands jerked up and clutched at Harp's. Until Harp reached the hollow of his throat, and twisted. Then the groping hands fell slack, the body hit the floorboards. By then Harp had spun to face his other captor. Izak's prone position was a gift he hadn't dared to hope for and he couldn't waste it. The man was sprawled out, taken by surprise. One hand was trying to disengage from his dick and the other was sunk into the mattress, all his weight above it. He'd have to raise himself out of the mattress before he could even try to aim.

He never got that far. Harp was on him first, left hand flying at his throat, the blooded blade aimed at the jugular, his right hand on the gun – and every bit of Harp was muscle these days. As the fat man choked and clawed at the descending knife Harp's right hand turned the gun, forced the fat man's finger to depress the trigger and blow a hole in his own gut.

Harp jumped back, the gun his now, and watched as Izak lurched off of the bed and staggered back into the wall and then slid down it, legs splayed, clutching at his stomach, eyes gone wide and frightened. Harp shivered, took a panting breath then steadied. Be afraid. But never, ever, show it.

'You… you.' Blood was seeping through the fat man's fingers.

'You think I'd have survived fostering if I couldn't handle your sort?' Harp held the gun steady, listened for any sound below. He'd settled for the best shot he could get with the gun wedged between them, hoped the man's belly would muffle a shot better anyway. Now, he hoped Izak wouldn't realise he didn't want to risk another. He ought to finish Izak quietly, with the knife. He ought. To his relief the man's eyes dimmed, he sagged and suddenly he was a... thing, laid in a growing pool of blood. 'OK.' He made the mistake of taking a deeper breath and gagged on the reek. Blood was soaking into cracks in the rough boards, it might start dripping through and there was still one man below it, so get moving. He remembered to search Wilky for the cellar keys – it sure would be nice if he was cool as he'd sounded – jammed the too-big gun in his empty holster, collected the second. Saw the coil of rope, still lying. And the slingshot.

The bar door creaked but the third man slept on. Without his boots Harp ghosted across and it only took a breath to drop the running rancher noose the rope had sported round his shoulders. A gag, using the man's own neckerchief and that was that, for now. Yep, between foster and farm he'd learned a lot his crewmates hadn't; herding, roping, butchering a steer...

Then he was sick till his stomach had nothing left to heave up. 'Dumb idiot, no time.' He checked the street, no sign of any of the gang; maybe watching Regis was keeping them busy. Then the room, to end up with one rifle, the two handguns and a knife. No spare ammo. But wasn't that why he'd grabbed the slingshot? Enough. He headed down the cellar stairs and tried the biggest key. 'Guys? It's me, OK?'

'Crip, kid.' Bays grabbed him. 'Where're you hurt?' The voice was angry but the face was worried.

'Not my blood. Come on.'

Folk grabbed the weapons. Mullah claimed the rifle, Ludwiz and Fellik had the other guns. 'Where's the men who grabbed you, son?'

'I took 'em out, Sarge. One's tied up, the other two...' He trailed off, the words stuck in his throat.

The sergeant clapped him on the back. 'Well done. Got any ammo?'

'Sorry, Sarge.'

'Ah well.' The sergeant checked his magazine then barrelled past him, everybody else ran after, leaving Harp to play at rear guard, happy not to be the leader. Back in the bar Mullah put his back to the wall, peering through the front window. Bays, a mirror image, peered in the opposite direction. 'I see one down the street, Sarge. She's got a rifle, but her back's to us, must be watching the cruiser.'

Mullah grunted. 'Car's still where we left it, that's something. You see anything in the upstairs windows?'

'Nothing – hang on, someone walked across the window facing us, it might have been that mayor woman.'

'Damn. They'd want to use her as a front, to do the talking when they challenged Regis that could mean the smugglers are all still in town too. There were six – no, eight, we saw to start with.' Mullah glanced at Harp. 'That's five of them, but you say they had more watching?' Harp nodded, grimly, not taking his eyes off the road. 'Crip, half the damn town could still be in on it. We'll need to work fast.' No need to say they were outnumbered and outgunned – they knew it – nor to point out Regis obviously wasn't racing to the rescue. While Mullah looked like he knew what he was doing, the rest... It wasn't the first time Harp had wished the Militia got proper training 'stead of being such a ragtag army. Mullah's gaze came back to Harp. 'Here, kid, you'll do more with the rifle than me.'

'No, sir, you keep it, I've got this.' He found a grin he hoped they all believed and pulled the slingshot from his pocket. 'Go a decent distance. Don't need ammo either, just some pebbles.'

Bays stifled a laugh 'All right, farmboy. Show us what you're made of.'

A rear door led into a cluttered alley and the backs of smaller buildings, largely domiciles. Harp saw a curtain twitch, but no one shouted; he ignored the itch along his spine and looked for pebbles. Others saw what he was up to, passed him more as everybody ran to where the alley met the street, in the direction of their groundcar. By the time they crouched, in tantalising sight of it, Harp had his pockets full of ammunition; all he needed now were targets.

For once even Mullah looked worried. They'd faced angry crowds a few times, but this was the first time the threat of violence had been so real, the first without their heads protected by their helmets – maybe the first time any of them had killed another human. And they didn't know how many there were, or if any of the locals were involved. Harp figured he'd fall apart later; for now he had to hold it together like the rest.

'Sarge, there were locals back there keeping their heads down. I think we aren't up against the whole town, just the smugglers.' He figured that was important. Maybe the govment wouldn't need to punish the town?

'Yeah, good.' Mullah took a breath. 'Cos that might be our best hope of getting out of this. Harp, what can you actually do with that thing?'

He could kill vermin, had since he was little. It'd been a game at first, then keepin' Missus' veggies safe and adding to the cookpot; sometimes stopped a steer charging. He could use the slingshot, hell he could throw the damn stones almost as far if he had to. Even at humans?

'I can hit what I aim at, Sarge.'

He thought Mullah relaxed at his answer, at any rate he shifted his attention to the others. 'Right, lads n lasses, Fellik and I keep people busy, Ludwiz has the other handgun so he covers Goss and they head for the car. Bays, you got the knife, you keep an eye on Harp. On three.'

Four of them moved, boots scurrying, eyes darting, wondering how far they'd get before the locals saw them. Maybe their greys, plus all that dust, gave them an edge. Goss, smallest and fastest, made it almost to the car before a shout rang out. After that…

Mullah fired once from the alley, covering fire, then Fellik, but they couldn't see both sides of the street. And didn't have much ammo. Stupid as it was, their plan could hinge on Harp and pebbles. And if he reached the car he would have cover *and* see both sides of the street. So he ran after Goss. Bays, cursing loudly, ran beside him. In the open, clutching at a useless knife, his only weapon. 'Damn it, kid, zigzag!'

Zig? Oh, *good* idea, something just flew past his ear. He zigged then zagged, the car a haven that he really hoped he'd get to. Goss had made it. Ludwiz sort of tumbled in beside her, but he hadn't dropped the handgun. Harp slid underneath the car and so did Bays; the heavens loved them. Or these locals couldn't aim straight. Breathlessly he crouched. He'd already re-knotted the leather thongs, testing their strength, but it was near a year now since he'd even held one. Never mind that. Bays had picked up Goss's gun, still hiding there, and hunkered in beside him. Goss was in the car, and thumping sounds suggested she was pulling the first aid kit. Then he heard her saying, 'Here, can you?'

'Yeah.' A wheezy Ludwiz. 'Yeah, I got this, take the gun. Keep watch.'

So Goss, above, was first to spot a target. 'Harp? My right and up, a window with a flapping curtain. Want to try? I'm not much with a handgun.' Harp saw a head above the windowsill – leapt up, the sling already spinning, let it fly and prayed. He'd aimed for the leading hand, the most visible target. He hit the face, a hair below one eye. The man cried out and disappeared, maybe with a broken cheekbone. By that time Harp was searching for another target. While a part of him was glad he hadn't killed, another part was terrified that leaving one alive would kill a comrade. Toughen up, you coward.

Nothing else was moving. The smugglers would have heard their man cry out but not another shot, they might not know yet what had happened. Once they did, the car would be a target. While the thing was armour plated there was only partial cover now without the canopy, and Ludwiz was already hurt. Harp needed to work fast; he couldn't till he had another blasted target.

'Damn it, stick your heads up.'

The lookout at the other end of the street had decided to

start crawling their way, with a rifle. From her position she might try a shot beneath the groundcar if she realised where he was. How close would she get before she stopped to fire? Above his head he heard Goss whistle, Mooner whistle-talk for Mullah, telling him look right. Harp left them to it, but if someone tried to give the woman cover...

Someone did. Harp saw the movement in an upstairs window that way; saw a rifle barrel poking from the window, farther this time, trying to get the downward angle. Heard Bays gasp. 'Kid, any chance you could hit the rifle? Like, knock it out his hands?'

Could he? It was all of fifty metres and he'd have to hit it really hard, and on or near the trigger. 'Cross your fingers.' He stood tall behind the car, let fly and dropped again, then realised that Bays had gambled everything and was already running for the boardwalk underneath the shooter's window.

But the shooter yelped, and lost the precious rifle.

Bays was diving, scrabbling. Mullah fired again, a ground floor window shattered. Something fluttered right above the sergeant's head. Harp couldn't help – the car was in his way – but Bays grabbed up the rifle, rolled came up again and fired; too fast to aim – he wasn't that good anyway – but fast enough to scare the smuggler into ducking out of sight again. And now they had a second rifle.

The street fell quiet. Bays ducked behind a heavy bench. Harp watched, aware of Goss's heavy breathing and of Ludwiz cursing just above him. Were the smugglers backing down? Regrouping? Creeping up on Mullah from that alley? Crip, he couldn't aim at what he couldn't see. And Bays was crazy – and deserved a bloody medal, if he lived to get it.

Still, with Bays one side, Mullah and Fellik the other and him in the middle, living began to look like an option. As long as they conserved ammo and only the smugglers fought back. If the locals joined in... most Mooners had projectiles. And made their own ammo, when they had the time and credit for the metal, which often meant the ammo wasn't perfect. And projectiles hardly ever came with autosights, another point in the Militia's favour.

It occurred to him to thank the rule that had them lock their regulation pulse guns. Even if some weren't disabled, the enemy shouldn't have the codes to change the guns from stun to kill, and from their current range the captured weapons couldn't reach them on their present settings. Handguns couldn't do much damage at this distance. But they shouldn't wait for closer contact. 'Goss?'

'Yeah?'

'Can you get the car to Mullah?'

'Sheesh.' The woman didn't move. 'What about you?'

'I'll hop in behind. I don't think we can wait much longer.'

'Right. You ready?'

Harp set one hand on the rear baffle. 'Go!' He almost didn't make it when Goss gunned the engine but a bloody hand came up and grabbed him, Ludwiz groaning as he hauled him over. Goss was ducked behind the windscreen's scant protection, putting all her faith in those still giving cover. Mullah saw them coming, kept the rifle steady on a barrel lid and grabbed at Fellik. Harp checked back and saw that Bays had seen what they were doing, firing across the street. Another window shattered; that might keep the heads down for a moment.

Only someone threw a window open over Bays, intending to fire blindly down into the thin wood awning. No. Oh no. Harp stood up in the lurching transport, Ludwiz shouting Goss to 'Keep 'er steady!' This time it was Bays who was oblivious to danger. This time Harp made no attempt to scare, or injure. Shifting stance or not the stone flew true; it struck the man between the eyes. Harp's stomach felt the blow, but he would not regret it.

The car slewed to a halt, dust rising on all sides. Mullah and Fellik piled in, Goss was already spinning them. 'Bays!' yelled Mullah, rifle braced against the transport's side as Goss was swerving in a wide half circle, veering out across the street again and raising lots more dust. And Bays was running, zig and zag, a ghost, and in the dust the locals surely couldn't see him...

But they kept on firing. Bays dived headlong in among their bodies, landing full on Ludwiz lying in the bottom. Ludwiz yelled and Mullah fired, so did Fellik, Goss revved madly, using all the feeble speed the transport had to get them down the street, toward the open ground, toward the *Mercy*, still sat on the hill, her hatches sealed, no sign of rescue.

Bays kept shooting, mainly into bricks and mortar. Harp let fly as well, each shot a broken window, anything to keep the smugglers' heads down, buy them time to clear the buildings. Then he didn't have a clear target any longer, and the men and women at his side were slapping others on the back and cheering. Harp dropped limply in a seat, his stomach churning.

'Take a breath, kid. Head between your knees.' The sergeant pushed his head down.

'Sarge.' Harp swallowed, tried again. 'I killed... three people back there. Maybe four.'

'And you saved six, you think we'd be here otherwise? We didn't start it. Now we need to focus on our jobs and get those folk arrested. Right?'

'Right, Sarge.' Harp straightened, hoping Mullah couldn't feel him shaking.

'Good.' The sarge looked back and smiled; the locals hadn't chased them. Then toward the cruiser, frowning, where the ramp was lowering at last, like everything was normal. 'Right, lads n lasses, we'll see this through then it's up to the Orbital and we'll get good and drunk. I'm buying.'

Of course it wasn't that simple. Orders from above had them staying put, the cruiser's guns aimed at the town, until not one but two more cruisers landed. *Mercy* wasn't part of the arrests but *Faithful* was, her captain nothing like so cheerful this time. Harp figured Mullah would report that the town had simply been afraid to help them. But that didn't seem to mean much these days.

6

'Damn that Regis.' Harp watched as Bays threw himself onto the nearest bunk. 'You're missing your own damn party.' It was three days later. They were offworld, docked at the Moon Orbital while a Militia refit crew swarmed over everything in sight and the crew finally had leave – except for Harp who'd been confined to ship because of "possible infection". Right now even some of his pets were cursing Regis. The fool in charge of them had Mullah on report for insubordination cos the sergeant tried, and failed, to make him issue Harp and Bays with commendations. Ludwiz – who *had* got one cos of being wounded – swore he didn't want it, much more friendly these days.

Bays sat up enough to pull his work-boots off and throw them at his locker where they clanged against the open metal door and bounced back out, to land on Goss as she slid past him, dressed to party. Goss swore too, then sighed. 'The other crews have been spreading the story. We should get free drinks all night.'

'So you'll drink mine.' Harp tried to smile. 'I'm fine. I like the quiet.' Much as he'd like to get drunk Harp wasn't convinced he'd have kept the drinks down anyway. Truth was, although he tried to hide the fact, he hadn't felt right since he'd killed those people; had begun to think he never would. It was all very well Mullah saying he'd only hurt smugglers, but what if some were simply too-scared settlers, doing what the smugglers said to save their loved ones? Each time the memory came back he started shivering, or sweating, or the two together. It was damned embarrassing, he'd had to say he must have caught a cold and then they'd dosed him, like a baby. And of course the captain stuck him back on cleanup then refused him leave again in case he was infectious. Anything to keep him out of sight, as if the whole militia didn't know he was in *Mercy's* crew by this time.

Of course the captain hadn't stayed on board, oh no; he'd disembarked as soon as the umbilical locked on, "to debrief on the insurrection", no doubt to explain the failings in his crew that landed them in danger and some reason why he couldn't come and help them. Odds on he'd somehow pin the blame on Harp, or Mullah. Harp let out a sigh. He'd got resigned to the fact Regis' version of World's obsession with 'family values' meant the man felt entitled to hate him cos he'd been born "out of wedlock" as they quaintly put it, like it was a prison, but it was totally unfair to take such prejudices out on Mullah. And there was nothing he could do to help except to keep Bays' outbursts, growing wilder by the hour, here in private.

The techs left him pretty much alone after the first day so he alternated the damn calisthenics they were supposed to use to offset the pull of Orbital's gravity with some reading Mullah left him. Newscom said there'd been another "minor altercation" on Moon's surface but at least nobody else was hurt. Nobody was going out undermanned or under-equipped now, even on the "friendly" missions. Squads kept open channels cars-to-cruisers. There'd been scuffles, but no bodies.

The crew were back three days later and the techs got off once Mullah signed the docket. Then the captain sauntered on, complaining that the ship was filthy and that Harp, 'on watch', had been responsible for keeping *Mercy* 'shipshape'. Docked his pay, again. And everyone was treating him like glass; perhaps they didn't trust him any longer either. Maybe him being a killer as well was the last straw for them all.

So when he got the call to report to Regis the following day his first thought was the man had finally found the excuse he wanted to get rid of him. He was already on permanent clean up, what else was left? He made himself as tidy as the worn uniform allowed and prepared for the worst. Citing failure to single-handedly clean the ship was a push, but if Regis had somehow managed to convince the brass up here he was responsible for the mess – the deaths – in Welcome, and was citing that as proof he was unstable … a dishonourable discharge didn't sound impossible, and the way things were, no one on the surface would even look at him for a job then.

+++

When the door sounded Regis sat more upright and used the stern expression he'd practiced. He'd been looking forward to this for hours. 'Come.' He made sure he didn't look up till he heard the bastard's boots come to rest on the other side of his desk. He'd raised his chair specially, but the damned mongrel was still too tall so he leaned back, fingers together, trying to appear at ease while Harp stood to attention. 'Private Harp.'

'Yessir.'

Regis stopped a scowl. Almost a year on board and the mongrel still had that appalling farmboy accent. It was a disgrace, especially attached to the patrician looks Regis secretly envied. And it always felt faintly… insubordinate. Not openly insubordinate, he could have dealt with that, but the dumb insolence was almost as bad. More importantly for Regis's peace of mind, the bastard had always drawn the wrong kind of attention. Yes, it was more than time the brute was gone. Nothing about him reflected well on Regis's command out here either. He took up too much room, and Regis was convinced he studied – trying to become his captain's equal – even though he'd never caught him. And half this damn crew had made a *pet* of the embarrassment; oh yes, high time it ended.

Harp stood waiting like a dummy. The close-fitting greys, designed for the close confines of a militia ship, showed off the hulking shoulders and washboard stomach, the unsightly muscle. Regis was convinced the galley gave the bastard extra portions even though he'd personally cut the rations to the lower orders, selling off the surplus for a tidy profit as he did the water. He'd always been an entrepreneur. Without thinking, Regis sucked in his own gut, then scowled as he felt it relax again of its own accord. Yes, those cheekbones weren't as knife-sharp these days as at the start. Though he was still leaner than most of the crew, the women included. Regis had to wonder how many of them, men or women...

Straightening, he pulled his mind off lower-deck perversions and back to the present, and the present almost made him smile. This was a day he'd wished for. 'You've been transferred, Private, effective immediately. And you're in luck, there's a navy frigate in port right now with orders to transport you.'

'Sir.' A pause, without expression. When Regis didn't speak again the bastard asked, 'Where to, sir?'

'After the debacle on the surface someone's obviously decided that you need retraining.' Regis glanced down at the less attractive details. 'Unlikely as it seems, you're going to World.' He watched the bastard blink, shock finally leaking out, then delivered the coup de grace. 'Your transport leaves at 1400. I'll send you your travel orders.'

'Yessir.' Disappointingly the bastard just about-turned and left, leaving Regis hovering between relief and annoyance. He was finally rid of him, but to World? It was well away from Regis but really, the last place the creature belonged. Given a choice Regis would have dropped him into that volcano the brass were so impressed by right now.

+++

A transfer, and to World? Harp stalled in the corridor outside, trying to take it in. OK. Orders. He had orders, and no time for panicking. He had to pack and board a navy ship, and fourteen hundred hours was only two hours away. Which navy ship? It was damned hard work, trying to run and read the orders now appearing on his wristcom at the same time, so he settled for the bare bones. When Bays met up with him in the lower deck corridor Harp figured word had gone before him. Bays confirmed it. 'Navy, eh? I wonder how you'll do with all those Worlders.'

Harp could smile. 'I survived this year with you lot.'

'Yeah, but they're a snooty lot.' Bays' smile died. 'You'll be better off somewhere else, but I'll miss you, kid.'

'Same here.' Harp meant it, but he figured yet another life was over. No one had ever kept him more than three-four years. This time he barely had time to say goodbye, and how he was to make it to his transport…

Bays hurried to keep up. 'Two hours, yeah? What berth?'

Harp sighed. 'Red ten.'

'That's right around the other end of navy's dock.' Bays tapped his wristcom. 'Crip.' His lips twitched. 'Have you seen the name of the ship?'

'Yeah,' Harp said grimly. Even running he could hardly miss that.

'Maybe it's an omen.'

'Oh yeah.' They had reached their quarters. Harp felt a bit adrift. He might not like everyone here – and he doubted anyone but Bays would talk rubbish about missing him – but it was probably the best year he could recall. And it was over, just like that in seconds.

Bays clapped him on the back. 'Go make us proud, kid.' They clasped hands. 'But watch out for those sneaky Worlders.' Bays swung the hatch.

Harp ducked through – into a wall of grinning faces. His bunk was stripped. His few personals were out of the net and laid on the bare mattress.

Bays pushed him in and grinned from ear to ear. 'We got your bedding handled, but nobody can crack your locker code. Not as anyone's ever tried,' he added quickly. 'So you'll have to pack your own gear.'

Harp swallowed. 'Thanks, guys. Looks like the grapevine's outdone itself.'

Goss snorted. 'Mullah was up on the bridge, just not soon enough; he leaked it as soon as he found out, but you'd already gone to report to Regis. Mullah checked the log too; Regis sat on the orders for six bloody hours.' Angry faces. 'We're damned if he's going to get you into trouble with navy for boarding late.'

'Well, I don't have much to pack, and you've saved me the detour to Stores.' These people weren't all friends; still didn't all like what he was. Maybe one or two still felt he shouldn't be on *Mercy*, same as Regis, that he made them less respectable – but they were crewmates, and that counted. It'd taken him a while to learn the difference, but he wouldn't forget it again. 'Thanks for everything. I mean it.'

'Aw, get on with it.' Goss punched his arm, then kissed him, then blushed. The other women followed. The men, thankfully, offered hands or nods.

His few personals, his militia issue, rolled, folded, shut down, packed; a textbook exercise, and he'd long since memorised the sketchy textbook. Turning in the hatchway, he gave the nod-and-hands-tucked-in salute Militia used onboard, that Mullah said they copied from the navy. There was silence for a moment then they laughed. 'Best practise that,' Bays added. 'I hear navy do a lot more of it.'

7

Jogging off the *Mercy* onto an empty dockside, he felt a little lost, a little… bereft. Telling himself grow up, get on with it. Posted, somewhere. He still hadn't had time to look that far ahead, but his first stop was a navy frigate named *Harpan's Luck*. Ouch. Good thing he wouldn't be on board long. Although according to these orders, now he quickly read the next part while a riser took him up one, her listed destination was the Orbital that served Harpan's World. Where he was supposed to transfer to the navy's own training centre? He was going all the way to World, being sent into the navy? Assuming Regis hadn't mucked up these orders he'd be there in five days' time. Assuming he boarded his lift before she left dock, cos he'd plotted a course now and he still had to get halfway round the Orbital's outer wheel, lower-deck crew naturally being barred from cutting across officer country at the centre.

Regis was a complete shit, but at least Harp was rid of him – hopefully for good. Stepping off the riser, Harp dodged a line of carts snaking across his path, hopped over one of the connections between them, round two of the ever-present construction crew, this time doing something with red cables, then strode on toward the walkway he needed next. It was too far to get there on foot, but also too far to spring for the price of a suspended railcar, something that *wasn't* included in his travel permits. That was Regis; mean and ornery to the last. He wondered, vaguely, if the navy would find as many reasons to dock his pay as Regis had. Small miracle he'd managed to save anything. And no time now to make the link to transfer what he had on his Orbital account, let alone he didn't know where to transfer it to. He should remember to do that though, once he found out where he was based. In the meantime, focus on getting to the first stage of his journey.

Luckily the walkway was nonstop, and not crowded

today. A few sideways steps took him from slow to high speed ribbon and off he went, scuffed grey kitcase at his feet, his old duffle at his back. He might even look like he knew what he was doing.

Two walkways later he was getting close. Red quadrant was the end of the line, but he was making decent time. Eventually he sidestepped back into another slow lane then off, and started counting berths. Red was a quarter of Orbital's cake, he thought, and navy-restricted. Having to show he had orders to be in there cost him some precious minutes. And according to his reading, *Harpan's Luck* was at the farther end.

He'd read up on the main specs of these larger ships after his first flight up here, yet another new thing he'd been ignorant of. Ship-gravity was supposed to be set the same as an Orbital's, at least in human-based habitats – some kind of average, one-size-fits-all, but there were sure to be a lot of other things didn't match, weren't there? Bigger, obviously. More than *Mercy's* two decks and a hold, so he'd have to learn not to get lost again, but the same ranks and rules, surely? Just more people, wearing dark blue uniforms instead of grey.

Red five. Six. Seven. According to the largely unlit overheads the navy berths were mostly empty. He wouldn't *see* any of the navy ships of course, any more than he could the *Mercy*, only the tube-like access where a ship would dock and be connected, most of which were only visible right now as giant, vac-sealed hatches. Even those were bigger than Militia's.

Red ten's umbilical stood open, had a six-strong team of red-tabbed Orbital Security hovering outside it too. The overhead said "*Harpan's Luck*" all right, and "Final Boarding". OK; made it. He strode to meet his latest challenge. 'Reporting in, Corporal.'

The Security com-synced, read his orders, raised his eyebrows then passed the buck. 'Cleared to board, Private.'

'Thanks.'

'Their Ops is on this deck, C11. They should have your

berth and such.' He still looked doubtful. Understandable; Harp wasn't navy.

'C11, thanks.' Repeating numbers had got to be a way of life but it did help a guy remember instructions.

His lone footsteps echoed more than usual, cos this umbilical was bigger than *Mercy's*. And there was more condensation on the gridded deck plates, where warmth escaping from the frigate hit the cold of dockside. So it was no surprise the inner lock stood wide, this time with navy uniforms on watch, stood idle, till they saw him coming. 'Hey, Militia, you get lost?'

'No, transfer orders. Which way's C11, friend?'

'Transferring, eh. Well, welcome to –' The man's attention sharpened, Harp had stepped into the light. He checked Harp's name tag. The other private straightened too, his gaze flicked to and fro between the name tag and Harp's tell-tale features.

Sure enough. 'We don't see many of you off World. Friend.' When Harp didn't object to the same greeting the man relaxed more. 'Not dressed as a private, and certainly not in the militia.' He tried a smile. 'You meant to be undercover?'

Made a change. Mooners usually jumped straight to the more obvious conclusion – at least, it was obvious to Mooners who knew damn well the Family never deigned to make the trip this way. 'No. Seems like I slipped the net. I was born on Moon, never been to World till now.'

'Oh yeah?' The private led him in then turned left; a smaller man, older and a lot better turned out. Harp had grown used to the drab grey he wore, but the three-piece blues the navy wore off ship, the trousers, tee and jacket, made him feel a very poor relation. Then he almost smiled. Poor relation was a polite term for him compared to some he'd heard from stricter, old school Mooners, and, of course, from Regis.

The other man led him along a metal passage, currently deserted, so far very like the cruiser. 'You've really never been to World before?' He sounded doubtful.

'Nope.' But he might as well ask. 'Is it like the vids?'

The other man laughed. 'All pretty and polished? What do you think?'

'I guess I figured they were the best parts, and maybe the rest was more like here, but I never thought I'd get to see. Still, orders is orders, heh?' And yes, perhaps he did exaggerate the Mooner accent, just a little. Not so broadly as he did with Regis.

'Usually are.' The man slowed by a closed hatch, turned and studied Harp a moment, obviously still intrigued. 'I'm Yats.' It said so on his jacket, but it was a gesture.

'Harp.'

'Yeah, kinda memorable.' Only this time Yats was smiling. 'Word of advice?'

'I'd be obliged, sir.'

'If you really were born on Moon, well, you can't help what you look like. I'm thinking you're used to that? You might not be popular – but most'll leave you be, you only being onboard the one trip and not navy anyway. There's some might not, though, might decide to show everyone how righteous they are, and it don't do to rock that particular boat so you're not likely to find much help. Watch out for Vengis especially. He's a petty officer, and a right–' A hatch swung inward and another crewman passed them, leaving. 'Ops, your stop. Good luck.' Yats turned and went the way he'd come, and Harp bent through the opening before him.

There was a general admin space inside, bigger than *Mercy's* wardroom: several desks in work mode, several crew sat by them, at least one inner hatchway in sight suggesting more. Voices layered the air, screens flickered. He identified two officers by the linked H and Ns on their jackets but opted for the nearest body with a sergeant's stripes as safer. At any rate the woman didn't seem upset to be accosted.

'Yes,–' Belatedly she realised he wasn't navy, straightened. 'Yes, Private?'

'Ma'am. Security said to report here for a berth.' He offered his wrist.

She swiped hers over it and studied the resulting orders. 'Private Harp, Militia, transfer to Foundation Training Centre.' A second look took longer. 'Going home, Private?'

She was only trying to be nice. 'No, Ma'am. Born right here.'

'Ah.' If she was curious she hid it more than Yats, tapping buttons instead of asking questions. 'Alright. You've been assigned a one-bunk, lucky you. D 215 aft. And D10 mess. Non-navy passengers are restricted to off duty areas. You'll need to review ship's regs and layout stat. Best to reset your com to the navy band, and use a tracker right away to get around, keep out of trouble.'

'Yes, Ma'am.' He'd never needed nav help on the cruiser. Nor been barred much anywhere except the captain's quarters. But it seemed fair; he'd had a job to do on *Mercy*. Here he'd be under navy feet. He stepped back, tried to nod navy fashion, keeping his hands down; probably not quick enough. About-turned, stepped outside again and tapped his wristcom to wake up its tracking system. 'Current location to D215, locate.' Hopefully it would organise itself to tap into the frigate's codes, get authorisation and access the deck plans.

Crew passed by. Some looked him over, others didn't, but he couldn't move yet cos it took the tracker on his com an age to synch with navy's system and respond with a direction. Eventually it flashed a back-lit map, a green line pointing onward.

D deck, helpfully, was one deck 'down', via grav chute; an actual down right now while the ship was in dock and the slightly heavier Orbital gravity ruled. Militia cruisers didn't rate or need such luxuries as gravs, but he had used one on the Orbital. This was one of the faster ones; his baggage damn near floated for a moment when he boarded. So he stepped off smartly at the hole tagged D, and yanked his gear free just in time before it went without him, following his wrist again past signs and numbers. This place was a mess of acronyms, an alien language. Grav felt comfortable enough but by the

time he got to D215 his bags felt heavier and he felt…
lost.

No lever on the hatch this time. Instead his wristcom
tripped the lock into his temporary refuge. And glory be,
it really was a one-bunk, even if it was a cupboard. The
narrow bunk filled half the space, with storage high and
low and yep, the usual thin mattress. Somebody had left
the bedding in a squared-off pile at its centre, so he
wouldn't have to forage; seemed the navy had good
manners. There was even a wall screen set into the
bulkhead at one end of the bunk. And a panel in the
furthest wall led to a tiny private head; a flip-down waste
disposal and a shower somehow shoehorned in an area
about as big as he was. Still. A place all to himself, the
first time ever. No one else's gear, or noises, or smells.
Wow.

He took a deep breath, and started stowing his
belongings.

8

Bunk made up and everything squared away – cos maybe someone would decide to inspect – he stretched out, trying to get his breath back. Then his wristcom signalled 'messages'. He took another breath and woke that nice big screen up.

Ship's comp had registered his presence. Ship's comp had manuals for non-navy personnel on board, and presented them in order of importance – to the ship. So regs, deck clearances and penalties came before mess schedules and course timetables. But it was all there and all useful and he figured he was meant to read it all before he ventured out to cause these people problems. He settled in and set the screen to vid and audio and started learning. He was halfway through it when the screen blanked and an override instructed, 'Militia Harp to report to Petty Officer Vengis, immediate.'

Vengis; the name Yats had mentioned, someone to stay clear of. Seemed that wasn't going to happen. A query to his tracker placed Vengis in D105, forward, but he was cleared for most of D deck. He tidied up, as much as militia gear did, reset his tracker with D215 as 'home' then set it to take him to 105, wondering why. He hadn't done anything wrong already, had he? Or had Regis set him up for something?

Turned out his existence was enough for Vengis. At first Harp thought it might be cos he was Militia, but he soon worked out that Vengis was another, lesser Regis; more belligerent, and weirdly less offensive with it, but another one who didn't want to breathe the same recycled air as Mooners, or a failure in planned genetics. He'd obviously checked Harp's file. Notwithstanding that he barked out questions, then he scowled and muttered 'rubbish' at the file on his screen, and then he pounced on Harp's apprenticeships. 'Militia as tithe payment? So two ranches got rid of you?'

'I guess tithes do have to be paid, sir.' A devil

prompted Harp to drop back to his dumbass farmboy drawl. He'd learned to tone it down, but he could bring it back when it was useful. Sometimes doing it made folk ignore him, sometimes it annoyed them. Vengis looked royally pissed by the time Harp got to the part about him being transferred although he hadn't actually applied to join the navy, not even knowing what kind of training was taking him to World. Then he outright snarled at his screen when the details didn't show in *Luck's* comp either.

If Harp was honest, which he wasn't going to be with Vengis, he found that omission a mite worrisome too. For once he actually hoped it was just Regis playing power games again. By then he was answering the petty officer on dumbass autopilot. Vengis wanted to put Harp in whatever place Vengis thought he belonged, make him feel ashamed? Try bashing through that shell. Better than him had tried, and when Harp was a lot smaller. The fact was he didn't belong anywhere, did he? He didn't like what he was, he couldn't ignore it, but he'd pretty much learned he had to live with it. Yep, he was a blatant Harpan bastard, a blot on a society that was convinced such stuff was all-important; but he hadn't asked for it, didn't trade on it and *wasn't* the one to blame for it. If there was shame involved, let somebody else own it; he'd grown past it. End of story, till the next new face thought different and he had to grin and bear it.

Maybe he'd sighed or something. Vengis stopped talking and dismissed him. Of course that might be cos when Harp hit the passageway and checked his com he found he should have hit the mess a half hour earlier. Deliberate? He'd bet on it. He'd met the type before. The more important question was would the navy feed him, cos he'd missed one meal today already and he'd lost the knack for going hungry.

'Get lost, did you?' Then the man looked up. The smile died. 'Or was you expecting room service?' Cooks Harp had known never liked latecomers; it seemed that went for navy cooks too, even if they weren't sure what he was. Prepared to glare at someone who might turn out to be Founding Family, because they broke *his* rules? He could respect that. If the man turned him away it'd be no more than he'd have done for everyone else.

'Well?' The cook behind the counter had a thick, black beard, maybe to make up for the bald head. Ranchers favoured beards but Militia didn't, yet another difference. Four more mess crew stopped to watch the interaction and the mess hall at his back, long tables still half full, went from the buzz since Harp had entered to an ear-flapping silence. Waiting for his answer.

'Sorry, sir, I had to report to Petty Officer Vengis. Am I too late?' Most of the counter racks were already gone. He could see huge pans being scraped and slotted into a giant washer unit.

Maybe he'd sounded suitably contrite, or the cook wasn't a fan of Vengis either. The beard stopped bristling. 'Huh. You're in luck, kid. This lot left a mouthful.' Someone laughed. Perhaps the tension eased a little. Cook's arms moved in a blur. 'Here. No choice, but come back if you fancy seconds. Only make it quick.'

'Yessir, thank you sir.' Harp grabbed the loaded tray and took it to the nearest empty table, more than happy to eat quickly. The food was warm but generous; he wouldn't need seconds so he slowed to enjoy an actual dessert, another change from *Mercy*. This one was a cake with lemon flavoured filling and a glop of white on top. It wasn't real cream – he'd tasted that a few times on the ranch – but it was close. OK. So he was packed alongside strangers yet again, and Vengis, but for now he had good eats and the amazing private cabin.

Then a shadow fell across the cake. 'Hm. Harp. That'll be short for Harpan, then?'

Harp laid down his fork, the bulky shadow blocking him from rising. 'Guess it sounds like, don't it?'

'Cept I never seen one of the Family in greys before, nor in the ranks. They decide you weren't good enough for World?' The mess went quiet again. Insulting someone who might be Family? Either this man was a fool, or someone had already leaked Harp's background. Harp might bet a cred or two on Vengis, which meant these were likely that man's lackeys.

So... back came the drawl. 'Never been to World, friend, so I couldn't rightly tell you.'

'That so?' The corporal raised his eyebrows, playing to his cronies. 'I'd have thought they'd keep their leftovers close to home, that's if they didn't put their mistakes down at birth. So why are you so different?'

He only wished he knew. 'Ah, maybe I'm not bright enough?' Harp smiled up at them. 'I was real good with steers though, and never met a ranger anywhere I couldn't saddle. Sure will miss that, less you guys have ranches.'

Idiocy nearly always worked. The speaker looked disgusted. 'Well you listen, bastard farmboy.'

'Yessir?'

'You just mind your manners, got that?'

'Sure, I hope I always do, sir.' Harp smiled sweetly. His tormentor stared, then found an ugly smile. 'Yeah, I see you do. Maybe we'll see you again.'

'I sure do hope so, sir.' He almost overdid it. The man's eyes narrowed then his brow smoothed out again. He shook his head, exchanged knowing looks with his friends and sauntered off. Harp returned to the cake.

This time the new arrival slid onto the bench beside him. Yats. 'You have a death wish, kid?'

Harp's shoulders loosened. 'Why, no sir.'

'Well you might when Wash works out you conned him.'

'Hmm. That likely though?'

Yats grinned. 'Not from me, kid, I'm enjoying it too much, but how long can you keep up the hick accent?'

Harp fought a grin of his own. 'Hell, I can keep this ole thing goin' till the lady steers come home for milkin.'

Yats laughed. 'Five days'll be no problem then.'

'Mm.' Harp dug fork into cake. Yats stood and followed Wash out. There was still some muttering, but it didn't feel so bad now and as Yats had pointed out he only had five days of it to deal with. Navy ate at the end of each watch like Militia, three times a 'day', so maybe thirteen more meals.

His second meal on board was more peaceful – Wash and his cronies didn't appear – but a little surprising, it looked like the navy Thanksgiving was worded a bit different to Moon's and Militia's. They said thanks to the Founding Family first and everything else after. Harp was careful not to comment, but it kinda made him wonder; what else would be different?

In the event he only got to eight meals, between time in the D deck gym and more on his bunk studying. He did have to dodge Wash and his cronies a couple times, once he figured was with Yats' connivance. Just as well he had that one-berth he could lock while he was sleeping. But on the third day he clean lost his appetite anyway.

His nice big bunk screen had fed him a lot of general data on the navy and some more specific details he hoped would make the move easier. With nothing else to do, and aware he was probably better off out of sight anyway, he'd spent most of his time between meals keeping fit or on his bunk learning what he could. That included the ship's regular newscom bulletins. Some were ship-based but others were sent from World, the latter mostly sports or politics or entertainment, more than he was used to getting on the *Mercy*, so he did keep busy. On a whim he even asked the comp to show him the location of some human-populated planets. Thoughts about how little he knew, World-wise, prompted questioning what more *was* out here. The data he could find was old – more like ancient – but it looked like there weren't *any* other planets, not in reach, cept mention of a couple Kraic-settled worlds. Which meant if there *were* any more humans now it wasn't for at least two star systems? He guessed that explained why no one ever bothered to teach him about them. Either they were so far away they weren't in touch, or all the so-called history was guesswork.

Or there *weren't* more human planets any longer?

+++

On his second 'day' on board there was some news from Moon. That made him pay attention.

'An update from Harpan's Moon reveals that the semi-dormant volcano on Collar Mountain, which we understand has been the cause of interest in government circles for some time, has now been officially classed as a regional health hazard.'

It had?

'The region has always been one of Moon's so-called hot zones, but sulphur emission levels have apparently been rising steadily there for some time and –' The civ onscreen stopped speaking, looking sideways. 'Breaking news, viewers. In the last hour flames have been sighted coming from the caldera, and it appears molten lava has broken through in one location just below the summit on its western slope. I believe we have vid of it, coming through to you any moment.'

Collar Mountain, where he'd seen only distant smoke and night-time sparks.

The vid showed a view not unlike he recalled, from several miles out on the surrounding plain; maybe from the edge of the very township he'd revisited. The mountain's peak, almost due north, was no longer topped by a hazy-grey, it was a mass of lurid smoke, like a distant campfire just visible above the lip. When the picture shifted Harp realised someone had switched to showing images up closer, from a second, moving camra. This one flew around the steeper west side of the mountain, sending images of lava flowing like a burning river. Eating everything before it, down the slope but thankfully not in the direction of the little township he had grown up next to. Trees were bursting into flames and massive boulders tossed and dragged along within the flood like they were pebbles.

'As a precautionary measure the Riverbend mining operation is being temporarily shut down and local inhabitants are being evacuated, as we can see.' There was a shot of assorted vehicles, from groundcars to steer-drawn carts, all going the same direction, a single Militia cruiser and the familiar grey uniforms; no one from *Mercy*. 'Experts have declared the eruption a possible threat to the local inhabitants. Although the threat is not extreme, the air quality in the region is slowly deteriorating, such that…'

The man talked on but Harp was focussed on the vid. The lava wasn't much like water, as he'd believed; more like a crusty-looking, surging mix of grey and crimson soup. It didn't look like it was slowing, and the ground didn't flatten out much at the bottom. He figured if the lava changed course it'd only have a few miles to go to reach that end of the township. Those experts might not think the threat was enough to panic about, but it sure must feel that way to the folk living there; looked it to him as well. Even the underground rooms a lot of the Riverbend houses probably had nowadays wouldn't protect them if that happened – in fact they'd be a death trap. Moreover, Collar wasn't the only mountain on Moon – what if they became volcanoes too? Was anybody checking others were still dead, or dormant or whatever, or could they be coming back to life as well?

When Collar first started smoking he'd been intrigued and read up on it, having seen the smoke for himself. The experts then, maybe the same ones this guy was talking about now, had said the smoke was 'negligible', and that any 'real' volcanic activity was a thing of the past, on both World and Moon. But he had wondered. After all, with drought, and prairie fires. And now this… What *couldn't* happen?

He'd put a tag on any news reference to Collar, or volcano, but after the first flurry the casters seemed to tire of the subject. Successive news bulletins only showed repeats of the images he'd already seen and there was no more mention of the threatened township, so he'd thought maybe things back home weren't as bad as the first panic envisaged. He'd wondered if *Mercy* had been part of the relief duty at some point, and wished that Regis could have held off getting rid of him for a few more days so he could do his duty to the folk who'd given him a roof those years before. It was frustrating to be sat out here above it all, in the most luxury he'd ever known, when folk back home were deep in trouble. When his com reminded him of chow time there was no way he could face free food again right now. Or careless Worlders. He would study some, and wait for updates.

But there wasn't any more word from home before he needed to think more about what lay ahead than behind. He had to think Vengis and Wash were a warning shot. Though what he could do about it…

+++

OK. Day four. Decision time. Harp sat on his bunk, no witnesses in here, and stared at the two little shot-caps the fancy comp system had ejected. One would change things, so it promised, and the other would reverse the process. If he wanted.

The first had just cost him twenty cred, the second his last thirty. Robbery, of course, because you couldn't call up one *without* the other. So fifty cred, because the comp insisted that the dosage was "cosmetic, non-essential". But what might be cosmetic to the comp could be an essential for him, if he was going to face a lot of Worlders. Simple truth; he might be a lot better off in the days to come if he could look at least a bit less Harpan. And to do that something needed changing, and his red-gold hair had seemed the safest option. Till he held the means to do it and became a coward.

But the comp also said it took about six hours to "activate" and that meant do it now, before he slept, or maybe never. Cept he wasn't even sure he wanted… Crip, just do it, fool.

Waking brought a rush of panic, what if…? When he asked, the comp screen made a bigger mirror than he'd ever seen before, and showed him… Short of breath, he faced this near-stranger. The features looked the same, but his hair was all dark brown now, maybe with a *hint* of red. His eyebrows too, the stuff was clever. And...? Yep, down below as well so even if he stripped. The darker colour made his tan look browner too, less golden; maybe it was worth the fifty. Looking part-Harpan should be less conspicuous than all-Harpan. Maybe he should consider tossing that reversal dose and staying duller. Even if it felt so weird.

When the frigate signalled World Orbital approach he stripped his bunk then watched that on his private screen as well. Tried to convince himself he was ready. He'd stood on the Moon Orbital's obs deck a few times and stared out at the sight of Harpan's Moon; the vast curve of planet with its huge stretches of browns and reds and greens turned to duller browns, the sharp edges of the three giant, funnel-shaped, deep-mine entrances, the blotches round them that were slag heaps, or scatterings of buildings, the rare splashes of irrigated green, usually muted by protective plex domes. He hadn't dreamed Harpan's World would look this different.

Swathes of blue and brighter green were broken up by much more tidy, geometric areas of white and grey and umber, which he thought were often buildings, interspersed with something the comp id-ed as gardens; land that no one seemed to classify as either farms or ranches. He had no idea yet what their use was.

World was so much bigger too. He might have *read* it was six times the size of Moon, but actually seeing it... And infinitely bigger than the frigate. He'd read about the navy, as much as he could, but how the hell was he supposed to find his way around all that?

Idiot. You'll only get to see the fraction someone grants you access to, like here on *Luck*.

Second shock; World's Orbital was also a lot bigger than he'd expected, the berths he could see from space suggested that it was twice the circumference of Moon's. Thankfully it did seem to be the same basic layout: concentric circles, brass in the bull, docks round the outer ring. His orders had him transferring onto the next available surface shuttle, but this time he had transport passes round the rim, and even clearance to bypass civilian formalities. Another difference, and perhaps a hint of how the navy did things.

He'd shared meals with a few of *Luck's* crew. They'd been OK except for Vengis and Wash, curious looks at the freak but polite enough talk in the end. It had been an easier time than he'd expected. He wasn't sure how to read that. Though he couldn't lose the feeling some of that was luck; he was sure Wash had intended to shake him down, both for the fun of it and whatever he could steal. The rest of the crew, it was almost as if they didn't really believe he was a bastard, even after Vengis made it pretty public. But he didn't feel obliged to say goodbyes, especially now he didn't want them looking closer. So when the tannoy announced the ship was docked and locked he donned his old grey jacket, pulled the knit watch cap low on his head, shouldered his duffle, hefted his case, signed off at C11 – and walked onto a spotless navy dockside. Bigger, older, obviously long completed.

No banging and rattling or bare power lines here, and the few trollies rolled almost silently. It wasn't as cold as the docks on Moon Orbital either. Even the condensation from the beams above had somehow been tamed, from intermittent rain to the odd drip. Amazingly it also looked like he was first to disembark. It was so quiet out here his footsteps sounded like they shouldn't be there. Where was everybody?

It was a relief of sorts when further round the dockside, minutes from the relatively quiet – restricted? – area round *Luck*, there was a sudden, almost welcome mass of folk to weave through, and a deluge of familiar dockside noises; cargo pods, cranes and heavy lifters, baggage carts and loaders. He must have disembarked so early such things hadn't got to *Luck* yet.

But if he ever thought Moon wasn't a backwater he sure knew better an hour later.

9

His route included some civilian sectors a step in from the workaday rim. There was quieter flooring in these inner sectors so his footsteps were a whisper, but the passages were more crowded and the folk here had fancier clothes – fancier voices too. Nobody *sounded* like him anymore. He found that more unnerving than expected. Inevitably he got stared at, even after he remembered to remove the cap so the new hair was visible, but he told himself it was probably cos he was the only one in grey.

An hour after he'd disembarked his wristcom told him to hop off a bright, purring trolley cart at a sign directing him to "Surface Transport, Military and Authorised Personnel Only" and follow his tracker down another interior tunnel. Turning off into this wider, quieter corridor was welcome. He guessed he had to get used to all this for a while, but he sure didn't object to a break.

Not far though, and this surface shuttle was at least smaller than *Mercy*. Another relief. And prettier, with cushiony seats maybe a third full. Mostly navy, the rest what he was already labelling the fancier class of civs, so he chose a seat in an empty row near the back and waited for folk to forget him again. Which they did, they left the row alone except one of the crew came back to check on him, ask if he was comfortable, locked down, understood about zero-g. How did the woman think he got here, magic? But he smiled back and accepted a sealed beverage.

Otherwise no one took much notice. He only figured as he joined the line to disembark the woman must still have thought him *real* Harpan kin, however distant, trying to go unnoticed. Had the others thought the same? Hadn't the colour change made any difference? Obviously not enough; she'd just flashed him her callup.

He smiled and ran, figuring that would be less embarrassing for both of them. Was that what being real-

Family felt like, being treated as special? Even when they tried to avoid it? He almost forgot he was now actually on World, still shaking his head as he crossed an open concourse that was very much like the one he'd just left, except gravity told him pretty plainly he was somewhere different. It felt like World was as heavy again as *Luck*. More muscle building? He hefted his gear, which also felt heavier, naturally enough, checked his wristcom for his next move – and barged into someone going the other way. 'Crip, sorry.' The body he'd hit was navy, and a lot smaller, and softer. 'My fault, Ma'am, I didn't –'

Double crip, this *was* a real-Harpan, had to be; the pale hair, the slanted eyes he'd never seen on Harpan's Moon, except in pictures or a bloody mirror.

'It's quite all right. It is a crush, isn't it?' Her accent was different again, kind of sharp but rich at the same time. Kind of like singing. But she didn't sound mad, or offended, in fact she'd smiled. Only now she frowned a little, taking in his face, his worn attire, maybe picking up his clumsy accent. And the way he'd frozen, arm still bent to see his wristcom.

Now she'd checked his shoulder. 'Were you looking for anywhere in particular, Private?'

A real-Harpan, one with dimples, willing to be nice to a nobody branded with Harpan looks who was probably supposed to stay well out her way. For once he felt like the public embarrassment Regis called him. He swallowed, then figured the fastest way to get clear was answer the question.

'Thank you, Ma'am. I'm supposed to report to the navy's Foundation Training Facility?' Too late, it occurred to him there might be more than one. And was he supposed to nod?

She'd turned. 'You're new intake? That corridor. Follow the orange stripes not the blue, OK?'

'Yes, Ma'am, thank you.' Checking out the wall stripes allowed him to look away from her. He probably looked pretty dopey anyway, staring and all.

She chuckled. 'Good luck, Private.'

She walked on. Bodies jostling him reminded him to move too, only not before he saw her looking back and frowning. Ouch. Best to remove himself. But turning eased the jitters somewhat cos he saw their blurred reflections in the polished surface of a passing hovcart; her so all-round paler, him… much darker.

Breathe, fool, and thank the stars you took that colour shot.

The orange stripes meant he didn't need to watch his tracker now so he didn't bump into anyone else, at least till he reached the Facility. He'd admit he gaped again then. The entrance was a mile-wide ramp up to a huge arch made of some kind of stone stuff, ten metres high, maybe twenty wide, and more tunnel than doorway. A stone umbilical. But it had the fancy H-for-Harpan logo, this time an HW, the navy's waving line across it, so it had to be his destination. The entrance stood open at this end but he spotted smaller doors farther in, split by bars – grilles? And armed guards, and the nearest had spotted him with his mouth open. Great. He closed the stupid mouth and climbed the artificial hill before him.

He might not look so Harpanish now, but he was still a hick and in the wrong uniform. But he had the right authorisations. Eventually they let him pass. After they'd called somewhere for verification, he'd passed a body scan and they'd put his gear through another.

That didn't stop the pattern repeating at the two other guard posts. It took him over an hour to travel maybe two hundred lead-filled yards, to reach the raised-up counter called Recruit Reception, where he found a queue of other civs, both men and women, most of whom had passed him in the tunnel. Inevitably heads turned at this oddity among them, but then every move he'd ever made – from Nursery to House, from House to Pre-Employment, ranches to Militia – each new 'home' had meant a sea of judging faces and another possibility of challenge.

Old habits resurfaced. He joined the back of the queue, kept his focus on the counter ahead and his thoughts to himself, even when the man in front turned round to speak, read his name tag, blinked then turned back quickly. It might have been better if he'd asked Mullah to switch his name back to Goss. But he hadn't had time to think let alone ask – and anyway he'd got used to this latest name change, and he supposed it *would* still be his lawful name. And it wasn't as if changing it would alter what he looked like any more than he'd just managed. They'd said there was 'no provision' for altering orphan faces when his eight-year-old-self had asked. That it was against the rules. He didn't suppose that had changed, but at least now he'd altered something.

The line shuffled forward, but it looked like he was almost the last. He'd studied enough to recognise the rank labels at the counter; a Petty Officer presided. He was near enough now to see the recruits being checked off yet again, then pointed down a smaller corridor. The PO gave Harp a look, but, give him his due, treated him the same as the rest, and Harp followed the line to a space about the size of his House assembly hall but higher-ceilinged. There was yet another, longer counter, fronting vast rows of shelves and cubbies, feeding stuff from somewhere behind. Recruits were filing along while navy pushed clear packets at them, barking at them to keep moving. Looked like they were being kitted out. The prospect of looking more like everyone else made Harp step forward a lot more eagerly than some of those around him.

He wasn't so thrilled by the time he left the counter. Presumably they had his file cos they hadn't once asked his size – which argued the operation was a lot more automated than the shouting made it feel – but there was one hell of a lot of stuff and with two bags already he felt like walking inventory. Still the rest were no different – in fact some were worse – and they were all herded direct from there to a platform and onto a tube train waiting, loudspeakers ordering boarders to take the next seat in line. It was almost full, so he didn't have far to go, though he noticed a lot of the bodies slouched like they'd been there some time. There was a collective sigh of relief when a klaxon blared and all the doors slammed shut a second after, except for a yelp from the last woman in who almost left a foot outside, and did lose kit – all over both the floor and nearby bodies.

Harp used his foot, the only thing free, to push stuff back her way. Others chose to do the same. A pair of other women smirked and didn't. Yep, just like House and Pre-Employment. Hmm. Was loading them up like this the navy's way of teaching them their place? That woman sure was blushing.

The train stopped at an unmarked platform and a blank-faced building. This time they got shouted at to disembark, a lot of shouts cos now there were a lot more navy.

'Team A, fall out left.' A lot of blank expressions turned to panicked ones, but one girl shouldered through the crowd, marched left until she reached a waiting uniform and stood at attention. What the…? Harp definitely hadn't had any team allocation in his orders. Regis, leaving something out? But then the credit dropped; he had an H on all his packets, and the girl beside him had a lot of Ss, and the guy past her… 'Hey, friend, your kit's got As on it.'

The guy's head swung to him, then down. 'Crip, thanks.'

'No problem, maybe pass the word?'

'Oh, yeah.' The guy rushed forward, pointing at his packets. Harp watched heads swing, other people moving. Gradually the turmoil eased, the PO that way stopped haranguing them and other teams formed up, collected a superior to tell them what to do and marched – if you could call it that – into this building.

1 0

And straight through it without stopping. The new team H straggled through the wide corridor after other letters, seeing nothing but closed doors until they re-emerged – into the open air. Yes, real sky up there, and air that didn't smell recycled.

'Hey you, never seen sky before?'

When Harp looked down the two-stripe corporal in charge was glaring and the rest had turned to stare again. He hadn't had a Sanchez for a year, but at least it felt familiar.

'Not lately, no, Corp.' Then he saw the guy's expression, not so Sanchez. 'Sorry, Corporal.' Thankfully the man grunted and walked on, so Harp hung back and hoped out of sight was out of mind. The earlier letter 'teams' were spreading across a sunlit quadrangle hemmed in by other block-like buildings. Glancing back, he saw the one they'd passed through was identical, fake stone, no windows and a lot of storeys. No windows? Folk here evidently built much higher too. He wondered briefly if they might build underground as well, like most of Moon did now. It wasn't near as hot here though, so maybe not?

Ahead, everyone seemed to be making for two blocks right across the square. It was a chance to breathe air that wasn't recycled, that moved against his face and made him feel almost welcome, though that evaporated once the Hs gathered in a barren lobby where their corporal stopped and faced them.

'Right, stand still and listen. You miserable lot are now H-team, and your asses belong to me and the navy. You will take that chute to deck 13, dorm 13-8. You will make up your bunk, change into your uniform and stow all your belongings, as per regulations. You will be standing at the foot of your bunk, at attention, in exactly forty-five minutes. Have you got that?'

'Yessir.'

'Yes.'

A lot of mumbles.

'Got that, recruits!'

'Yessir.' This time halfway to a chorus; some learned faster than others and some, like Harp, had maybe been there before?

'Forty-five minutes from… now. Dismissed.'

A taller girl near the corporal made a beeline for the chute he'd pointed to, stepped onto the narrow, moving ledge and whisked from sight. Harp noted it was labelled 3, for future reference, hefted his belongings and decided to follow. Good thing it wasn't a grav chute or there'd be packets floating everywhere.

The chute made a wheezing noise, was maybe a lot older than the ones on Moon Orbital, but he was used to old. The big 13 marker fed him into a long corridor with more signs, though he hardly needed them when the girl was already striding away to his right. 13-8 was a long, narrow dorm – more Orphan-House parallels – so he figured the single door in the far wall would be a shared head. Mepal bunks lined both sides, only two high which was a nice surprise. Tall, mepal lockers sandwiched between, and that was it. Some of the recruits arriving looked appalled. Harp merely noted the mattresses were full size and not as thin as orphan issue.

His packets said H, and sometimes a size, but nothing else, so he figured it was first come first served and zeroed in on the first bunks left of the entry, tossing gear onto the upper mattress. Wedged into a corner with two walls was as private as this was going to get, plus he was well clear of the general to and fro of the room, and any smells nearer the head. He grinned. Being orphaned taught you all about communal living.

He knew about keeping to tight schedules as well. His arms ached in this grav, and his legs, but his wristcom said he had thirty-eight minutes left and he didn't think the corporal would be late. All right. Change, gear, bunk? Change first. The packets were good quality plas with touch seals; waterproof, maybe even airtight. Serious stuff Militia didn't have. Designed for use on navy ships like *Luck*?

One packet held new name tags with a navy logo, soft ones for clothes and tougher ones for… whatever else turned up. He'd need to seal those on but couldn't yet, unless the head boasted the press to do it; surely the corporal couldn't expect that in the time he'd allowed them. Either way, that would have to wait. He left those in their packet.

The new outfit wasn't the smarter three pieces the navy wore in dock. It was a navy one-piece, not unlike his present greys, but better fabric. Not surprisingly there were shorts and tees, also navy coloured. And some superior boots. So far so good. As he started stripping off another guy claimed the lower bunk, hesitated then offered a hand. 'I'm Hendriks.'

'Harp.' He'd never shook hands before but he'd seen it so he put his hand out too; turned out there wasn't much to it. Then he went back to getting naked. Hendriks reddened, turned away and stared down the dorm; not used to this then. Harp took pity. 'Hey, you heard the man. We have… thirty-two minutes?'

'Hell.' Hendriks turned back, blushed again but nodded. 'Right. Yeah.' He pawed at his packets, opened one up, straightened then froze.

The girl who'd got there first had chosen the top bunk opposite. Now she was standing below it glaring at them both, in pale pink scanties. 'Seen all you want, have you?'

'No!' The smaller guy went even redder. 'I mean I wasn't even… sorry.'

She sneered, turned her back and pulled a navy tee out of its packet. Hendriks spun toward Harp, now shoving a leg into a blue coverall. Hendriks gestured helplessly. 'They put girls in here?'

'Looks like it.' Orphan Houses didn't, but he'd had his year on a cruiser. 'You get used to it.'

'I doubt it.' He realised Harp was pulling boots on and he'd still done nothing. A flurry of activity ensued. At least the guy had nimble going for him, with his slighter build and long, thin fingers. Unlike Harp, he'd find this mattress ample. He was still red faced, but he wasn't alone in that. It looked like a lot of these folk were used to pampering the navy wasn't so inclined to give them.

Harp's study time on the frigate had included "squaring away". There were rules to it. Surprise. His old boots, and a second, lighter pair, went in the bottom of the nearest locker. So did his bags, folded flat. Wash kit and small personals went in handy pockets in the door, everything else onto shelves, but in a prescribed order, and folded square. Hence "squared away". He gave the result a look-over and hoped it would pass, pretended not to notice Hendriks copying and moved on to his bunk.

Mattress and pillow, rubbery but not bad. He'd been issued a bottom sheet, pillow case and a thin padded cover, like Militia issue only blue and better. And his time with Regis finally had some use; the man had been a pain about inspecting their berths, always trying to find some small infraction for which he could dock their pay. Harp went into auto, flipped the mattress, flapped the sheet, tucked, smoothed it out and gave it knife sharp corners. Placed the pillow underneath the recessed wall light and the stow-net. Finished with the cover, smoothing that as well, securing all the corners to the links the bunk provided. Changed, bunk, luggage stowed, and… eight minutes to go. So what had he missed?

The empty packets. He gathered them but couldn't see a waste disposal. Maybe in the head? Was he meant to just throw them away though? They were suspiciously tough. His gaze fell on his open locker. 'Crip, of course.' Now he had six minutes to put all his unused items *back* in the packets. Tidily, of course. That left the empty ones. He folded them and stuffed them in his duffle; probably wrong but he was out of time.

When he straightened Hendriks had changed, half stowed his gear and just about made his bunk; not bad for a guy who'd started so late. The girl had finished. She had obviously left *her* spare kit sealed. When she saw him looking she looked smug. 'You *almost* got it right.'

'You did.' Harp eyed her; not far short of him in height, brown hair pulled back, all pockets sealed, no bulges anywhere except where bulges should be. Creases from the packets but the rest... He tried a smile. 'You'll be a navy brat, I'm guessing.'

She smirked. 'And you're a Mooner.' The inference was clear; he ranked lower. Only then she added, 'Saw your name tag.' One brown eyebrow lifted.

Harp's smile died. 'Yeah? It's Harp.' The brow stayed lifted. 'Just Harp.'

Pursed lips. 'Not...?'

'Not.' He waited for her to turn away.

'O-K.' She thought about it for a moment then she nodded, some decision reached she wasn't telling. 'Hissack.' She stepped up and held a hand out. Her shake was firm, her fingers slightly calloused much like his, not soft like Hendriks' – though he thought the rest of her looked pretty soft and pampered.

He stepped back. 'I guess we're all aitches.'

'I guess.' They weighed each other up. 'Why'd you choose that bunk, not my side?'

So she didn't know everything. 'Dorm door swings not slides. So your side gets the draught more.'

'Damn.' She looked annoyed. 'I should have thought of that.'

'It comes with practice.' He didn't say where from. She'd behaved decently but they were still strangers, neither ready to share. As if they both knew that they turned and surveyed the rest of the room. There were twenty bunks set up now, one untouched, so nineteen recruits. Less than a House dorm, more than *Mercy*.

Harp figured they were all roughly the same age – no one more than mid-to-maybe-late twenties – but the view made him feel a lot older. Some recruits had completed their orders, in varying fashions. Others were obviously not going to meet the deadline. One girl was slumped on her bunk, in tears. If the corporal was anything like Mullah, let alone Regis... 'We should help out.'

'What? No way.' The girl looked scornful. Hendriks turned from straightening his bunk and listened. Harp waved at the mess. 'Look at it. What are the odds we'll *all* get penalised?'

Hendriks gaped. 'But that's… not fair.'

'Who said all this was going to be fair?' He saw their disbelief; they obviously wouldn't act, so he guessed he'd better. He raised his voice, 'Hey. Four minutes left, people. You might want to hurry along there.'

Bodies scurried, like vermin caught in a light. Hendriks started snatching up empty packets, hiding them under pillows. The floor looked tidier if nothing else. Harp slammed his and Hendriks' lockers shut – leave resetting codes for now – and pulled the covers on the next two bunks out flatter, snagging at the corner clips he'd learned to deal with on *Mercy*. Hissack didn't bother doing anything, but it was she who hovered by the door and called out, 'Someone coming.' So when the corporal, whose tag said Bigg, marched in there was some vague attempt at order, even if half the recruits were still moving and the rest still didn't know what attention meant.

Bigg stalked down the nervous room, then curled his lip. 'You call this shipshape?' He pulled a loose cover off one bunk. Moments later the entire contents of someone's locker sprawled across the floor. The victim opened his mouth, then wisely shut it. 'You *will* learn to stow your gear navy fashion. You *will* learn to make up your bunks correctly.' He rounded on the shuffling recruit behind him who had rolled his eyes. If it was Mullah he'd have known that too. 'And you. You will learn to respect your superiors, and Pay Attention At All Times. Got that, recruit?'

'Yessir.' The guy stood straighter, showing the whites of his eyes but not, quite, rolling them this time.

Bigg humphed and turned back to the room at large but the guy had learned and didn't fidget this time. 'A vaccing shambles, that's what this is. All of you, empty your lockers. Now!' Hissack locked stormy eyes with

Harp, then started grabbing her gear and lining it up on the vacant lower bunk. Her every move was precise, controlled. He had to hand it to her, her expression was impressively neutral.

They stowed, and removed. Stowed, and removed, then did it against the clock, until Bigg decided the result was "adequate". Hissack calmed down as far as precise and cool. The eye rolling guy turned sulky, which didn't help anyone as Bigg soon spotted it. Hendriks went from jittery to resigned. Harp? Found all the repetition restful. Told himself the mindless repetition counted as muscle build. Plus it gave him time to think. There was even time for a grin or two, safe inside his own head. For one thing, Bigg was actually pretty small, and maybe tried to hide it, the way he stretched his neck every time he gave a command? Harp'd found before the smallest were the loudest.

Watching the other recruits had a lighter side too; they might be used to the grav but most of them weren't any way used to being ordered around, or at least not like this. While he'd had Mullah, Bays and even Regis. The Militia were a pretty rough setup compared to here but he'd learned something. Hell. After Regis, Bigg didn't even seem that unfair.

On the downside he was the only one with a Mooner accent and as always, the only one here with the distinctive Harpanish looks he'd never be able to hide. While there were three other pairs of slanted eyes further down the room, and one set of sharper cheekbones, there was no one matched his more extreme features. He stopped a sigh, just in time. He wouldn't have minded looking like one of them instead, less obvious, more acceptable. And maybe he shouldn't have been so quick to stow things away right, that might set folk against him too. But then he was always going to be the odd one out so keeping in Bigg's good books was probably the best he could hope for.

After that Bigg had them standing at attention, the right way, then at ease, then repeating it. Harp put himself in the zone, as Mullah called it, the way he did for target practice, and the world kind of blurred and closed in to just him and Bigg. He didn't get bored or annoyed, or feel the increasing fatigue, cos he simply lost track of time. It was like waking up when Bigg rapped, 'Right. H-team, *on* my command you will form up by the door in two columns and *march*. That's assuming you useless cretins know your right from your left now. *Do* you know that?'

The "yes corporals" came out pretty smartly by now, the forming up not so much, so that got repeated a few times. Nobody had had time to visit the head. Harp figured he was good for a while yet – he hadn't eaten all day. He'd spotted some folk casting anxious looks in that direction but obviously no one wanted to ask. He wondered if it was deliberate, another way of intimidating newbies.

Bigg led them back to the ground floor, barking at them to form the two lines again when they exited the chute, chivvying them about staying evenly spaced. Harp, nearest the door so first in line his side, focussed on shortening his natural stride a little to match Hissack's. The way she marched he figured a navy background for sure; her head stayed up, eyes front, arms swinging. He was plodding along, but she made it look easy. He'd seen Militia officers move like that. No one had ever expected it from mere grunts like him, but it looked like navy was all-round pickier. His few days holed up with those navy manuals had sure been worth it.

They 'fell out' at a navy barbershop for what Harp still thought of as an orphan-cut; meant to last. Shorter than Bigg sported. Another way to teach them their place? Sitting down was heaven, even for a few minutes. Creaking up again to make room for the next recruit, he found his hair barely moved when he brushed it back. On the bright side there'd be no cracks about his curls for a while. The girls fared no better; Hissack's hair ended up as short as his. He thought it suited her. She obviously didn't, though she tried to hide it with a grim expression.

It reminded him of the real-Harpan girl he'd walked into, but her hair had been pulled back somehow, rather than truly short – and even the navy he'd seen on *Luck* hadn't been shorn this close. Wasn't there a word for this... not intimidation, they didn't call it that... yep, acclimatisation. He had heard it in the Orphan Houses. Supposed to make everyone look and feel the same. Of course it hadn't worked for him, but he'd got the idea of it: it was meant to make everyone act the same; think the same, toe the same line. The Houses had played the same game, just shouted a bit less.

And Bigg had the game down pat, a siren sounded as the last recruit stood up. 'Right, you lucky lot, now you get to eat. Form up! Left turn, march!'

The mess wasn't far, but they weren't the first. A good hundred shorn, blue-clad recruits were sat at the long mepal tables or queuing at the server counter. For whatever reason Bigg made them hang back till the previous bunch were served. Harp's legs protested. The team already shuffling along in line looked larger. Cos they all had the same first letter to their names? That simple?

Turned out the wait was cos the Thanksgiving was coming through the tannoy a moment later; Bigg had obviously known it. Like on *Luck*, the mess went quiet and the galley didn't serve till it was over, then picked up again like nothing happened. And once again the Founding Family were first in line for thankyous. Something the navy did, or World too? Probably best not to draw attention to it by asking? Odds were if anyone was in the wrong it'd be Mooners.

Bigg was talking anyway. 'H-team, advance. Freetime for chow is one half hour. Muster at the exit.' As soon as Bigg stepped aside some of the team made for the nearby door marked 'head'. When Harp nodded Hissack to take point she approached the counter the same way she'd tackled everything so far; efficient and cheerless. She took what was doled out, marched the shaped tray to the next empty seat, slotted herself over the long bench and started eating, with no appearance of enjoyment. Harp took the seat opposite. He couldn't help watching, but it was impossible to tell if she liked what she ate or hated it.

But the food wasn't at all bad, he'd had both worse and less, and sitting gave his legs another breather. Finished, they copied those ahead of them, ditching utensils in a deep bin, scraping their trays and sliding them into a half-filled rack Harp knew would go into the industrial-sized wash units behind the counter; pretty much like on the ship. None of the corporals ate, just stood at ease around the walls and talked among themselves. And watched, which muted other conversation. Bigg snapped back to life as Harp racked his tray. 'Harp, Hissack, collect your columns and lead back to your dorm, understood?'

'Yes, Corporal.' Hissack's response was a tad faster; Harp thought that pleased her.

'Lights out comes in forty. Recruits *will* wash. Clear?'

'Yessir.' Two could play at that game. Harp's reply matched Hissack's. She stiffened – sure was into competition.

Bigg's grin was evil. 'Since it's your first day you get to lie in. Rouse-up will be oh-five hundred.'

'Yessir.' Crip. Harp figured Hissack was thinking the same thing he was; they'd just been landed with prefect duty, which might please Hissack – only did she realise that meant they'd also likely get the blame if someone else screwed up? Bigg stood to one side, a silent reminder as the rest rushed up and fumbled into lines again, then nodded. 'Dismissed.'

Hissack shot Harp a look then they marched their lines forward together, past the barbershop to the chute. A break in the rhythm told Harp someone still hadn't mastered marching in step, even in a straight line. He quashed a sigh; there was always one, and it only took one to cause grief for all. Thankfully Bigg didn't stop them for it, this time. At the chute Harp stopped anyway, minding his manners.

'Easier if one line goes first?'

Hissack nodded. 'My column, move up!' She vanished

upward, her recruits following like baby birds. Yep, she had the knack. She'd likely be a corporal herself in no time.

Harp half turned to watch for the end of her line. Not far off, rolling-eyes guy managed to tread on the heel of the girl in front, then smirked when she yelped. Hmm. When the girl reached the chute the cretin stepped up too, in close again. Trying to take the same ledge? Not happening. Harp "stumbled", knocking him aside. 'Crip, sorry, friend, not used to the grav yet.' The girl rose out of sight. The guy threw Harp a filthy look and fixed dark eyes on Harp till he too vanished. Yep, always one, and it looked like Harp'd just found him.

Most of Hissack's line were in the head by the time Harp's lot reached the dorm, and they didn't seem to have got the memo about time. No choice, was there, his lot needed in the showers too. He planted himself in the head doorway.

'Bigg said lights out in thirty, folks, suggest we don't dawdle?' He must have channelled Mullah. His line gasped and scurried, the first line speeded up in reaction, and Hissack's mouth curled up at the corners as she walked out, washbag in hand, wearing her pants and tee. Harp figured if that was what she'd chosen that was what they were meant to, so he doubled back to his locker, ditched the coverall, grabbed his washkit and winced through his 'ablutions' as Bays called it. By the time he got back to his locker, what hair was left still damp, there were five minutes left. He stowed his stuff and just about managed to heave himself up to his bunk.

'Aah.' Too much too soon; he felt like he'd been washed and hung out to dry. It was going to be tough till he adjusted. He needed sleep but his mind didn't seem to have got the memo. Was he supposed to wear a fresh coverall tomorrow or not? Should he have got one out ready? And what about those name tags in his locker? Ah forget it, no way was he moving till he had to. But he thought to call out, 'I make it five minutes left, folks, and if you didn't hear it already we get up at oh-five.'

A chorus of groans told him Hissack hadn't shared that tidbit, followed seconds later by some actual protests as the lights flashed on and off. Like anyone'd listen.

'Figure that's our warning.' Hendriks was in the lower bunk, his wall light on already; Harp had pegged him for a thinker. Most of the room were now in bed. Not all. Harp hesitated, but a real crew stuck together. 'Guys, there's only – '

Either his com was two minutes off or Bigg was, cos the dorm plunged into darkness. Someone down the row clanged into something mepal, bunk or locker, started swearing loudly. Across the way a female voice cried out, and someone sniggered. Somebody inevitably farted, drawing several disgusted comments.

Welcome to communal living. Worse, there was a tiny glow near the ceiling at the other end of the room, tucked over the door to the head, so small he hadn't seen it when the dorm was lit. It could be a poor nightlight to the head but he'd vote the dorm was under navy supervision. Were they meant to notice? Safer to pretend he hadn't? Harp pulled the cover over his body, turned to his bonus wall and told himself to sleep, and now. He figured he was going to need it.

11

He was so right. A siren woke them at oh-five as promised, at the same time all the lights blazed back on. The grav still pulled at him, but maybe not quite so bad as yesterday? Determined to deal with it Harp was first up, but not the first into the head. Hissack beat him there, but evidently wasn't washing yet. Instead she made fast use of the little press in a corner alcove, sealing name tags to her clothes – fresh clothes – she evidently aimed on wearing. That made sense, they'd cool off while she showered. So again he copied, letting others grab the showers first.

On past experience he figured Hendriks checked what he was doing – Hendriks being quiet but maybe cunning – but he left the rest to keep their own selves out of trouble cos there wasn't time for too much being helpful – and he really didn't want folk thinking he was used to giving orders, let alone expected them to listen. Some folk got the picture, found their own tags, muddled through the seal, washed and got themselves in order. Amazingly, in all the to-and-fro, one guy and a couple girls were still out cold. Old habits raised their heads; he pulled the covers off in passing, grinning at the shrieks and curses.

Not everyone had reached the point of planning ahead. When Harp finally exited the shower the girl that smirk-guy had stepped on the previous night had just come out of the next stall, with a towel wrapped around her. As if on cue the next stall down slid open too and smirk-guy stepped out right behind her, towel round his waist. It looked like he had clothes in hand but hadn't dressed. The fellow pushed himself against her rear, saying something in her ear. The new girl gasped, went red and fled. Smirk smirked again and strolled out after. When Harp reached the dorm he saw the guy was still following the girl, then realised that was cos he had the bunk above her. That explained them being next in line.

But by the time Harp reached his own corner the other man still stood there, towel discarded, dressing very slowly, very occupied with watching while the girl pulled on her clothing. She looked mortified. But he wasn't doing anything reportable; no flagrantly improper moves, no actual contact, and unfortunately for the girl a bunkmate acting crass was hardly that unknown in such communal living. Harp knew from experience she'd have to either ignore it, accept it or step up and deal with the crud; herd law applied to humans just as much as steers. The weak got stepped on. You had to stand up for yourself. He turned away and counted off ten squats; the sooner he got the hang of the grav the better, before it was his turn to get hazed.

The outer door clanged open on his thoughts and Bigg marched in. Harp shoved his locker shut and leapt to stand before his bunk, and once more Hendriks copied. Hissack, big surprise, was at attention staring back at them already. Would he call that expression bland, or smug?

The bunk below her was still empty, others having passed her corner cos she hadn't looked too friendly. Hmm. But that would have to wait till Bigg was finished shouting.

Naturally a third of the dorm weren't in position. Eight got black marks – the navy said "demerits" – and everybody got bawled out; oh yeah, the honeymoon was definitely over. Harp wondered what punishments navy blacks earned; on past experience he'd go with cleanup and/or loss of wages.

He was right; Bigg promptly tagged the worst offenders for cleanup duty, in their own free time, which turned out to be swabbing the dorm for some, including of course the head, and the corridor for others. Harp wasn't included, *nice* surprise. Recalling how much of *Mercy* he'd worked on he wondered how much of the base Bigg was prepared to make use of.

Heading to breakfast he rebuked himself for feeling surprise when Hissack waved his line into the chute. So navy brat could be a lady; turn and turn-about then? This time Bigg didn't make them halt – so Harp joined the long mess queue, took a tray then found a vacant table. Others followed, looked at how Harp ate and speeded up more. Harp concealed a smile, he was simply used to orphan meals, and hired hand meals, and cruiser meals with Regis counting every 'lazy' second. They'd work out soon enough he didn't know much more than they did.

Smirk, now labelled Hoik, had chosen the next table, next to the girl again. Too close. The girl was only picking at her breakfast. Even in the heavy navy coverall she looked a waif and no, he didn't like the way she edged away from Hoik and kept her head down. He waited until Hissack rose to ditch her tray then followed. 'Hissack?'

'What?' Did she ever sound friendly?

'A word?' He kept his voice down. 'There's a girl on your line might be a lot happier bunking below you.'

Hissack gave him a blank stare. 'Yeah? She tell you that?'

'No, but – '

'But you're in charge, right?'

Dammit. 'No.' He took a breath. 'I think she's frightened.'

'Oh, so you're a white knight.' Her lip curled. 'If she's scared she shouldn't be here. Now she'll have to lump it.'

She wasn't wrong, but…

But Hissack was already leaving, obviously annoyed he'd even asked her when he'd only… only what? Was she in the right; did he think women needed protection? Hissack obviously didn't. OK. He supposed he was still pretty new round womenfolk. House Matrons hardly counted and Missus Destra, well, she'd been a boss as well; he guessed he'd only learned to deal with females in his time with the militia. And the ones he'd…interacted with… were mostly slightly older, more like Hissack; didn't look to need protection either. And he wasn't sure, really, how women usually acted. Or what they liked.

And could admit he had no notion how they thought.

His chin came up. But he did know fear; he'd been there, and that girl was scared – and Hoik sure looked to be the reason. Maybe he didn't know women but he didn't think life here was that much different. Problem was he didn't know what he could do that wasn't just a temporary fix, and those usually made stuff worse rather than better.

Bigg appeared as H-team gathered by the exit, bawled at them for ragged lines again then marched them down new corridors into an empty warehouse of a space tagged Training 2. There were already three more teams inside, at attention, each group well apart, and H-team took the final quarter of the floor space.

+++

Bigg left them to find their own way to the mess with one hour to get lunch and report back to Training 2. It'd be more half an hour for those on cleanup. Some might get short rations. Wherever Bigg went his ears must be red, and not just from those who had to bolt their food and run. They'd stood to attention, at ease. They'd marched, wheeled, about-turned, double-timed – man had that been a sight. Attention *again*. Parade rest. Harp had identified the rest of the navy brats from how they got most of it right. He hadn't. He wasn't exactly at his best in this grav, plus Militia crews didn't get that sort of spit and polish; and *Mercy's* didn't get much of any formal training, courtesy of Regis. But he thought he was starting to get the hang of it, once he listened to Bigg less and copied Hissack more.

Hissack had taken zero notice what anyone else did. That was one girl real determined to get ahead, and he figured she wouldn't mind walking on others to get there. Harp sighed; in his experience being in charge, or that way inclined, never made folk nicer. All he'd ever wanted was to go unnoticed. Since he'd never had much hope of that, he'd pretty much settled for avoiding trouble.

Lunch was a scratch meal, even the Thanksgiving seemed shorter, so the rest of H-team had no problem being back when Bigg returned with his punishment detail. Instead of looking impressed he just took them through everything again. And again. Then, when even Hissack was wilting – Harp's legs quaking – he marched them to a chilly cream-walled classroom with no windows, sat them down in rows of creaking mepal desks and turned them over to another guy, a sergeant this time, who went through the different navy ranks in detail: what to call them, when to salute, and not, who never to speak to unless they spoke to you first…

Then another corporal walked up and down the rows while they sat a test on the old-style flat-top desk screens, first on what they'd just heard then what the corporal called basic maths. Harp used some minor aerobics to release the tension in his tired limbs and forced himself to focus. He'd been considered pretty good at maths but he discovered orphan standards didn't cut it here. There was stuff he'd never even heard of. Though he might not be alone in that: when Bigg dismissed them others too wore glum expressions.

Supper. No one supervised them anymore, and the big wall screens, blank till now, had come alive too, showing some govment channel; news and such, about things that meant nothing to Harp. They were allowed to linger for an hour after supper, bar those who hadn't completed their chores; Bigg disappeared. Even so there wasn't much talk at table, nor later in the dorm, and what there was, was more in groans than conversation. Harp's com said he had nearly an hour till lights out so he washed straight away, dodging the end of the head still in cleanup, squared his gear away and settled limply in his corner eyrie, thinking he should go back over all those ranks he was supposed to know now. Figured if it was one of the first things they pushed at him it was one of the most important to them.

Down below him folk moved in and out the head – most had waited till the cleanup crew were done, seeming embarrassed by it – or started making new connections. But he was too exhausted and unsettled – the test had been the *worst* thing so far. He'd adjusted to Orbital gravs, he could surely do it again here, but he'd thought being on World, around its more sophisticated folk, would be a lot tougher in other ways. World was the source of the fervour about breeding and ancestry that had lurked around him, spoken or not, all his life. Plus he'd got the impression Worlders didn't think so much of Mooners either, so he frankly didn't understand the non-reactions. So far people were distant, but still polite. He figured the brown hair had helped, but maybe there was some sort of etiquette here too, like on Moon you didn't drink water without offering to someone didn't have any. World, its navy anyway, seemed more straight-laced than home, less rowdy. But he couldn't help but wait for that to alter.

So he felt safer being left alone, for now at least, until he knew more – or he would have if he didn't notice that the waif was also in her bottom bunk, head down, although the nuisance bunked above ignored her. So maybe that problem would blow over, maybe Hissack was right. Only the girl made him think of new-made orphans coming in wide-eyed and trembling, tossed into a system that essentially ignored them, clumped them all together. Like them, she was in a system now; like them she'd have to channel her survival instincts, grow a thicker skin, as he had so much younger. Even if he wished she didn't have to.

At which point he realised Hendriks was calling to him, head sticking out from the lower bunk. 'Sorry, what?'

Hendriks decided standing up worked better. 'I said what did you make of the second test?' He gestured to the next top bunk. The male recruit there sat, his long legs hanging, bright teeth smiling at them. 'Hamud here seems to think it was straightforward, but I'm not so sure.'

Hamud was big and more olive. Harp recalled he'd had long crinkly locks before the barber's crop. It must feel odd, losing that mass of hair; draughty too. He found himself grinning. Thankfully Hamud grinned back, teeth flashing as Harp answered, 'You might think so, but for me some of it was pure gibberish.'

'Really?' Hendriks' eyebrows rose. 'Which questions?' The three of them ended up reviewing the entire test. Hamud could quote it word for word, even better than Harp. But it was Hendriks who understood the most. Harp figured the guy was pleased about that but not in a bad way, more like relieved, as if he'd felt left out? He didn't need to. Hendriks didn't have the height or muscle Harp and Hamud did – the darker guy was obviously an athlete – but when it came to maths he easily outstripped them. That discovery increased the smaller guy's confidence. As did the fact Harp shared his amusement when he spotted Hamud's bunk-companion, something red and fluffy tucked beneath his pillow.

'What the crip is that thing?' Hendriks blurted.

Hamud ducked his head. 'A mascot, just for fun like.'

'Yes, but what is it?' Harp inspected it as well. The… thing, just about small enough to sit in Hamud's wide palm without tumbling off, was worn red plush, rotund, with four squat legs, a tiny tail and an enormous, hose-like… nose? From Hamud's expression it was something he'd maybe had from a baby, like a safe sort of toy, but why bring it here where it would surely get him laughed at?

Turned out he had his reasons, and they might be crazy but they worked for Hamud. 'It's an elefant, a legend, of an Old Earth creature, like from when Old Earth was young. And it's a luck symbol, see, a red elefant, something that goes way back in my family.' And he looked embarrassed. Harp didn't question it out loud, in any case, and draw attention; show them they knew stories that he'd never heard of. Besides the Worlder hadn't finished. 'My little sister was worried about me leaving home, so…' He shrugged. 'Besides, I like it, OK?'

Harp, and Hendriks too, quickly changed the subject. Well, everyone had their quirks. He'd have liked something special like that growing up; something that was his and no one else's. And this was Hamud's childhood proof that someone loved him. Sure there was still the odd remark Hendriks couldn't resist, about needing something to cuddle up to in bed, but by lights out Harp thought maybe they had formed the start of a relationship. Maybe crewmates? He realised he wanted that as well; his time on *Mercy* must have spoiled him. He was no longer so comfortable as a loner.

Lights out came as suddenly as before, with exactly three minutes of flashing for warning. So now he knew. Hamud laughed when other folk ran round like headless chicks. Harp smiled as well; some people always took a while to learn stuff. Hissack in her upper bunk looked scornful. Shame she never smiled.

'Night,' he tried, since they'd already interacted. She ignored him this time.

Hamud rolled his eyes. 'G'night, all.' He swung the long legs under the cover. Hendriks disappeared below his covers as the lights blinked out for good, though a faint gleam said he was still using his wristcom. Folk settled down, with groans and curses. Day two over.

+++

Soon the days acquired a pattern. Bigg had meant it about the first lie-in, after that the lights came on at oh-four. There was more marching, tests and lectures, more chores as penalties – some impressively inventive. Being bawled at was their new existence. Harp got tagged for cleanup – at least once for what he was sure was just Bigg putting him in his place, but it was almost a relief; it felt more normal.

The gruelling routine had one benefit. Harp's muscles stopped protesting, adapting quicker than from Moon to Orbital, which let him focus on the other challenges. One recruit went home, a failed medical. Folk looked surprised, like being fit was normal. But no one in charge said anything else, so Harp figured his blood test had passed for ordinary again. The need to make a wish for that to happen always felt so stupid now, so childish, but he guessed it'd got ingrained. He'd become superstitious about it, like it was bad luck not to. So yeah, he'd worried a little; who knew how much stricter the navy was than what he'd always dealt with back home.

After making the first approach Hissack had apparently changed her mind. She stayed aloof, forming a clique with six other navy brats; maybe the hair had made him less interesting. Those seven formed a club-of-the-initiated, while the rest tended to group by which side of the dorm they slept, which line that put them in. Hendriks and Hamud stayed friendly, either they genuinely didn't care who he was or they were intrigued by it, he still hadn't decided, but it did mean he wasn't a loner here. The few who looked a bit like Harp kept their distance, clearly didn't want the association in other minds, but that was fair. He caught the nuisance, Hoik, watching from a distance. The waif continued to cower, like a ranger that knew it'd done something wrong but whose brain hadn't worked out what.

Enough. What girl-wisdom Harp'd picked up said girls didn't like being cornered in private areas, like in the head or at their bunks, without an invitation. But he could manoeuvre next to her in the lunch queue. 'Oh, sorry, didn't mean to take your place.' He found it telling that she hadn't even tried to stop him.

'That's OK.' Damn, her voice was as soft as she looked.

He grinned at her. 'I guess I lose my manners when I'm hungry. What little I ever learned.' Blue eyes went wider, shocked. 'Now you, I'm guessing you were brought up better.' This time she blinked, then almost smiled. Good. Harp moved forward with the queue, loaded his tray, noticed she took a lot less. 'These rolls are really pretty good, you should try one.' Wonder of wonders that worked too; she took a roll, the fish paste with it, hesitated but sat down with him. When Hoik shoved in the other side of her she turned her shoulder, answering more willingly when Harp made conversation.

Hoik stabbed his food. The girl – turned out her name was Hunley – started eating properly then walked with Harp back to the dorm and was still smiling when Hoik shouldered past them, grabbed his washkit from his locker and strode off toward the head. But now she'd stopped, mid-sentence, watched him disappear – and shivered.

Here was the time. 'Hey, that guy being a nuisance?'

'Oh.' She bit her lip. 'Not…not really, he just…'

'Gets too close?'

She nodded, blatantly embarrassed.

'Hm. He try anything he shouldn't?'

'No.' She finally looked up at Harp. 'He just… crowds, you know?'

'I know.' He'd met pretty much all the bully tactics, including the sexual kind, but it looked like Hunley hadn't, and had no idea how to deal. So he grinned at her. 'Nobody ever teach you how to send a guy packing?'

'Well, I. No.' She blushed.

'But you know where to aim for, yeah?' Damn, now she was bright red. He persevered. 'One knee, fast and hard. We're all real vulnerable that way.'

'Oh.' She cast a panicked look toward his groin. 'I couldn't…'

'Oh, I'd say you could if you needed, you girls are a lot tougher than you like to pretend. Goodnight, Hunley.' He'd done what he could, now it really was up to her.

12

The fitness regime had kicked in on day two. No big problem, though some recruits seemed to find it a nasty surprise. What had they expected, armchair duty? Oh, it hurt at first, but Harp still found it comic; he was used to hard work but apparently the navy weren't ready to give them that yet. They'd had to invent all sorts of faked ways to make him sweat instead, like running up and down steps and lifting weights that were just weights, not cargo or kit. His favourite so far was running round and round the big 'quad', as they called it. Being in the open air, that wasn't trying to cook him, was a novelty, and getting away from Bigg's voice a bonus.

And on day four, it rained.

He thought he was imagining it at first, the feel of a spot of something wet on his neck. Maybe sweat, cos they had been going a while. But then it came again, and again, and someone running round in front of him put out a hand and looked... disgusted? And the moment after that the quad got washed, water pouring from the sky. And people were complaining? How could they complain at such a gift? Harp stopped, head tilted, letting others pass him as he savoured water running down his head and shoulders. It was really raining, not a short-lived shower but real, steady rain. How long was it since he'd been in rainfall? Little wonder World was so much brighter.

'Harp? You OK?' Hendriks, always near the back, drew level.

'Yeah. Fine.' He took the hint and ran again, Hendriks beside him. 'Does it rain like this often here?'

Hendriks frowned. 'Like this?'

'Heavy rain.' Still no reaction. 'Good for the land.'

'Oh, I guess what you'd expect.'

The point was Harp didn't know what to expect, but he let the subject drop, promising himself to learn more later. To discover no, World didn't have a drought, maybe not a food shortage either? Certainly not crop-stuff anyway. They had some kind of automated farms, all undercover, sort of growing things in giant trays it looked like, as if the ground wasn't good enough. There was something about "protein production" as well. He wasn't sure what that was exactly; it sure didn't sound like meat. Another unsettling difference; he'd always been told Moon fed World…

They started Unarmed Combat on day ten.

'And… again.' They'd rolled mats out to pad Training 2's floor, four sets for the four teams, E, F, G, H. They'd hardly set eyes on the rest of the letters and the four teams still trained apart, but there'd begun to be some furtive interaction in here or the mess, either the top dogs eying each other, or the plain curious. Hissack had been swapping stares with a big guy in G, Hendriks with a skinny redhead guy in E who smiled back shyly. Harp half smiled if someone else did first, but as usual few did. Hell, some of H team still looked sideways at him though it seemed there really was some rule about politeness operating here that Moon had missed. But darker haired or not, he had to think his face still said, at best, some sort of Harpanish connection.

And no, that didn't earn him any special treatment from their betters. Bigg for one didn't make things easier, so folk soon figured out he wasn't useful to them. He was surprised Hendriks and Hamud stayed friendly, especially Hamud, whose physique and calm approach to everything was making him a favourite of several instructors. Hamud was picking up new skills like he'd been born for navy.

Otherwise Harp's body was back on track now, but he found the Unarmed Combat…odd. Not unlike the fake fitness workouts but less pleasant. He'd grown up scrapping, often as the underdog, and then there'd been his time in the Militia, facing angry townsfolk. This though, this was… regimented, so polite. Your opponent did this, you countered with that. It seemed to work, he only had to watch Hissack dump much heavier opponents to see that. After the first few sessions she, Hamud and the other navy brats were separated out to do more than the slow-mo he and Hendriks needed. Hendriks was fine studying the moves but seemed determined not to put his weight behind them, basically faking. The sergeant was soon onto him. Predictably that didn't help; Hendriks just wasn't a fighter.

After ten days of "basic tuition" they were paired off, their sergeant butting in when he felt like it. By sixteen days in it had got more competitive. A rumour had started that those who finished lowest could get booted out.

Apparently people here didn't want to be rejected. Apparently everyone else, in team-H at least, had volunteered; a detail Harp had only tripped over in the last few days. In the pre-lights-out lull, almost the only down time they got, Hendriks and Hamud had started chatting about grouping them by initial, Harp barely listening till Hendriks got to given names. 'I'm Ivo by the way.'

'Oh yeah? I'm Abdu.' Both guys looked expectantly at Harp.

He shrugged. Might as well get it over with. 'I'm Harp. Well, Harpan.' Hoping no one else was near enough to hear.

Hamud laughed. 'No, really? Harpan Harp?'

'No, well not both.' He might as well clarify. Hamud might let the details drop but Hendriks wouldn't. 'My given is Harpan, and my last house name was Goss, but –'

'Whoah.' Hendriks pounced. 'Your *last* house name? You've had more than one?'

'I've had seven. Eight if you count Harp.' They looked mystified, so maybe it was different on World. 'Orphans on Moon take the house name they're living in, so my birth name, then Nursery name, Education name, pre-Employment name. Then I had two apprentice placements.' Which he didn't like admitting cos it smacked of failure. 'The last one of those was Goss.'

'OK.' Hendriks' head tilted, a tell that he was thinking hard. 'So why aren't you still named Goss?'

'Cos I went to Moon Militia and my cruiser captain

wouldn't have two crew with the same name. I was last in so they retagged me.'

'Harp. Not Harpan.' Hamud's turn to doubt.

'People called me Harp when I was a kid. And I had a good sergeant, he accepted the shorter version too.'

'Hm, I guess Harpan was a bit... you looking...' Hamud had the grace to leave the thought unfinished, for which Harp was thankful. There was nothing respectable about looking like a Harpan if you weren't one that resulted from a marriage contract, "breeding" that you could lay claim to. Surely they'd guessed he was what he'd found these Worlders called a "breeding error"; firmly bottom of the social ladder, not someone you wanted to be seen with. He probably knew that even better than they did.

'Yeah.' The talk went back to training and Harp figured that was that. He hoped.

But Hendriks wasn't finished. 'Hang on, you've been apprenticed twice *and* in the Moon Militia?'

That was worth the wince. 'Yeah, but I only spent a year in my first placement; they said I didn't suit.' He felt compelled to add, 'The second place was better, I had four years there before they had to tithe me into the Militia.'

Hamud's mouth was open. 'Hell man, how old are you?'

'Twenty now.' He thought. So said his orphan-file.

Now Hendriks looked astounded. 'But, but, how old were you when you were apprenticed?'

'Usual age, thirteen or so.' What was the fuss about?

'You were apprenticed at thirteen?' Hendriks' eyes...

'Yeah, we all are, 'less someone thinks we're worth more education.' Which he obviously wasn't, though if he had been he suspected someone with his awkward looks would be rejected anyway. He'd always figured it no accident that both his grownup placements were remote from townships. But they were still staring. 'Look, it's how being an orphan works. They can't feed us for ever.'

'Crip.' Hamud drew breath. 'Sorry, I never met anyone orphaned before. I didn't know it was that tough.'

Harp shrugged; as far as he was concerned it wasn't. It was only his looks made things harder.

Hendriks' eyes had narrowed. 'You know,' he said slowly, 'I've never met an orphan before either.'

Harp smiled, trying to lighten the mood. He'd guessed they came from nicer backgrounds. 'Well, there's probably a lot of us about.'

Hendriks was still frowning. 'I'm not so sure about that.' He tapped his wristcom, frowned some more and finally looked up again. 'There's no index for orphan housing in Foundation, nor anywhere on Harpan's World. Not one entry.'

This time it was Harp who stared, but Hamud got in first. 'There must be, surely?'

'Look for yourself, there's nothing.' Hendriks tapped some more. 'But under Harpan's Moon there are five mixed sex Nursery Houses, six segregated Education Houses and five called PreEmployment.'

But none, at all, on World? Harp let that sink in. World sent all their orphans to Moon? Was just being *any* orphan an embarrassment here? Was – crazy thought – the fact these two had never met an orphan one of the reasons he was having it so easy; cos their minds couldn't quite get to grips with the idea he was one, let alone a bastard?

Which thought, naturally, he didn't voice. Didn't have a chance to if he wanted. After that disclosure Hendriks and Hamud fell over themselves trying to measure more differences between their lives and Harp's. Turned out kids here on World didn't just have real families and stick to one name, they also had education a lot longer. Hamud was twenty, Hendriks twenty-three, but they'd both enlisted straight from Education. Different sorts of schools, Harp gathered, but they'd never earned a living, never really been considered adult by themselves or others. And Hendriks said the same applied to all the other recruits, nearly all of them were out of "college". And were volunteers.

Harp supposed it explained why they were all more worried about failing. When lights-out came he lay up in his bunk and weighed that difference. While he found the navy training a vast step up from Militia's, he wouldn't exactly be heartbroken if he didn't make the grade. After all, he figured if they didn't want him they'd only send him back to Moon and the Militia which meant going back to what he knew, with all he'd seen and learned here as a bonus. Not to mention he could go back with his new, less awful image. So as days sped by, and other H-team faces tightened, Harp was fine with learning what he could and keeping out of trouble, doing cleanup when he couldn't, fine with being less than perfect. He was more concerned for others.

Hamud and Harp had taken to coaching Hendriks in Unarmed Combat, Harp playing opponent and Hamud coach. In return Hendriks was coaching Harp in Worlder maths. Hamud didn't seem to have any weaknesses; he was starting to rival Hissack who had pretty much established herself as top of their class. That hadn't made her more likeable but now she was aiming that basilisk stare at Hamud. Who naturally grinned at her in an attempt to rile her. So Hamud was one of the in crowd, and being in Hamud's shadow seemed to make Harp generally accepted, something he was trying not to take for granted.

At the other end of the unit's spectrum little Hunley continued to shy away from Hoik and flinch in Combat class. But then she was hardly alone. Hoik had taken to Combat like it was a special treat, eyes brighter every session. Their sergeant, seeing obvious enthusiasm, put the minor injuries he regularly caused down to exuberance, especially when Hoik was always so apologetic. After. Well, except the smirk that always showed up once the sergeant wasn't looking. But the sergeant never saw that.

'Slow it down a fraction, son,' the man kept saying. 'Show me more control, then I can move you up.'

But Hoik couldn't seem to curb his 'enthusiasm' so he continued against lesser opponents. Including Harp, but Harp had learned to roll with blows; he won or lost but didn't have the bruises or the cuts that others suffered. Harp was ranked among the bottom third in Combat? Fine. He was more interested in the fact he was edging up the list in maths and the assorted theory classes. He liked learning, and it looked like he had been more ignorant than stupid, even judged by Worlder standards.

But his safe middle-ground status suffered when it came to Weapons training.

+++

He'd figured he'd do OK there but the navy brats would still head the field. Especially when the first practice weapons they were assigned were pulse handguns. With autosights. They'd have to be blind to miss!

Apparently not. True, the navy brats did OK; almost all of them hit the inner rings on their projected targets by the end of the first session. But a surprising number of the rest still missed an outer. Maybe it was the noise – for some reason these things were seriously noisy, more than anything he'd ever handled – but two recruits even managed to hit someone else's targets, which earned them a rude-sounding buzzer and ironic cheers. And the second one of these was Hamud, in the bay beside him. Hamud used some words Harp didn't know. His hands were shaking.

'Ham, take a breath, OK? Another. Now plant your feet, aim, and squeeze it gently, like a saucebulb.' The night before, Hamud's muscles had drowned his supper in the mess's lethal hot sauce. There had been applause and catcalls. But the image worked. Hamud snorted but his hands relaxed, his next attempt was in the outer circle. 'Better,' Harp encouraged then shut up as Bigg popped up behind them.

'Taking a break, Private?'

'No, Corporal.' Mullah's training had Harp lower his

gun but stay facing the targets, one rule where Militia matched the navy.

'Huh.' One could almost hear the cogs whirr as Bigg decided to set him down. 'Well then, let's see, shall we? Six shots, rapid fire. Now!'

Harp reacted to the shout instantly like it was Mullah; lifted the gun, hands steady, shoulders turned. Didn't wait for auto to react, just fired: three across the inner circle, three centre, in three seconds flat. Then lowered the gun, powered down and set it on the rack in front of him; stood back and turned to hear the verdict. Truth to tell he was a mite annoyed. He'd been so careful not to hit too many bulls all through the session.

Maybe the staccato bark of the – unnecessarily? – loud weapon had put others off too. It had certainly drawn attention, there was silence in the weapons bays by then, one broken only by the rapid footsteps of the sergeant heading fast in their direction. 'You order that, Corporal?'

'Yessir,' Bigg stood stiffly.

'Well now.' The sergeant studied Harp with new attention. Darn, as fancy folk like Hissack said it here. 'Where'd you learn to shoot like that, son?'

'Moon Militia, Sergeant.' Harp stood easy, such things now a habit.

'Hm.' The sergeant consulted his wristcom, pursed his lips then raised his head and shouted down the alley. 'Master Sergeant Zeiz?'

'Yep?' Another man appeared in the furthest doorway.

'Got one for you. Seems to have slipped through the cracks.'

'Oh yeah?' The man stepped out and started down their way. He didn't look too thrilled about it.

Their sergeant grinned. 'Could do with your special touch, Master.' Not encouraging. The second "oh" sounded more resigned than intrigued and by now the other man was halfway down the alley. He was smaller, and bow-legged, like a long-time ranchhand, with the rolling gait Harp recognised in riders. Harp was head and shoulders taller but at least two decades younger, and of course the new man was at least three ranks above him. And it was pretty obvious what was coming.

It was like his first day in the Militia. The master sergeant picked up his gun. 'Move down the end, private'. But the time they got there the man'd disabled the auto. As if that would make a difference. 'Three shots again. Take your time.'

Fast or slow… Harp shot three centres.

That led to checking the first gun in, requiring a walk back past the other bays full of gawking recruits to the counter-window. This time he left with a small-fire projectile. It was older, heavier, and again the auto was disabled so again his shots depended on his eyesight. It also threw left and kicked like a steer but after a couple of trial shots he was back in target-centre, angrily aware other recruits were casting sidelong glances. At that point the session timed out, but he knew the damage was done; he'd made himself noticeable again. And it was his own stupid fault for not swallowing his pride when he was challenged.

13

Next morning's lecture was about navy ships: the difference between frigate and destroyer, destroyer and battleship, battleship and their single, brand new arc ship. Crew numbers. Crew roles. Recruits sat taller and took notice; this was what they all aspired to. What Harp wondered was why, when there were so many ships, and so many eager recruits to choose from, somebody had felt the need to transfer him – a very small cog in such an enormous wheel. Had Regis just found this a convenient way to get rid of him, before his stupid looks could draw the wrong kind of attention? Because now he looked back he was certain Regis hadn't been much of a captain, and for certain no way an honest one.

Reasons aside, everyone around him came from wildly different backgrounds from his own, with vastly different expectations, and ambitions. No way he belonged. The ranch had been the only portion of his life so far where he'd felt normal, or accepted, and he didn't figure he'd be going back there if he washed out here, even if the drought was beaten. And the drought wasn't beaten. From what little he could glean of Mooner affairs from the screens in the mess hall it was worse; small wonder he hadn't been alert enough that day in weapons practice. His mind had been on Moon, and he'd reacted as he would with Mullah. Something he could see, too late to matter.

Two days earlier the early morning mess screens had been all excited at the rebirth of a *second* Moon volcano, this one also in the northern hemisphere. Only fumes and sometimes gouts of dust so far, but… So while others found the talk exciting Harp just felt depressed, and when they were dismissed, with all the standing to attention that required, he almost missed the slight vibration from his shiny, navy-issue wristcom. When he woke and checked its screen it posted him new orders to report to 'Tac-Training 7' immediately after chow.

Not Unarmed Combat? Had they all… no, no one else was checking messages. Huh. 'Listen, guys, I've got to report to something called tac-training, right after lunch. Can you tell the sergeant in Combat?'

Hendriks nodded, looking… worried? But by now Harp only had thirty left to reach the mess, eat and report to wherever it was. In the rush he ended up too far away to ask the guy about his odd reaction, and when H-team exited left Harp's wristcom tracker took him right so that was that. He only hoped he wasn't in trouble.

Tac-Training lit up a completely different block, maybe a good ten-minute hike across the open quad, then a door check, then hopping a chute up eight new floors and, time ticking down, a sprint along three corridors. Was it a test, to see if he made it in time? Being singled out was a lifelong curse, and he hadn't learned the rules enough to weigh the challenge.

Outside TT7 he paused to get his breath, then touched the access panel. A voice inside called out, 'Come in,' the door slid open. The woman inside the small, nondescript office was a corporal behind a desk, and not much older, so that wasn't so bad. Till she looked up. 'Recruit Harp, yes?'

Seen properly she was so pressed and polished he immediately felt sweaty and out of place, and her voice was very Worlder with the mix of clipped-off words and flatter vowels, and the slightly singsong rhythm he still found so foreign, and so redolent of every Worlders' better lifestyle.

'Yes, Corporal.' He wondered what he sounded like to her, probably nothing good.

If so she didn't show it. 'Good, on time. You're to go straight in.' She looked toward an inner door. Maybe she activated the lock cos it slid aside before he reached it. The room beyond was even smaller, empty cept a fancy seat and real big wall screen, but a disembodied male voice gave crisp instructions.

'Private Harp, please sit.' When Harp sat down the chair conformed to suit his shape; he'd heard of that but never seen it, had to stop himself from squirming.

'Place your head and hands onto the rests.'

Once he did a slew of sensor wires curled from the chair, across his wrists and hands, around his throat and forehead. That was new. They weren't tight. They didn't hurt. They were just… there. He figured he could tear them off, but no doubt that would only get him into trouble so he tried ignoring them, which wasn't easy.

'Your heart rate is elevated, recruit. Try to relax.'

So that was what the sensors were for. He followed orders – well enough apparently to satisfy whoever watched him since the wall screen flickered and white dots appeared.

The screen took up all one wall, and the head rest had closed in, so much that now he couldn't turn his head to see its edges. Then the voice said there were buttons recessed in the armrests and he was supposed to press them when he lost a moving dot, again when he reclaimed it. He didn't think he did too badly; Mullah had always said his 'peripheral vision' was above average.

After that the screen fed him numbers, then a slew of letters, which was pretty much like orphan medicals, except these marks kept getting smaller. And smaller? How far were they going to test his eyesight?

After that came pictures, indoors and out, well-lit and dark. This time he was told to pick out objects, doors and switches, things on shelves. A sort of virtual reconnaissance. Then seek out people. Some were "friendlies", others "enemies". They could appear from anywhere. He had to push a button when he found one, right hand for an enemy and left for friendly. Damn, wrong button. Had somebody rated him as unobservant? That annoyed him; he tried harder.

His eyes plain hurt by the time they went back to the dots, and there were crowds of the things this time, in different colours too. 'Follow the red' would suddenly switch to 'Follow the white' or 'Follow the blue' while the damned dots bounced all over the wall, and sometimes each other.

By the time the voice said to stop and the sensor wires snapped off and slid back into their slots he'd lost all sense of time and started feeling dizzy too. He had to blink to clear his vision when the voice dismissed him, blinked again when peering at his wristcom showed him it was chow time. He'd spent half a day in here? He was still blinking when he reached the mess and tagged onto the serving line. Still having trouble even after the Thanksgiving interrupted progress. But as soon as the recording ended...

'Harp, hey, over here.' Hamud waved and he and Hendriks shuffled up to leave a space between them.

Harp nodded – big mistake – let the counter staff fill him up then wove a less than perfect path to join his comrades. He misjudged the distance to the table top as well and let the tray go early, so it bounced and rattled. 'Crip.' He used his hands to guide himself onto the bench and blinked some more. He could still see the damn dots, making everything blurry.

'Hey man, what'd they want? You OK?'

'I will be.' He hoped. 'They gave me a whole pile of eye tests, I'm still seeing double.'

'Eye tests, you? After all those bulls?' Hendriks still looked worried. 'That doesn't make any sense.'

Now he had time to think Harp was afraid it did, afraid he knew now why he'd been transferred without being asked. Damn it, he shouldn't have got complacent. But he wasn't about to voice his suspicions, or have to talk about killing people. He'd made some unexpected friends here, people who accepted him, he didn't want to lose that gift until he had to. So he shrugged. 'Navy doesn't have to make sense, does it? We just have to do as we're told.' The food kept swirling round on his tray, making him want to heave, but he knew he needed to eat so he tried looking up then closing his eyes and shaking his head. Several times, like a ranger shook off midges. When he reopened them Hissack was gaping at him from across the table but the room stayed still at last. 'OK, that's better.' Digging into the chow meant he could also take his time answering more questions and try to play it all down. 'Usual stuff though, small print and such. And watching dots move till I couldn't see them any longer.'

Hendriks still shook his head. 'Testing the rest of us would make more sense than you.'

Hamud, also chewing, mumbled, 'Or me after I hit the wrong bloody target.'

'Yeah, exactly.' Hendriks nodded, tact not being what you'd call his strong point.

Harp resorted to another shrug. 'So maybe you'll be blurry-eyed tomorrow.'

But no one else was called out, so obviously it had related to his shooting. Except no one mentioned it, or came back with results either, and the following day his life went back to trainee-normal. If he didn't count the looks he got now both from H-team and from corporals and sergeants in his classes. So he did what he always had; he kept his head down, scoring in the middle of the team now, not too dumb but not too clever, even if he had to fake it. There were only two places he couldn't do that well enough; Weapons practice, and with Ham and Hendriks.

He figured he'd shown his true colours with weapons and it was too late to change but at least Master Sergeant Zeiz, as Harp had guessed, was another Mooner and more friendly, for a sergeant. Maybe their shared background made a bond he hadn't had with others here. The one-on-one lessons were good anyway; relaxing, not to mention peaceful.

A lot of the theory classes were easier too. He'd discovered he took in the terse lectures – often full of words he wasn't sure of – better if he hit the manuals before as well as after. The result was he and Ham and Hendriks started betting favours on which topic the next lecture would cover. Hendriks beat them both the first few days, until Harp realised the subjects were, more often than not, in the same order as the recruits' basic training manual. Called out, Hendriks only grinned. 'Wondered how long it'd take you.'

'Just cos you live for book learning.' Harp shook his head. 'Some of us had to work for a living.'

'Yeah.' Hamud smirked. 'And some of us have actual muscles.'

'And between you, you owe me five favours,' Hendriks retorted. 'And I won't forget.'

If the manual was any guide Harp figured Hendriks might not have much time left to claim them before they all passed out of training. Assuming they all did. Talk in the dorm was starting to get obsessive, folk checking their rankings on this or that list, adding, dividing, trying to find some reassuring magic number. All exacerbated by a rumour that the bottom twenty-five percentile of the Weapons and the Combat scores would rate unfit, no matter what they did in other classes.

'Trouble is, we don't know how the other teams are doing,' Hamud commented one evening. 'So the best of H-team could be bottom overall. We have no way of knowing.'

'Oh great.' Hendriks, who'd been whinging about being right on the line, looked up to Hamud's bunk in horror. 'Now I know I'm sunk.'

'Or H-team could be good enough we all of us mark higher,' Harp suggested. 'After all we've got those navy brats to skew things.'

Hendriks wasn't reassured. 'It's fine for you two. Ham's up top in Combat, you're too good to even practise with us on the range, but me…'

A snort from Hamud. 'You think my weapons score will top yours, after I hit someone else's target? I reckon the only one of us safe is Harp.' Ham smiled across at him. 'They'll probably take you even if you fail everything else, which we know you won't.'

Which was more or less true. Even his maths was respectable now, thanks to them, and he suspected they knew he could do better in the other classes, if he wanted. It belatedly hit him they might think he wasn't trying because he'd got big-headed; thought he really was a shoo-in. 'Look, it's not…' He groped for words that wouldn't sound too stupid. 'I don't want to look too good.'

Hendriks gaped but Hamud didn't. 'Huh, I guess that makes sense.' He smiled again. 'You ever do your best, at anything?'

'Not if I could help it, no.' Except maybe on the ranch. He saw the understanding dawn on Hendriks' face. For once it didn't seem so hard to say it. 'If you look like me it's not so clever.'

Hamud nodded. Hendriks winced. That seemed to sum it up, at least they didn't talk about it any longer. He realised he was starting to take the strict Worlder manners for granted. A real shame those hadn't travelled out to Moon – he'd have been a lot better off.

The next evening saw a sudden change in their routine. Wristcoms pinged or buzzed or shook and everybody stopped undressing, checking out new orders. Harp heard someone mutter, 'Finally,' so maybe he was the only one caught by surprise. As of three days ahead all lecture schedules had been replaced with Assessments, a whole heap of them over the next fifteen days. This was where they passed or failed.

Hendriks went straight into panic mode. 'We all know I'll fail Combat.'

'Rubbish,' Hamud countered.

Harp… wasn't so sure. Actually he wasn't that sure he'd pass there either. If he and Hendriks had one thing in common it was their dislike of Unarmed Combat. Except where Hendriks' problem was his naturally scrawny body, Harp knew where *he* failed was aggression. Hendriks lost most of his bouts because his opponents were bigger and stronger and, face it, he wasn't the combat type. Harp lost them cos he couldn't bring himself to hurt folk. He wasn't a child. He knew what hurt was all about. He'd killed. But these folk weren't a real threat, only a pretend one, and he didn't like it – seeing bruises, seeing people gasp or struggle to stay upright. So he'd compromised; with a stronger opponent he accepted a defeat, with weaker ones he made each bout as short lived as he could. Sometimes that meant winning fast. Others, not losing too obviously.

Result: he and Hendriks were currently fifteen and sixteen out of the eighteen in H-team. Seventeenth was a gangly youth called Hogg with no coordination. Hamud said he couldn't shoot much either so the guy was in despair. 'His friends keep trying to cheer him up but he just doesn't have the skills.'

Harp figured the guy for one of those late developers who still had to grow into his height and reach, but he'd enlisted straight from 'college' like the others.

Last of all was Hunley, no surprise. She'd spent almost every active session backing off and being bawled at by their various instructors, even after they tagged her for extra attention. Harp had weakened to the point of talking Hamud into offering to coach her in between; that hadn't done any good either.

'I give up, she's hopeless,' Hamud had declared, fresh out of patience. 'Sorry, Harp, she just won't try!' It was obvious Hunley hated the whole navy experience. She'd made few friends and by now even they looked annoyed with her behaviour. To Harp the mystery was why she'd joined up in the first place, not to mention why she hadn't quit already. He had heard a few from other teams had changed their minds about a navy future, yet she hadn't. For himself, he had to admit he'd never been better off.

Though he couldn't help thinking Hunley might have managed better if Hoik had been in some other team.

Hissack never had suggested Hunley take her vacant bunk, and though there was another bunk not being used now Hunley never moved to that one either. If her friends had suggested it she either hadn't chosen to or hadn't dared to; she stayed put, too near Hoik. And trembled.

There wasn't any obvious reason, no repeat of crude intimidation in the showers, not that Harp had seen and yep, he'd kept an eye out. But he couldn't watch her all the hours there were, and something wasn't right between them. Hunley still avoided Hoik whenever possible, and when it wasn't Hunley froze if Hoik so much as looked at her and reddened if he bent and murmured in her ear.

But if she wouldn't quit, at least the end of her ordeal was closer, pass or fail. They wouldn't stay together after training. Still, Harp was struggling with a mix of anger and frustration. He couldn't 'deal' with Hoik without doing more than talk, and that would bring too much attention. And he couldn't ask his friends to intervene. They'd volunteered for this life, he couldn't let them risk their own ambitions fighting. So there they were. Hunley wouldn't or couldn't help herself. Nor apparently could the instructors see a problem. That was that, and it wasn't as if he didn't have his own problems in Combat.

A fact both Bigg and their current instructor were currently pointing out. The sergeant looked exasperated, Bigg disgusted. Harp was tagged for extra combat training, before breakfast, him and Hendriks. Hamud ambled in the first time claiming he could use the workout but his plan to help misfired. Yep, he paired with Hendriks as intended, but that meant odd numbers so the sergeant paired himself with Harp. It wasn't pretty.

'Move. Now *hit* me. Not some pussy tap, lad, put your vaccing weight behind it! Harder, damn you!' When the man stepped back his face was red although his breathing hadn't altered by a hair. 'C'mon, kid. Scared?'

'No, Sergeant.' And he wasn't, even as the blows came faster, harder. Nobody was trying to kill him, were they? He'd been beaten up for real, worse than anything they did in here.

Wrong answer, if there was a right one. The sergeant prodded him in the chest, hard enough to push him back a step. 'No?' Another prod, not real blows but taunting. Harp could feel the others slowing down and watching. Maybe that was why he finally reacted.

'No.' He looked the sergeant in the eye and blocked the move forward, sticking stubbornly to a defensive action.

'Aargh.' The other man threw up his hands. 'I read your file, kid, I know you can do better. You know you can do better. Pull your stupid finger out and do it.'

'Yes, Sergeant.' No. They might think he was a killer

but he wasn't. Harp watched the man grow redder. Happily the session ended, and no worse had happened. Dismissed, they ran to shower. Being late to mess meant even more demerits.

Ham fell in beside him as they headed down again to breakfast, looking sideways at his bleak expression. 'Same again? You know he's going to make you suffer.'

'Yep.' Harp was already cross with himself; talking back was always a mistake.

'So hit him harder. Or hit someone.'

'Don't feel like it.'

Ham flung his hands up. 'Man, it's not a choice.'

'Yes, it is, Ham, that's exactly what it is.' If he'd learned nothing else he'd learned that much. 'If they want mindless they can get it somewhere else.'

'Crip.' They'd reached the counter. Hamud shook his head and turned attention to his breakfast. Their meals had gradually improved, now only the pickiest and the most pampered groused about it. Or they were all too hungry these days to care.

Meal over, more assessments. Today it was ships' regulations. Hendriks, hot on stuff like that, had teamed with Harp to push the final details into Hamud. For some reason Mr Memory had found a blank spot where rules were concerned, though Harp noted once he got them down they seemed to be stuck forever. All three walked into that with fair assurance and came out with smiles.

Hissack did the same. That figured. Others didn't look so cheerful; Hoik was scowling. But he brightened noticeably after lunch when H-team headed down for Unarmed Combat. Was this the day they got assessed there too?

Hoik's 'clumsiness' had continued to keep him out of the more challenging group but Harp was convinced that was deliberate, figured the guy didn't want to risk facing better opponents like Hissack or Hamud, he just wanted to have fun winning easier bouts. Hoik liked to win, to feel he was superior, but not to earn it. When folk studied in the evenings he would often disappear, word was sometimes for an assignation, others gambling. There had been a couple times he'd crept back after lights out and he didn't walk straight. Only a couple times, but that was likely cos he'd got bawled out next day in every single session, trying to manage with his eyes half shut and zero concentration.

But their Combat sergeant still maintained the guy had promise, and Hoik still played him for a sucker, saying 'Sorry, Sarge,' whenever somebody he faced came off the matting hurt or bleeding. By now nobody in H wanted to spar with him, especially one on one.

'Pairs today, hand to hand.' The sergeant looked them over. 'Winner takes on winner. Group one get three points for a win, one for a loss. Two get two points for a win.' A nasty smile. 'And nothing for a loss. Three extra for the last man standing.'

Assessment it was. Harp worked out the maths. They were still split in their two groups, ten advanced, eight not. His group meant three rounds so the worst four would score zero and the others two, four or a miraculous six, cos forget any hope of winning against whoever won in the advanced group. Even so this could seriously alter people's final rankings. Faces round him showed they realised it too – this wasn't going to be a friendly contest.

'First up, group two.' Group one sat down to watch and feel superior. 'You two. The bout's over when someone's down or off the mat. Go.'

The first pair were evenly matched and the bout lasted a good five minutes. There'd be no calling time today then, it was all about winning or losing. When they limped off the next pair called was Hoik, and oh crip, Hunley. Hoik strolled forward smiling. Hunley looked defeated long before he touched her. It was quickly clear she was trying to lose, as fast as she could, backing away on a straight course for the edge of the mat. Probably her best bet; if she got a foot on the floor beyond she'd be counted a loser.

It took her an endless two minutes to get there. Two minutes in which Hoik skated all round her, blocking her from escaping and putting his paws everywhere he could. When Hunley threw herself away at last she hit the plascrete floor so hard she skidded, ripping skin off, and she was in tears. But the blasted sergeant didn't bat an eyelid, only grunted, 'Win to Hoik. Next pair…'

Hoik sat down and smirked, while Hunley huddled by herself. And still it wasn't Harp's turn. It was Hendriks versus Hogg. As Hendriks rose, Harp muttered, 'You remember?'

Hendriks nodded curtly. Harp sure hoped so. Hogg might lack coordination but he did have muscle and a lot of reach. The three friends had talked through the group's strengths and weaknesses so Hendriks knew what tactics to employ that might offset his lack of muscle. With Hogg they'd all agreed on getting in real close before the other guy had time to settle. So he'd either win, and fast, or finish even lower.

Hendriks, looking nervous, took position facing Hogg across the matting. The sergeant called, 'Begin.'

Before he'd closed his mouth, Hendriks was running straight at Hogg, head down, arms tucked, to hit him squarely in the ribs and stomach, both fists pumping. There were whoops all round the mat as Hogg went flying, on his back, mouth open, struggling for breath. Whatever breath he hoovered in whooshed out again when Hendriks fell on him. Hogg gasped for air then slapped the floor. The bout was over.

Hendriks, looking dazed, walked off the mat then found a beaming smile when Harp then Hamud slapped him on the back. Two points to Hendriks.

'Last two up.' Harp rose, to pair with Hunley's best pal Halviez. Crip. Halviez wasn't much good either, so win or lose the most important thing was not to hurt her. As he stepped onto the mat his mind was on the fastest way to get this over.

Maybe Halviez thought likewise. As soon as they got the word she rushed at him, clipping his jaw with an uppercut that made his teeth rattle. Maybe it was the surprise, their training, or some memory of orphan conflicts, but he blinked then simply reached and pushed – and Halviez went stumbling off the mat onto the plascrete. Not best pleased the bout was over from the scowl she gave him. 'Sorry, Hal,' he muttered, offering a hand. She didn't take it, but at least his friends were smiling. And he had two points, no matter it was more from luck than prowess.

The sergeant didn't comment, simply turned to the advanced group, pairing them against each other till he had five victors. Was it chance he didn't pair Hamud with Hissack? Harp didn't think so. One of those would surely be the final winner.

In Harp's second round a guy he didn't really know hit out before the word was given. There was outcry round the circle but again the sergeant made no comment, Harp thought he had almost smiled. Suddenly old orphan rules kicked in; this *wasn't* friendly, this was war. Before Harp knew it he had got in close, to hook a leg behind the other guy and dump him on his back then fall on him as Hendriks had to stop him rising; didn't stop him cursing.

'Result, two to Harp.'

By the time Harp rose the guy below looked suitably embarrassed; this time it was his turn to say sorry as he slunk back to the circle. Harp, his temper over too, might easily have felt relieved that it was done, except the next bout up was Hoik, and Hendriks.

T2 went quiet, and when Hoik got in a blow – a low one followed by that trademark 'oops' expression Hoik had used so many times now – there were hisses from the sidelines. But it didn't go too badly after that. Maybe the foul blow shook Hendriks up enough he really applied himself for once. He mainly stayed on the defensive but he was avoiding trouble, holding things at stalemate. But a stalemate couldn't win, and everybody knew it.

The impasse lasted until Hoik tripped Hendriks up and Hendriks tumbled backward.

It wasn't a bad fall. And Hendriks' head and shoulders skidded off the mat; the bout was over, honours even, practically a win for Hendriks. Only Hoik slammed down on him before the sergeant called a halt, and one knee landed squarely on his stomach. Everybody heard the crack, the scream as Hoik pushed off his knees to rise, arms out, and step away. 'Oh crip, I'm sorry, Hendriks. How bad is it?' Any fool could see the cretin didn't mean a word of it, his lips were twitching, he could hardly stop himself from laughing.

Hamud grabbed at Harp. 'No! You in trouble too won't help.'

Yet again their mad, sadistic bloody sergeant nodded Hoik away, and didn't see it was an act? 'Bout over, points to Hoik,' the fool was saying as he strode across to check on Hendriks, still flat out and pasty faced and groaning.

The medics arrived fast – that was something – took one look, immobilised Hendriks, loaded him on a hover and sped away. The sergeant still resumed the bouts as soon as they were gone, despite set faces all around the circle. Hoik, across the ring from Harp, turned back from watching Hendriks leave and aimed a non-existent gun at Harp, and smiled. Harp, blank-faced this time, stared back.

Others took the mat. Harp didn't see them, all he saw was Hendriks falling, screaming. When the sergeant called, 'Third round,' then, 'Next up, Harp and Hoik,' he didn't hear the murmurs either, didn't feel the tension in the others. All he saw this time was Hoik get up and bounce onto the mat; the black eyes narrowed in anticipation. Hoik was in position quickly, Harp much slower. Neither looked toward the sergeant.

For a time the two men circled, looking for advantage. Harp stepped in a couple times, misjudged Hoik's reach, got hit and backed away. His lip was bleeding now. Hoik's smirk grew wider, and the next time Harp advanced Hoik went in for the kill, a flash of kicks and punches, all connecting. Harp backed off; Hoik followed.

'Harp, get on with it,' the sergeant shouted.

Harp's head turned toward the reprimand. Hoik sprang – into a straight-arm jab right in the throat.

Hoik's mouth was open, wheezing, and it looked as if his legs had turned to jelly but that wasn't stopping Harp, not this time. Solid blows knocked Hoik clean off his feet; he hit the mat. Harp straddled Hoik, continuing the barrage, steady and relentless, deaf to shouted orders to desist. Eventually it took the sergeant and a corporal and three recruits to pull him off his sobbing victim, still with no expression. Till the sergeant slapped his face.

Harp blinked, and swayed, his fists still clenched, his gaze still fixed on Hoik. The sergeant muttered, 'Crip, don't let him go, not yet. Private? You hearing me, son?'

Harp's head refocussed on the sergeant. Then he shivered. 'Y-yessir.'

'Can you follow orders now?' The man relaxed when 'Yessir' came out firmer. 'Go clean up and then report to medical.' The sergeant watched him carefully. 'Repeat your orders.' Harp repeated it verbatim, staring dully at the sergeant as another set of medics bustled in and zeroed in on Hoik, still down, still sobbing, till the sergeant swore and turned him bodily to face the exit. 'All right, dismissed, Private.'

The hands stopped holding him. Harp stumbled then recalled his orders, walking out with even paces, half aware now that recruits made way. It wasn't till he reached the dorm and felt the rush of water in the shower that the world came back completely and he realised what he had done. And faced the comeback.

He'd lost it, hadn't he. They called that insubordination. Another recruit had been kicked out for it, and he hadn't even been in a fight.

The water washed the blood away, he thought it was mostly Hoik's. He must have caused a lot of damage. He had meant to. If they hadn't pulled him off... Crip, he could have killed the guy. He put a shaky hand out to the tiles and saw his knuckles, raw and bloodied. They were going to throw him in the brig. And when they let him out – or if – what chance they'd even ship him back to Moon? A passage home would surely cost a fortune and he had no funds to pay for it himself. That hair-shot and the antidote had taken almost all the cred he'd carried with him, the rest was gone, and he had no idea how to live if he was stuck on World. Crip, being kicked out might be the *best* he could hope for. Maybe they would send him to a navy prison, or to rehab. Bays had said that World had rehab. Said it changed a guy forever. But the sight of Hunley cowering, then Hendriks' scream...

The water started running clear at last. So did his thoughts. He'd done what needed doing, and he wasn't sorry.

He reported to Medical where they shone lights in his eyes, inspected a bump on his head and sealed up his cuts and bruises. They acted surprised there weren't more, but he'd never marked easy. His hands were the worst of course. The orderly tutted then applied layers of plasskin, but whatever antiseptic gunk he'd sprayed beneath it was a purplish colour and the plasskin made it all look shiny so it looked like somebody had painted both his hands. When the orderly told him to go eat it was hardly surprising folk stared at him as he walked stiffly past them.

He'd vaguely assumed his team would be there as well – it must be about that time – but H-team weren't among those seated. He hadn't felt this alone since the day he'd left the Gosses. Yeah, something else he'd have to get used to again. He aimed for the counter, took whatever they offered and turned to find a seat.

The mess was quiet, no one talking for a moment, then the heads turned back to eating but a murmur spread around the tables. Had they heard that he'd lost it?

There was space at the end of one table. He took the end of the bench, looked at his tray and remembered he'd been told to eat, to counter any nausea from the meds. As if he wasn't feeling sick enough already. So he ate. No one filled the empty spaces. He didn't taste the meal and he sat cocooned in silence. And this time, when Thanksgiving sounded, didn't join the final chorus.

14

With no orders to do anything else Harp went back to the dorm. It wasn't long before the rest joined him, but the usual bustle was subdued and more so when Bigg appeared in the doorway. Everybody straightened to attention but the corporal just stood there, looked Harp up and down then about-turned and departed.

Hamud stuck his hand out. 'Here, shake man. It was high time Hoik got a taste. I only wish it had been me.'

Harp didn't move. 'How bad is he?'

'Nobody's saying and nobody cares. They've suspended all assessments for tomorrow so we all get extra time to study. Good result all round, eh?'

'Yeah.' Harp still felt sick, so eating obviously hadn't helped. The atmosphere in here wasn't helping either. It felt like someone's funeral, and he didn't think it was Hoik's. 'Oh crip, how's Hendriks?' How had he forgot the most important question?

Hamud smiled. 'He's in regen, but the word is he'll be good as new in no time.'

'So they won't need to reject him?' Maybe there was something to be thankful for.

'Nah. It might even work in his favour.' Hamud grinned. 'They can't take today into account so much, can they?' He saw Harp's face. 'Hell man, we all saw what happened, so did Biggsy and the sergeant. And if anyone else is in trouble it ought to be them, for not stopping Hoik earlier.'

Somehow Harp didn't think it would work that way. He nodded though, to end the conversation, cutting off his comrade's indignation.

'Sorry, Ham, I'm tired. I'm going to crash.'

Ham's features softened. 'Yeah of course. Meds kicking in?'

'Maybe, yeah.' He did feel kind of heavy, and what sounds there were around him sort of stuttered. And he ought to try to sleep, to get some energy – and nerve – to face whatever came for him tomorrow.

'Here man, you'll never make it up into that bunk, take Hendriks'.'

'What?' He tried to focus but the face kept moving.

'Here. There you go.' There seemed to be a lot of faces now above him. 'Call out if you need us, right?' Or maybe he was seeing double. He tried to feel for that lump on his head but someone eased his hand down, and he lacked the energy to argue.

+++

When he woke the dorm was empty. Hell, he'd missed rouse up, now he was in more trouble. The dorm lights made him wince but he swung his legs and made himself sit up. And why was he in Hendriks' bunk? But his wristcom flashed from where he must have left it hung above the pillow so he twisted back to check the screen. New orders. Of course. He took a breath then started frowning. H team were on exercise all morning, but he was excused? A small relief. Reading on he found he wasn't on the schedule at all, except for Weapons Practice later. What was left of the first half of the day was all his. It didn't even say his movements were restricted. But then, where would he run to?

OK, he was awake, sort of, so he shuffled to the head, took care of business then considered a shower. It seemed like a lot of work but he ached, so if there was any hot water left it might help.

The water ran hotter than he remembered, maybe cos no one else was using it? It sniped at sore spots, but he did feel better. Dragging himself out, he remembered he was supposed to take more pills. With food. How late was he? Past breakfast, surely? But when he ventured down a cook soon spotted him and waved him in, then pushed a covered tray toward him. So he'd been expected?

He ate awkwardly, hampered by a split at the side of his lip he hadn't noticed. Took the pills and nursed a caffee till it cooled enough it didn't hurt so much to drink it. By the time he saw the bottom of the mug his head felt almost normal. He rechecked his wristcom and confirmed he really wasn't wanted. Maybe someone somewhere was still deciding what to do. But the mess crew kept looking and when he rose to leave he got more looks from people entering. In the end he holed up in the dorm and read the manuals again. The regs on insubordination were depressing but he fell asleep again before they made him suicidal, sleep beset with images of smugglers; settler bodies; Hunley crying; Hendriks groaning.

His wristcom jerked him back into the present. Crip, he only had minutes to report to the weapons bay. Scrubbing at his face he tugged his coverall as straight as it would go, figured the penalty for being scruffy on duty was the least of his worries and staggered out. Jogging hurt, he settled on a rapid walk and just, about, made it.

Naturally Zeiz was already there, but where was the rest of H? He gave up wondering and headed for the far end bay, his usual position these days.

Zeiz came too, and looked him over. 'Huh, you see straight?'

'Yes, Sarge.' Maybe.

'Let's get on then.' There was a long-range pulse rifle on the counter and a thousand metre target glowing in the distance. Crip, a thousand metres? But it wasn't a request; he reached out for the rifle.

Zeiz's hand got in the way. 'See your hands, private.' Harp let the Mooner turn his hands, inspect the purple plasskin, which was practically glowing round his knuckles. 'Young fool.' Zeiz prodded. 'Someone with your skills needs to take care of these, not bash people with 'em.'

'Yessir.' He tried not to wince and bit the lip instead. 'Crip.'

'And mind your manners.'

'Sorry, Sarge'

'Huh. Five rounds to start, fire when ready.'

Harp had to think five was Zeiz being kind. Or maybe not. With the weight and the recoil on this thing even that was a punishment. Harp foresaw a blinding headache in his future but he used the ledge to take the rifle's weight and focussed on the tiny target.

His first two shots were way off but the rest were a mix of inner and bull, and yep, his head was already aching.

'Not bad, considering.' Zeiz confirmed the score then took back the weapon. 'I guess this was why you enlisted, eh?'

'Sarge?' He'd assumed Zeiz knew how he'd got here, even wondered if Zeiz had been transferred in too.

'Well, not many Mooners cross to World, I guess you volunteered to use what you can do to make a good career? Not a bad idea.' Zeiz was racking the first gun on the back wall and choosing another from a row he'd obviously already signed out. 'Ten rounds this time.' He punched up the target.

Harp took the bigger, even heavier gun with clumsy fingers – his arms ached at the thought of firing. 'I, er, didn't enlist, Sarge.'

'What?' Zeiz's head swung back his way.

'I got orders, to transfer here from Moon Militia.'

Zeiz's eyes narrowed. 'So yesterday was you trying to get tossed out?'

'No, Sarge,' Harp said stiffly.

'Cos you do know, don't you, that they're not going to *let* you go, not when you can take painkillers and still shoot like this.'

Crip, if that was true… Harp took a breath, and a chance. 'What *will* they do, Sarge?'

Zeiz grinned. 'Well son, they have options, so the sergeants' mess has bets on. Now get shooting, private.'

Stance, sight, shoot, repeat. When his hands started to seize up Zeiz let him switch to handguns for the final stand, confirmed his scores and then dismissed him with a 'Get to sick bay, tell 'em I said to put more coldgel on those knuckles, then eat and get some sleep. A busy day tomorrow.'

Somehow he'd finished almost at the normal hour, so this time he found H-team in the mess, along with others. Conversation hitched then swelled back louder but his own surrounded him and practically dragged him to a table. Hamud made him sit and Hissack, on his other side for once, demanded, 'Well? What've they said?'

'Don't know.' Her mouth reopened but he beat her to it. 'Really. All I know is I've been pulled off schedule.' Except for Zeiz's comment; why "a busy day tomorrow"?

'Crip. Are you sure you don't have any useful connections? You know? Someone to put in a good word?'

Obvious what she meant. 'No. None.' Probably the opposite.

Hissack scowled, not at him but for him? 'No one's questioned us. That means they'll go on the instructors' reports, and the recordings.' Of course – there would be vid. He hoped he wouldn't have to watch it.

Hamud's turn. 'The vids'll be clear though, show Hoik was asking for it.'

'Unless they only show the last bout.'

Hamud stared at her. 'They wouldn't, would they?'

'They shouldn't, but recordings can be twisted.' Hissack looked... frustrated? 'And without Hunley there's a key witness missing.'

'What?' Harp's turn to frown.

'Hunley up and left as soon as they dismissed us, went straight to the commandant's offices.' Someone none of them had ever set eyes on. Hissack scowled again. 'Word is she declared herself unfit to serve. It would have been a damn sight more use if she'd done that earlier. But the point is they let her quit. They could have insisted she hung around for a hearing.' She saw the stares. 'Ma's Navy Legal. I was aiming for – never mind. Hunley was a witness and they didn't keep her, which has to make me wonder who's in charge, and whether someone has it in for Harp. Because we know Harp isn't *everyone's* golden boy, even if some do think the sun shines out of his arse.'

Harp choked. 'They do? That's news to me.' They laughed, but folk had always found some way to lay the blame on him back home and he didn't see that changing in a hurry, more polite or not. 'The best thing you can do is stay out of it.'

'Bollards to that.' Ham's scowl challenged Hissack's. 'They can't reject you cos of Hoik. We're all witnesses too.'

'If they call us,' Hissack interjected. She even looked bothered.

'Then we say so anyway, whether they ask or not!'

'No.' Harp sat straighter, food forgotten, talking to the entire table. 'You'll every one of you keep your heads down and your mouths shut. I don't want you lot on my conscience too.'

Some faces looked recalcitrant, but others showed relief. He hadn't volunteered for this, but they had and they shouldn't sabotage their futures. Hell, if Zeiz was right the navy didn't mean to lose him anyway. Why should they when they had much worse alternatives to choose from. But Hissack's scowl and Hamud's still worried him, almost as much as his blank tomorrow.

'Drop it for now, guys, OK? Let's see what happens. Now, how's Hendriks? Anybody seen him?'

Apparently Hendriks was already eating solids. He'd be back with them tomorrow, but excused any physical exercise. Hamud's frown had cleared as he said that. 'So the lucky sod gets to complete his theory assessments but miss the stuff he'd score worst at. How about that?'

+++

H-team were rescheduled before lights out; back onto Final Assessments. Including Harp. To his profound relief, that turned the rest's attention back to studying and off his 'situation' as their would-be Legal called it.

Hissack wanted Navy Legal, eh? Yep, he could see that, but he hoped she wouldn't jump to *his* defence. It would be best for everyone, himself included, if his bloody 'situation' got him out of here so they all forgot him. But there was another theory test tomorrow he apparently was meant to sit, so he supposed he ought to do the same as all the rest and study. Just cos it wouldn't count didn't mean he had to look stupid as well.

15

The big wall screens were on as usual in the mess, on opposite walls so no one could miss the latest success or the prettiest pictures or whatever govment or navy wanted them to know. Only today there were lists. They looked like names and people ahead were reading them before they ate. Some walked to the chow line smiling. Others didn't.

Hissack's face went sharper. 'They've published the first results. Come on.' Harp, tugged forward by both her and Hamud, had no choice as Hissack elbowed through the growing crowd with total disregard for other people's feelings. Harp was forced to smile; Hissack might have turned into an ally, but she *was* still Hissack.

The words at the top of the screen announced final assessments in three areas, two of them theory. And Unarmed Combat. Harp slowed, what curiosity he'd had abandoned, but Hendriks' face appeared from the crush and his beaming smile diverted Harp's attention. 'Hey, how are you feeling?'

'Harp.' The other guy's face sobered. 'Hell, I heard what you did, the med orderlies couldn't stop talking about it. You shouldn't have. I mean…'

'Forget it. What's with the smiles?'

'I scored gold in Threat Assessment and a merit in Astrogation. And a pass in Unarmed Combat.' Hendriks' smile widened. 'And that's not even the best of it.'

'I thought there were only three scores up.'

'Come on. Hey, let us through, guys.' People moved aside as Hendriks hustled Harp toward the nearer screen and pushed him to the front, then people clapped Harp on the back. He'd managed silvers on the theory lists. And 'special merit' in the Combat?

Hamud whooped and Hissack pushed across and punched him, hard enough Harp rocked back on his navy heels. Read the lists again. They hadn't altered. 'What the?'

Hissack's voice cut through the babble. 'Don't you get it? That's why you haven't heard anything, and why they didn't stop Hunley leaving. You're not being penalised at all. Darn it.' Hissack's scowl resurfaced. 'They were waiting to see who'd deal with him, and I missed it.'

All those times the sergeants didn't notice. Times they should've paired Harp off with Hoik but hadn't. It'd been a test? For everyone? Or him?

'Man, you're off the hook.' Ham hugged him!

Oh yeah? Harp figured the navy would still find some way to punish him, but that meant he had three more days of assessments. Thank the stars he'd studied, though it felt like everybody else in H was pulling for him this time – throwing questions at him, checking that he had the answers.

Hendriks, still reporting in to Sick Bay every day, came back with news that Hoik was out of regen but had been transported to the brig, the navy prison, and the orderlies were laying bets he'd be dishonourably discharged rather than the easier rejection out of training. Apparently that meant he wouldn't be allowed to re-enlist so his career in the navy would be dead before it ever started. His civilian future might not be too rosy either. Hissack reckoned World's employers would take notice too, that they were bound to see it on his record.

Harp pondered sympathy, but couldn't feel it. Hoik had earned it and he'd got it. Harp was more concerned about *his* future. It seemed pretty sure he was going to pass out of training. The question was what would they do with him next? Were they going to keep him in the navy, or return him to the Moon Militia? More worrying, when they all had to fill out final questionnaires, why did it sound like Harp's was the only screen didn't include a question about what posting he'd prefer?

16

Hissack got Legal and smirked. Hendriks got Technical and did a jig. Hamud got Marines and cheered. Harp?

'Armoury.' Ham threw an arm round his shoulder. 'Big surprise. You pleased?'

'Yeah, I guess.' It felt wrong though. Armoury was about caring for weapons, testing them, maybe teaching them, but not real combat, and somehow he'd expected… but it didn't matter what he might expect, the navy had decided for him here just like others had so often.

He wasn't staying on this base though, he was going to a ship. The same ship as Hendriks, and Hamud. Not only that, it was the fancy arc-ship, the *Defiant*. That was worth a second look. *Defiant* was brand spanking new, barely out of the World Orbital construction derricks; scarcely out of her initial trials.

Hendriks was ecstatic. It was his idea of paradise, but really it made reasonable sense. The *Defiant*, a new ship, was filling in gaps by padding her no-doubt hand-picked, experienced crew with beginners. Beginners who might benefit from the best officers and non-coms they could ever hope for, all keen to prove *they'd* been selected on merit not luck.

So the recruits, recruits no longer, handed in their dull coveralls and changed into the proper three-piece day dress, pants, tee and jacket, they were now allowed to wear in public from that moment onwards. Then tried to pack the rest of their new gear into the two duffles they were allowed to ship out with.

Hendriks groaned. 'I'll never do this.'

Hamud forced his lucky mascot into the top of the second bag. A faded, red plush 'trunk' poked out and had to be shoved in again. Despite the ribbing, he was taking it along with him. It didn't stop him poking Hendriks. 'Thank your stars they don't issue evac suits till we're onboard.'

Harp was finished – almost. He had permission to

"retain" Militia's bulky dockside jacket, till the navy found another. When he'd tried the brand new navy version it turned out at least a size too small – unless his muscles had grown muscles during training – but he was to leave the rest of his Militia gear with Stores, and didn't have much else to pack, so finishing was easy.

But Hendriks had gone paler, though he should have known they'd get their vac training on *Defiant*. Harp'd only ever had one dummy run at it himself, on Moon's Orbital, a poor attempt to show him how to get a badly-fitting suit on and confirm its systems. He wasn't sure the navy even used the same suits. But he had been into space that once, aboard the frigate, which was more than Hendriks. Even Hissack hadn't, he discovered, and she wouldn't now; she'd been assigned to World's main base, down here in Foundation City. She already knew the capital, and had even offered to give him a tour before he shipped off planet.

She was treating them all differently these days anyway. Especially him? She'd stopped acting like he was some kind of threat, which was even weirder when he considered he'd lost it and almost killed someone. In fact she had a look in her eye he wasn't unfamiliar with these days. It wouldn't be wise to make assumptions, not least cos Hissack had scored gold in Combat. But if she sent clear enough signals – well, it'd been a while but he hadn't forgot how and she did have a great body. Very… flexible.

Though odds were she wasn't thinking anything like that. She was still a high-priced Worlder, he was still a lowly Mooner, sunk still lower as an orphan lacking a reliable genetic record he could parrot. Couldn't see her fancy Ma would want her close to either. But he'd settle for the tour with thanks if she had meant that offer, mind his manners so as not to show her up in public like some farmboy.

Trouble was he *was* a Mooner, and a farmboy, and an orphan. He was hardly used to towns on Moon. He'd seen a fraction of the orbitals. He'd never seen a City.

+++

They'd taken another train from the base. That was OK, crowded again but mostly with other uniforms. Like theirs. They'd shared a grin at that. The train was yet another solid tube – no windows, no real sense of motion – but when he asked how far it was…

Hissack shrugged. 'Don't know, it doesn't take long though.'

That puzzled him. She really didn't know? On Moon, and on the ranch, everything was about distance. Hell, even on the weapons range. He *thought* in distances. But then all that was reaching, seeing, even on a map, and so far he hadn't *seen* anything on World, so maybe city folk didn't think like that. It wasn't about how far, just how long. And how long would depend on how fast, which he'd already found he couldn't guess. Enough deep thinking, he had felt the slight vibration; that meant slowing, and arrival.

When he stepped off a sign announced Foundation City, capital of Harpan's World. The seat of power, of the govment that ruled both here and Moon. His legal guardians, he supposed. He'd seen a vid-tour once when he was little, but he'd never dreamed he'd see the place for real.

'Hey, fool, you're blocking the doors.' Hissack tugged him on, toward a tunnel.

'Sorry, I was, er…'

'Staring. Yeah, I got that.' But she grinned and pulled him to a moving walkway. 'Anything you want to see first, farmboy?'

Harp groaned. 'Is it that obvious?'

'No.' She made a show of inspecting him as they sped on. 'You clean up as well as any of us. Till you open your mouth anyway.' Grin.

Crip. 'I've been trying to talk better.'

'Oh, you do all right most of the time, but the drawl's still there, just slighter.' Another grin. 'But never fear, as long as you're in uniform the girls'll love it.'

Harp stopping looking round. 'But not you.' It wasn't, in the end, a question.

Hissack's turn to blink. Her mouth half opened. 'No.' She said it slowly. 'I guess not. I like you, Harp, more than I expected, and you strip off worth inspection, but…'

'We're horny cos we've been without, not cos we really want each other.'

'Horny? Never heard it called that before.'

'Guess it's a Mooner word then. Steers on a ranch have horns, and fight with them in mating season.'

'Horny.' Hissack smiled. 'So you're saying that's why we've been eying each other?'

'I wouldn't have said no, you know that, right? I mean.' Harp floundered. 'I knew you were out of my league, but a guy can always dream.'

'Private Harp, don't you dare say I'm better than you. It's high time you lost that chip on your shoulder. You're a citizen like anybody else. Scrub that, you're *navy*. That puts you ahead of most.'

Harp swallowed. He had meant that as a compliment but it had made her mad. Was that what others saw, a guy who thought he had no value? Maybe she was right? OK, so they were equals. On the surface. He'd pretend to think so anyway.

'So, friends?' He held his hand out.

Hissack took it. 'Friends. Let's find a bar and drink to it.'

'OK.' He followed where she led. 'We need a cheap one though. I don't get paid until I'm posted.'

Her steps slowed. 'Harp, how broke are you? Far as I recall you never sprung for any extras.'

He debated lying but it felt dishonest now they'd settled on a friendship. 'Right now all I have is fifty Hendriks loaned me, that I'll pay him back on the *Defiant*.'

Hissack looked more curious than shocked. 'How come?'

Harp sighed. 'When I was transferred my back pay wasn't.'

'From the Moon Militia? Didn't you chase it?'

'Yeah, I asked, but my account was emptied days before I got here.'

'What? That's theft. Please tell me you reported it.'

He sighed again. 'No, cos I knew it wouldn't do any good.'

'Harp!'

'Crew credits went missing a lot, some of that was mine too.' And Regis walked off *Mercy* in a fancy-label jacket. As if all the pay he'd docked them for 'infringements' wasn't insult enough. 'I should have realised it might happen but my transfer was so rushed I didn't have time to think.' Probably another reason Regis waited.

'Whoah, you should have had plenty of time to organise your affairs before leaving Moon.'

That led to explanations. How he'd only had a few hours; how he hadn't come to World by choice; how Regis had delayed his orders, almost certainly on purpose. By that stage Hissack had found a bar she said was cheap, although to Harp it didn't look it. Well, the place had cushioned seats, for cripsake, and a lot of glassite tables he could see right through to fancy patterned flooring. And the human barkeep's clothes were better than he'd ever owned, before the navy.

At least his uniform made him presentable. It even got a respectful nod, and no one had ever given him that before. So he straightened his shoulders and pretended to belong. If strangers he'd never see again wanted to think his looks meant something they didn't, well, let 'em, this once. Less embarrassing for Hissack. He just wished she'd asked the price before she ordered the beer.

Hissack's mind was still on what he'd told her. 'I still don't get it. I mean, space knows why they transferred you without warning you, but I really don't understand why this captain would deliberately try to get you into trouble, much less cheat you.'

Harp tried the amber beer, which tasted every bit as pricey as it looked. 'I'm guessing Regis fixed the transfer to get rid of me. There was a limit to how long he could keep me out of sight, cos I was too… noticeable, for the wrong reasons. You must have worked that out by now. Regis only wants notice for the right ones, the things that benefit him.' He took another sip; confession needed beer.

'He was jealous?'

Harp's hand stopped midair. Regis jealous? She'd got that wrong. Hadn't she? He shook the idea off. 'The man's ambitious and he's got some wealthy family behind him here on World. Someone said it was their clout got him his captaincy, which figures cos a meaner, lazier son-of-a-bitch you never met. He liked being in charge, and he liked to spend. His few favourites got an easy ride while the rest of us covered half their duties. And he'd find reasons to dock our pay, and we all knew the credits ended up in his account instead, but there was nothing we could do about it. There was one time he had leave arranged here on World and suddenly half the crew discovered their accounts were short.' Harp took another drink before he lost his temper.

Hissack didn't try to hide her anger. 'He transferred you to World with no warning so he could rob you?' She scowled, very much the Hissack of their first encounter. 'How much did he get?'

Harp gulped more beer. 'I had near two thousand in there. Militia grunts don't get much but I'd saved half my pay.' Because he'd wanted, finally, some sense of independence, self respect, a nest egg for a future that was still uncertain.

'He took the lot?' Hissack's fist clenched round her glass. 'There'd only be three access points, right? Your own code, your superior officer's and Militia Accounting. So it could be someone in Accounting.'

'Yeah, but we knew Regis; we just couldn't prove it. Ship's records always showed the debits as crew making sports wagers that lost.'

Hissack studied his expression. 'And no one argued because his family is influential, maybe enough to buy him a career on Moon when he didn't have what it takes to get one on World?' She smiled, and it wasn't friendly this time. 'But I have a mother here in Legal, and Navy Legal pretty much trumps anyone outside of the Founding Family. All I have to do is ask and she'll start digging. Hell, she'll want to.'

'But… can Navy Legal even investigate anything to do with Moon Militia?'

'Navy Legal can investigate anything that affects Harpan defence or security,' Hissack told him smugly. 'And this comes firmly under both Theft and Conduct Unbecoming.'

'Crip.' The mere thought of sticking it to Regis, after all his petty tyranny… was worth another beer, never mind the prices.

Two more beers cost him ten cred. He called it extortionate, Hissack insisted it wasn't, then insisted on paying the whole tab, pushing her wrist at the small table screen before Harp could prevent it.

'Today's on me, no arguing with your tour guide. I have a city-size allowance and if I don't spend it my father starts talking about reducing it. Since it's the only thing he does give me I have no intention of giving him any excuse, so you're doing me a favour.'

By the time Harp had untangled the clues in that they were walking down a busy thoroughfare; still underneath a roof – albeit one with images of plants and flying things. The walls got slowly higher, making room for bars and fancy eateries, some overhead, and stores with merch on show to tempt those passing into spending yet more credits. Some passersby sent stares at them, then looked away. A couple even made a space for them to pass when it got crowded. He pretended not to notice; that felt safer.

He'd thought the first stores fancy, but they soon got fancier, from two-d screens to holo images, then some stores boasted real-space displays out front, which said a lot in places where he figured space of any kind was valued. Hissack slowed, she said she liked to 'window shop'. He guessed he understood that. If he'd ever seen places like these on Moon he'd have had his nose stuck to the show too. Although the prices might have sent him running. But it looked like Hissack had never had to look at price tags. An important, navy mother and an absent, credit-paying father, eh? He watched her inspect a belt behind the plas, peered closer, saw it was described as "Genuine Mooner leather" and tagged at seventy credits! Hissack said it was a bargain and debated buying it.

Harp started laughing; couldn't help it. He had a hide belt in his duffle; older but it even had a hand-tooled buckle made of steer horn, birthday treat from Mr Seth and Missus Destra. Bet she'd think that even more exotic!

Hissack heard him laugh and looked the question.

'I got a wider one, only mine's buff hide.'

'Bufflo?' Hissack's mouth stayed open.

'Yeah, it's tougher so it wears real well. That's lam,' he said dismissively. Mr Seth had reared bufflo, wouldn't touch lam, even though they needed less water. And luxury market or not was still down to counting every cent when he'd left. But he had clearly soaked up better standards cos he answered her with, 'Lam hides tear too easy. Only good for standing round in.'

Hissack laughed. 'And I suppose you paid less than seventy too?'

'Paid nothin', made the belt myself. The buckle was handmade, and given.' He couldn't help but feel smug when Hissack looked so impressed, but he hadn't been trying to put her down or anything. 'Never saw anything like that on Moon though,' he admitted quickly, pointing to a life size statue in the even bigger next-door window, wearing what he had to figure rich folk here thought was fashion, silver boots and pastel coloured pants more tight than looked respectable, except there was a hip length tunic, tarted up with silver edges.

Hissack looked, then smiled. Uh-oh. But she'd already grabbed his hand and pulled him through the silver coloured doorway, underneath a sign said *Kissel Fashions*, and a human clerk was coming forward. Hissack beamed at him.

'My friend needs something for this evening and was

admiring your displays.' She smirked. 'I'm thinking something casual and understated, just like him.'

'Hiss, no!' Too late. The woman had already turned to lead them deeper into trouble.

'Yes.' She tugged again. This time she couldn't budge him. 'Do you realise I haven't shopped for months. I'm in dire need of splurging.' Once again she tugged, in vain. 'I told you, helping me is doing me a favour, and I owe you for Hoik and I like to pay my debts, OK?' She studied his reaction. 'If you don't behave I'll… I'll tell the nice clerk you're a paid escort and make you model everything in the store.' Her eyes danced. 'I might even tell everyone I meet what you charge.'

'Hiss!' He could feel himself go redder.

'Give in?' She only grinned. 'I can fight dirtier, if I have to.'

'Crip.' The clerk had turned to see why they weren't following. Any second she'd come back, and Hiss would do it, wouldn't she? 'OK, OK, but nothing fancy, and I'll pay you back.'

'Of course you will.' She was patting his arm. The damn woman was humouring him!

'I mean it, Hiss, I –'

'Shush.' She spoke up louder. 'But darling, you know you have absolutely no fashion sense. Just leave it to me and this nice assistant.'

It wasn't as if he had a choice, the two of them talked a foreign language anyway, and when he tried to argue both of them behaved like he was ten, all smiles and patience. It was easily an hour before they left the place, still empty-handed. Oh, not because they hadn't picked an outfit, as they called it. No, cos Hissack told the clerk to send the purchases direct to her apartment. Harp hadn't thought to stay here overnight. What's more he hadn't even known she had a place here. It turned out her father bought that too. Who the hell paid space-knew-how-much to keep a place she hadn't set foot in for months?

At least after that she behaved, taking him places he'd actually heard of, like the Government Assembly and the famous Founder's Mansion. He'd vaguely known these were on opposite sides of the same central 'square', which turned out to be a pretty stretch of parkland in the open air and reached through covered walks that opened out like funnels and showed holo images of Founders, looking solemn, other folk between Harp guessed must be important too, cos many of them looked like Harpans.

It'd have been easier if he'd been born looking more like these early pictures, where the faces were the same but all the hair was so much darker, but no, he had to come out lighter, like the later, more unlikely generations, didn't he, so no mistaking or assuming some long-dead connection. Cept he did look like those early Harpans now, so maybe changing his hair colour had been more believable than he'd realised?

Even that confusing notion didn't hold his attention when they exited the last funnel, cos this was the first natural-looking space he'd seen since he left Moon. And was it all the time he'd spent indoors or was the sky a different blue than home? As for the park…

He could only stare. There were stone paths and benches, all too white, like someone scrubbed them. At least he thought they were benches, but they might be artwork cos the park was decorated here and there with things no one could ever sit on. But it was the colours stopped him. There was grass here, startlingly bright and thick enough for carpet. It wasn't there for feedstuff either. Hissack said they cut it short like that just to make it pretty. And the flowers… Big, blowsy things in red and white and gold and colours that he couldn't even name, whole banks of them, some even growing on the trees.

And water? It was coming from a fountain, running down into a fancy pool, there just to look at. Hell, even bare patches of dirt were different from home, dark and soft instead of hard and pale. He bent to touch, his hand unsteady.

'Harp?' Hiss looked confused. 'I thought you came from a ranch. Anyone would think you'd never seen grass before.'

'I haven't, not like this.' Too awed to shrug it off he told her, 'Moon is dry, and getting drier. If the drought goes on it won't be long before there's no more forage for the livestock. Or the people.' He looked up at Hissack. 'That's how come I got in the Militia, cos my fosters couldn't raise the cred to pay their tithe. A lot of folk are getting pretty desperate back there.' He saw her face. 'Folk here don't know that?'

'No. Well, I never heard it on the public channels, and Ma's never mentioned it either. Crip.' She looked around them at civilians strolling, children playing, everybody carefree. 'The government must know though. Maybe they're afraid there'll be a panic?'

'Maybe.' But Harp had to wonder. Was *this* where the tithes went, to pay for flowers Mooners never saw, with credits they'd have used for water, medicines and feedstuff? His gaze returned to the Assembly building, all five storeys, vaguely cuboid with a covered entrance opening onto the park. He watched as people, more bright colours, scurried in and out like insects; purposeful, intent. Complacent.

It was made out of the same stone-stuff he'd seen everywhere else here, only where the stores and bars went in for fancy shapes carved into the surfaces this frontage had inserted coloured stone – and even metals? – in the walls, and an impressive row of balconies all hung with shiny banners, where the famous Harpan H stood out, picked out in red and gold above them. It impressed all right. It must be reassuring to these Worlders.

He was trying to decide why it didn't reassure *him* when Hissack pinched his arm. 'I'm sorry Moon is having such a hard time.'

Crip, their first day of freedom, she offered to show him round, spent her own credits on him, and he was moping, and spoiling her day too. He found a smile, which came easier when she returned it. 'Yeah, thanks. I know. So, can we get closer to the Mansion?'

'Oh.' Hissack relaxed, her mood improving instantly. 'Not much, but there's a good view over that way.' A brisk walk – he figured neither of them knew how to stroll like civilians now – took them to the top of one of the grassy hillocks. It felt wrong to walk on this grass – but he forgot that when they reached the top. The Founder's Mansion lay before them, like a fancy painting.

He'd seen pictures, but it really was a work of art. His teachers had described the big-name artists who'd designed it and embellished it; how it had taken generations to complete and there were still 'improvements' being added.

It didn't *look* like it needed improving. It looked huge, and awe-inspiring, glittering in all this sunlight. It looked powerful, much more so than the building it was facing. But then he guessed the Founding Family *was* more powerful than the Assembly. It was their world, after all, they'd built it, they owned it. They could pretty much do what they wanted.

Yeah, like take a family embarrassment and send the shame away to Moon? Harp took a breath. At least they'd taken the trouble to find him a family; it wasn't their fault those people'd been killed, so soon he couldn't even say what they had looked like. And it wasn't so surprising they'd forgot about him once they'd done that, never knew he'd ended up in Orphan Houses. It wasn't that they hadn't cared at *all*, just that their caring had been… distant, like the way the Founder's Mansion stood apart from all these other buildings.

Hissack was gazing at the place with pride. Pride in her world too, maybe; probably the reason she enlisted. He should pay a compliment or something.

'It's impressive.' Well it was. 'Or don't you notice any longer?'

'No, I notice.' Hissack went on staring. 'Do you think there could be grander places, like on other worlds?'

He'd never even thought of other worlds before. 'I can't imagine them. What makes it glitter?'

'New security screens. They went up last year on both buildings; complete sensor domes. They can block signals, and stop missiles dead.'

'Yeah? Crip.' He stared up, trying to trace the curves, then gave up, but looking higher made him realise the light was fading.

Hissack saw him check his wristcom. 'Time to eat? Then we can think about what you want to see tomorrow, over dinner.'

'OK.' It looked like he was staying; couldn't claim he wasn't willing and she didn't have to pay for her apartment so he wouldn't really owe her. What the hell; she could afford to let him have a couch or something and he'd pay her back, somehow, in credits or in favours.

'Yeah, OK,' he said more firmly. 'Lead the way, Private.'

'Yessir.' Hissack grinned and pulled him back across the grass, toward the way they'd entered.

17

The new 'outfit', all dark reds and greens – thankfully no silver edges – didn't feel like him, but it would have been churlish to say anything or refuse to change into it. Especially when Hissack went to civvies too as soon as they arrived at her apartment.

So this was what Worlders called home? Actually, she'd called it 'a box' and apologised that his bed folded out of the main room's wall. And that she only had the one washroom. She was still apologising when they took a sort of minitrain that curved and lifted them to what she called a "reasonable eatery". He'd had to smile. More glassite tables, presumably in fashion, more very fancy human staff instead of auto, even saying welcome at the doors then showing them to table. Which he gathered she'd reserved. And then they poured out water and set breads, at least three kinds, all in a fancy woven basket.

Hissack saw him frown. 'Perhaps you'd rather find a hostel? I know it's small. I won't be offended.'

'Hiss, your place is more than fine, believe it, better than I'm used to.' Shortening her name was starting to feel comfortable too. He'd told her that it suited her, and had the bruise to prove it. It was easier to be more honest with her too. 'I wouldn't even know how to register somewhere else, nor how to behave.'

'You really do have an inferiority complex, don't you? I never realised. I guess because you never said much. Try the wine,' she said abruptly. So he did. It wasn't bad, a softer taste than beer, fruitier perhaps; he wouldn't know what real fruit would taste like, though on Founder's Day the orphans got to drink the synth kind. Hiss sipped too. 'I didn't like you much, you know.'

He was relaxed enough to grin. 'I kinda figured.'

'You were so… contained. And knew what you were doing.' She mock-scowled. '*And* you grabbed the best bunk.'

Harp laughed. 'You thought I knew everything? I

thought you did, you and all the other navy brats in H-team.'

She gaped at him. 'But you were so aloof, even when we worked out you weren't Family. To be honest, you were scary. I'm sure Hendriks was relieved you acted friendly.'

'Hell, I was relieved someone would talk to me; it didn't always happen.' Annoyed with himself, he cut off there. She was right; he did need to stop thinking he wasn't as good as anyone else. As good as any other navy grunt anyway. 'Now you, you were the scary one, especially in Unarmed Combat. I was quite happy not to be in that group.'

She looked pleased. They toasted the end of training then she led him through the menu and he could admit it was the best meal, perhaps the best day, he could remember. The only shock was when he realised that there'd been no Thanksgiving all the time they'd sat there. Hissack looked surprised he'd noticed. 'Not in a restaurant, no. People are coming and going all the time. It'd be rude.'

'But we all stopped eating in the mess, and when I was on ships.'

Her turn looking doubtful. 'I suppose so, but it's not expected, not in public places; not for civilians anyway. It's more something for at home, or formal gathers.'

So there it was, another difference. Or maybe not, after all Harp hadn't exactly been used to eating out either.

So they went back to her 'box', stripped off and showered, in and out around each other without any awkwardness or hesitation, just like in the dorm room, and he figured that was how it should be. He had played in the Militia, up on Orbital, but never on his ship. Perhaps the same rule would be best with Hissack. And with other crewmates in the future, now the future was upon them?

She had caffee for them both next morning, that she even brewed herself, and long-life rations from her storage. She didn't say Thanksgiving, but he didn't comment. He thought about that though. It looked like the navy were keener to put the Family first than Mooners, but maybe Worlder civs were less enthusiastic than both? Except when other folk could hear them? For show? He didn't know enough yet, better not to jump to such conclusions.

After eating they headed out to "see the sights" again as Hissack put it, still in civvies, on a route march that she said would take in all the major landmarks they could find the time for; the largest gallery, the fanciest museum, both as big as Mooner townships. They saw the Harpan River too. Hiss said it ran right through the city, for a while aboveground even. And the Harpan Bridge, which spanned that portion and had fancy lights that Hissack said they ought to come back later to admire.

The visible river was over a mile long, the biggest stretch of open water Harp had ever seen. Hiss said she wished they had the time to travel to the ocean. Harp was less than certain he'd have coped with that; the open river shocked him into silence.

They ate a complicated sort of rollup, meat paste, sauce and veggies in a wrap made out of something very white and smooth, another Worlder luxury. To top that off they ate beside the water, on a stone veranda, watching folk float past in tiny boats. Hiss talked of hiring one but he declined; the thought of having only water under him was somehow scarier than going into space. They walked some more instead to fill their final hour before reporting back. Hiss chose a different route this time. They passed through somewhat poorer districts for a while where his new clothes made him better dressed than locals, but of course that didn't last. Hiss wanted him to see impressive, not what she considered normal. Harp was simply pleased to see there was a normal here, that some of World was maybe fractionally closer to what Mooners lived with. Pleased that he could walk around without offending Worlders with his mere presence. Maybe he should keep the darker hair and just forget it?

Eventually they went back to the box, changed into

uniform, collected their duffles and went to grab a shuttle from this city proper to the outskirts where they'd take the tunnel train to barracks. They were walking past those fancy stores again – Hiss needed one last look, 'to tide her over'. He was still figuring out what that meant when she grabbed his arm.

'Hey, what's going on?' She tugged him forward. 'There's a crowd.'

To Harp a crowd spelled caution, always had. 'We need to watch the time, Hiss.'

'Oh there's plenty yet, don't be a spoilsport.' She started weaving through the crowd, pretty much towing him. 'Look, it's Kissel's place, and there's Security outside.' Short of digging in his heels all Harp could do was follow her or lose her.

He recalled the elegant interior, the valuable merch. Had they been robbed? It was the sort of place that folk might envy, right enough. Had anyone been hurt?

Maybe she was concerned about the polite clerk too. 'You're taller. What can you make out?' Harp stretched a bit and peered over intervening heads, to see the doors swing open. The security outside moved quickly to surround a man with greying hair – and telling, knife-sharp features. Hiss had obviously caught a glimpse as well. 'Oh, look, Harp, it's the Founder! Maxil Harpan, in person.'

The greying man was smiling genially at the crowd as his security formed up around him, leaving him a clear space to walk in. People stepped toward him, surging forward, leaving Harp, who hadn't, with a sudden space before him. Founder Maxil Harpan turned toward a waiting auto, even though it was a walk-place so it shouldn't be there.

Hiss was hanging on his arm. 'Well, there's your final landmark, the Founder himself. How's that for luck.' Then Hissack realised that Harp was backing off, and pulling her as well; her smile faded. 'What?'

'I shouldn't be here.' Harp tried to turn, still blocked by Hissack's hold.

Too late. That older version of his face had stilled; the gap in front of Harp had opened up enough that he'd been visible. The current ruler of the Harpan Worlds was peering at a Harpan bastard.

Harp recovered first. 'Let's go.'

This time Hiss moved on without more protest, only glancing at him when she thought he wasn't looking, till they veered off into a side street. 'I forgot. Would you believe, I clean forgot who you, er, resemble.' She looked back then ran to catch him up. 'Are you OK?'

'Yeah. Let's go for that train, all right?' He figured he could slow down now, but couldn't seem to do it without conscious effort.

It was a relief when the train wasn't far to go, another that she didn't speak again until they boarded. 'Harp, You want to talk about it?'

'No.' He'd got to staring at his boots, high time he found his manners. 'Not much. Sorry for rushing you.'

'Mm.' A pause. The shuttle raced them ever closer to the barracks. 'You'd fit right in though, wouldn't you? You don't just look a little like them. If it wasn't for the darker hair you'd be exactly… and you even have the name.'

'No, Hiss, I wouldn't fit, at all, I'm still a farmboy. And I only have half the name, and that much was probably someone's idea of a joke. And it didn't help me fit in anywhere, all right?'

'Right, hence the complex.' Hissack *hugged* him, in her uniform and all. 'So you're the black lam, who cares? Promise me you won't ever think you're less than them, because you're so not.'

Hissack was delusional, but who was he to say so. He just – he hadn't realised how very much, how *exactly*, as Hiss said, he'd matched. OK, now he knew. The years, the reactions, made a lot more sense now. And he needn't ever feel so chilled again about it.

18

Officers got to sit at the sharp end, grunts at the rear. And it was easy to tell which end was which. In that respect the navy's newest atmospheric shuttle was the same as his old cruiser, arrow shaped to fly through gravity. In sharp contrast the shuttle's overhead screens showed the *Defiant* didn't remotely subscribe to any rules of aerodynamics, but then why would it: it would never travel anywhere that wasn't vacuum. The immense craft resembled a giant wedge of grey cheese roped to a thick, crescent-shaped plate. Only the ropes were half a mile thick and both the cheese, and the plate behind it, looked like space mice had been nibbling all over them, cos every surface Harp could see was full of hollows and protrusions.

'Small' craft, dwarfed by the *Defiant*, darted round his current ride, in and out his view, and lights flashed here and there. Last-minute maintenance? A final polish? Because *Defiant* was due to release and leave this outlying spar of World's Orbital two days from now, and he'd be on it.

On his other side, Hendriks was pointing out technical details to Hamud. They'd finally stopped exclaiming at how much lighter they felt once the shuttle's grav matched the Orbital's. Harp, who'd expected the change, and already memorised *Defiant's* specs – what was available – half listened and let the sight of her sink in. Hoping he really did have all the deck layouts fixed in his head so he wouldn't embarrass himself. Yet. They already had their cabin assignments so he didn't see a problem there; his was way forward in J20. J deck, practically the bow. He knew areas nearest the hulls were largely docks and holds, for safety. According to his search, anything forward and higher was listed as senior officers' quarters, and a whole block that was bridge. As far from that as possible the tail-end 'plate' was the huge power plant. Fitted with the "pulsetec" engines Militia ships never got, that he still couldn't read up on. From what he *had* been able to read, it was safer to make it detachable. It would be nice to feel stronger again in less grav though, even if it was an illusion.

Hendriks was going to H203, Hamud way back in F348, where the Marines' quarters were semiautonomous, with their own arsenal and armoured bulkheads. The three had made promises to hook up when their off duty allowed, but looking at all this Harp wasn't so sure how. They were the only H recruits posted here but he'd exchanged odd words in the wait area with folk from other teams. As he'd guessed the virgin ship was taking on some virgin crew, but he figured the *Defiant* might be almost as strange to seasoned ratings, and give them almost as much to learn. Hendriks said she was chock full of new tech and new design, some of it traded with the weird looking Kraic in the neighbouring sector. He was in a whole new world, where even aliens he'd barely heard about before were suddenly a lot more real; he might even see one. And if Hendriks was right, as he usually was, maybe he was too, and being rookies here might even be to their advantage; they wouldn't have to un-learn so much. The thought was something to hold onto, looking at another new existence looming ever closer.

By then *Defiant's* hull was close enough there was nothing else to see, then the shuttle docked with a clang, a red light flashed up front and the pilot's voice said, 'Welcome to *Defiant*, people. Don't forget your bags and baggage.'

Harp exchanged a look with Hendriks at the less than regulation language as a hissing noise accompanied a rush of air, the red light changed to green-for-go and then the forward hatch slid open.

Officers disembarked first, then senior ratings then grunts, rookies and old hands mixed. Joining their new ship meant a short sharp walk through the cold of a docking umbilical then swiping their wristcoms past a wall plate at the inner airlock. A Petty Officer and several ratings weeded the just-passed-out from the rest and marched them to an empty hold. Told to stand easy, maybe two hundred new recruits set down their duffles and... stood easy. And then stood some more, in an unheated cavern.

+++

Hendriks was shivering and Harp's fingers had about lost all feeling by the time the sound of clicking heels and their muddled echo heralded some new arrivals, but Harp knew better than to turn and sight-see. Mullah cured that impulse long before he reached the navy. He could track the new arrivals anyway; a shuffle then a solid step proclaimed a pair of heavy feet, and then a second, lighter, set had cleared the hatch behind him. Finally a woman officer stepped into view and turned to face them. And behind her came a man, so quietly Harp wondered if the rest had even heard him.

They made an interesting contrast. The man wore a Petty Officer's stripes, was slightly built and greying at the temples, with a face that showed about as much expression as the metal bulkheads. The woman wore the interlocking Hs of a senior brass. He counted, four; commander. Phew. The highest rank he'd ever seen. She was stocky – explained, the heavy tread – and had red hair, another rarity to ponder. For the rest he put her age at maybe thirty-five or forty, surely very young for a commander. Cos she'd had enhancements? Or had spent some serious time in space and was really much older? Or because he thought, despite the hair, she was a real-Harpan? Yep, the ochre skin and narrow features definitely had a Harpan look about them; maybe not a direct line but very possibly related. Would a real-Harpan get promoted faster?

Harpan-looks-wise, she was not as close as him, even now, he was relieved he'd found a spot toward the rear. With any luck she wouldn't notice him. Or come across him later.

Either way she looked athletic and determined, and

when she spoke she had that clipped World accent, even more than Hissack. 'Listen up, recruits. My name is Commander Soffi. I am your XO. The man you see beside me is Chief Pak, who is *Defiant's* Training Supervisor and from this moment owns you, over and above your immediate superiors. You have been fortunate enough to be posted to *HNS Defiant*. There are many more than willing to replace you. Anyone who fails to deliver everything the chief expects *will* be transferred out, and someone else shipped in. That clear?'

'Yes, ma'am!'

'You should already have your quarters and station assignments. You now have one hour to stow your gear, change into work uniform and report to your Head of Section. Anyone who does not have both these assignments, report to any of the senior ratings round you. Anyone who fails to report in on schedule will be leaving on the next shuttle. Is *that* clear?'

'Yes, ma'am!'

'Dismissed.' Soffi turned to talk to the Chief. Recruits began to disperse at a fast clip. Hendriks checked his wristcom then gave Harp a farewell nod – as did Hamud, heading for another hatch. Harp prayed he'd been mistaken, drew a breath and headed for the nearest rating.

'Problem, crewman?'

'Yes, Corporal. I have quarters assigned but no station posted.'

'Let's see.' The man swiped wristcoms then consulted his. 'Harp, private 1?'

'Yes, Corporal.' It would surely be a comp glitch; he just wished it wasn't his.

'Huh, J20 is all I have too. No other orders?'

'No, Corporal.' Please don't put me on the shuttle.

'All right, I'll send it in to Ops. Meanwhile you better find your cabin and get stowed away. Stay put till you get further orders.'

Thank you. 'Yes, Corporal.'

A sniff. 'And if you want advice, don't annoy anybody else on the way.'

'No, Corporal.' Great. He'd barely arrived and he'd already ticked someone off. And no doubt next someone would bawl him out for not reporting to a duty station. Being innocent had never stopped folk being mad at him yet. No matter, just do as you're told. He gave the required brisk nod – regs said shipboard crew didn't throw their arms around– and got out of there. All he could do was get stowed away as fast as possible. With his luck he wouldn't get his duty station sorted out before he missed the deadline.

A quick glance at the signage told him he was aft on R deck, which meant a long hike; he set off briskly, consulting his wristcom for the fastest route. Five decks higher he began to think all that physical training had been worth the pain; by then he'd negotiated twists, turns, raised hatches and three cliff-face ladders when he couldn't find any handy chutes, all carrying his two duffles. Lighter or not, his legs were beginning to feel it, his wristcom said he had another three decks to climb, *and* he'd used up nearly half his hour. Crip. Ship's regs said he couldn't run except in an emergency. He jogged a few times though when nobody was around to see him.

He could feel the sweat trickling down his back by the time he identified the hatch tagged J20. If his missing orders came through now he'd have to dump his gear, run and pray. Deep breath and here went nothing.

The hatch was green-lit so he could at least swipe the autoplate instead of needing to force the safety lever. The hatch slid open, Harp threw one leg over, duffle in each hand, bent through and straightened up again – to find himself the centre of attention.

Getting wholly in and swiping the hatch closed gave him a moment to recover, and wonder what the crip he was doing there. A single glance had told him J20, however narrow, was a six-berth cabin, three up three down, on a ship where most ratings, junior or not, would sleep at least three up and five deep. There was no way a raw recruit rated such an almost-private allocation. Damn. They'd not only messed up his duty station, they'd given him the wrong berth as well? Had they mixed him up with someone else? He certainly couldn't blame these folks for staring.

There were five other crew present, three of them female, those all shoulder-tagged as medical orderlies. Armoury berthed with Medical? Another sign he shouldn't be here. What else could go wrong?

'Whoo-ee. What have we here?' A guy had stood up from the farthest bunk. He looked no more than thirty, but Harp instantly distrusted that impression; reminded himself again that spending a lot of time in space made folk look younger. He was small and wiry, but apparently their spokesman, strolling forward, blocking Harp from going farther in. As if he'd intended to. 'Well, now. And you'd be?' Glancing at his name tag. 'Harp?' Black eyebrows rose in the dark brown face. 'Is that supposed to make you incognito?'

And it starts again. 'It's my name –' What was he, private, corporal? The way he talked Harp would guess worse, but the guy's shirt tag only said Delom, and he didn't have the right shoulder markings either. In fact the only label other than his House name and *Defiant's* shield was just a weird letter R, above his name and on his shoulders.

Apparently Harp's hesitation was amusing. 'That'd be sergeant, to you, sonny. Haven't got round to fixing the stripes on yet. But you seem to have lost a couple letters to your name there.'

And again. 'I got tagged Harp on Moon Militia duty, Sergeant, cos my *given* name is Harpan.'

This Delom stepped back and looked him up and down. 'Hey, people, do we scent a story? Shall we hear it?'

The nearest female did wear sergeant's stripes, was at least ten years older than Delom, a great deal paler, a handspan taller, and frowning at him. 'I think we let the poor guy get settled in, before somebody wants him.'

'Oh, but I want him, already,' said the oldest woman there, a corporal, a solid-looking figure, olive skin and greying hair pulled back severely as required on duty.

She gave Harp a leer. 'He's so pretty.'

The third girl – smaller, classic round-faced-dainty and another corporal, scowled downward at the speaker from the higher bunk. 'Hands off the Harpan. He'll want higher game than medics.'

Crip. He could take the hazing. Well, he'd have to. But the mistaken identity… tempting as it was right now it wasn't worth the payback later. 'I'm not Family. I'm Mooner.'

Delom looked unconvinced. 'You don't look it, but you do look like a Harpan, and I don't like being lied to.'

'I'm not lying, I was on a farm before I went to Moon Militia.'

The last guy, still flat out across a lower bunk, joined in at last. 'He's got the drawl.'

Delom considered. 'A Mooner. No kidding?'

'No kidding.'

'Well, OK. So what's a Mooner doing in the Specials?'

'Specials?' This sounded like things were even more messed up than he'd thought.

The rest swapped glances then the leading orderly took over. 'I'm Mac.' The female sergeant had an R tab too. 'You don't know why you're here?'

Harp dropped a bag to nod uncomfortably, very much aware he would be sweaty. 'My posting said Armoury, but I don't have a duty assignment yet.'

'That'll be because your station isn't listed either.' Mac looked scornful. 'As if everyone hasn't tagged us as Specials anyway.' She saw Harp's face. 'We're off the books, kid. Special duty. Supposedly R is for research personnel. Putting Armoury on your transfer orders was probably someone's notion of an amusing cover.' She saw Harp's puzzlement. 'A joke, like sending you behind blast walls?'

It wasn't funny. 'There must be some mistake, Ma' – he caught himself in time – 'Mac. I'm straight out of training.'

'So what can *you* do other rookies couldn't?'

Light dawned. 'I… can shoot?'

Mac nodded, visibly relaxing, and Delom cut in. 'And that makes three. Let the party begin.'

Mac frowned him down. 'All right, kid, you're last in, you get the last lower bunk and the last locker. And what do we call you?'

'Harp, Sarge.' Since she and Delom were both stepping aside he edged past, trying not to slam anything into them.

Mac stood and watched him, close enough to make a mere farmboy nervous. 'I'm senior crew in here but otherwise we're all in the same game. Which means everyone bar Sufi and Oko are rated as acting sergeants, you included, Sergeant Harp.' She smiled grimly when his mouth fell open. 'Better close the mouth and stow your gear. We don't know when we'll be wanted.'

Harp took the point. 'Right.' Till someone rescued him he'd better go with what he'd got; a crazy situation.

The younger woman sat cross-legged up above. The guy below was still in shadow; just a long thin shape that stretched the full length of the mattress. The older woman pulled the last tall locker open for him. Harp dumped his duffles on the deck in front of it and started his unpacking. That at least felt normal. If he didn't count a dress uniform he'd never had before or the lighter weight ships' coveralls that would replace the clumsy ones he'd worn in training.

There was a neat pile of bedding on his bunk, standard issue, so he made it up then stowed the last of his personals in the wall net behind. While J20 might be semi private it was still close quarters, and close scrutiny, but he'd survived in worse conditions.

Mac wasn't done. 'This joker's Delom. This is Sufi.' Pointing to the older female. Sufi blew a kiss. 'That's Yentl.' The stretched out guy gave a limp wave, hand almost greyish when it met the brighter overhead that lit the cabin. 'And that's Oko.' The younger woman who had frowned at him still looked suspicious, but she nodded.

Which meant Harp was the youngest in both years and

experience. It didn't make any sense – but what the navy said went, till they said otherwise. Since the rest were in the thinner coveralls he figured he should change to match and an inner panel light suggested J20 even had its own head. 'Am I OK to shower?' What did he call people if everyone was supposed to be a sergeant?

'Go ahead, through there. If we get word to move we'll bang on the door.'

'Right, er, thanks.' He laid out a clean coverall, still bearing its packing creases, grabbed his washkit and shut himself out of their sight and sound. They'd talk about him now of course, but thankfully he wouldn't have to hear.

The shower stall included air dry. That explained why he hadn't been issued towels. And everything looked new, which he supposed it was. Everything sparkled. It was like being back in Hissack's apartment.

The cabin went quiet when he stepped out, in shorts and tee. Sufi grinned. 'Yeah, definitely the prettiest.' Oko scowled. Mac shook her head. He got the sense that was a pretty standard interaction. Mac started talking again as he pulled the one piece suit up.

'You'll need to add tabs before you go anywhere or you'll get stopped. You too Delom, unless you want Security all over you.'

A suddenly helpful Delom dug the patch kit out of Harp's locker and tossed it across before moving away, opening up his own locker and foraging for the same. And suddenly it wasn't a mistake, cos both kits were stocked with curving sergeant's stripes, and Harp's included R tags like these folk were wearing. Unlike the recruit issue that needed a machine these were hi-tech, self-fixing versions. Self-*un*fixing? With the suit already sealed to his waist he twisted, positioned an R patch carefully, smoothed it down the regulation right shoulder, then added the stripes beneath. Still crazy. Then he took the time to add them to the tee he was already wearing, then his other tees and all his work gear. He would finish later, if he needed. By the time he'd got that done Delom had too. Four sergeants and two… corporals?… sharing a berth. Three medical staff and three… whatever… berthed together. None of this made any sense.

Mac still wasn't finished. 'I'm assuming you haven't been on this kind of op before so this is how these things work. Delom and Yentl, and you, are the specialists. We three are here to keep you three operational, so whenever you're on duty so are we. And no, we haven't been told yet who's paired with who.'

Given a choice Harp figured Mac would be the easiest to work with. Thinking of work… 'Do you know what I'm here for, cos I sure don't.'

'Presumably your awesome skills.' Delom grinned at him. 'I'm a pilot, Yentl's a navigator, you can shoot. So friends, we see a picture forming?

Harp closed up his suit, and his mouth. One thing he did know, pilots, especially ones who flew solo, weren't sergeants, any more than new recruits. Nor were navigators. More like lieutenants, or captains. He was beginning to think Mac wasn't necessarily a sergeant either, though the corporals might be genuine. But in Yentl, Delom and himself the navy had mixed three different skills and ranks, and made them temporary equals. And felt they needed orderlies to keep them fit for duty? And while Mac might well pull rank in here Delom, as pilot, was the likely leader if the three men had to work together. For a mission?

If. Whatever. Screw it. 'When do we eat?'

Yentl chuckled, lifted his arm and checked his wristcom then unfolded from the lower bunk to show he was as thin and bony as he'd seemed, with pale, practically translucent skin and short-cropped hair as grey as Sufi's. All of which suggested he'd spent more time in space – perhaps a scary amount more – than Delom. He clearly wasn't overawed by anyone as Harp was. 'It's near enough. We might as well head out, now we're all here.' He sealed the neck of his suit, instantly presentable in a way Harp could only envy, and stepped toward the hatch. 'Everyone?'

'Lead on, friend.' Delom gave Harp a small shove, then

fell in behind. The women brought up the rear. That didn't feel right, but they didn't comment so maybe they preferred it. Somehow Yentl led them forward anyway, without once checking his screen, until they reached a hatch marked J-Mess 10. The usual tables and benches were shorter than in Training – these, though, bolted to the decking ship-style – and the usual long counter, cept this one had a pull-down shutter – raised right now – and fancy safety fittings.

Better food as well. Mac spotted Harp's expression as the mess crew doled out ample portions. 'Only the best for *Defiant*, eh? Starting to feel glad you came?' When he gave her a less than happy look she rolled her eyes, then smiled at her dinner.

This mess was smaller than he'd expected too; would hold at most two hundred at a time out of the several thousand bodies must be on *Defiant*. Right now it was less than a quarter full, untidy clumps with careful gaps between them. As far as he could see the other diners all wore the normal shield-like patch, with a fancy gold-scripted D at the centre. But they also had the normal ranks he didn't. Then he spotted R tab lurking in a distant corner.

Delom had seen them too. 'Ah, fellow travellers. What d'you think, shall we go say hello?' He'd spoken loudly, as he always seemed to. Heads looked up. His distant 'comrades' stared, then turned their backs. 'Ah well, maybe next time.' Yentl was already settling at the nearest table anyway. They followed his example. 'So, they've brought in at least two teams.' Delom chewed slowly, studying the other group, then saw Mac frowning at him. 'Only mum's the word on that out here, eh Mum?'

She smiled and shook her head at him, so Harp was right about it being her default reaction. Delom was probably right though. If they really were an unlisted unit it stood to reason they weren't meant to blab about it. But a pilot, a navigator and a rookie marksman, one who hadn't even trained on any of the bigger ordnance yet? It sounded like a bad joke, but what was the punchline? What sort of trouble was he in now?

19

Harp spent most of that night lying awake. There was surprisingly little ambient noise this end of the ship, no engine vibration, almost no coming and going, and the boots outside only made a dull thudding sound cos of some kind of noise absorbent flooring Yentl said *Defiant* had in her accommodation sections. Yentl added, in his quiet way, they had a raft of senior officers' quarters on the decks above them. And he knew the multi-level bridge was forward, three decks higher. Harp figured that accounted for most of what was over his head, and put them in maybe the most rarefied air in the ship. With that in mind he'd tapped his wristcom for another look at the decks directly below them but it gave him only "cargo" and "restricted access".

So that was it; a fake promotion and a quiet berth in a too-small cabin sandwiched between secure cargo holds and higher ranks. No wonder J20 felt *too* quiet. If he didn't count Delom's loud snoring. Harp pulled his pillow over his head and tried again to sleep. He had no idea what tomorrow held. It'd been a while since that had happened, and he couldn't shake the feeling that he wouldn't like it.

When he did drop off a whistle sounded, it was second watch, already. All the cabin lights came up, then Mac called, 'Orders up.' There was a flurry as they all reached up and checked their wristcoms. Seemed they had an hour to dress and eat and then report down to a K deck cargo hold, one of those still tagged "restricted".

The new orders also set restrictions on their movements. Till told otherwise J20 crew were confined to forward J and K decks. Which didn't include the ship's armoury, or the ordnance he'd expected to train on. Yep, he knew he wouldn't like it.

Mac was quiet, Delom cheery, everyone else in between. Sufi patted Harp's bare back and made him jump as he was pulling a clean tee over his head. Oko glared, at him, and got an evil smile from Sufi. Everybody ate well, gearing up for... something. When a Thanksgiving sounded, Family first again, Harp was the only one stopped eating, though everybody said the usual thank you when it ended. Yet another change of manners, nothing ever simple.

There were marines on guard outside K7. For some reason it hadn't occurred to Harp marines might be armed on board, except maybe in dock, but these obviously were, and they checked nametags – wristcoms too – before they let anyone pass. And K7 wasn't a cargo hold. Maybe it had been designed as one but it had been divided up. The part they'd entered was prepped as a classroom, chairs and desks in five rows of... ten each. Less than half were filled. Two other groups of six sat, well apart, toward the front, one lot all male – the people from the mess last evening – and the others four women and two guys. All R rated, and a lot with sergeant-stripes. A handful of other folk Harp pegged as officers either sat or stood around the back. Harp saw his new XO among them.

Some of those wore Rs as well, but others normal patches. All wore active duty coveralls, but some looked new like his, their owners' bearing more civs than navy. Or civs pretending to be navy? Those wore R tabs and either slouched or didn't seem to know how to sit still, and they were looking at the sixes like a rancher would a bunch of steers at market. Harp noticed Mac was eying them as well, and he'd begun to trust the older woman's instincts.

J20 settled in the middle, choosing isolation like the others; evidently last but no one looked annoyed about it. Well, they were dead on time; Harp put a mental tick against Mac's mothering skills. And dead on time, in navy fashion, someone at the back walked forward, followed moments after by another. One pure navy, big and bald and stern, and then a smaller, thinner man whose coveralls still bore their packet-creases.

'There will be no recording. Total com shutdown will

apply till you're dismissed.' The man speaking looked pointedly toward the back rows. 'That goes for everyone.' There was some shuffling behind but eventually the man seemed satisfied. 'I am Colonel Ngow, officer in charge for this operation, codenamed Flashback.' His attention shifted over the sixes. 'Some of you have been selected to meet very specific requirements. This includes the ability to keep your mouths shut.' He glared around the room again. 'That clear?'

And there it was again, dead giveaway. The 'Yessir,' muddled by the mumbling. "Yesser" too, cos "ser" was Worlder, wasn't it, just mumbled. Ngow's brows dipped lower; clearly not an officer who liked civilians cluttering his mission.

'As you will have noted there are three potential teams in place. Each will have a complete support network. Each support unit supervisor will submit daily reports on health and progress, where possible.' Ngow stood easy, signalling his warnings over. 'This is new ground, people. You will be assigned emergency stations, but otherwise you are outside the normal chain of command unless I say otherwise. There will be no assumptions, and no pulling rank, other than where appropriate. Good luck.'

When he stepped aside the other 'officer' stepped forward. Harp felt those round him stiffen. The man might wear *Defiant* patches, and an R, but everyone round Harp had picked up the civilian vibe; the rounded shoulders and a way of looking at them down a pointed nose that any training sergeant would have bawled him out for. The fellow had a touch of gold in his skin though; a coincidence, or indication of a 'favoured' background which ought to be a warning? It occurred to Harp his own skin probably looked like that too these days. Those browner tones from years of outdoor life were likely fading. Crip, that would make him look an even better match to everything he wasn't. Thank the ever-living stars he *had* gone darker.

Meanwhile…

'My name is Professor Simshaw.' The man's gaze strafed the seated sixes. 'You men…' A woman in the other unit snorted. Simshaw bristled then decided to ignore it. '…are experimental operators. You are not required to comprehend the complexities involved, merely to follow my orders, to the letter. I understand your units have been designated code names Hawk, Eagle and Falcon. You will receive schedules accordingly which must be adhered to at all times.' The man paused a moment as if he expected something, then continued when no one stirred. 'Very well, let us begin. The unit designated Eagle will proceed at once to the Medical Suite. Colonel?' Like the colonel was his lackey.

'Professor.' Ngow smiled sweetly. 'For those who don't know, the professor is here to assess the results of the tests we plan to run. Not to monitor them directly. As such,' Another wintry smile. 'Your teams will not regularly interact with him.' The atmosphere in the classroom subtly shifted; other navy didn't favour prig-civilians giving them their orders either. 'You will however deal with me if any of you are found wanting. Sergeant Farah, you're now Eagle team.' A tall man nodded. 'Delom, Hawk. Hund, Falcon.' A woman nodded. Delom just smiled. 'Doctor?'

A navy doctor – looked like the real thing – stood up and led the Eagle team across the floor and through a hatch marked 7-2, set in a temporary bulkhead. Harp noted there were three internal hatches, labelled 7-2 to – 4. Three more then.

'Hawk. Falcon. You lot are relieved till called for. Dismiss!'

The two teams left sprang to attention, left-turned and fell out. And yes, Harp thought, there might have been a hint of show-the-civs-the-proper-way-to-do-it. Harp was halfway through the outer hatch when Simshaw's voice protested, 'Colonel, time is precious. I can't have two thirds of my test subjects sitting idle!'

'Professor, the other teams have nothing *to* do until

Medical confirms they're fit for purpose. Let's let the medics do that first, shall we?' At that point a marine had shut the outer hatch behind him. J20, now the Hawks, returned without discussion to their mess, now empty bar the galley crew still doing cleanup.

'Caffee.' Delom headed for the dispenser and concocted something complex, adding extras. By the time he finished, everybody else had full mugs too. They settled in the corner farthest from the galley and Delom looked round the table. 'Three teams, so we'll be in competition.' He looked revved.

The quieter Yentl merely nodded, but Mac sighed. 'Please don't let all this get stupid.'

Following pattern, Sufi looked more cheerful. 'A separate medbay, eh. Wonder what they've got. Think it'll be the same as one of ours?'

'Suf, if I knew that I'd know a lot more too. We're next up anyway.'

Delom grunted. 'I hate being poked and prodded. And they didn't give us a time.'

'So we stay close.' Mac shrugged. 'It's not like we can go far anyway.' She pursed her lips. 'I'm cleared for main sick bay and I know a couple people on *Defiant*; might as well say hi.' "And ask around" remained unspoken, but the other women rose at once to join her, leaving them to drink their caffee, and Delom to dip his head toward his wristcom.

Yentl looked across at Harp. 'You're quiet.'

'I'm not that keen on medicals either.' Didn't like being prodded. Didn't like being stared at, and talked about. Didn't like the lifelong, superstitious need to *fix* his blood tests. 'Why didn't they tell us what we're here for?'

Yentl nodded. 'Maybe because they won't, until we pass fit?'

Crip, so obvious. 'Sorry, wasn't thinking straight.'

'Relax, son, we've all been there. You'll feel better once whatever this is gets started.'

Across the table Delom's head came up. 'Or not,' he

said cheerily. 'More caffee? Or a roll or two? The good news is I just checked and they've taken us off standard diet too.'

+++

They weren't called for three hours, and Eagle team were only just leaving as Hawk team arrived. That should have warned them; Eagle's three orderlies looked subdued, the 'specialists' exhausted. The unfriendly Farah, who they'd figured was the Eagle pilot, muttered, 'Good luck, suckers,' as he passed them. Hawks exchanged uneasy glances.

Past the 7-2 hatch the first unwelcome sight was Simshaw, but thankfully he was also on his way out, in a rush, clutching a carton of record chips to his scrawny chest. He looked pissed off, and almost walked right into Harp, Hawk's tail ender.

'Good reflexes, kid.' Mac nodded approval. 'He wasn't stopping.'

'Shame though,' Sufi murmured. 'I'd have enjoyed watching him bounce off.'

Mac shook her head, and went to greet these mission-medics. Harp figured she'd want to set a pecking order; like if she wasn't happy – if they started to look like those Eagles – she'd pull the Hawks out whether these people liked it or not? He was starting to think she might manage it.

The women got to keep their clothes on. Harp, Delom and Yentl got to strip down to their shorts and had to leave their wristcoms with their suits and boots. Delom puffed out his surprisingly broad chest; Yentl shivered. The place was still essentially a cargo hold and background heat was minimal. Harp told himself to ignore the cold, the way he always had the heat back home, and catalogued their new surroundings. Hull-grey metal walls and floor, presumably the outer skin, a lot of tec that didn't look right cos it didn't fill the space available. That didn't count three open-ended bays partitioned off along one lighter-coloured bulkhead, and equipment that included three big diagnostic-couches.

Into those they went. The walls between them meant they couldn't see each other – so they wouldn't know how well, or badly, each was doing? Couldn't hear each other either. Harp at once suspected baffles built into the tall partitions. Mac went with Delom, Oko with Yentl, and Sufi, grinning, partnered Harp. Each got a medic to themselves, all Rs, but officers, so said their shoulders this time; two lieutenants and a captain.

It started simple enough; measurements, pulse, bloods. Harp sat still and Sufi did some of it while their medic looked on. Harp was guessing the medic was more than he seemed and figured Sufi thought the same, the way she followed orders. Their navy records were to hand but obviously these weren't trusted, even Harp's which were so recent.

As usual it was a relief when that was over, but then came the physicals; hearing tests, eye tests, those bloody dots again, although at least this time there weren't so many and the screen they raced across was smaller. So that *was* why he'd been picked. They were allowed a break after that, issued loose, insulated coveralls and water tubes and told to stretch out and relax, in a sort of common area out front with comfortable chairs and couches. Harp had barely stopped seeing double when they were called back to their bays and onto treadmills. This time the bulkheads weren't enough to block the sound of Delom swearing, and an overtaxed generator, half an hour later. If Harp's own experience was any guide the pilot had also got his running rate increased, again, with very little warning.

When the shrill whine of the treads lessened Harp figured one of the others had stopped running, but the wall meant he couldn't see who walked away. When it went quieter again he waited for his own medic to call time as well. Alas, his guy turned out to be a sadist, leaving him running for a while longer.

When Harp finally escaped Yentl was coming back into

the room – not from the classroom but from another hatch set into one inner corner. The guy looked finished, much like Farah had. Delom was being led that way as well, patting the slighter man's shoulder as he vanished. Yentl spotted Harp. 'It's –'

'This way please.' Yentl's medic urged him firmly through the hatch, back into 7-1, the classroom. Gone without the chance to pass on any useful intel. Deliberate? Harp had to think so.

An hour later Delom only had the time to huff and roll his eyes before they whisked him after Yentl.

'This way please, ser.'

They might be logged here as sergeants, but nobody in this navy called sergeants 'ser'. These guys were treating them like officers. Or civs. He stopped thinking about that when the 7-3 hatch swung open, to reveal a tiny antechamber. And an airlock. And the medic handed him a small rebreather unit.

What the? Harp couldn't see what lay beyond the sealed hatches but evidently air wasn't included. The guy wanted to know if Harp was familiar with the breather – luckily he was – and checked the unit was secure against his chest, and the clear mask snug over his face, before doing the same for himself. When the inner hatch popped open minutes later Harp's feet tried to hover off the deck. Vacuum *and* zero g?

This wasn't another bit of equipment, this was an entire chamber. One that looked like a cross between a torturer's lair and a giant spider web. No – maybe the cat's cradle game poorer kids played, only woven out of curving, blue-metal girders. With a shining ball of clearer lattice floating at its centre, like him almost floating in the entrance.

'This way, ser.' Ser, again? The man was pointing at the centre, where there was a hefty-looking chair inside the hollow lattice. Harp's every instinct said to run. He took a breath and told himself Delom and Yentl had survived it.

Yeah, but obviously not enjoyed it.

But they'd lived, and he was curious as hell what this thing did.

The man stood waiting, patiently. Ah, yet another test then? 'Fine.' There was maybe half a g where he stood, and he was looking at a thread of metal ramp, a walkway barely wide enough to put both naked feet together, from the hatch up to the crazy ball of wool suspended in the centre of the chamber. So he slid his feet that way, inside the lattice, felt what gravity there'd been recede, till by that centre sphere he was floating freely, grabbing at the strands to make the last few paces. Hollow footsteps said the medic following had cheated, come equipped with boots that could become magnetic. Great for some.

The chair was high backed, and well padded. If that was meant to be reassuring it'd already failed but he pulled himself down. The medic clumped around him, pulled across a lap-strap once he'd put him in position as he wanted, silently adjusting everything until the headrest fit his height and gesturing for him to lay his hands flat on the armrests. Sensor wires spun out to wrists and hands and he felt more across his head, his chest. His thighs as well this time? He slowed his breathing, tried to settle deeper in the seat. All this felt serious.

Proof that he was right came seconds later. Mepal bands, their inner surface also padded, sprang across his body, round his forehead, chest, above his elbows, at his thighs and ankles. Everywhere except where it could damage the rebreather. All clicked home. He couldn't budge, except his toes and fingers.

'Comfortable?' The man stepped into sight. There must be com installed in the rebreather, space knew where.

'You're joking, right?'

The solemn medic grinned. 'Let's say as comfortable as we could make it? Ready?'

'Huh.'

The grin resurfaced. 'You'll do fine. I'm betting on you, ser.'

Betting? If this was some crazy medic game…

The man was turning, looking to his right, Harp's left,

and damn if there wasn't a horizontal slit across the bulkhead that way, patched with glassite tinted bulkhead grey. Between his focus on the lattice and the colour-camouflage he'd missed that. Observation window? A control room? He saw a flash of movement through the grey, made out a ghostly silhouette, but then it faded. But a female voice announced, 'Hawk. Test 3 commencing.' And the chamber's lights began to flicker. Power building.

Harp forced tensed muscles to relax. No one was telling him what to expect but for sure panicking wouldn't stop it. He needed to stay calm, and focussed, like when he was shooting.

Course, it'd be nice if someone told him what to focus on.

The medic left. The hatch clanged shut, the ramp sank slowly out of sight and merged into the deck. Harp heard a second muffled clang as that connected with the floor below him, then he felt a faint vibration underneath him. No, all round him, like his old days on the cruiser, like an engine idling in the background. So this ball was going to move? Well, here we go then.

When movement came there was no warning, nothing. One moment he was sitting there the next…

Crip, he was being turned inside out! Which way was up? Down? The bulkheads spun and shuddered, he was being tossed inside a Mooner hurricane, the monster trying to tear him limb from limb. He yelled out loud when it began, then clamped his lips together, challenging the tempest. Trying to scare the rookie, were they?

At that point he gave up trying to reason and defaulted to endurance.

20

'Ser? How are you feeling?' Harp had had to learn to use that Worlder 'Ser', not 'Sir' when he 'dined' with Hissack, yet another readjustment, but it wasn't much, he figured he would cope.

How was he feeling though? Like he'd been washed and wrung out, but he wasn't about to admit it. So much for feeling stronger. When 'OK,' came out a croak he cleared his throat and tried again. 'We done then?' The medic had his breather off, so they were done, and pressurised as well. Harp forced his mask off too. And at least some gravity was back as well – it felt like somebody was sitting on his shoulders.

'Yes, ser.' That smirky grin again. 'Water?'

'Yeah.' Harp took the bottle, pleased to see his hand obeyed him, even if his fingers maybe shook a little. He could hit the target though, and swallow fine. The water cooled his throat, and cleared his head. It also had an aftertaste; he'd ask about that later. Right now the sensors and restraints had vanished and the ball was motionless again, suspended by whatever forces ruled inside its lattice. And the ramp was back.

Of course it was, fool. Time to get his act together. Damned if he was going to stagger like Delom and Yentl. Mooners had a reputation to uphold, the pioneers of Harpan's Worlds. The cowboys. 'So, what now?'

'I believe you're off duty till second watch tomorrow, ser.'

Harp raised his wrist, then remembered his wristcom sat with his suit. 'What time is it?'

'Thirteen-oh-five, ser. I believe you call that third watch?'

So he was more used to a surface dweller's fifteen-hour clock than a spacer's eighteen? Definitely civ, not navy. Harp pushed himself out of the chair, wobbled, then found his feet. He figured the chamber still wasn't at full onboard-g. Ignore that; focus now was walking down the blasted ramp without falling off. Would it have killed them to put a rail on the thing, or make it wider? Correction; he also had to get his clothes back on with limbs like rubber. Which would be another challenge

It was and it wasn't. He had assistance so he didn't fall over or anything, but Sufi's hands weren't exactly impersonal. Thankfully she stopped feeling him up when he growled at her. The way she jumped was funny enough to calm him down a notch, until he spotted Simshaw in the doorway, staring rudely. Pissed the man had seen him fighting Sufi off, Harp stared right back. The man at once retreated. That reaction pleased him on some distant level, and relieved him too cos for a second there the room had shrunk and he had felt a crazy urge to go for Simshaw, all guns blazing.

He blinked, took a deep breath and told himself to cool down. It was obvious enough why the man stared. Crip, could the guy be wondering if they were related? Forget it, Simshaw had his file, didn't he, and blaming other folk because the weird ball had rattled him was wasting energy he didn't have. And more importantly, he had a lot of questions, and he was off duty. Hopefully by now the others had some answers.

+++

Mac shrugged. 'You'd all have passed any fitness tests I ever handled, but I'm still trying to work out what these guys are looking for, OK?'

The Hawks had retired to the privacy of J20 and Delom had finally woken up. Mad. Mac said the 'naps' he and Yentl had taken had lasted over four hours. Harp had surfaced after two, but then he'd set his wristcom to alert him so he didn't miss this debrief. Result: he was awake enough to listen but he wasn't sitting up yet. Nor was Yentl. But Delom had moved to slouch across the foot of Yentl's bunk. Out of the women, Sufi knelt up on her bunk and Oko sat cross-legged on the padded deck, her back against a locker. Mac stayed on her feet, her back against the shower access, where she had a clear view of all the others. She looked harassed, little wonder when Delom kept on demanding answers and she clearly didn't have them.

Harp figured it was time to change the subject. 'Mac, did they say what happens next?'

'Only that you're off the hook till second.'

Sufi raised a hand. 'My civs were muttering something about Simshaw not being happy about some of the evaluations. I'd say they won't want any of us back till they've organised all their results.'

'Yeah.' Oko's gaze slid over Harp. 'Until they know who they're rejecting.'

Sufi punched the woman's arm. 'They won't reject ours, you've only got to look at them.' That earned another glare from Oko. 'Oh, come on, you know I'm only playing.' Sufi stroked the arm she'd hit and smiled winningly at Oko.

Crip, so that was why Oko had it in for him? At least it put Sufi's groping in a new light; not stalking but tormenting him to make her lover jealous? When he laughed she joined him, eyes plain daring him to gripe. He didn't, he was too relieved to bother. 'So, can we eat now, cos I'm starving.' Despite the fact Mac had pretty much forced a hi-pro bar down his throat before she'd let him close his eyes.

Delom sat up. 'Being hungry seems like your default setting, kid, but this time I'm with you. Anyone else?'

Yentl declined. The rest got up. Mac didn't argue but the first thing she did when they reached the mess was order a tray to J20. Mother hen was looking after her chicks, and had authorisation to demand room service? Harp and Delom exchanged looks; someone in charge had foreseen the need?

The Eagles were in there too, though three of them didn't look too cheerful. Only two Falcons, both orderlies, so likely the Falcon crew were still sleeping it off, maybe with the missing orderly on watch? Did Mac's leaving Yentl alone suggest she wasn't that concerned?

Delom exchanged politer words with Farah. He looked dwarfed, but neither Farah nor his crew were acting so obnoxious this time, so once he'd filled his tray Delom strolled back their way and settled at a nearby table; talking-distance, with the option to ignore them if he wanted. Mac sat opposite, the two of them effectively a buffer. Yet more mother-henning. Harp tried not to smile as he joined Delom. The lovers sat by Mac and kept their heads down.

It was like a chess game. Delom had advanced a piece for the Hawks. The next move was the Eagles'.

'You're one short.' Comment, or sneer? Harp reserved judgement.

Delom grinned. 'Yentl likes his bunk.'

One of Farah's crew, the oldest by his looks, groaned. 'Tell me about it.' Farah scowled; his guy had lost him points. The guy ignored him. 'If this one hadn't dragged me here I'd be in mine.' He turned toward Delom. 'D'you think they'll make us do that ball thing again?'

'Who knows.' Delom sat, outwardly relaxed, the opposite of Farah. 'What will be will be, friends, but I know they haven't stopped us drinking, cos I checked my orders.'

By the time the Falcons turned up and joined the general cursing the three teams were at least at nodding level and the evening turned into a low-key party. 'Here's to us, the birds of prey, friends, and surviving what the stars that Sim-freak's up to.'

'Birds of prey!' the others chorused.

But the amped-up Farah added, 'May the best birds win,' and crushed his glass. Mac shook her head. The silence after pretty much shut down the party. People nursed their final drinks then wandered off, one Falcon needing redirection by a team-mate.

'That Farah's going to be a pain in the ass.' Delom nodded wisely. 'You know that, right?'

Mac grunted. 'More than you? Come on, people, busy day tomorrow.'

Delom wagged a finger at her. 'Unless we're kicked out, Mum. Unless we're kicked out.'

Mac left him calling for another drink. Harp followed her, and hoped the pilot had a harder head than he did. Though that wasn't hard to manage. Drink and him weren't really meant to go together; two beers were his limit.

+++

Delom woke up as if he hadn't had a drink at all, impressive. The teams made breakfast by the end of first watch and strode into the classroom as the second whistle sounded. Some looked more alert than others. No one, bar Delom, was smiling.

First thing all nine orderlies got called next door to 7-2, their private med bay. They were gone some time, while everybody else sat waiting. There were fewer officers today, muttering between themselves and largely ignoring the birds. With nothing else to do, Delom looked round as Harp did then played endless games of Havoc on his wristcom. Yentl slumped and closed his eyes, and Harp looked at his feet and tried to eavesdrop. Missus Destra always reckoned he could hear a slider right across the paddock. She exaggerated, but he thought the odds were good these strangers wouldn't think that anyone could hear them right across the classroom.

Annoyingly, as soon as he started to concentrate the murmurs stopped, but after another half hour someone finally got bored.

'How much longer?' said one voice. 'I'm down for a surprise inspection.'

'It can't be long now,' said another. 'They're only talking through results.' The second voice was female, higher pitched and easier to hear. Harp restrained a smile.

'Can't see why they're telling orderlies at all. Crip, I've got better things to do than waiting.'

'Probably don't trust us to keep our mouths shut in case we let out who's flunked.'

'Someone failed the medical?' Harp strained to hear.

'Don't know for sure, but –' She broke off. The 7-2 hatch creaked open. Mac came through, as calm as always, so he switched his gaze to Sufi, then to Oko. Sufi twitched a tiny smile; was she trying to say he'd passed, or sympathising?

Oko sniffed. At him or not? She'd partnered Yentl yesterday, and had to wake him up for breakfast. Crip, he hoped the older guy had made it through, he'd be the perfect antidote to having Delom in the pilot's seat, a steady influence against that flash and challenge. Yeah, if he was going to be shooting at something he'd rather have both of them steering him into a fight. And out of trouble after.

A medic came forward, consulting his wristcom. 'OK, they want Hawks in 7-4.'

They were still wanted? And going first? Was that random or not? 7-4 – that was the door they hadn't used yet. He was curious to see what lay behind it but annoyed he wasn't going to see who'd failed. If they had done.

Mac led the way across the classroom. At the hatch another whitecoat split them up, directing them down three new passages; occasional support struts made them more like forgotten gaps between the bulkheads than deliberate paths. This time Sufi sauntered off behind Delom and Mac stayed with Harp. He liked that change, no question. He'd have liked it more if he knew why.

By the time they arrived at another hatch he'd worked out the sim chamber inside must butt against the back of yesterday's raised-up control room. Sure enough, there was another grey-slit window, easier to see this time because the metal walls, the ceiling and the floor were mirror-polished. Everywhere he looked, a glaring dazzle.

The bad news; this sealed chamber might be half the size of the other but it too had a chair dead centre. The good news was they hadn't said to strip today, plus this chair was fixed. So no zero-g, and no rebreather mask to make him feel claustrophobic.

'Sergeant Harp.' It sounded like the same female voice.

'Ma'am?' It was vaguely annoying, the way her shadow popped up without warning; he could usually hear a click when someone activated a com. Hopefully he didn't let that show.

'Take a seat, please. Orderly, get him settled then sealed in.'

'Ma'am.' Mac's voice was wooden; mother didn't like this either, likely didn't want to leave him, but she followed orders. She also muttered, 'Smooth your clothes down, kid.' He heard the hatch clang shut behind him. He wouldn't have minded some time alone, in different circumstances. This chair could have been built for him, it felt so good, but Mac's advice had sounded like a warning; not so reassuring.

This time the chair fell back into a couch, and a whole web of restraints snaked across. In seconds he was trussed up like a dinner joint, his lower arms still moved but not much else. A visor had dropped down as well. He forced tight muscles to relax and waited. What was coming this time?

'First, we'll get you familiarised with the programme. If you have any difficulties we want you to say so at once. Clear?'

'Yes, ma'am.' As clear as anything else here.

The couch beneath him started spinning slowly, in a circle. 'As you can see your seat is gimballed. It will turn. And tilt.' The couch demonstrated. On the second circuit Harp noticed the inside of the hatch was polished, barely distinguishable from the walls around it. Then the lights went out.

'Try to relax, Sergeant. This is purely a familiarisation session.'

Why did he not believe that when – surprise – the damned dots reappeared, only splashed on every vaccing surface in here.

'In a moment we're going to set one or more targets moving. You will find that your muscle movement can create a response from the chair. We want you to attempt to track targets by directing your chair. Clear?'

'Ma'am.' Maybe.

'Here we go then.' Why did people always sound so cheerful?

One dot expanded – presumably to make sure the stupid grunt didn't miss it – then slid across the wall. Was it *inside* the wall? Hendriks might have some idea, if Harp could ever ask him. He stopped trying to reason and sat a moment. Muscle movement, eh? Like this? He thought about turning left, against the restraints – the couch jerked wildly.

OK, gentler. Still too much. By now the vaccing dot had changed direction. He ignored it. On his fourth attempt the couch moved smoother. After a while he tried to make it tilt instead of turn, and still ignored the dot. She didn't bawl him out though. Maybe she'd decided the stupid grunt might do better bumbling through by himself.

He was beginning to get the hang of it so he checked out the dot, as per instructions. At first he was too jerky. Too tense, that was it. He closed his eyes and took some slow deep breaths.

'Mr Harp, are you still all right?'

'Yes, Ma'am.' He kept his eyes shut, went on breathing, hearing Zeiz reminding him to squeeze not pull; to focus. There. The dot – the bull – was drifting slower now as if the woman up above had picked up what he wanted. He pictured targeting the inner ring; imagined easing sights into place. He wasn't tied down on a couch. No; he was prone in the firing bay, his body loose, his mind a tunnel, fixing on a moving target. Fire when ready. Seek. Line up…

'OK, Sergeant, I think we're getting there. Shutting down in three, two, one…' The dots blinked out, his visor lifted and the chamber lights came on again.

'The hell?!' The sudden glare was blinding off the all-round mirror.

'Ah, too bright?'

'*Yes*, ma'am.' Yes, he'd almost sworn, and no, he didn't feel guilty.

The glare dimmed, now he was just seeing double. 'We'll bring them up gradually in future. How do you feel otherwise?'

Unbalanced. Exhausted. How long had it been? He winced as the restraints retracted. 'Crip.' Tugged feebly at his coverall. 'Ow. Crip.'

'I take it the suit isn't optimal?' She didn't even sound surprised.

'No, ma'am.' Creases were embedded in his legs, and other regions. If his lower half wasn't numb anyway he'd be swearing a lot louder.

'Good to know, we'll deal with that as well. Dismissed.'

'Ma'am.' He'd barely managed to get his feet on the polished floor before the hatch swung open. Mac came striding in to help him stand. He needed it, his legs were jelly. Sufi would have struggled. Was that why they'd switched?

'Easy, kid, just take it slow.' They reached the swaying open hatch. Mac gripped his right arm so he used the left to help, but as his feet hit corridor the pins and needles hit his body, insects nipping at his feet, his legs, then climbing up his body. 'Ow' was more a plaintive whisper than a shout this time around, he had no breath for shouting, or for swearing, much as he would like to. Walking just plain hurt, was getting worse, and now the vaccing corridor kept shifting so the struts attacked him.

Someone grabbed his other arm. Big grip. Marine. 'Hey, thanks.'

'No trouble, ser. You make it to the Med bay?'

'Yeah.' His bunk would be much better but he didn't think they'd listen.

They gave him another damn medical, pretty much a repeat of the last, bar – thank stars – the treadmill. It took what energy he had to wish away the blood test this time. By the time they let him sit and take a break his legs worked but he ached all over. And his stomach screamed at him. They hadn't even let him have some water. Mac got some but they wouldn't let her hand it over till they'd finished.

The first bottle emptied in seconds. Bless the woman, she already had another. This one he drank slower. Mac sat on the padded bench beside him. 'We can leave when you feel ready.'

'Give me a minute.' He stank; he was surprised Mac sat this close. 'Mac? How long was I in there?'

'Four hours, give or take.' She looked grim.

'That long?' No wonder nobody was bugging them about the calisthenics, or the treadmill. He'd been in the zone. It worked, but there was always payback. 'They said it was only a familiarisation!'

'You want your meal in J20?'

'I want.' He thought. 'I want to compare notes. Are the others free yet?'

'You're the last. And you're not doing anything right now except eat and sleep.'

'Yes, mum.' He tried to smile, it seemed to make her feel better if nothing else.

The same Marine escorted them back to J20, sticking close, but he made it unaided. Inside, all the lights were lowered. Sufi had a folding seat by Yentl's bunk. Two lower ones were occupied, Delom was here then. Sufi looked like she'd been playing something on her wristcom but she shut it down when Mac appeared. 'Sound asleep, Sarge. How's our youngest?'

'Sarge?' Harp murmured. 'Figures.'

'Shut it.' But she smirked before she changed it to a scowl, at Sufi. 'Where's Oko?'

'Went to eat.'

'Go join her, I'll eat after.'

'Right, S– Mac.'

'All right, kid, before you stick to the sheets. Need some help?'

'Best offer all day, Sarge, but I can manage.' He stumbled to his locker, pressed his thumb against the pad and grabbed his washkit.

'Cheeky little sod, aren't you. If you're not out in ten

I'll come get you.'

'Promises, promises.' Half out of his coverall he had to lean on his locker to manage the rest, and his underwear felt plastered to him so he banged about. But the other two never stirred.

'Hmm, maybe not so little.' Mac went on her toes to tug his tee up past his head. 'That's it.' Then she reached for his shorts.

'I c'n do it.'

'Course you can.' She steadied him as he stepped out of them then slapped the shower panel for him. 'Ten minutes.'

When he made it out again she tossed clean shorts his way, and nodded when he caught them. 'Put those on before you hit the bunk, so Sufi doesn't have a field day later.'

His teammates slumbered on. 'Huh.' Thanks be for lower bunks. He felt Mac pull the cover over him; he hoped he thanked her. Delom's snores felt reassuring this time, almost soporific.

21

When Harp resurfaced Oko was on watch. Yentl was still down. Delom was up and dressing. 'Hey, kid, how're you doing?'

'OK.' In fact surprisingly good. The aches had gone, he didn't feel sore any longer and his head was clear. 'Except –'

'Don't tell me, you'll be starving? Makes two of us, so get some clothes on.' He turned to Oko. 'Tell Mac we'll be in the mess?'

'Ser.'

Harp grabbed fresh clothes. Oko went back to her reading. It occurred to Harp she hadn't frowned at Delom even though Sufi was paired with the pilot now. The corridor outside was empty, nearly always was, so he felt free to ask. 'Delom? Why is Oko all right with you but not me?'

Delom grinned as he walked. 'Maybe cos I'm only pretty but you're a vaccing wet dream?'

Harp's breath deserted him, it took a moment to translate. 'Ah, cos I look Harpan.' Delom meant it wasn't what he looked like but who.

Delom glanced back at him. 'Kid, how many Harpans you come across?'

'I've seen images,' Harp said defensively. And in the shopping mall, and that one who'd briefly acted friendly.

'So not many, right? Well, trust me, you're a whole lot prettier than most of them. You have to know that.'

'No, I don't.' They were rounding a bend so he could see Delom in profile, watch for the reaction. 'I'm a freak. You know and I know it.' Delom was too sharp not to have guessed by now, as he figured most of H had.

'Kid, if you won't see it I can't make you.' Delom pushed him ahead, into the mess. 'But the way your hair's been getting paler, no one's going to miss it any longer, are they?'

'What?' Harp stumbled in the entry.

'That dye job you arrived with? Nice try but it's been wearing off the last few days. You didn't notice?'

'But…' It was supposed to be permanent, unless he used the other shot. He hadn't. Like a fool he hadn't thought to check his image lately either, too preoccupied with everything around him. 'Crip.' He took a step outside again. Another.

'Running away, are we? A bit late now, don't you think? We've been watching the change for the last three days so it's not like others haven't seen it too, is it?'

'Oh.' Harp's gaze darted left, right. The mess wasn't empty. There was a marine-claimed table in one corner, gone from eating to talking. A couple clusters of crew looked up. Then looked away as usual, like he and Delom weren't there.

The galley chief acknowledged them, but only to inform them, 'Orders say you R crews get to eat whatever you like from now on. No limits cept your orderlies say otherwise. That suit you, sers?'

'Oh, you have no idea,' Delom said fervently. 'Let's go with two of everything to start with and the same for him.' They didn't speak again until their trays were empty and they both sat back with caffee, when Delom said, 'Calmed down, have we? Let's get back to what's important. Anybody tell you not to talk, between us?'

'Nope.' But how much paler was he? Maybe he should act like it was nothing special, as Delom was doing. No one *seemed* to be reacting.

'That's nice, so give.' Harp took a breath, gave up on useless panic and conceded that for now a blow by blow of his 'familiarisation' mattered more. By the end he *had* calmed down, enough to feel resignation. His disguise had failed. So back to bastard-normal?

At least Delom's attitude hadn't changed; his next words showed it.

'You got four hours? Then it wasn't as bad, cos you woke up minutes after I did.' Delom paused to drink. 'So we're both testing new systems. Wonder if Yentl is too.'

'Or if the other teams are testing the same things?'

They mulled over that possibility till Yentl entered, loaded up a tray and walked across to join them. He didn't act any different either. He too ate before he talked but an hour later they knew everything each other could recall. Including the fact that Mac really was a sergeant.

Yentl didn't look shocked. 'I'd guess Master Sergeant, she has the look.'

Harp winced; he'd been calling her mum, to her face. He was better off cheeking an officer any day than a senior NCO.

Delom just nodded. 'That sergeant nonsense has gone out the lock anyway. They're all forgetting' Harp froze. OK, so Sufi and Oko might still be corporals, but *he* was totally out of his league. Maybe he slumped or something, Delom prodded him. 'Hey, don't look like that, we can't all be the pretty one. Some of us need stripes.'

Yentl chuckled.

Harp didn't. 'I. Am. Not. Pretty. Will you drop that? Don't I have enough to cope with?'

Delom shook his head. 'OK, you're not pretty. Message received. What we need now's the other birds so we can grill them.'

The younger, slighter Hund, her Falcons too, came in an hour later, more than willing to combine their intel and no, apparently not going to comment on the youngest Hawk's hair-change. Trust Delom to be the one who called him out. Hund's sim matched Delom's, right down to the depressing two-hours. Her navigator, name of Sorrel, barely older, compared quieter notes with Yentl. They agreed their sims had probably been closest to the stuff they knew already. Sorrel sighed. 'The main difference was they wanted me to keep tabs on a lot more traffic, a lot faster. Plus they've added a damage control function to my boards. That was fun.'

Hund summed it up. 'So what we're meant to fly is fast, and maybe has a three-man crew. That makes it bigger than a dart then.' Harp could follow that. Darts had a crew of two, the pilots doubling as gunners. So whatever this was had more weaponry than pilots could handle.

His Falcon counterpart leaned in, a grizzled block of muscle, massive thighs and biceps. Jayson said he was a heavy gunner and he'd rather have his mounted cannons than the "hop-n-skip" he'd had to mess with in the simulation. He'd timed out at two hours twenty and "good riddance", but they'd told him he'd be going back in "that damned lattice".

Hair-related embarrassment took a back seat. Delom didn't mention Harp had done four hours, nor did Yentl. Harp was happy not to either. He must have done a lot worse, to need so much longer. What had they expected from a rookie?

Sorrel remarked that Farah's team still hadn't appeared. He saw Delom and Hund exchange a look but Mac turned up before they commented. 'Come on you lot, sleep. Cos I predict another fun-filled day tomorrow.'

Harp followed orders when Delom did, nodding to his Falcon opposite – the older man did likewise –trailed Mac back to J20 and used the shower as a fair excuse to confirm Delom's bombshell. His hair was almost back to normal, paler brown now, even lighter at his temples. Warning that it wasn't finished. How had he not seen this?

Delom mentioned three days; sudden then. Something in Simshaw's tests? If so that meant repeating the dose – assuming he could even get hold of one here, the way everyone watched – would fail too. And it wasn't as if folk didn't know now.

Harp resigned himself to being back to what he was, and hoping folk here really didn't care. OK, and hope to hell that state of play continued.

When he came out, Mac said the Hawks were scheduled for duty second watch, till further notice, and they all turned in. What would they throw at him tomorrow? Would he manage any better?

+++

The next day's biggest trial was Simshaw. When the Hawks walked in the man was addressing the civs. Addressing was the word, too. Simshaw waved his hands and strutted, while his minions hung on every word – but didn't look directly at him. It reminded Harp of Regis.

The day saw one immediate change. The 7-2 medics issued them with skintights. That meant they had to strip off, to the buff, and replace everything with thinner, two-piece, stretchy garments, in front of everybody there. Typically, Delom showed off his muscles, and the rest, Yentl blushed and Harp… got through it by turning his back. Especially on Sufi. Given their respective body types he guessed they'd had these garments made to measure, which, alas, suggested they'd be wearing them more often than he wanted.

Then it was back to 7-4. The dots weren't so horrendous second time around. He even came out feeling not so dizzy, but a glance at Mac – him being once again without his wristcom – told him that was cos he'd only done three hours. Maybe he was getting better.

There was no sign of Yentl or Sufi when they let him out, but Delom was lounging in the common area, evidently waiting for him. Or was flirting with the navy medic. 'How're you doing, kid?' He tossed a water bottle. They'd agreed the water they were given had some additive; Delom thought it simply glucose.

'Better. I think.' Harp sat down and drank. He did feel clearer headed this time.

'Sergeant Delom, you were dismissed an hour ago,' said a familiar voice. Harp looked round, confirming Simshaw was behind them, his superior expression morphed to peevish. 'Sergeant Harp.' A sniff. 'Proceed to 7-3.'

The bloody lattice, after three hours in -4?

Mac cleared her throat. 'With respect, ser –'

'You are here to follow orders, orderly, not have opinions.'

'Ser.' Mac's teeth were gritted.

'Sergeant Harp! Why aren't you moving?'

He'd been meant to jump? His, 'Oh. I guess. Yessir,' came out pure Mooner drawl. Their project leader didn't like that, not at all, his eyes went narrower, but Mac approved his small rebellion. He could tell that from her blank expression; if she hadn't, he'd have got a warning look instead. There was no dodging though. He tossed the empty bottle at the chute and headed off to face another challenge. Crip, he stank already; he hoped Mac could stay upwind of him cos he'd smell worse before this ended.

Only two hours lattice this time, but he was convinced they'd set the thing to go round faster cos he still felt sicker. When Mac and a marine supported him he didn't even think to argue; figured he'd be on his face without them.

The medics fed him fancy water – he'd become a vaccing desert – followed this time by a shot of something and a while on his back in 7-2 till they were happy he could walk straight. Thank the stars that seemed to be the lot. He was supposed to eat and rest till second watch again; six hours on, twelve off. Hooray. Or not, cos when he got his wristcom back he saw that half the third had passed already.

The last thing he saw as he walked through 7-1 was Simshaw, conferring with the officers who never ventured farther than the classroom. Simshaw's beady eyes tracked Harp across the room; some officers' did too. He had to figure all that didn't bode well for his future.

22

These vaccing corridors were too narrow; the damned wall had hit him, again. He straightened up then aimed toward the grav-chute; he was late already. Mac had gone ahead for once without him, maybe cos he'd snapped at her again and told her not to mother him when he'd had trouble dressing. He was getting temperamental; didn't mean to, but she always looked so vaccing worried, and it bugged him.

Dressing. Yet another thing that tried his temper nowadays. She'd got them larger shipsuits, but the damn things still felt awkward with the skinsuits underneath them, only it was that or walk around in just the skinsuit, and he wasn't doing that in public, thank you, after Sufi's comments.

Harp let out a snort, part groan, part laughter. Del was happy to display himself, and Hund. It figured the pilots would be exhibitionists. Although he couldn't say if Farah was. They hadn't seen the Eagles since that second day. But rumour said that team had failed and the brass had so far failed to get another team together to replace them. He couldn't say he missed the Eagles. They'd been more stand-offish than the others, never shared their intel.

Ah, the grav chute, finally. It seemed to take him longer every time to get here. Right then, best foot forward, grab onto the ledge and down you go to K deck, on your lonesome. Yentl and Delom were often scheduled together these days. They were doing fine, while only Harp was poor enough to need so many extra hours.

And he was so vaccing tired. He leaned on the descending wall to keep his balance as it wavered. Signage flashed, to tell him K deck was approaching. Crip, his torturers in 7-2 were going to take one look and give him booster shots again, and Mac would try to talk them out of it, and they'd ignore her, as per Simshaw's orders. And he hated boosters with a vengeance; hated how they dried his throat and how he never felt like eating after, then felt sick when Mac insisted. Which was pretty hellish when you came out seeing double anyway, with whirling dots all round you.

Unbidden, the demented dots began to dance before his eyes again. He closed his eyes; that only made them fizz round faster. He was drowning in them when he stumbled off the chute and down the corridor to 7. Was he down for 3-d targeting or lattice? Did it matter? All he had to do was get there then they'd shoot him up and feed him to whichever torment they'd selected.

Today was the worst yet; wall signs kept blurring, and where once he'd paced this corridor in minutes now the walk took hours. But he plodded grimly on. The corridors were chilly but with all these layers he often felt too warm; until he couldn't wait to lose them. A relief to register the brighter light ahead; the hatch to 7-1 was obviously open. Only once he stumbled through, the classroom wasn't glaring bright as usual, they'd dimmed the lights. And taken out the desks? 'Hello?' He looked round owlishly. This… wasn't 7. He turned himself round, then had to hold onto the hatch to climb back out. OK, so which way had he come from?

'Hey!' More trouble. Boots on metal, getting louder.

'Ouch.' Harp swayed, the noise vibrating.

'What d'you think you're doing– Harp?'

Was he imagining it? Hamud? 'Hey, long time no see. I think I'm lost.' Ham – really Ham – had somehow got an arm around him. Good idea. He said so.

'Crip, what's happened? Are you ill?'

'OK, just need another booster. Always needa booster, I'm a weakling. Did you know that?' He was getting maudlin. Shouldn't. Tried to pull away.

But Hamud wouldn't let him. 'Come on, man, I've got you. Sarge? I gotta man outside M12. Needs help. Whoah, easy does it, Harp.'

Harp snorted. 'If it was so easy, wouldn't need the extra training, would I.' But it was kinda nice to lean on someone. 'Wish you were around more.'

'Oh man. What the hell are you on?'

'Nothing, only tired. Always tired.' He had no idea where he was going but it was OK cos Ham did. Had he just said M12? Wrong vaccing deck. 'Think I fell asleep in the chute.'

'Crip. OK, just a few more steps, if you can? Hey, Sarge, that was quick. I think we need to get my friend here up to Sick Bay, stat.'

Somebody had Harp's other arm, then there were voices, someone pointing out he had no proper patch. Of course he didn't. 'R,' he stuttered, 'R for reject.' All the noise went quiet. Hamud eased him down onto the deck. 'Help's coming, Harp, s'OK. Stay put a minute while my sergeant calls it in, OK?'

'OK?'

'OK.' Things drifted. Coloured dots swam past his eyeballs but he couldn't focus. Simshaw would insist he did it over.

+++

Something kept beeping, annoying as hell. Harp tried to turn over and go back to sleep but the cover was too tight; it wouldn't let him. He supposed he might as well wake up. But then he wasn't in his bunk, not even in J20, he was in a Sick Bay cubicle, the beeping was a monitor above him. And Hamud sat beside him, studying his wristcom.

'Hamud?' He'd got lost. No, he'd zoned out and left his area. Now Simshaw would create another scene, report him to the colonel.

Hamud must have heard him groan. 'Harp? Shall I call a medic?'

'Hell, no.' If there was anything he didn't need. Please let them not have needed blood tests. He tried to sit and found he was strapped in. 'Ham? Can you get these off me?'

'Sorry, orders. They weren't sure if it was safe. I mean, you did seem out of it.'

'Crip.' He was saying that too much these days. 'No, I was only tired.'

'Yeah, you said.' Ham looked uncomfortable.

'Said?' Harp studied the averted features. 'What else did I say?'

'Enough I've been warned to keep my mouth shut.' Hamud stood to check around the bay's partition then returned. 'I had to tell them everything you said as well as where I found you. Then I got confined here with you. Does that mean this thing's contagious?'

'Damn, I'm sorry. And it's not an illness, so you're fine.'

'OK, that's good.' Ham sat again. 'It's more interesting than patrolling cargo holds, which is about all they've let me do so far.' He leaned in closer. 'I didn't know what to do, barring act like a wall till someone said otherwise. The medics hardly got you down before some civ barged in here, throwing orders like he owned the place. You can imagine how that went down; they wouldn't let him near you, but next thing some colonel turned up as well.'

'Ngow.' Harp slumped back. 'So I am in trouble.'

'I don't think so, cos my sergeant was still here. He had a word and then they went into Medic's office, but it had a glassite wall. Your colonel and that civ were arguing; a real row. Then the civ stormed out and the brass gave orders you're to be left alone till told otherwise.'

'So.' Harp tried to sound casual. 'They never got round to the usual tests, even?'

'They'd stripped you off. They were just going to hook you up to the machines when the fuss kicked off, then that colonel told them to hold off and report to him when you woke.'

At that point an orderly – not Mac – turned up; must have seen he was awake. Soon after Hamud stepped outside, then Mac arrived, then Del, apparently surprised to see him conscious. Mac immediately checked his file on her wristcom. 'How d'you feel?'

'OK.' He actually did, for the first time in who knew when. So she was back in charge? 'How much trouble am I in?'

'How about none?' Delom looked grim. 'Is it your fault you were so exhausted you could have killed yourself?' He saw Harp's disbelief. 'You were groggy, in a vaccing grav chute. If you'd fallen at an opening it would have chopped your stupid head off. We should have gone over Simshaw's head before this. We were worried when they took you off the schedule, but they kept on saying it was normal, and we've hardly seen you lately cept when you were sleeping. And all the time…' He threw his hands up.

Harp went cold, a sudden image of the chute, the always-open holes onto each deck, expanding then contracting as he passed them, like a guillotine, a giant pair of scissors. 'So I'm not in trouble. You're sure?'

'It's Simshaw's in the shit, not you, kid. Ngow didn't know how far he'd pushed you. Sounds like Sim-freak's been fudging his reports for weeks.'

'But, why?'

'Who knows, but Ngow's moved himself into Simshaw's office down on 7, and kicked Simshaw out into a file room.' Del's expression eased. 'Which no one's smiling about *too* openly.' This time he grinned. 'Which means we're all stood down until you're cleared for duty, after which Ngow says we'll be training as a team. No more splitting us up. We'll be able to keep an eye on you again.'

Harp sagged, relief robbing him of what energy he had. Then realised. 'Does that mean we're finally going to find out why we're here?'

But neither Ngow nor the sulking Simshaw let them off the sims, or gave them the disclosure they'd all hoped for. Events outside conspired to make their small frustrations unimportant.

23

Simshaw glowered, but Ngow took very visible charge, or people would answer to him; from now on there'd be strict limits on hours in the sims. Despite that, Ngow seemed to think Harp required an escort whenever he left J20. Presumably in case he tried to kill himself again. The upside was the duty went to Hamud.

Ham claimed he hadn't volunteered. 'My old sergeant griped it was the simplest way to keep me quiet. Not that I have the slightest idea what you've got yourself into here. Or why you were in such a state. But you do look better.'

'Oh yeah, I'm fine now the colonel's in charge.'

'So what's with the hair? This the real you?'

Damn. 'Yeah. Sorry.'

'Hey, I get it, man. Guess they don't let you fake it any longer, huh? Seems a bit mean, if you ask me.'

'Yeah.' Harp decided to leave it, it was too complicated to explain.

They were nearing K7. Hamud lowered his voice. 'There's a lot of civs down here so I figure it's all hush-hush?'

'Science types, and medics, yeah. Watch out for Simshaw, he's the guy who had the row with Ngow; hollow chest and prissy manners. He's been sidelined and he gets vindictive.'

'Saw him when my new team leader gave me the walk-through. Man, the gear you guys are using is too weird.' Ham whistled. 'And no one wants to explain anything either.' He went deadpan as they reached K7's hatchway.

Days went by. The Hawks and Falcons were on different shifts, lucky to cross paths in the mess. It was like the world had shrunk. The Hawks were now on call through watches two and three, but never both. It might sound longer, but it felt more settled. They were sleeping better; Harp felt sure he was improving. Well, he wasn't doing all those extra hours. They spent time together, as a unit. In the chamber labelled 7-5 they hadn't known existed, fitted out some distance from the others.

Wherever it was, this sim sort-of faked the nose section of a small three-man fighter craft. And it operated in zero-g. Delom and Yentl probably felt right at home, Harp, not so much. He'd had a short lecture on zero-g before his first flight to Moon's Orbital, and brief experience of how it felt, suspended in the lattice, but diving head first into an entry hatch, then sort-of swimming through nothing to his seat inside, well, that was different.

Yentl said his layout was different as well, because Pilot and Nav boards were in separate cubicles, directly beneath Harp's; they couldn't even see each other once they locked in, let alone him. All Harp could see was an enormous hemisphere of view-screen showing, Yentl said, the patch of vacuum right outside *Defiant*.

While Harp was down-timed, Yentl had had time to find things out, like what was happening outside their K7 bubble. It seemed *Defiant* was at best a mere hundred thousand klicks from Harpan's World. So close? But Yentl didn't seem surprised. 'It's just a shakedown, after all, to test the systems.'

Mac had added, 'And keep Flashback close to base until the navy makes it public.'

J20 was in general agreement; Operation Flashback had to be the navy's latest weapon, hence their isolation even from the regulars aboard *Defiant*. Or as Delom put it, 'So vaccing secret even we don't know about it. But,' he'd added smugly, 'can't be long now, can it. Then we'll stick it to the pirates, cos what else are we here for? Once we prove it works, whatever *it* is, I'll lay odds *Defiant* won't be coasting any longer.'

Harp hesitated, but… 'There really is a pirate threat?'

Both men looked startled. Delom answered. 'Something make you think there wasn't, kid?'

'It's just, we never saw a sign of any, all we ever heard on Moon were rumours, and the govment saying they were raising tithes to build the Orbital to guard against them. So the folk back home, they started wondering…'

'If you were being conned?' Del whistled. 'Folk on Moon are that suspicious?'

It felt like when he talked to Hissack, so again he chose the honest answer. 'Folk on Moon are practically starving. Makes it kinda hard to trust in strangers.' Crip, even a lower deck Militia like him was questioning stuff by the time he left. Talk about defending Moon had sounded pretty thin when all their gear was so substandard. Then the thoughts had sort of sidelined, what with all his other troubles.

But clearly Del and Yentl did believe the pirates real. 'So this really is about the pirates.'

Yentl shrugged. 'If you mean they're a menace, yes. If you're talking about Flashback, it makes sense. They're the obvious threat, and we haven't argued with the neighbours in decades, human or Kraic.'

Harp was suddenly very aware how little he knew, about World politics, *or* the surrounding universe. He'd even forgot about the Kraic. But then he'd only ever seen one image of the 'neighbours', just enough to know they're weren't remotely human, though his teachers reckoned they were smart as. So all right then. Flashback was a weapon, probably a fighter craft, and it was about the pirates. And it had a fancy weapons system Harp, and Jayson, were supposed to master.

But still failing to, cos Simshaw was back to badgering the colonel, calling it "imperative" they both improved. Or so said Hamud who updated Harp on all the rumours, cos Marines could find more time to eavesdrop than the crews they guarded.

Ham collected data elsewhere too. He'd met with Hendriks on the quiet, who'd been shocked because according to *Defiant's* log Harp wasn't there, had taken sick an hour before *Defiant* cut its cables, and been shipped straight back to Barracks. Hendriks had been 'fishing', as he put it, but with no success despite his crazy comp skills. He had been annoyed at failing. Now he was relieved, so Hamud said, to know that Harp was healthy.

Then of course he'd gotten nosy. Ham became the go-between, enlivening their daily walk from J to K deck, dropping back so Ham could pass on Hendriks' latest update.

'Hendriks swears none of your team are on *Defiant*'s roster, not even your orderlies. So the way you're restricted, he thinks most of the regular crew aren't meant to know you exist. Even our Marine detail is quartered apart from all the rest so stars know where the others think I've disappeared to.' Hamud slowed his pace. 'Whatever you're doing must be a damn sight more secret than secret if they're hiding it from their own side as well.'

Hendriks' reaction, surprise, was a burning desire to find out anything and everything about *Defiant*'s real mission. So far Hendrik's access to the new, bridge-based, upgraded firewalls — "Radical" he'd called them – hadn't been discovered, though if it were…

Harp stopped worrying about Hendriks breaking regs, and looked at the logistics. 'If the pirates are such a threat, and we're going after them, it makes sense the brass are trying to keep it quiet.'

Ham nodded. 'Officially, *Defiant*'s shakedown run is having teething problems, hence her hovering around in-system. Hendriks says that's nonsense, what they're hiding must be you guys. But they can't use that excuse forever.'

No they couldn't. Flashback was a lot to hide. Which said it was intended to be a big surprise. And if that was right, Harp was biting at the bit to get his hands on the real thing. But all he had were sims, and more trials, and more complaints from Simshaw. How much longer?

24

They were off duty and gathered in the mess when the tannoy squawked. The XO's voice came next. 'Hear this. All crew to transit stations. Repeat, rapid transit imminent.' The voice dropped a notch. 'This is not a drill, people. We are abandoning our trials to answer distress signals from Harpan's Moon.' Pause. 'You'll all have further info when I've got it.'

The com cut off. The mess erupted. Sufi was the first Hawk to react. 'To Moon? But navy doesn't operate on Moon. That's their Militia's job.'

Then Mac said, 'No, we don't.'

Harp studied her expression. 'Mac, what aren't you saying?'

Mac's face softened, mother hen again. 'Sorry, Harp, but... Sufi's right. The navy's never *needed* to deploy on Moon, which means...'

'The Militia must have more trouble than it can handle. How can we find out–'

The wall screens Harp usually ignored stopped playing Worlder sports, blanked out, which suddenly felt rather shocking, then lit up again. It looked like somebody had bounced a local feed to the *Defiant,* showing them a view of Moon from orbit, probably its Orbital, half hidden in its shadow, and the XO had then patched the images from the *Defiant*'s bridge to general quarters.

Things looked normal enough. Harp almost relaxed. But it couldn't be, could it, or *Defiant* wouldn't be diverting. Belatedly he realised the shifting clouds that blocked his view weren't clouds, cos clouds meant rain, and he had never seen this many clouds together, not in his whole lifetime.

Smoke?

From prairie fires? The risk of fire was ever-present, and a blaze could spread in minutes, eating everything before it. But Militia cruisers scooped tons of dirt to douse the fires, while settlers on the ground cleared firebreaks, risking life and limb to save their homes, their crops and livestock, all they'd sweated blood for. And of course to save them from the slow starvation many teetered on the edge of. And they'd never had World navy charging in before. A new eruption then? Had Collar finally exploded?

The tannoy squawked. The XO's voice again. 'Hear this, all crew. General quarters. Repeat, general quarters. Marines and gunners to condition amber.'

Sufi gasped. 'They're arming the cannons? At Moon?'

'What?' Harp's gaze was riveted. The wallscreens split to multiples. More gasps spewed out around him. Moon's new orbital, three quarter-built, had turned into a broken wheel, almost half its ring a mass of tangled wreckage. Several of the docking areas and makeshift outer habitats, the areas that Harp knew best, looked like they had imploded. And a riot of detritus drifted aimlessly in space around them. Debris that included bodies.

Other screens showed Moon again, in closer focus this time, clear enough for Harp to see that in the gaps between those clouds the Moon itself was similarly wounded. Fires cast lurid light on scorched terrain and what he thought were burning buildings. One screen briefly showed a tiny township. Nothing moved on empty streets, and when that screen zoomed in again he counted bodies, but no sign of fire on the ground around them. Something – somebody? – had killed them.

Then another camra panned across a downed Militia cruiser, showing gaping holes midsection.

'Cannon fire.' Mac had seen it too. 'That ship's been fired on. So's the Orbital.'

'But.' Harp stared at her 'There isn't anything on Moon *to* fire on a cruiser, nothing big enough to do that kind of damage.' Except, horrific thought, another cruiser? Or a visiting supply ship? Or the navy? No, that made no sense...

'The pirates,' Mac said tightly, 'It's the only answer why our guns are live. In case we sight them on our run-in.'

Other tables heard. That raised a storm of protests. Pirates, in this close to World? It was impossible, unheard of.

'*Was* unheard of,' Mac insisted, eyes still cataloguing details.

Then the XO's voice came back. Now every corner listened. 'Moon reports no further sign of hostiles, people. We'll keep watch, but it looks like the attackers have run.'

Harp swallowed. They would be too late to stop the carnage – to even find the criminals? He gnawed his lip. He had *heard* about the 'pirate problem', thought he had accepted it was real, but till now it always seemed a very distant threat, to other people's planets – Worlder stories Mooners sneered at. Or a threat to people who had more worth stealing?

But there had been whispers up on Orbital, hadn't there? About the pirates getting braver. So now he knew, it really was the reason Harpan govment had upped the tithes; to build Moon Orbital, and to expand the navy to protect them, with an Arc ship like *Defiant*. Only they had been too slow, Harp figured grimly. And they'd focussed more on World than Moon, the poor relations, so that Mooners who'd already been impoverished to pay for these 'improvements' had lost everything they had now, to a threat they'd stopped believing.

25

Harpan space was too damn big; it took even *Defiant* two more interminable days to get to Moon. Updates continued to come through, presumably the XO's way of keeping people calm and focussed. In their off hours all the birds sat in the mess and watched, and waited. Watches changed, fresh crew took over but the men and women in the almost silent mess sat frozen, listening when the patchy feeds became more personal, when Moon's survivors spoke into the cams describing what had hit them. The Orbital's Chief Admin, face turned grey with dirt and tiredness, told a camra what she knew so far. The XO shared a chunk of that transmission too, and Hamud muttered it was being bounced round Moon where possible, and through *Defiant* back to World as well, the sound improving now Defiant was much closer.

The woman said two vessels posing as World traders had signalled approach and requested berths in the civ sector of the docks. Everything appeared normal till they diverted from their assigned courses and headed straight for the sectors reserved for navy or Militia. Some bright spark in Orbital Command had cottoned on, and triggered mayday signals, both to World and down to Moon, but that was all they managed. Minutes after that the Orbital was in the middle of the battle for its own survival. Meanwhile four more pirates, maybe more, had raced in past the outer markers no one on the Orbital was watching any longer, heading for the surface.

The woman licked dry lips. 'We were under fire, anything in dock a sitting target. There was nothing we could do for those below except to pray for you guys' intervention. But the pirates up and left less than an hour after we got you on approach. Have to think they saw you coming somehow, but at least it scared 'em off.'

Another screen reported World, now pretty much obscured by Moon 'beneath' them, was deploying other navy vessels – some to hunt the pirates, others, like

Defiant, crossing to their sister planet, taking days, at best, where Moon had needed moments. Most of these would head straight for the surface. Logical. The Orbital would still have some resources left in its undamaged portions, but whichever settlers had been hit were likely left with nothing.

More news. This time round Moon's Admin looked defeated. 'So here's what we know now. They targeted ranches. Shipped out whole herds, looks like. In some places there's barely anyone left. But that's not the worst. We think some of the bastards killed the men and took the women and kids. In fact.' She cleared her throat. 'It looks like they hit ranches first then aimed for townships. Like they hit Riverbend and Bedrock, with the biggest Orphan Houses.'

Riverbend? Where they'd evacuated? Hmm. Folk had only returned to Riverbend a few weeks ago, when it was declared safe enough to reopen one of the shafts, and they'd have gone back as soon as it was allowed cos the town depended on the mine – not least cos miners rated extra rations. Which posed the question: how had pirate been that up to date? Unless they'd had informants in the Orbital, or on the surface?

On screen the woman's hands went whiter as they clamped together. 'A couple kids in Riverbend managed to hide. From what they say it was all real organised.' Another pause, a deeper breath. 'I don't rightly know how long it's going to take us to rebuild, start supplying World again…' Harp watched the woman fight off tears. 'But we sure do thank you for coming so fast and scaring them off before they did worse.'

The image blanked, the mess stayed silent. Harp sat frozen. She had thanked them, when they'd failed her.

Sufi was in tears. 'Children.'

Oko put an arm around her. 'Navy'll go after them, Suf.'

'But how will they find them? We haven't spotted anything and we were nearest.'

'Ion trails,' Yentl muttered. 'If it's not too late the techs'll trace their course.'

'Or courses,' Hund cut in. 'They'll split up, that's what I'd do. Well, I would,' she said to angry faces.

Delom nodded. 'Yeah.' Then brightened. 'But so many working together succeeded so well they'll do it again, and that's how we'll trace them.'

Sufi sniffed. 'Yeah, but not till they attack some other poor –'

The wall screen shifted half its length to column data. Data. Damage. Casualties. The first came from the Orbital. They'd mostly finished seven of the final nine sectors. Three of those that had been operational were bared to vacuum. Thankfully they'd closed the sector doors in time to save lives in the others, and only one of the core sectors had been holed. The message was pretty clear; the pirates had only targeted the docks, and opposition. There'd been five Militia cruisers, one navy frigate and two genuine World supply ships in dock, those just loaded. The frigate was probably a write-off, so were three of the Militia ships. Both the supply craft had tried to run but they'd been hijacked, cargo, crews and all. Harp wondered dully if they thought themselves better off or worse.

But given all that, Orbital casualties were surprisingly light; it looked like the pirates had concentrated on keeping civilian personnel pinned down and unable to help.

Harp knew that left three more Militia cruisers. They'd have been on duty, spread across the surface. One of those was *Mercy*. He nursed yet another caffee, jittery enough already.

Evidently *Defiant* thought her crew were entitled to know the worst. The big screens continued to display both words and pictures as *Defiant* raced toward its destination. One screen started showing interviews and such again, from newsfeeds on the govment channels. Lists began to scroll, sent up as Moon compiled them. First came which areas were hit the most. Then names of people, healthy, injured, dead or missing, scrolling, always scrolling up that portion of the screens as further names got added.

Harp only recognised a few. A couple of Orphan House supers, a teacher who had helped a toddler with his numbers. Then another foster, one he'd met with on that first, unhappy farm. And some time later, when he almost started to believe... the Gosses' names appeared. No survivors. It sounded like the isolated ranch had been among the early targets; and with only four of them, two past the age for fighting...

'Harp?' Mac's hand was on his arm.

'They hit the ranch I came from,' Harp said dully, staring at the names, already scrolling upward.

'Oh. I guess you knew a lot.' She jerked her head toward the streaming data.

'No, not really.' How could he explain there could be people there he'd played or learned with, but he wouldn't know their names now? Never had it felt so *wrong*, the way the orphan system altered names to match them to locations, making every orphan change identity so often. Meant to make them feel they belonged was the official explanation, but he'd always figured it was more convenience for bureaucrats; to make them almost non-existent.

As for younger kids, he wouldn't know at all, and now he never would. Someone onscreen was saying that they'd lost at least a quarter of those kids, from House to Pre-Employment, five to thirteen years. Getting on toward a hundred of their future population. 'Mac?'

'Hmm?'

'What will the pirates do with all those kids?'

'Crip, I don't... could be they'll sell 'em.' Mac said softly, softer than he'd ever heard her.

'Crip.' He didn't have the words. She nodded.

Navy and Militia casualties scrolled up on another screen. It looked as if most of the frigate's crew had been on the Orbital. The reduced crew manning the ship were dead but the rest had pretty much survived, sealed up inside the core; full marks to navy discipline and training. A fair proportion of the docked Militia had survived as well, though Harp suspected more by luck than judgement. But the three ships down on Moon…

It looked like they'd been hopelessly outgunned, outnumbered. *Hope* and *Trust* had tried to engage and been shot out of the sky. *Hope* was another write-off, *Trust* repairable, but both had some survivors. According to their reports *Hope's* captain had bravely – and, face it, stupidly – squared off against two pirate ships, trying to head them off Riverbend. So who knew, maybe those two orphans owed her their freedom. *Trust* had been powering up, too late, and strafed from above; someone on watch had been slacking but the crew weren't naming names, at least in public. But no word of *Mercy*?

The next interview looked like Orbital dockside, noise and movement in the background and a glimpse of damaged deckplates. This time someone mentioned *Mercy*.

Harp sat up, his drink forgotten as a civ, a newscom interviewer, asked a spate of questions. Answers seemed to echo this time like his ears were underwater. Stupid notion. *Mercy* had been on the ground as well. A sitting target. Eyes fixed on the screen, Harp stood up from the table, drifting past those ruled by Simshaw, till he stood before the screen wall where the man onscreen was saying *Mercy* had been hit, disabling her engines, and her crew were gunned down in the open, trying to return to duty. 'Master Sergeant Mullah?' So he'd got promoted? So his wife would get a better pension. 'Private Bays', reported "missing". Still a private. But he'd liked it that way, hadn't he?

More names. This time he knew their names, and faces. Ludwiz dead, Goss critical.

The speaker smiled. 'But we at Channel One are proud to tell you the remaining crew managed to return fire and the survivors are already back at work, helping to transport much needed supplies to the surface.' The man was turning round to talk to –

Regis. One of the survivors. Not a mark, except a bit of dirt, and smirking at the camra. 'Yes indeed, duty comes first, of course, but I've always kept a reserve crew on board, six being the bare minimum to get the ship lifted and man our two small guns.' Regis and his pets, all seven.

The other man went back to solemn. 'I understand your largest gun jammed, captain.' That forward so-called 'cannon' Mullah always said was useless anyway, a waste of–

'Sadly, yes. We think our forward cannon was hit almost at once, and with only one gun left operational, well, there was nothing we could do to help our comrades on the ground except try to scare the pirates off.' A sigh. 'Of course I mourn our losses, but they all died heroes.'

'Harp?' Hamud stood beside him, looking troubled.

The interviewer gushed. 'I'm sure all our citizens, both here and on World, feel better knowing you brave boys have our backs, ser. Did I hear there's a rumour you about to be given a citation?'

'I couldn't say, ser,' Regis said. And smiled.

'Harp? Harp?'

Without replying, without looking, Harp swung back and slammed his fist into that smile. Gasps, a cry from Sufi, made him blink and swing around to see a mass of faces turned his way. Mac grabbed his hand. He wondered vaguely where the blood had come from, and why Simshaw, sitting just beyond her, looked so pale.

'Come on, let's get this taped up', 'Mac was saying.

Harp let out a shaky breath then let her tug him out to 7-2 where it turned out all the blood was mere dramatics, actual damage superficial. Maybe hitting Hoik had left him harder knuckles. Mac prescribed some food, and no more caffee. Hamud walked him back into the mess and sat beside him while, still dreamlike, Harp downed double portions that the galley crew were very quick to serve him.

'Feeling better?'

'Yeah.' Harp raised his head then shivered at the splintered wallscreen – hadn't realised they were that flimsy – then ducked back to focus on his meal.

'Thank the stars for that.' Ham sipped. 'I tell you, man,

that took me back to when you flattened Hoik. You were growling then as well.'

'I… growled?' Surely not. He must have shouted.

'Growled. Well, sort of. You've been known to do that when you lose it, didn't you know?'

'I. No.' He'd really growled? Nah, Hamud was exaggerating. But the man was right, he had to watch his temper.

Hamud, more relaxed now, chuckled. 'On the brighter side I don't think Simshaw will be hassling you any time soon. Did you see his face?'

Harp pushed his plate away. 'He's going to report me anyway.'

'I don't think he'll want to talk about it cos, talking of crip, there was a real whiff from his direction. Did you notice?' Hamud's smile was evil.

'Simshaw…?' Harp gave in and grinned, then straightened. 'Vac it, what more can he do.'

'That's the spirit. Honestly though, I don't think Freak'll risk upsetting you, after today.' Maybe he saw Harp sag. 'Come on, I'm supposed to get you to your berth. You look as if you need it.'

Maybe Ham was right; maybe not, but the next time Harp returned to the mess he thought Simshaw and his cronies *were* more subdued. But then they'd been watching the screens as well. In any case, the birds were still in training and now they had the same clear goal; to take the battle to those pirates, soon as they were ready. In the meantime *Defiant* was on final approach to Moon Orbital, her crew were champing at the bit to join the rescue operation, and the shore assignments were coming through. Like everybody else, the Hawks and Falcons had already volunteered; all they needed were their orders. Harp could finally stop sitting here and help his fellow Mooners.

Mac and all the orderlies got theirs, and went off to collect the kits already prepped by Sick Bay. All the others waited, till their mess crew were the last still with them. Eventually Delom and Hund tapped in, then both swore at their wristcoms. A tight-lipped Hund explained it, Del still cursing. 'Our orderlies are gone to the Orbital's Chief Medic. The rest of us are stood down. We're not cleared to take any unnecessary risks.'

Harp half rose but halted when Del started grinning. 'Yeah? Anyone fancy a few *necessary* risks?'

Hund vetoed that straight away. Del subsided. 'Ah well, just a thought.' He waited till the three remaining Falcons left before he looked at Harp and Yentl. 'Well guys?'

Yentl eyed him. 'Still no clearance, Del. How'd we get off the ship?'

'Oh, I think I know a way to swing it, a way to boost morale too.'

'How?' Harp's frustration lifted. People needed help so if there was a way, he'd take it.

'You leave it to me, kid. All you have to do is follow my lead. OK?' Del knew the navy after all, while Harp knew almost nothing. And Yentl wanted in as well. Perhaps they both knew things he didn't.

Though Del's smile really should have warned him.

26

Eight hours later Harp was sitting in the cabin of a heavy-lift four-track, at one end of the navy's share of what had been the Orbital's three-quarter rim, the elevation giving him a clear view of the dockside ten feet below. Not a pretty sight, despite the progress; buckled deckplates, scorch marks, water damage. But at least now it was airtight so they could repair it. Someone had told him the Militia's sector was so bad they still hadn't patched all the holes. *Defiant's* three remaining corvettes – mini cruisers, shuttles really but with weapons – were ferrying supplies and personnel between Orbital and Moon, using the small, single dock round the rim normally reserved for visiting VIPs that Bays once mentioned. So the civilian sectors had to take most of the incoming traffic, navy and civilian. Problem was there were more ships than berths. Even when the dock was intact they often had to repair umbilicals or cargo ramps before relief crews and supplies could be unloaded.

But *Defiant's* marines had managed to seal the last patch in their own sector four hours ago and their repair crews had flooded in. First objectives were the few remaining bodies, those who hadn't been sucked out to vacuum. Utilities came next: power, water. That meant replacing ruined pipes and cables, wiring, switches, comp connections, not to mention drying out the areas still flooded. Harp had spent his first few hours on pump control duty. Operating a pump, not getting half as wet or dirty as the others. Not getting into anything or anywhere these people didn't think was reasonably safe for him to venture.

His present position was higher, colder, and less comfortable. And infinitely better.

+++

Delom had got them off their ship all right, by using Harp

as their free pass. Oh, he never *said* he and Yentl were escorting a member of the Family, but he'd sure behaved like it. Most of *Defiant*'s crew hadn't even seen Harp anyway so Delom's whole scam had worked like a vaccing charm. 'Head up, kid,' he'd said, 'leave the talking to me.'

By the time Harp caught on the damage was done, they were being waved through and arguing would only have got them into more trouble, faster.

Then of course every gullible civ they met, and normal-navy, took one look at him, compared his old, grey jacket and his private's tags with all the spit-and polish worn by Del and Yentl – and of course their real captains' patches – blinked, assumed that his was borrowed camouflage then rushed to do whatever either 'minder' asked them. Crip, they were so pleased to see him they fell over themselves. And, kept on thanking him for coming, and Delom was saying, 'Suck it up, kid, you're a one-man morale booster, only doing what some Harpan should have.'

It was beyond embarrassing, made him cringe inside. But Del was right; his presence, fraudulent or not, had made a difference to these people. Heads came up and shoulders straightened. Weary faces started smiling. World had sent a *Harpan* to support them and assess the damage, one who didn't shy at getting dirty either, joining in the effort. As a private, Harp should have got the worst of it. As 'Private Harpan' he'd got pump control, and then a rest break two hours after starting.

So when the lift operator climbed down, practically asleep on her feet, Harp grabbed the chance. Perched up here in the cab with only Del and Yentl and a dockworker on com below, this felt like heaven.

The lift's normal job was shifting overweight cargo but right now there was no cargo. He was shifting massive slabs of metal; deck plates, girders, to a heavy loader for removal to recycling. Till the decks were safe they couldn't berth the smaller ships still queuing with the able bodies and supplies they needed. Plus Del reckoned the navy wanted its own docks back, civilians out from under and their own marines in situ. *Defiant* hadn't come into dock at all, operating her shuttles instead, and Del reckoned that was as much for security reasons as her need to take up more than one berth.

But keeping *Defiant* far enough away not to see him was a plus right now, and Del and Yentl and the docker were below him sorting out the jigsaw puzzle, picking out which bit of debris he should lift that wouldn't smear *them* across the deck plates. And he was useful here, his extremities gone numb but near-invisible behind the streaky glassite canopy that kept the condensation from above from landing on him.

Folk hadn't really forgotten him though. For the last four hours he'd been a vaccing landmark, somewhere folk could visit in their break times, peering up and trying – hopefully in vain – to take a picture until Del or Yentl caught them.

Del waved; another chunk of something broken hooked and waiting. Harp refocussed. The work wasn't that hard. It was just so vaccing cold.

OK. The three below had moved out of range? Check. No one else coming his way? Ah great, a bunch of civs in coveralls and insulated jackets – how he wished – were crossing deck he'd need to swing across, most probably on break and heading for the next-door sector where the bars and eateries were back in operation, where the air was warmer and the food was courtesy of the *Defiant*. Hurry up guys.

One was hanging back; a male, hunched, as many were right now, his jacket ragged at the edges. Harp would have to wait for him to go as well. Meanwhile, he rubbed his hands together to unfreeze them; doing nothing was the devil. Then the straggler raised his head. It was Regis. What the…? Harp leaned forward, peering closer. All the rest were civs; civ clothes, civ walk and several had scruffy beards. But, looking closer, Harp could see that Regis wore his greys beneath the crappy jacket.

Had he lost that coat he usually swanned around in, that

he'd bought with creds he'd stolen? Was he slumming it because he didn't want to get that dirty? No, not Regis. Every instinct argued.

Regis wouldn't be seen dead dressed like this. In fact everything felt off. The man had no reason to be in this sector. Yet there he went again, looking round, like he was worried, keeping surreptitious watch on Del and Yentl.

Yentl's voice came from the speaker. 'All clear?'

'Yeah, sorry.' Harp powered up and raised the girder, slowly, slowly, stop it swinging…

Regis' head jerked up, in Harp's direction. 'Crip.' His hand had slipped, the load was swaying. 'Double crip.' He got a grip; the girder slowly steadied. 'Idiot.' He concentrated, got the thing across and on the heavy loader that would take it to be smelted and recycled. Regis scurried. Had he noticed?

'Hey, you OK?' Del's voice this time.

'Yeah, sorry, fingers slipped a minute.'

'Vac it, I forgot the cold up there, kid. Time you took a break before you drop one on us.'

'No, I –'

'That's an order, *ser*.' Because of course their com had docker-ears.

When Harp looked again Regis was gone, so he followed orders. The docker was happy to recommend one of the civ eateries. When Harp, with Yentl – cos space knew a supposed-Harpan couldn't possibly go anywhere alone – got there he found a table waiting, food and beer already on it. The docker must have called ahead. The civs and navy all pretended not to notice him as Del had earlier 'suggested'. Harp sat down and started eating, aiming to get back on duty asap. Till he spotted Regis, hovering outside a nearby store. Had Regis seen him? Was he double checking? If he recognised him, realised what Harp was doing, he'd take pleasure in reporting all of them.

Or maybe not; he seemed more interested in something further down the dock. Let's hope he stayed that way.

Harp ate as quickly as he could, considering his fingers had reached the pins and needles stage of thawing and now felt twice their normal size. If he was fast though, maybe he would take a minute, see what Regis was intent on?

'Slow down,' Yentl muttered. 'We need to warm up before we go back anyway.'

'Yeah.' Harp hesitated. After all it might be nothing. It would sound so silly. 'Sat too long, I guess. Thought I might stretch my legs, just for a few.' He went on eating, keeping half an eye on Regis.

'Fine.' Yentl started eating faster.

'No, don't rush, I'm in disguise, see?' He pulled out the knitted cap someone had offered him hours earlier. It hid his hair, always the first thing noticed. 'I won't go far.'

Yentl studied the result then nodded. 'OK.' The usual slow smile. 'Call if you need us to ward off admirers.'

'Up yours.' Harp flashed a smile. Should he explain…? But Regis was checking his wristcom, straightening and moving off. Harp drained his mug and rose. 'I won't be long, I promise.'

One minute Regis was standing around looking shifty, the next he was striding away and making a poor stab at trying to look casual. Harp only had time to say a short thank you to the cook and speed walk to the next corner. Then slow down again. Regis was slowing too. What was he up to? People doing nothing wrong didn't look so shady.

He'd paused outside a grimy warehouse frontage, hardly his sort of establishment. There'd be no fancy merch in there – unless it was illegal? Was he buying stuff he shouldn't?

If he was, it was a court martial offence. Militia was search and rescue, courier service – and Customs and Excise. While black deals were increasingly common as Mooner credits ran low, for a Militia officer to be caught doing it… if Harp could show Regis breaking the law, especially that one – if he could record it on his navy wristcom, so much sharper than his old one – he could get Regis kicked out. It was too late to help his old crew but at least the new one would benefit.

Regis took another look over his shoulder – Harp stepped behind a group of dockers – then dived inside the warehouse. Follow, or stay put? Staying put wouldn't prove anything, would it?

27

Most of the warehouse frontage was a drop-down plassteel shutter, serious protection that was not uncommon for the valuable cargoes might be in there. This one was still down though, which was odd when every other warehouse seemed to be so busy shifting what supplies they had to where they were most needed. He supposed the merchant could be dead or injured, but it must be partially in business, since Regis had got access through that narrow side door. He guessed he still needed to check.

The door creaked. Harp found he'd closed his eyes, stupid move, then went for broke and slid inside. The warehouse was open, after all. If necessary he could say he was checking what could be useful for the repair work.

No one was in sight though, and the interior was blessedly dim, only one dull emergency light flickering high over the door. The rest of the space got what little light crept through a strip of grimy plas set high above the shutter. So far so good; no staff in sight, no Regis looking at him.

This was the only place still intact he'd seen wasn't a hive of activity of one sort or another, but it looked like there wasn't a lot here and judging by items on the nearest racks the main merch was rust. Which made it even odder Regis came here.

Somewhere, mepal clanged against mepal. Another door?

The floor was uneven, he'd have to watch that, but there was enough light to stroll casually down one of the side aisles, and avoid the large pallets left at floor level. But then the warehouse ended at a solid mepal bulkhead. He made a careful survey of the other aisles. No activity, no Regis. Nor had he heard footsteps. But the man had vanished, somewhere.

He walked, slowly, the length of the rear wall. It was built in the normal prefabbed sections, each bolted sheet about two paces wide. Except for the end section, cut down to fill the final gap. A section that didn't quite touch the floor. And had faint scuff marks at the base, in just one corner?

It took him a few minutes to suss it out, finally risking a narrow beam of light from his wristcom, but those marks had given it away. Somebody, like Regis, was in the habit of kicking the panel right... there. The noise it had made meant kicking it probably wasn't a great idea; he knelt and pushed. Eventually he got the right combination of position and force and heard a muted click; a strip of metal swung a fraction inward. Harp stepped quietly through then stopped and listened. Anybody hear him?

Apparently not. There wasn't much light back here either, but enough to see a second decent storage space, stacked anyhow with cargo. No rust back here. And he could hear voices. First things first, he set his wristcom to record, then dived into the maze of pods and cartons. Most of the stacks were taller than he was. Where they weren't he ducked. Straight lines were non-existent, sometimes he was forced to back and try another gap, and stop to scout out every corner, but his ears kept him moving in the right direction, told him he was getting closer.

The mepal all around created echoes. At first even his hearing only picked out the odd word, but he knew Regis was complaining about something; that was very familiar. Harp slowed even more till he was crouched behind a final row of cartons, picking up at least three voices now, including Regis.

'Don't tell me that's all there is. One million up front and two more after, that was the deal.'

'Ah now, Captain, shouting won't change anything.' A throaty voice, male. Avuncular. A stranger sounding patient. 'Expenses came higher than anticipated, didn't they? Everyone got a bit less. Sure we'll make it up to you next time.'

'There isn't going to be a next time,' Regis scoffed.

'Sure there is, Captain. Resigning isn't in the contract, is it, once you know about us?'

Crip, what had the fool got into? By the sound of it Regis had got paid a lot less than he'd expected, and was in their clutches now because they could betray him to his own Militia. This time Regis had been caught by his own greed. Harp glanced down to check his wristcom was recording this, which meant he had proof Regis was some kind of crooked. Only, what in the stars was worth the promise of three million cred? Not his problem, he'd got enough.

Which of course was when he heard the hidden door behind him click, and heavy footsteps coming up behind him. Crip. No need to panic though, he'd just slide back and sideways till the cartons hid him, wait until these people finished then.

A screech, then half that secret wall he'd thought was fixed began to rise, another shutter, and the only reason anyone would raise it was to reach this cargo. Bringing in or taking out, that was the question. Harp reverted to his childhood, crossed his fingers, listened as the new arrival greeted Rusty-Throat as 'boss', and made it pretty clear he neither knew nor trusted Regis cos all talk of credits ended. Regis obviously didn't trust him either cos now he was in a hurry to leave. Seconds later Harp heard Regis striding past his current shelter, heading for the dockside. At least with Regis gone there was no one who knew who he was.

Other than that his luck was right out. An engine growled, too close, a four-track, and the sounds that followed said they had started loading. How much were they taking?

Over the next half hour Harp played a tense game of hide and seek in a playground that shrank, slowly but steadily. Del and Yentl would be wondering where he was, probably starting to worry, but he'd turned his wristcom to silent mode so it couldn't give him away, so he couldn't call out without turning that off, which he now regarded as a serious design flaw. He'd marked five voices now; one female, one of the males driving the track. When the earlier arrivals went forward he crept back, hoping for a second back door, but if there was he hadn't found it. Either he found a way out through the front, past the black merchers, or he stayed hidden behind what they didn't remove. Problem was he didn't know if they'd leave anything behind.

Climbing the stacks seemed the best bet. Yes, he could creep forward up here, and none of them seemed to think of looking up. OK. Five enemy. The heaviest steps belonged to a hulk doing most of the work. No wonder Regis had changed his tune; Harp wouldn't have bet on himself either, even one on one.

He stayed up there a while, flat on the biggest cartons, but the track kept coming back for more; he had to keep retreating. They wouldn't be handing all this over to Orbital Admin to help the repair effort. No, they must be loading a ship. Wouldn't anyone think that odd on a dock where all the other supplies were coming in?

But they didn't seem worried. So someone out there was looking the other way; Regis wasn't the only one they'd bribed. By now Harp was convinced he knew why. The only thing Regis had worth millions to crooks was information; Militia schedules, Orbital security procedures. And which townships housed a lot of children.

So he had to get out, cos now he really wanted to murder Regis.

Cept his maze kept shrinking, and they didn't take a break. In fact in one exchange they seemed to be concerned about a shift change. The track came back for more. Harp shifted backward, found he had to jump around into another would-be aisle – and kicked a crowbar lying in the shadows; bit his lip to stop a curse. Space knew how he had missed it earlier. Raised voices said they'd heard, and footsteps pounded. Only one thing left to try then.

He scaled the nearest stack and *ran* across it, jumping to the next, and then another. If he made it to the open he could run ahead toward the track and then the outer warehouse. It was all about surprise and speed. Shouts behind; he didn't waste time looking back, just sprinted. There. The four-track faced the exit and – his luck was in – the driver had gone hunting with the others, and the cabin door was open. Harp jumped in and grabbed the lever. Or he would have, if someone hadn't slammed into his legs and yanked. His head hit something; maybe the step; the tracks were jagged, would have sliced him open. But the warehouse tilted. By the time it straightened up he was surrounded and that hulk was pulling him onto his feet, and he could hear that outer shutter rattling, closing. The hulk had pinned Harp's arms behind him, not that he was fighting; still too dizzy.

'More Militia? Dearie me, you're Navy aren't you.' Throat still sounded deceptively friendly, mild-looking, in a jacket Regis would approve of but Harp would lay odds if he wasn't the top man, he was close.

Now the woman, not much smaller, pawed his pockets. 'No ident. His patch says he's *Defiant*, but he's just a private.'

'Well now, that's good for us but a shame for you, son. Cos that means you won't be missed for a while, doesn't it? So there's time for us to have a little chat. See, I'm wondering why a navy private would be off his ship without his ident. How about you tell me?'

Harp's head was buzzing but he got the gist. Trouble was he couldn't think of a convincing story didn't feature Regis, and he needed Regis free cos Regis could identify these pirates. So, 'My captain... has my ident.'

'And why would he do that?'

'I... lost it. He kept it.' He could see three, where were the other two? Or was he seeing double?

'Hmm. So why are you in here? Now, think carefully, son, cos Red here doesn't favour liars, and she doesn't always know her own strength. Isn't that right, Red?' Red promptly demonstrated by punching him in the gut, harder than Hissack. Then smiling at him. Till he spewed all over her. The hulk behind him laughed as Red used words a lady shouldn't, leaping back too late to matter. Her bad luck he'd just devoured a greasy dinner. Figured he'd come out the winner, bar the gut ache; while his mouth was like the inside of a sewer pipe the spew had largely missed him. Only Red was pulling off her jacket, dropping and turning back; this could get ugly.

'Oh now, that wasn't nice.' Throat raised a hand to Red. 'And I'm sure you don't want to annoy the lady again?'

'No.' Harp spat, politely sideways. Blood was running down his face, the track-step must have had sharp edges after all.

'You were explaining.'

'I was… on my break. Civ eateries. Wondered why… this place was closed.'

'Why notice that, son?'

'Only place… was. Didn't seem right.'

'Ah, an observant young man. So you came looking and couldn't get out.' Harp nodded weakly. 'And who did you report it to, clever lad?'

'I couldn't.' Harp retched.

'Because?' For a moment there were two Throats raising eyebrows at him.

'No wristcom. Left it… on dock. To keep dry. Pumping out.'

Throat looked at Rat and Rat confirmed, 'No wristcom, boss.'

'Well now, while I do admire your attention to detail, son, see now you're one of *my* details. Nothing personal, but you just became something I need to cross off my list.' His gaze went past Harp to the giant. 'No blood. No play. And don't leave him anywhere close, where they'll find him too quick. Understood?'

'Boss.' The meaty arm came round beneath Harp's chin and pulled. Harp's head was trapped against the chest behind him, struggling for breath that wasn't coming. And his cap slipped sideways.

'Boss?' Red sounded shocked. 'Lookit his hair. There was a load of talk…'

'Hold it.' Throat tugged the cap free to reveal the near-red-gold beneath. 'Hmm. So that's why there's no ident. Let him breathe.' The hulk relaxed his chokehold, Harp indulged in coughing.

The woman had stepped close again, but this time only staring. 'There was rumour someone from the Family was here. What're the odds?' Her smile grew wider.

'Son, I do think you just earned yourself a rethink. Long as you behave. All right, we take him with us.'

'Boss?' The hulk was slower on the uptake. Save that fact for later.

'Turns out our alert young friend is worth a lot more alive than dead. Aren't you, Mr Harpan?'

Great. If he told the truth they wouldn't believe him, thanks to Del, so he might as well prolong the scam and live a while longer. Time to channel wealthy. Think like Hissack. He risked a weary smile, gracious-loser-fashion. 'Honestly, I don't know.' (*Think! And don't slur all the fancy words.*) 'It's quite possible my grandfather would be willing to spend more avenging my demise than saving me. He's not entirely logical when he's crossed.' There, pretty clear, he hoped, and as near Worlder-speak as he could manage, plus a hint killing him might be more trouble than they'd like.

'Hmm.' Harp was really starting to dislike that sound. But Throat pulled out a cloth and dabbed Harp's face with dainty fingers. Harp remembered to wince. 'There, that's got the blood off; hardly shows at all along your hairline. Now you and me are going for a short walk across the dock to my ship, all friendly like, and my two smaller friends on watch out there will be beside us, see? Or you might try to shout for help.' He waited.

'But they'll kill anyone who comes to my aid.' He was vaguely proud of such a Worlder word choice.

'Ah, you have quite the old head on young shoulders, don't you? I can see we'll get along famously.' Throat nodded, the hulk let go, Harp swayed. Throat peered into his eyes. 'A touch of concussion, son? Better not fall and draw attention, which reminds me.' Back went the cap,

Throat adjusting it with care. 'Maybe I should take your arm, like we're still having that chat. There we go.'

Hulk and Rat tailed them as far as the dockside then split off. Two other men fell in beside and behind. At least he thought so, sometimes it looked like four. But Harp noted all of them had one hand in a pocket. He thought Hulk's bullet head popped up above a bunch of dockers exiting one bar but Rat had disappeared. There were lots of folk out here, all civs. He fought to focus. Throat had smiled and raised an eyebrow; mockery, and almost challenge? Needed intel.

'Straight across, you said.' Harp checked the overhead. It shivered but… 'The *Bounty*? Apt.' If the sign was any guide he *was* seeing double.

Throat laughed. 'I thought so.' He was right about it being a short walk, short enough Harp held his breath all the way, only drawing air again when the *Bounty's* umbilical hid them from sight. OK, stay focussed, noone died out there because of what he looked like.

OK, thinking. Civ umbilicals all looked alike, being mostly one size fits all, so it wasn't telling him what sort of ship he was boarding, even if he'd known its real registration. Though in the present chaos what were the odds Orbital Traffic would have taken time to check a ship apparently coming to their aid? An incoming navy ship might note the hull shape didn't fit the call sign. If they found time or reason to look, which no doubt they didn't either. So the *Bounty*, on the board out there as an independent coming back from the nearest neighbour system, could be a mere super-shuttle or a vaccing warship. Simply put, the notion of a pirate returning for leftover booty was so outrageous no one would believe it, if they didn't trip over it like he had.

The important question was did they have the firepower to do more damage?

The first passageway didn't make him any wiser, apart from the trouble he had observing much, but he felt his captor's relaxation; Harp had done as he was told, protecting other citizens. A very proper Founding Family reaction, worthy of the newsvids. Though he couldn't help but wonder if a real-Harpan would have been as altruistic.

Not important. Somewhere in there Red had joined them too, to pat him down again for hidden weapons.

'I don't think you'll find anything there.' Had he really said that? Real-Harpan him must be a lot more forward.

This time she responded with a crooked smile that could have been engaging. 'Oh, I think I might.' But thankfully she stepped back, studying the navy-issue knife from his boot. 'Nice. I'll think of you whenever I use it.' So now only the walls were swaying, and he had two wiseasses he'd be better off without. By the time they got him to a cabin he'd seen enough to know the *Bounty* was an outer-orbit shuttle, very like a cruiser. And short range, which meant she'd come from Moon, or off a larger ship. He'd bet the latter. Then they shut him in and left him, Throat apologising smoothly for the "somewhat Spartan quarters somebody like him was hardly used to". Hah. It was only the second time in his life he'd had a single berth. But his smile had obviously confused Throat, so he needed to be more careful. Concussions wore off, but till then he shouldn't look *too* helpless.

The cabin, when it settled, matched the rest of what he'd seen, clean and neat and nothing to arouse suspicion if it was inspected. There were a few red hairs on a brush in the locker; that was a tad worrying, but there was no point borrowing trouble. He'd already guessed Red was Throat's second in command, so it wasn't odd she'd claim the better, single cabin – maybe one of a very few. At least he'd rated a cabin, not an unheated hold.

Easy then. All he'd got to do now was rest up, recover, and stay alive.

28

Back in captivity…

Harp's thoughts derailed. He couldn't have fallen asleep in here. Could he? Never say he'd fainted. But the bulkheads were vibrating softly, made his stomach lurch again and added to his headache, and his temple itched. His fingers came back red, still bleeding, but his brain was clearer. Up and moving. Time to prove it.

Since Red had lent him her cabin he checked it out again for anything useful. No weapons; disappointing, he'd have bet good credit she'd have had some ; he could only think she'd sent someone ahead to move them. But it wasn't a wasted effort. First find: a small first aid kit, which gave him painkillers and a couple of the same hi-pro ration bars Mac had been feeding him. Hmm. He ate one and tucked the other in a pocket. Figuring the pirates wouldn't be back to him for the hours it would take them to leave the home-system he decided it would also be real-Harpanish to make use of Red's washing facilities, cramped or not. He grimaced; he was really getting into the part. After that he stuck a med-patch on the gash on his head and replaced his uniform tee shirt with one of hers. She was as tall as he was. It was a bit tight, but a lot cleaner and might make him more civ-looking. Then he checked his image in her screen-mirror and practiced looking calm and dignified, the way the real-Harpans did on newsvids. Then since he had no way of knowing what would happen next he lay down again and tried to rest while he could.

Nor did he know how long it would be before the navy tracked his wristcom, hopefully still under the driver's seat in that four-track, putting out the SOS he'd programmed. He'd set it to activate half an hour after he'd made that last ditch run for the open dock, figuring the pirates might have had detectors, but they hadn't looked that efficient – maybe in too much of a hurry to leave. Maybe he should have raised the alarm sooner but by now it should be calling for help, and once Delom couldn't find him hopefully the navy would add two and two and make four. They would after all have the recording, whatever happened, and Regis' voice pattern was easily confirmed. He had, at worst, done that much. Plus he'd pinpointed the warehouse for them, even named the *Bounty*. The four-track hadn't been so far away, across the almost empty warehouse, that the wristcom couldn't pick up that last detail.

So he'd be missed; believe in that. Meanwhile, unarmed and outnumbered, all he could do was wait it out and continue to fool them. *Bounty* could still change her call sign again but she couldn't change her engines and according to the manuals he'd read they were like fingerprints. The navy could identify her from the record of her departure and then track her hoof print – as long as they caught up before she left the system. Nothing left to do but lie here.

Or was there? He had to wonder about the cargo they'd come back for. What was worth the risk, however low, of coming back on-station once it was teeming with troops? He should have tried to open something, or made sure he mentioned that for Del to hear. No, idiot, that's hindsight talking; too suspicious.

Was there any way to find out now though, if only to satisfy his own curiosity, find out what he was maybe going to die for?

Best to concentrate on living then. First things first, maintain the role of Worldly, sheltered Harpan, like he'd always been a real grandson. Cos it was all about time; he had to play the part well enough to make them hesitate, even when some real-Harpan laughed at them and refused to pay. He found Red's internal com, selected some gentle, Worlder music and settled down – and fell asleep in minutes. Yet another trial-turned-benefit of his concussion, and his real, communal-orphan background.

When his eyes opened at the snick of the hatch she stood in the entry holding a tray. 'Sleep well?'

Harp stood up, more slowly than necessary. 'Yes.

Thank you.' Wealthy Harpan manners, in whatever situation. She didn't look annoyed, nor especially surprised, though he'd bet their usual prisoners didn't wash and change and take a nap. But then that was the point. 'I borrowed a few small items. I hope you don't mind. I didn't exactly have time to pack.'

That crooked smile. 'The shirt looks good. You borrow my shorts as well?'

'Too small.' Harp tried the almost-smile he'd practised in the mirror, like a little flirting was a reflex action. Worked; she laughed and stepped inside. Which showed him two men in the passageway, both holding weapons. Ah well; it wouldn't have done him any good to try anyway.

Red set the tray down on her tiny table. 'It's the chef's day off so…'

Harp eyed the tray; soup and a rollup, better than he'd hoped for. He allowed a touch of hesitation, real-Harpan feigning being easy in an unfamiliar situation. 'I wasn't entirely sure you'd feed me.'

'Oh, we want to keep you healthy.' Once again that up and down, this time it lingered on the straining tee shirt. Was there a tiny frown? 'Work out, do you?'

Harp shrugged modestly. 'Some gym time. And a little riding in the country place, you know.' He didn't start to eat, he didn't want her noticing his hands were calloused.

'Riding?'

'Rangers.' If they stole steers, they knew rangers.

She pursed her lips. 'You're used to rangers?'

Look curious. 'We all grew up with them. Is that relevant?'

'Could be, sugar, we'll have to see how it goes.' Did that mean there were rangers where they were headed? One of the men fidgeted, maybe that broke her mood. 'Don't go anywhere now.' She backed away, still cautious.

'No, I don't suppose I will.' He sat down again, glanced at the food then back at her, hungry but well mannered. 'Could you tell me the time?' Cos let's pretend we aren't used to ship hours, or operating our own cabin controls, why not? What he wanted was some idea which watch they were keeping.

'Just into third, sugar, so sleep tight. Maybe I'll bring you breakfast in bed.'

Long breath, look confused, resigned, then half a smile. 'I'll look forward to it.' That got him a chuckle; she left still smiling. He must be her best prisoner in years.

The bread was fresh, probably baked on the dock. Synth cheese inside it, and the soup no worse than orphan fodder, and there was a mug of caffee. The mug was beneath Harpan notice but the caffee was excellent. He wondered if they'd stolen it or bought it.

He'd checked for surveillance three times over by then, but he hadn't figured Red as someone who'd stand for having that installed in here. The com system was a possible spy, but he'd also learned a lot about those in the last few years of his life; he was pretty sure the most this model could do was listen. With that in mind he made all the right noises: eating, moving around, squashing back into the head, letting his navy boots hit the deck then scraping them aside. The boots would need to stay off too – they were too noisy. So would Red's clean shirt. He replaced it with his own, dried blood, sweat and all, then sighed and rolled onto the bunk again, made sure his breathing hitched, then steadied. That's it, finally got scared but still determined not to show it. Every now and then he moved a bit, a restless sleeper, till he figured it was two hours later. Which left him maybe four to go exploring.

29

He had two choices, hatch or air vent. The vent came off easily but the pipes beyond it were too narrow for his shoulders. Not the first time he'd wished he was smaller. He put it back and checked for scratches. Hatch it was then. If it was alarmed… he'd tried it without thinking, so surprised cos he'd assumed she locked it. Might work. Might not. Just stick your head out, look surprised and cross your fingers.

Once again the thin spoon made a reasonable screwdriver. Off with the door's control panel, splice the wires then put the panel back so everything looked normal. Almost there. He found he was biting his lip, made himself step back and wait a moment. What was he, an amateur?

People he'd left behind knew he was orphaned, but they didn't really know what that meant. They didn't, for instance, know that some orphans learned very early how to break rules. Break out. Or break in. Harp was by no means the only orphan who could charm a lock – they taught each other. One place he'd lived, it was about the only way anyone ate enough and him, he'd always needed extra rations. All right, calmly does it.

He pushed the button, and the hatch swung open. So he stuck his head out. That's it, clueless, all surprise, no caution.

No alarm. No guard. What sort of security did these folks maintain? Right, off we go. He figured the best cabins, like his, were forward, so the hold should be down and aft, standard for a smaller vessel. His stockinged feet made no sound, though the occasional grid dug into his soles. It was surprisingly quiet out here, almost eerie, with only the faint hum of the engines aft for company. A deck lower, he heard voices and laughter – one sounded like Hulk – but he wasn't staying and they faded as he went on, down again. So far so good, although he held his breath at every junction.

The hatch outside the single hold was old-style, with a wheel. And a crowbar wedged across it? It took him minutes to ease the bar out again, and then the hatch squealed. He froze and listened. No alarm. No outcry. His instructors would have bawled them out for being sloppy but he cracked the hatch and eased inside, to chilly darkness.

Only a panicked gasp saved him from another blow to the head, or worse, but he picked it up in time to duck and swing and catch the arm, more luck than judgement. Crip, he had to keep this pirate quiet. Then he realised the arm was small and bony. 'Hold it, kid, I don't want to hurt you.'

The slight form he had backed into the bulkhead stilled abruptly. 'Mr Harp?'

Who? There was only one way to find out. Harp let go and stepped away. The shadow he could make out now moved sideways, reached up, and the overheads flared back to life. 'It is you!' Kids, at least a dozen of them, flocked around him, full of questions.

'Keep it down, OK. I'm not supposed to be here.' Kids, including two he'd met before; the boy who'd meant to brain him and a girl, much smaller. His sister, that was it – the kids he'd talked to, given sweets to. This was what Throat had come back for? How many trips had *Bounty* made since everybody thought the raid was over?

'So you're like a spy, not Militia at all?' The boy – Mik, wasn't it? – looked pleased; it wasn't time to disabuse them.

'I'm supposed to be a prisoner like you, so you don't know about me, right?' A lot of solemn nods. Mik's little sister tugged his trousers. 'But you're going to help us?'

'If my plan works.' Plan. That sounded so much more professional than he felt. Kids, damn it. 'The navy should be tracking us but we have to be patient and we have to be ready. Are there places in here you can hide, so they don't find you too easy?'

'Yeah,' Mik spoke for them, 'We already scouted it out. But I only found the one wrench, and some of these aren't big enough to fight anyway.' At least half. But a wrench? Harp had to wonder what the boy had hoped to do once he'd clobbered a pirate.

'Very good.' Hark at him, all spy-like. 'No more fighting then, unless you have to, but hiding will give the navy time to get to you once they board, OK?' Cos kids would make perfect hostages, especially against a navy wouldn't be so nice if the pirates could only show *him* to make threats about. So hiding really was their best defence until the navy made it. 'When they come, you'll hear them.' Let's not sound depressing.

'Right.' Mik nodded wisely. 'Plans don't always work, I gotcha. We'll be ready. What will you do?'

'I have to go back.' Harp felt the small hand tighten, smoothed the curls. This was one kid wasn't going to grow into another Red, if he could help it. 'But they mustn't know you have a plan, alright?' He smiled at the girl. 'You have to pretend nothing's changed.' Essentially it hadn't, but that wasn't what they needed. Hope was more productive.

'OK.' She held onto her brother.

Harp looked at them, still huddled together, still scared, with the tear tracks to prove it, but so trusting. 'Don't give up, OK?' They nodded. When he looked back from the hatch Mik was already organising, pointing them in different directions. 'Mik? I need to lock the hatch again so nobody suspects.'

'OK.' No hesitation there. Harp couldn't either; he'd been down here longer than intended, he was running out of time. 'See you, kids.'

'See you.' Shaky smiles.

Crip he hoped so.

He was a deck higher, trying to decide whether to head straight for the cabin or complete the recce as planned, when he finally ran into pirates, rapid footsteps growing louder like their voices. 'Navy? You sure that's what it said?'

'Sure I'm sure, I'm not deaf. They're on our vaccing trail, same course. And vaccing faster. What I want to

know is how they vaccing tracked us.' The answer
crouched beneath the mepal stairs they ran up, but the
clang of their boots made it harder to pick out the words.

'You think it... the Harpan guy? Shiv said... too damn
cool. Maybe they... kinda bug an it's... signalling all the
time.' Their voices faded.

The guess wasn't so far from the truth, but he could
sure do without the pirates digging holes in him to find
one. Or tossing the rest of him out an airlock when they
didn't. But they had confirmed the navy were behind
him. Now if he could stay alive, and those kids could stay
hidden. Cos now the navy was close – relatively speaking
– and the pirates knew it, it was all about time; the faster
the better. But one of the first things Throat *would*
probably do was check on him, so there wasn't much
point going back to the cabin and risk being cut open or
worse. So, hide? Maybe try to access an escape pod and
hope the navy picked him up rather than blow him apart?
Hiding would be sensible; he was still unarmed and
outnumbered, not exactly at his best either.

He really wished he was sensible.

The passages aft stayed quiet – he only had to duck into
a locker once. No alarms rang, even as they must be
preparing for attack. There'd been no general alert, none
when he opened that locker either. Dreadful safety
standards. Maybe the *Bounty* carried a smaller crew than
he'd assumed. Or maybe they were all manning whatever
guns her hull concealed.

Leave that happy thought for later. Next stop,
Engineering. Even the best ship design still meant big
blocks of mech; to propel them forward, create internal
grav, pump oxygen. Stuff they couldn't survive without.
A lot of that lived in Engineering, and with so much of it
there were so many things could go wrong. And funny
thing, they were always harder to put right than they
should be. Harp had skinned his knuckles way too often
in those cleanup duties. Access panels never big enough
or in the simplest places. It was a recurring gripe with
every crew he'd ever known, a major failing – till it was

an asset. What he needed was to break stuff, preferably important stuff, to slow the pirate's flight and cause a panic.

He needed a weapon.

Throwing caution out the lock he opened every hatch and locker he came to. Still no alarms. By his reckoning there was barely an hour left of this watch, the maximum he could hope for before someone found he was loose. Assuming they hadn't already gone to haul him to the bridge, to wave him at the navy as a real-Harpan hostage. If they were already hunting him he'd still heard nothing over shipcom, which meant if they *were* talking about him it was some other way. Forget it. On he ran, opening doors right and left.

And found a vaccing weapons locker.

He allowed himself a silent cheer. The locker was covered in dust, and there wasn't much in it, but if his luck held he wouldn't need much. He checked a small pulse; in better shape than he'd feared and carrying half power. Almost as an afterthought he shoved two grenades in his pockets and shouldered an ancient rifle. He could see the rust in the barrel, wasn't sure he'd risk using it, but *kids*; sometimes needs must.

The hatch to Engineering wasn't locked either. Did these people have no rules? Harp hung onto the hatch, using it as a shield as he peeked round. No one shouted. No one vaccing noticed. Two pirates sat at monitors, one of which was showing porn. Another was intent on something she was eating, three more had a slew of mepal spread across the deck – good luck with that – it sounded like they disagreed about the problem. No one had glanced round to see who'd cracked the hatch and entered.

Miracles did happen.

Harp had three objectives, but first he needed to get forward a bit, till he was out of sight; don't rush, don't draw attention. Where though? Based on all those lectures… Sure enough… he eased the locker open, very gently, latched the door back so it would stay open. Then he headed for his next objective, which alas was in the open.

When he'd read up on all those ships' safety regs he'd thought it was weird that an engine room's emergency shutdown controls weren't locked, neither by code nor key. Surely, he'd thought, that just meant any idiot could walk in and turn off the engines? But according to the manual that was the whole point; if the engines were about to explode there wasn't time to wait for someone authorised to stop them. Right now he was really happy about that.

All he had to do was open the box on that bulkhead, the one with all the fat cables, and press the big red button it protected. Or lever. Oh, who cared.

He almost made it.

'Hey, you.' It was the woman who was more awake but she alerted everybody else, and every one of them was armed. A bullet flew – a vaccing bullet near the engines, were they crazy?! *And* it missed him by a mile. They were either panicked or they couldn't shoot for caffee. Stars knew what they'd hit instead.

He only hoped the rubbish aim would last; firing back wasn't in his game plan. He wasn't holding either gun. But dodging was; he flung himself toward the box, flipped up the simple latch.

It was a lever. Red though. Grab, yank down, the engines shuddered. Pull the handgun out and fry the cables underneath it; two objectives dealt with. That was when the pirates stopped missing. Searing heat across his shoulder put his right arm out of action. Something slammed into his side as well, he *heard* the ribs crack. Time to fire back.

They weren't so brave after he hit the first, though he heard someone yelling into com for help, which seemed excessive when he was outnumbered five to one already. He wasn't sure he'd make his third objective any longer, or if he'd survive to worry, so he'd aim to slag as much as possible before they got him. Not life support of course, cos kids, but any wiring, or the coms. The coms would be a bonus once the navy boarded, which they surely would now *Bounty* was inertial.

The main console took three shots, the wall speaker one, but the subsequent flare up took a lot more wiring with it, plus a pirate who was too close to the fire. Four to one now. Since his legs were fine Harp chose to find his next objective, dodging round the bulky fixtures, crawling under counters. That hurt, and colliding with things was a bitch, but he was stubborn, and being blocked from his last goal wasn't acceptable; he'd had a plan. He'd got this far. He wasn't stopping till he'd vaccing finished.

Unlike the weapons range he didn't have to worry about hitting a 'friendly'; there weren't any. And with all *Bounty's* power and propulsion turned to giant blocks of useless mepal, all the lockers and the storage tanks, he wasn't short of cover either.

He was however leaving a trail. Very annoying, and a real-Harpan would probably bleed blue or something, so all that red was a dead giveaway. Dead, hah. He hunkered under a nice mepal bench and grabbed a rag to pad inside his sodden tee shirt, wincing at the pressure and at all the oil and grease that would infect him. Where was a sterile field dressing when you actually needed one?

Then he crawled down an aisle that led him, in a weaving fashion, back toward the hatchway he'd come in from. Wishing very much he'd thought to lock the vaccing thing before he left it. Had to shoot another pirate, sorry. Not. But he had reached a corner where the hatchway and that opened locker intersected, only he was closer to the hatchway than he'd planned – but hey, breathe out, take aim and squeeze. Then duck.

He'd opened a fuel locker. And in all the fuss the pirates hadn't noticed that small detail. All it needed was a spark; the fuel cells ignited and he had himself an instant prairie fire. Shards of red hot metal flew like fireworks on Founder's Day to drill new holes in the controls and generators, cut more cables, melt more wires. Killed the male pirates. Vac it, women *were* the tougher gender, only she was choking anyway; the flames and fire suppressant gas were mixing up a stinking, noxious fog bank that was giving him some welcome cover, though the blast had knocked him off his feet. Bad news, that hatch still wasn't locked. He got himself back up and found some balance, smiled behind the basic breather he had liberated from the fuel locker, lurched toward the exit.

He thought he heard the woman fall and vaguely hoped the gas had only rendered her unconscious. Then he changed his mind; he didn't hope at all. Nice-Harp wasn't playing this time – this Harp was the one who'd battered Hoik into the flooring.

Hatch. Lock it down and jam it with a wrench; the basic tools were never out of fashion. Harp slid down and rested for a moment, trying not to breathe too deeply cos his ribs hurt. It was quite a while before he heard the banging on the other side he'd been expecting. Getting through it wouldn't help them anyway, they were a sitting duck now, but he didn't see why they should get to take their anger out on him, if he could stop it.

OK navy, up to you now.

It was getting hot in here but he'd been hearing, feeling, impacts he hoped devoutly was navy boarding. Shame the missiles or whatever had to hit so hard, each strike played havoc with his side and shoulder. Still, keep coming guys. He wished he could have warned the navy not to hit the hold and scare the kids – at least they wouldn't be the real targets. Fingers crossed, kids. Now he'd pray to someone's deity the navy got to him before the pirates outside, or the fires in here.

But the *Bounty* didn't seem to be *under* fire any longer – no vibrations and no impacts. But he'd better stay awake until the navy boarded, so they didn't think *he* was a turncoat pirate!

Crip, these fires were getting hotter.

30

'Hello sunshine.'

'Wha–'

'And a good morning to you.'

There was only one person Harp knew who'd do this to a guy when he'd rather be dead. 'Del?'

'Your ears still work then. How about your eyes?''

'Too bright. Go way.' For a miracle he did, but of course it was too late now. He could feel... bunk. No pillow though; some rat had pinched his pillow. Beeping, crip. Sick Bay, again. He'd gone off sickbays, but at least this time they obviously hadn't given him a booster.

No booster, no Simshaw. Pirates. Fire. He'd had the strangest dream, cept some of it was real; the pirates, being real-Harpan, actually flirting. Fire? Yep, the fire was real too – he'd started it – just not the growling or the swirling iridescence; that would be the meds or the concussion. Yeah.

The kids were real. Crip. He told his eyes to open, winced, then told himself to suck it up. You're in the navy now, you laugh at pain and spit out dumb projectiles. 'Ow.'

'Hello, you back?'

'Still... here. Never ... left. Kids?'

'They're fine. One said you ordered them to hide till you came, and she wasn't coming out!''

'Little girl. Curls.'

'Oh yeah, new girlfriend, eh? She was asking about you as well.'

OK. He'd so much like to go back to sleep, but. ''m I in trouble?'

'You? You were never off the ship, were you? Just like you aren't on it now.' Del chuckled. 'Tough job charging someone non-existent, eh?'

Couldn't be that easy, could it? He'd been out on those docks, space knew how many folk would swear to that. Forget it, eyes too heavy, he could always panic later.

Only the colonel said it too, in much longer words, and glaring not laughing. 'You three are involved in a highly classified mission, and were not cleared to leave the ship, under any circumstances, a fact two of you were certainly aware of.' Another glare, but not at Harp. 'Definitely not to risk injury playing around with dock repairs. That alone should have all of you up on charges.' The glare refocussed onto Harp, let out of Sick Bay just in time to join them. 'As for playing junior spy, and wasting time in regen… So my schedule is now even further behind.' A sniff. 'Unfortunately, the fact there can be no record of your presence on *Defiant* makes charging any of you *another* security breach. For now. But my patience is not infinite. Understood, gentlemen?'

Harp said 'Yessir,' with the others, followed them outside. Delom was grinning, Yentl shook his head. Harp figured he was gaping. He was going to get off all the things he'd done because no one wanted to admit he was here? He was in the clear?

31

'Excuse me, ser, a security signal'. His secretary's voice said in his ear.

Ser Feldin Harpan III inclined his head, still obviously engrossed in what the senator was saying, but the whispered message meant the senator discovered Feldin was all sympathy; he "very much appreciated she had brought the matter to his notice; he'd investigate it, personally". As the woman left his office Jontig Chan, a distant cousin, led her out then hovered in the doorway.

'Come in, Jon. What's up?'

'Ser, the military have picked something I thought you should see.' The younger man brought up a blurred image on Feldin's main screen then added on another, larger, somewhat sharper.

Feldin straightened. 'Is that Moon Orbital?'

'Yes ser, two days ago.'

'Ah, the cleanup. That explains the damage. But who's that? I don't recall us sending anyone over.'

'That's just it, ser. According to our logs no one was cleared to go. Of course it's possible one of the younger Family decided to go incognito…' Jon's face said he didn't think it likely. Nor did Feldin. Inner Family reported, and had escorts. Who reported. If any left Security would know it, not the least because all closer Family were shot with tracers practically at birth.

'So… Who is this one?' Feldin peered closer, curious and puzzled.

'Ser, they don't know, facial recog hasn't so far matched him.'

'Oh, come on.'

'The best they've come up with is a trace several months ago, inside the navy's training centre in Foundation. The individual appears to have arrived on a navy frigate, *Harpan's Luck*, returning from a run to Moon. Ship's records have him down as transferred from Moon Militia. A Private Harp, ser, not Harpan. A listing for that name has someone orphaned aged four, reared by the state then fostered to a Mooner ranch, and then enlisted into their Militia as a tithe payment.' Jon looked disapproving.

Feldin frowned as well. 'A tithe payment?'

'Ser. Apparently it's become the custom for Mooner families unable to pay tithes to pay with some form of indentured labour and Militia duty counts as public service. He'd have been free to leave after the five years anyway, if he wanted, as long as the fosters could pay by then, though they wouldn't have had custody by that time as he'd be overage.' Jon's forehead creased. 'I must say, it seems very…'

'Outlandish. Have someone look into the practice, including who authorised it. But about this… Harp, you said?'

'Yes ser. I have the foster records if you'd like to read them but they're sketchy at best, even worse than usual.'

'Later. Where is he now?'

'Er, I'm afraid Security don't have his location, ser.'

'What?'

'It appears they didn't put out an immediate alert because he was on camra talking to another member of the Family, just after his arrival on World. Someone assumed that made it non-urgent even when his ID didn't register; probably assigned it to a systems glitch. They've since back-traced him through naval training, where he passed out with credit, then onto a trainee posting on *Defiant.*'

'So he's on Defiant?'

'No, ser, that's where they lost him. According to ship's log he was taken ill before she left and sent back to the centre's infirmary. Only local surveillance has no record of him reaching it, and they'd lost him again, until these images popped up in some private transmissions on Moon, describing a member of the Family who'd arrived, unofficially, to help the relief effort. It would actually have been very good PR, ser, except–'

'Except the fellow's an imposter.' Felin scowled at the frozen close-up.

'It would certainly seem so, ser. Ms Chan sent a local agent to investigate but by the time he got there the target had vanished.'

'They think he knew we were coming? And left no trace?'

'Nothing so far, ser.'

'So. An imposter.' Feldin studied the image, which certainly looked like a Harpan. Almost too-Harpan, hence Ms Chan's alarm. Someone had gone to a lot of trouble, and expense. For what? 'My guess: sending him to Moon could be a test run, to see if the impersonation worked.'

'Possibly, ser.' Jon still looked doubtful. 'Except it looks like he's been on Moon, all his life in fact.'

'That could be false. We'd have picked up any reference in public record.'

'We would here, ser, but the local agent reports Mooners don't take the same care any longer. I believe he claims to have sent some memos on the subject but the matter wasn't considered urgent enough to pass on to Ms Chan, since it didn't impinge directly on the Family. And of course the man would have been on record under several names, the custom over there with fosters, as they call them.'

'He could have grown up there, all this time? Pass the word it's definitely time to review Moon's record keeping. Meanwhile we need to find out who sent him. Use whatever it takes, and keep me informed.'

'Ser.' Jon departed, leaving Feldin to inform his father.

+++

'Feldin, how goes it, boy?'

'There's a small Family matter, ser.'

Maxil Cho Harpan V, current Founder, raised his brows and switched to scramble mode at once, he wasn't one for pointless conversation. 'Go Ahead.'

The tale unfolded. It wasn't the first time someone had tried to impersonate Family but Maxil agreed with his son; this one was both odd and potentially dangerous.

And possibly suggested very long-term planning, hence Feldin's concern.

'Witnesses now say the man always looked like one of us, Father. One has admitted to thinking he was illegitimate, and I'm informed some were more uncomfortable about it than alarmed. It appears that Moon has lapsed in its appreciation of genetics law. Security's read is that public officials were surprised we asked; that they'd thought it politic to sweep the child under the carpet, as it were, perhaps in an attempt to curry favour or possibly wary of causing us embarrassment. There were no recorded images after the first entry, only facts; height, weight, education levels etc., and the toddler's image back then is hardly a true indication of the adult.'

Maxil Senior waved that aside. 'There'd be something if he left Moon though, yes? No one's that careless. So what, we should assume he was selected for a basic likeness, either bribed or coerced, the constructive surgery to polish the act was carried out somewhere on Moon?'

'It seems a likely explanation, ser, since our first reliable visual shows him boarding *Harpan's Luck*, leaving Moon for World.'

'But nothing earlier.'

'Sadly, the installation of the Moon Orbital surveillance systems was low on their priority and behind schedule. The only camras up were in high security areas, the core and the armoury, and some of those were lost in the damage, because they hadn't yet linked the new system into World backup.'

'So we don't know much at all.'

'No, ser. He could have originated from Moon, or World, or even outside our local universe.' Feldin contemplated outside agencies, a covert operation by these pirates, worse, a bigger, more historic 'neighbour'; reminded himself the spectre of NewEarth was so far lost in time, and space, it surely couldn't be a factor, while the Kraic simply had no motive. No, their long 'lost' overlords were an irrelevance, a boogie man they could forget as much as NewEarth had forgotten they existed.

Maxil broke the silence. 'I assume you'll handle it personally? Good. Keep me updated.'

+++

Meanwhile, on *Defiant*…

It really had worked out. According to *Defiant's* medic the navy had used some very expensive drugs and equipment to ensure his rapid recovery. According to one of the orderlies, not one he knew, the medic was a bit peeved. Apparently Harp had recovered a lot faster than he wanted; the man had wanted to hang onto him, to work out why the treatments had exceeded expectations. Happily, it looked like Harp would escape any more prodding; the colonel only being interested in whether he was fit for duty.

He was barred alcohol so he had to stick with juice while the others drank for him; both sets of birds and Hamud who had left his trooper-table for the night. It was, weirdly, very good to be there. He supposed he'd adapted, again. Hey, a wall was a bulkhead, the floor was the deck and he was navy. And according to Delom he was a temporary sergeant and "a vaccing hero".

'No, I was stupid. I should have told someone as soon as I saw him.' Instead of being sure no one would listen. Face it, that was far more likely, and he would have lost Regis' trail. Regis who, Ngow had confided off the record, didn't know he had been rumbled. Ngow said Security were hoping he would lead them to Throat. Space knew how, but the pirate had escaped the *Bounty* before the navy took over, likely taken Red with him. Delom and Yentl got reminded, navy fashion, that they'd never left *Defiant*, and Harp was finding it increasingly difficult to remember what he knew and what he didn't.

Meanwhile, Del was shaking his head. 'You played the odds you were dealt and you won. So, gentlemen, and ladies, raise 'em. To *Defiant's* first hero, who never existed.' They raised their glasses; some would have sore heads tomorrow. Harp's stayed clear. He wasn't a hero, he'd just been in the right place – at the wrong time. He'd probably used up his whole life supply of luck. And so what if a few of the abducted kids were safe now. There were far more still in pirate hands; he hadn't saved *them*, had he?

His objective now? To find the other orphans, taking down the vaccing pirates in the process. It was time he went back to training.

+++

So much for a fast return. Ngow gave him a mandatory three days of light duties, aka extra rations, off duty two out of three watches, and a heart monitor when he talked them into letting him on the treadmill – and never say that didn't shock everyone rigid, including him. Three days was enough though, even if he had to stomach Simshaw again. The sims, the lattice, that was fine, he couldn't wait to get back into them, because they were the way back to the mission, and the mission was now all.

Getting shot might even have helped, at least the regen after. He felt stronger. He was pretty sure his reflexes were faster. That impression was confirmed when he joined Hamud for some gym time, and pinned the guy face down within a minute.

'Crip.' Ham tapped the floor, submission. 'How'd you get that fast? I've been keeping up my training, you haven't.'

'Guess I finally got motivated.' Harp hauled him up, idly noting that seemed to need less effort too. He'd definitely gained some muscle. Good, now all he needed was for Ngow to switch the training to the real thing. It couldn't be much longer.

32

Instead he got a covert talk with Hamud.

'Hendriks says he needs to talk to you, he says it's urgent.' Hamud kept his voice down as they walked toward K7. And no wonder. Flashback's areas were out of bounds to Hendriks and all normal crew. Plus Flashback's teams were all restricted to K7 and their forward quarters. Their marines were practically the only personnel with clearance to move between them.

Harp and Hamud knew that neither he nor Hendriks would be cleared to meet each other, now or in the near future. Harp stopped walking. 'Can't he send a message?'

'Says it's complicated.' Hamud nudged Harp forward, looking worried. 'Says he doesn't want to risk it.'

'Crip.' Harp moved again. 'He suggest how?'

'Yeah. A gun bay. Bring a jacket.' K7 loomed. 'I'll tell you later?'

'Right.' They reached the hatch and entered. Ham went one way, Harp the other.

Back into the lattice chamber. Rest. Water. Sim chamber, repeat. Treadmill, repeat. The usual monitors for pulse and heart rate, dehydration. Nothing more intrusive any longer. Maybe Ngow was so pissed at Simshaw he was being ornery about the blood tests and the cheek swabs. Long might it continue, if it meant Harp could relax a fraction. After all, the readings didn't matter if they rated him as fit for purpose, and he thought he was reacting faster every session. All those endless hours of practice might be worth the torture. Space, he hoped so. All those missing kids. And murdered crewmates.

Orphan-Houses taught their charges it was righteous to forgive, and that revenge was sinful. But revenge was burning in his heart and mind these days, in his defective bloodstream, and he knew the fire wouldn't die until he found those pirates.

Maybe Hendriks knew something. Though if he did why would he keep it secret? Why tell Harp, not shout it to the ship? Or did *Defiant* command know more than they'd admitted?

Turned out what *Defiant* command 'knew' was the last thing he wanted them to.

+++

'This civ Simshaw Ham's talked about, I found out he went over your colonel's head and made a formal complaint, about you. It went into the captain's log.' Which Hendriks definitely wasn't authorised to access.

'Hendriks, if they catch you snooping your career is over.'

Hendriks waved off Harp's concern. 'I'm covered. No way I was losing track of you a third time, so I put a tracer on your name, and Ham's, and all your crew.' All names he wasn't even meant to know. 'And Ngow's.' Hendriks grinned. 'I added one for Simshaw when Ham said he had it in for you, so when his name flagged up, along with Ngow's, it seemed worth a look-see. I had to be discreet about it so it took a few days, but when I did get in… Look, I don't understand some of it, and I didn't dare make a copy, but I memorised the gist, OK? According to the log this Simshaw was complaining he was being blocked, at Ngow's orders. It didn't give your name, but it was pretty plain.' Hendriks's boots made scraping noises on the deckplates, maybe his feet were cold down here in the ice cold gun bay; Harp was finally around the cannon he'd expected to be trained on. 'See, Simshaw was complaining he was being prevented from investigating what he called "genetic anomalies in one of the restricted personnel". He was citing risk to mission and demanding he be allowed to continue his original research.'

Harp's breath puffed out in the freezing atmosphere down here. 'What made you think…?'

'It was you? Ham said you were Ngow's blue-eyed boy, and he'd heard comments you were scoring way past what Ngow expected.' He was? 'Plus he told me Ngow's not a fan of Simshaw. And, well, to put it bluntly, Harp, you've always been different, haven't you? Ham and me, we figured you were special from the get-go; figured that was why you always tried to stay unnoticed. It was no big stretch to fill your name in.'

Harp hesitated, but he needed info. 'What are they going to do?'

'Ah well, that's the good part. According to the log the captain sent for Ngow, and Ngow argued Simshaw had been prejudiced against you from the start.' Hendriks winced. 'Cos of your looks. But Ngow said if any anomalies existed they certainly weren't affecting your mission-readiness. He said in his opinion, what was it – "the aggressive interference Simshaw advocated would be detrimental to the team's morale,"' the small man quoted smugly, '"which could be disastrous at this key stage in the mission".'

'So they aren't going to follow it up?'

Hendriks' smile faded. 'Not right now. But maybe once your mission's over.' Having passed his news along the other man's concern tipped over into normal curiosity. 'I don't get it. We know you're, well, unusual. I mean, it's hardly something you can hide, but I don't see why this guy's making so much fuss. I mean why get all het up now when no one ever did before?'

Harp felt an unaccustomed stab of guilt. Hendriks had taken risks for him, deserved a truthful answer. So did Hamud. But he couldn't tell them; that he was abnormal. He could only mumble that he didn't know why Simshaw had it in for him and urge his friend to drop the subject, for his own sake.

'Yeah, well, if you say so.' Hendriks shrugged, but maybe looked relieved as well. 'Does any of that help though?'

'Honestly, I don't know. Just, don't take any more risks, OK? I've survived this far and I don't want to bring trouble on anyone else.'

'Harp, trust me, no one's going to spot I've been there.'

'Crip, I hope not, but you promise you won't do it again?'

'If you're that bothered then yeah. I'll leave the tracers in place so they flag activity, but I won't hack into the signals. How's that?'

Sharing what he'd found had relaxed the guy, made him confident again. Could Harp talk him into stopping altogether? Not much chance of that with Hendriks. No, he'd have to settle for what Hendriks offered. 'Hendriks, I appreciate it, really, but be careful or you'll land us all in trouble.'

Either way they'd risked being there long enough. Hendriks headed aft, Harp forward, spent an hour thawing out by exercising in the gym then put himself to bed when all his team did. In the darkness of his bunk he replayed everything that Hendriks told him. Simshaw wasn't going to get his hands on Harp, at least before the mission ended. After though?

He tried to reassure himself. He'd slipped because he'd been unconscious when they brought him back. The medic who had treated him had obviously talked to Simshaw who was nosing round him anyway. If Simshaw had come running this time, and he had been bleeding? Or they'd taken samples while he was unconscious? He wouldn't put it past the man to filch a sample.

Still, one sample, when he was already injured; surely they would think it was a glitch, or that his blood had been contaminated by the engine room explosion? If they took another one to double check he could just make it all look right again, the way he always had.

Except for that initial slip, so long ago now, with that unsuspecting Orphan medic. Fooling Simshaw might be tougher this time. Yes, but he could do it. All he ever had to do was wish – and he was normal as the next guy.

Normal. Harp looked round but nobody had heard his snort of laughter. Old Seth Goss had had a saying: "if wishes were rangers, beggars would ride". He'd had another, not so nice, but they had meant the same. It was about how it was no use wishing. But for him at least one wish kept coming true. The others hadn't, but he'd come to count on this one. Drowsily, he thought it must have been a miracle he'd understood he was in danger all those years back, when he'd barely understood the world around him. Guess he was a born survivor…

+++

Memories. He remembered the roaring noise, and flames around him. Everything was shouting, creaking, screaming. He was flying, floating. Falling? Even now, some twenty years on, he wasn't clear about what really happened. He had been asleep perhaps, and woken in the middle of a storm a toddler couldn't make much sense of. Then there'd been a noise so loud he knew he'd screamed, the juddering, and then, well, nothing, for a while. Hindsight told him he had been unconscious. For how long he'd no idea, only that he woke up on the fringes of the debris he had later understood was both a shuttle and his homestead, burning, hopelessly entangled. He remembered he had seen a toy just lying there, untouched, a soft, stuffed ranger. He had picked it up and held it for a while then had started walking on unsteady feet toward the rising sun. With no idea of course where he was going.

They had found him some hours later; he had left a trail, little footprints and some blood they told him. At the time they'd only promised he was safe now, asked him, 'What's your name, son?'

He had *told* them Harpan, something he had never shared. Perhaps they'd thought he'd meant the planet, but he'd always let folk think it was the Orphan House that named him.

He had seen their quickly-masked reactions though. It scared him, made him careful after. He had watched, and listened.

He must have been a truly weird four year old, when he looked back. He didn't think he'd cried or asked about his parents. No, he'd watched and listened, and progressed from puzzled to… suspicious? Given in to some emerging instinct?

Or maybe that was hindsight too, and later life was colouring his recollection?

But one thing from that day was very clear, because he knew he'd done it, and repeated it in all the years after. Otherwise his life might be much worse than what he did have. When they looked so startled he had hugged that ragged ranger and he'd *wished*, that they'd stop staring, that they'd treat him normal. Oh, he'd wished for other things in later years, like changing what he looked like, but it seemed one wish was all he would be granted, and the way he looked was less important after all; those medics had still smiled, once he hid the wrong inside him.

Until now. If Simshaw had found his "anomalies"? He didn't think Simshaw was the type to give up and it looked like whatever had caused the fuss when he was little was still there.

What next then. Simshaw was persistent. And ambitious. If he figured Harp had something that could make him noticed… Simshaw would complain until he got his way. Eventually the navy would give in, if only in the hope it kept him quiet. And Simshaw was just smart enough he might work out that Harp's anomalies had only shown when Harp was unconscious? How could he expect to dodge forever? Simshaw would be watching, waiting.

Face it, Ngow wouldn't keep their Freak away for ever, or completely off the mission. Simshaw would be watching *all* the Hawks by now; he'd realised at last how much they stuck together. Del was sure that every move they made was under scrutiny by someone who could still report to Simshaw. It was getting on their nerves in any case; the training sessions were increasingly bad tempered, they had almost pull Del off one medic two days earlier when the idiot had parroted his overlord's complaints about their "lack of effort". Simshaw made their gums ache, even at a distance.

So it was every kind of relief when the next day started with the word for Hawk team to report to cargo hold P12, and not K7.

Del summed up the general reaction. 'I don't care where as long as Simshaw isn't with us.' But the colonel stood outside another sealed hatch – what else – and so did Simshaw. 'Crip,' Del said, but Harp slowed down and pricked his ears.

'I'll remind you that I selected these candidates, colonel. And their training programmes!'

'With the navy's supervision, doctor, and within the navy's programme.' Ngow's feet were planted. 'May I remind you Flashback is a *navy* operation centred on a *navy* prototype. Your team's involvement here is purely medical in nature and my crews have passed all aspects of your fitness training.' Ngow paused for breath. 'Which means your job is done, unless we hit a problem that requires more medics. I'd start packing, doctor.'

'I still require –'

'No more testing, doctor. No more contact that disturbs my crews. I trust that's clear?' Simshaw practically stamped his feet. Ngow remained expressionless, and Harp, behind them, dared to hope.

Till Ngow added, 'Perhaps when the mission is over someone else will re-examine your concerns. That's not for me to say. But definitely not at present. Crew morale is more important.' He noticed Del's approach. 'Now, if you'll excuse me, you are not required at this juncture.' Simshaw stuttered something. Ngow turned to meet the Hawks and blatantly ignored him. Simshaw huffed then marched off in the opposite direction.

So Harp's safety wasn't permanent, not once the colonel felt no need to keep him happy. Harp's existence, always primed to blow up in his face, could still be on a countdown.

33

Lost in thought, Harp trailed his crewmates as they followed Ngow through this latest guarded hatch. Again marines secured the hatch and checked their idents. Once inside his first impression was the cold; a real cargo hold this time? For real, or another alteration?

Where he stood looked real enough. No K7 classroom here, just a drab expanse of deckplates rimed with frost and wet with condensation. This hold hadn't seen much action in a while. Or at least not this half. The far end of this cavern had been plas-screened off, and shadows moved beyond the giant curtain.

More marines outside the plas-screen meant the usual precautions were repeated, but eventually they entered, Ngow leading. Their arrival caused the mix of civs and navy personnel inside to stop and stare, but Hawk team barely registered their interest.

'Whoah.' Del's head tilted back. The vessel in here wasn't huge, no larger really than a super shuttle, but its shape…

Harp stood there like the farmboy he still was, just gaping. This was… it was like a silver sphere, one that made him think of insects' eyes, and wedged into a flattened, spiky oval.

'Gentlemen. Meet *Raptor*.' Ngow watched their faces. 'When prepped it will be housed in an airlocked bubble on *Defiant*'s outer hull, painted to look like any other part of the superstructure; hence your zero-g entry training. Once released, the bubble will eject her into vacuum.' He grinned. 'Fast. Care to inspect her?'

They hardly needed to answer but Del nodded for them. Harp wasn't sure he could have managed that much, his mouth was dry just looking at her. Somehow *Raptor* suited. Ngow stepped forward. 'She's locked down, but essentially she's finished so I think it's time you got acquainted. I need you to tell us if there's anything about your respective stations doesn't match what you've trained for. Or anything that doesn't suit you.' The colonel headed for the rear. At least Harp guessed it was the rear. A narrow ramp there looked out of place, a temporary measure; which it was of course, they'd trained to enter in a vacuum, zero-g. They wouldn't need a ramp once *Raptor* was on-station.

Reaching the ramp meant walking under *Raptor*. The polished hull rose up, and out, as if it was going to gulp them up and swallow them whole. He guessed it would do. Walking underneath it took a conscious effort. Even Del had faltered for a moment, but he followed Ngow up the ramp and through a tiny hatch that brushed at Harp's broad shoulders. And he'd been right, a lot of this outer hull – the sphere part – was made of hundreds of separate segments rather than larger plates, very much like the multi-facetted eye of some insects back home.

The immediate interior matched what Harp had seen in training. In some ways. Ngow, acting tour guide, led them up a narrow, curving tube. Harp reasoned that the ladder bolted to one side – which they ignored at first, then had to use as horizontal shifted on them – was a sop to gravity, and maintenance; they wouldn't need it once in action. Now though, everybody bent and climbed and shuffled.

They'd continued aft. The tube dead-ended at a cramped work station, with a *lot* of console, curving round a couch that almost filled the space inside it. Overheads showed views of the exterior; the hull, the hangar and the operations crew below them.

'The Nav station doubles as damage control as you know, Captain.' Ngow spoke to Yentl who, as always, simply nodded, but the colonel had unthinkingly confirmed Harp's guess. So much for calling him a 'sergeant'. Yentl was still studying his station, what he had no doubt trained for in that other chamber Harp had never been in.

Ngow wasn't finished. 'We think it's a match but if there's anything we can improve, however small, then say so. Clear?'

'Yes, sir.' The smooth way Yentl slid into such a

cramped space already proved the training got something right.

'Now the cockpit.' Ngow twisted himself round and out the entry, and about-turned. Since there was no room to pass that put Harp in the lead. Del, contorting round to face the other way as well, sent Harp a look and groaned. 'I'll be so glad when we can float through this.'

'Hey, be glad you're smaller than me.' Right now it didn't feel like *Raptor* had been built to take him.

This time they manoeuvred Del into a cockpit that Harp assumed was the front end, where the obs-screens showed the hangar and the crews from different angles. Everyone below had stopped what they were doing. Harp supposed it meant a lot to them as well, this moment, when a flight crew took possession of their project.

Del's territory – there was one couch here too – was hardly bigger than the pilot. Del didn't wait, he slid straight down into the couch and rubbed his hands together. 'Hel-lo, darling.' Ngow snorted, obviously used to pilots. Much as Harp now figured Del was used to Yentl? Both stations, like the tube, smelled very new and some things didn't look quite finished off yet, bare, dull metal where *Defiant* would be plas or polished. Ngow grinned. 'Get settled in. She's safe to touch. Again, make sure she suits you.'

Del was reaching out by then to stroke the centre console. 'When…?'

'Not yet, but soon now, hopefully.' Ngow turned around again. 'And now the turret.'

Harp and Ngow took the tube halfway back, till they hit a small hatch opposite the ladder. They were entering the central sphere, through a narrow airlock. It felt uncomfortably, yet comfortably, like his sim chamber, down to the rebreathers and spare skintights docked in a cubby. 'You'll need the rebreather but you can do without the rest this time.' Ngow helped himself to a rebreather too. Once through the lock Harp's couch, a brand new version, floated in the centre. Ngow had told Del she wasn't powered up, but that couldn't be entirely true, could it, or the couch wouldn't be floating.

'The couch should fit you. Try it.' Ngow drifted, staying by the hatch. Harp pushed himself across the void. The couch whined softly as he settled into it; an exact fit. He couldn't stop the smile.

'Good?'

'Yessir.' It all looked so new; no wear and tear, all polished edges. He supposed all that would change soon, hadn't realised how worn the other one had got. But this was real. The buttons here would really fire, not just activate an image.

It struck him Ngow hadn't brought the others here. He'd have thought… but Ngow started talking.

'Check everything. We've brought the couches online so they'll configure. If not say so. We need you to be completely comfortable, all right?'

'Yessir.' The couch was shifting round already; it would fit him even better. In fact. 'Sir, has this been built to fit me?' It was no good to Jayson.

'Tell the difference, can you?' Ngow nodded. 'Yes, this one's all yours.' The way he said that…

'Ser, what about Jayson?'

Ngow hesitated, a first. Then settled his back against the curve of the wall, one hand against the inner hatch for anchor. 'Need to know, Sergeant. Understood?'

'Ser.'

'Jayson can fire the guns, but that's about it. He doesn't have your reflexes so *Raptor* is being tailored to you. Our current hope is that if we can record your operation in action we can write programmes off that to let others follow your lead. That's our hope.' Ngow looked sombre. 'Whether we succeed… we've been searching for similar candidates but we haven't found any, so building software off what you can do may need to be the next step. Last option, *Raptor* might need to operate AI instead of human gunners, which no one's happy about. All of which is classified.'

'Yessir.' He was the only gunner they'd accepted; Ngow had a brand new weapon, probably incredibly expensive, with a single gunner? Little wonder Ngow had stopped smiling.

'So now you know, son. Make sure everything suits, cos we need your optimum performance. And don't tell anyone else, even your team.'

'Yessir,' Harp said faintly. Ngow hesitated – that made twice – then ducked into the lock and left him to it. Time to try things then. His couch moved at his whim – like the sim only better, maybe cos it fit him so much closer. A reminder of his new significance to Flashback. Crip, he couldn't be the only crewman who could run this station. If he'd never thought he was a freak before…

The thought of his reflexes – his brainwaves? – being downloaded into navy comp systems didn't make the situation any more palatable. But it would go into his records too, wouldn't it? He'd been thinking he was starting to blend in at last, but there wasn't much chance of that now. He was going to be singled out for good.

When the hatch clanged and Ngow's head appeared Harp realised he hadn't done much. So when Ngow asked him if he wanted extra time he only had one answer.

'Yessir.' And Ngow didn't argue, just backed out. So now or never. 'Sir, what happens after this? To me I mean?'

Ngow looked surprised, then nodded, maybe with approval.

'Points for forward thinking, Sergeant. It's unlikely you'll be posted to general duties. You have something the navy can use. I can already think of other operations you could transfer to. You can expect your temporary rank to be made official as well. In fact.' Ngow began to smile. 'You're probably already rated as a valuable resource, to both our planets.'

'Ser.' Harp tried to find the words. 'I don't want to be some kind of…'

'Hero figure?' Ngow's smile broadened. 'Son, I may not know you as well yet, but I do know that about you. Relax. Wherever you go next is hardly going to be public knowledge.'

'Oh.' Hero wasn't the word he'd had in mind but the answer was still welcome. He sagged a little in the couch. It settled with him.

Ngow watched him. 'That sort of thing worries you? From now on if you have any worries at all you bring them to me, understood? And again…'

'Don't tell my crew. Understood, ser.' Back to keeping secrets, this time for the navy. Part of life's rich pattern. Harp couldn't help thinking the secrets were reaching critical mass, but there didn't seem to be anything he could do about it.

34

He was supposed to be comfortable. Joke. He'd better try though. He had no sense of Del or Yentl's presence near. If those two were communicating then he wasn't hearing. Which was fine, he had enough to cope with.

Without thinking, his fingers clenched on the arms of the couch. Good thing those weren't active, or he could have put a vaccing missile through *Defiant*.

Add it all up. The bad news: he'd be tagged as different, on official records. But the good news was it looked as if his difference would urge the navy to conceal it; he'd become *their* secret. As long as he could keep the rest – the things he wasn't even sure about himself – out of their notice. All right. He could do that if he had to. Maybe. Crip, at least he'd had a lot of practice.

When Del's voice reached him from the speaker at the hatch, he pushed out of the couch and swam out of the sphere, the turret, meeting Del and Yentl in the tube and squirming out into the hangar. Ops-crew asked them questions; did they need adjustments? Turned out Yentl wanted one board moved completely, overhead. He said it would be faster. Del said he was fine and Harp just nodded, staring up at *Raptor*'s hull. He got it now; the hull was so segmented cos each separate segment was a gun emplacement. *Raptor* was a honeycomb, with missiles and the like instead of honey. *Raptor* was a flying armoury with a ginormous payload, pockmarked with destruction. Nobody bothered explaining how they loaded it. Nobody ever explained anything.

Del rubbed his hands together. 'Two more days until the test flight.' Yentl murmured an agreement.

Harp swung round. 'A test flight?'

Del looked startled, maybe Yentl didn't. 'No one sent you word?'

'No, nothing.'

Del looked at Yentl. Yentl shrugged. 'Just us then. That makes sense, I guess. I mean we're only testing the propulsion, not the guns, so not much point you sitting there for nothing.'

Turned out Del was right. The two flew *Raptor*, and enthused about it. It left Harp on edge. He wondered if it was deliberate, letting him see everything then yanking him off her. But his training had intensified. They all knew prep was almost over.

Harp's role was becoming automatic. His left hand got to choose what he wanted to deploy; missiles, pulse charges, chaff. His brain targeted. His right hand got to push the triggers. Or not. In an emergency he could now go to voice activation and fire two-handed, but there was a tiny corresponding time-lag Ngow didn't like; he said that was a backup. Harp kept wondering if he could do it better.

Dealing with these final nuances meant hours of extra practice. He knew now the weapon system was the focus of the operation; Raptor, genius or not, was just the vehicle that moved it. *He* was what the colonel planned to aim at the pirates.

+++

And… this was the day. He was finally going to try for real. Harp told himself to keep his cool and pushed off, hand to hand along the tether line the techs had rigged to *Raptor's* access. Yentl was ahead of him, his face concealed by his rebreather, making light of zero-g while Harp was still the novice. Del, of course, had scorned the line and pushed himself into the gap between *Defiant's* airlock and the *Raptor's*, showing off by somersaulting. Harp could hear him laughing in his earpiece. Del had really fallen for the *Raptor*, calling her "a real lady, with a real temper". Harp just hoped she would behave until he got the hang of everything inside his sphere. Del and Yentl were pretending to be comfortable with it now, but it was his first test flight.

Through Raptor's tube, like swimming this time, much less energy required in zero; twist and dive into the turret's tiny, one-man airlock. Strapping in, including sanitary hook-ups, telling Del – and through him to *Defiant's* com as well – that he was in position. Moments later *Raptor* hiccupped, clicked, then thrummed with power; Del had fired the engines.

Ngow's voice came on. '*Raptor*, you are cleared for final trial. Passing control.' Harp breathed deeper. Ngow said the drones they'd target mimicked ship specs. With specific weapons.

Del's voice: 'Harp?' Too loud. His fingers made adjustments automatically, the shout became a murmur.

'Hear you, pilot.' It was so familiar. Were they still pretending?

'All set, turret?'

'Yeah, just floating here, doing nothing.' Sounding brash because he was so nervous; cos he knew stuff now that Del and Yentl didn't – like that he was all there was to make this happen.

Defiant-com was confirming Del's checks, giving them the all clear. They were really taking *Raptor* into vacuum. *Defiant's*, Del's then Yentl's voices wove together in a dance of information. Harp fiddled with the com, to shunt *Defiant* to the background, Del into the fore. When he brought his weapons up it would be Del he'd want to hear, not *Defiant*; didn't need distractions. But he heard *Defiant* saying, 'Bubble open, Launch when ready, pilot.'

Del responded, then a word from Yentl, followed by, 'All systems optimal, *Defiant*. *Raptor* launching in…' The bubble must have irised open. *Raptor* was already moving, racing into vacuum. Harp heard Del say, 'Oh, you beauty,' but his only other sense that they were moving was the changing images around him. *Defiant's* hull was gone, receding twice as fast as he'd expected. He sat very still and watched the bubble close behind them, and *Defiant* shrinking. There were muffled protests, words like "excess speed, uncalled for, untoward acceleration". And a laugh, pure Del. 'You wanted to know what she could do, didn't you?'

Typical fighter pilot. Thrill seeker. Risk taker. Hair trigger. Except maybe that part of the job was Harp's now? *Raptor* was programmed to keep her pilot *away* from her armaments except as last resort, if Harp was out of action.

Ngow's voice cut in. 'Gentlemen, this scenario puts you only one hundred and fifty thousand klicks off Moon. No retreat. Feel free to attack on sight, assuming pirates.'

Yentl's calm voice broke into *Defiant's*. 'Turret, I'm tracking pirates emerging jump point at...' Harp's brain accepted the coordinates as he watched his turret walls display them, several lit-up icons, colour coded to identify each threat and let him prioritise. There'd been reason for those different coloured dots he'd blinked at.

'Wow.' *Raptor* was fast. *Defiant* had become a toy behind them, was still shrinking. He could hear Del whooping in his ear as *Raptor* slowed its pace – a relative assessment – just as sharply. Harp knew Del and Yentl would be feeling that acceleration, but he wasn't. He was in suspension in his turret, g-force couldn't reach him any longer. Weird, considering. He sat in an explosive bubble; feeling more a part of space than part of *Raptor*. According to Del she was one of the fastest craft he'd ever heard of, with superior speed and acceleration compared to his old dart plus what he called "more staying power". Harp wasn't sure exactly what that meant, but he accepted it was good for keeping them alive in combat. Frankly, areas outside his sphere now had minimal importance.

His sphere was his world, his focus. His walls displayed all space around him, and he meant all. Like the sim, he was seeing 360 degrees. A twitch and he tilted, another and he spun. He was aware of everything both Del and Yentl would be viewing via their banks of screens, and more. He simply saw, like he had the eyes in the back of his head kids thought their teachers possessed.

Ngow's voice cut in again. Annoying.

'Let's see if what we've spent on you was worth it, shall we?' Then dead air. *Defiant* wouldn't talk again, unless there was a glitch, until this test run ended. Del and Yentl were the only other people in his world now.

The early targets were easy, so slow Harp figured Ngow was easing them in, except that easy here meant seconds. After that he had to keep his wits about him, but his walls kept telling him he was succeeding. Coloured markers flashed then disappeared. Then single targets multiplied, became attacks from different vectors, became...

Time had frozen. Harp was floating in the zone and nothing now existed but the targets. And he could destroy them with a thought, the pressure of a single finger.

Then he missed one.

Out of twelve incoming missiles, one got through and past, but it was close, too close. He heard Del cursing, dimly registered that Del had been too busy playing audience and wasn't on it fast enough. Harp cursed out loud and–

shifted Raptor.

One second she was idling in space, the next she was careering off toward *another* missile. Harp's instinctive play succeeded, when he shifted course a second time the enemies locked on and struck each other.

Del was whisper-shouting, *Raptor* getting showered by flying debris; even Harp could hear the impacts though he didn't feel them in his bubble haven. Del and Yentl did of course – more curses – from the sounds Harp figured Yentl had to put out fires. But the *Raptor* had survived his error.

Del's voice cut across *Defiant's* garbled interruption. 'What in the stars? You override my boards?'

'*Raptor*, that's a negative, no override. What just happened?' Harp could only sit and listen.

'Ah, then I dunno, ser. The engines cut out just before I altered course, it had me worried for a minute but we're all right here.' Del's voice sounded so convincing, did he actually believe that?

'Engine failure? Test suspended, pilot. Bring her home.'

'Received, *Raptor* returning to base. Turret? I guess you can shut down whenever you want.'

'Got that, pilot.' But he didn't, and not just cos it would have left him sitting here in darkness. He wanted to see everything, and he wanted to think. Badly. He'd just overridden his pilot's controls, hadn't he? Worse, he had no vaccing clue how he'd done it. And he suspected Del had just covered for him.

+++

The official verdict was something had "misfired' for approximately 1.2 seconds", then come back on. No one seemed to think it strange *Raptor* had veered off course as a result. Hull and engines got stripped down to their nuts and bolts, rebuilt, and some connection got the blame. Del didn't argue, didn't comment. The ensuing silence on the subject made Harp nervous, but he hoped he didn't show it. Well, there were no awkward questions. He risked breathing a bit easier and swore he'd never do… whatever he'd done… again.

Finding the "malfunction" took days and put *Raptor* out of action, so no more test flights, but this time no one moaned about returning to the sims. In fact the Hawks all volunteered. Del even asked the techs to make his programme harder.

'Give me unexpected,' he demanded. 'That thing nearly caught me napping when our boy here actually missed one.' Near miss or not, morale was high around them. Word had clearly filtered to the techs, and even medics seemed to know the trial had essentially succeeded. That or they had noted Ngow actually smiling.

Simshaw likely wasn't, but it sounded like he wasn't part of Flashback any longer – word was Ngow banished him to other parts of the *Defiant* when he tried to interfere. Long might that continue.

Unsurprisingly the only not-so-happy faces visible belonged to Falcons, especially Jayson. Hund tried to hide chagrin.

'We heard you aced the trial, kid. Well done. There's a rumour about feeding your moves into a sim.'

Beside her Jayson winced. 'Yeah. Should be interesting, being you, huh. Think they'll make me diet?'

Harp shrugged, in sympathy. 'Only if they want you to fit my chair. Can't say I see how that'd work. Will you have to?'

'Looks like.' Jayson grimaced.

'Crip, I'm sorry.'

'Not your fault, we're different styles is all. You're faster all the time than I am.' The heavy gunner smiled at last. 'I'm starting to think they gambled on that; me heavier, to suit the fire power, against you being, what, a sniper?'

Harp nodded. 'Pretty much. Although I always thought they picked me cos I didn't know enough to doubt the orders.'

'Huh, mebbe you're right too. This don't match anything I did before.'

Did Jayson relax? Harp thought Hund had, and her next words seemed to say that. 'Whatever, as long as one of us hacks it. Buy you guys a caffee?'

Cos they couldn't order stronger. So they whiled away the time in sims or conversation with the Falcons. Hund and Del put heads together trying to outthink their trials, and their navs did likewise. Ngow looked approving. Jayson asked a lot of questions but was philosophical when Harp too often couldn't answer.

'Told you. It's a different skill set, kid. You're born with yours and me with mine. Don't sweat it.' So he didn't. But he itched to go back into *Raptor*, to the quiet, the silence. Into space.

Then, vac it, they got news of pirates, on the very day they heard *Raptor* was back in one piece.

35

The big mess screens flashed a lurid orange, making Harp look up from his food, then the XO's voice cut in. 'All hands hear this. Scan has possible pirate presence, currently outside our sector.' Followed by something about "going dark in one hour", and then the wall screens went black. First time he'd ever seen that happen.

Harp looked across at Mac. 'Going dark?'

Mac blinked. Del started laughing. 'It figures you're the only one onboard wouldn't know.' He grinned. 'Means hiding ourselves from enemy scan. You'll be the only rookie here who hasn't had the drills.'

'But...' Harp looked from Mac to Del to Yentl. 'How can something the size of *Defiant* hide?'

Mac shook her head. The other orderlies looked genuinely puzzled. Once again it fell to Del to answer.

'You're still thinking like a civ. It's not how big she is, kid, it's how quiet. We don't really *see* anything out here, do we? Not till we get close. We pick up ident signals.'

Light dawned. Harp recalled thinking no one on Moon Orbital would realise what the *Bounty* really was unless someone looked out a ship's port at it. They'd believed the *Bounty's* faked call sign, 'saw' her as a trader. 'So *Defiant* will put out false ID?' It made him wonder what name Throat was using by now.

'Easier to be something else than invisible. She'll shut down inessentials and hide enough mass so anyone looking picks up a smaller signature. It's not fool-proof but with luck we'll get close in before we're rumbled.'

'Close enough for *Raptor*?'

'Be nice, wouldn't it. But that'll depend on the brass, eh Mac?'

Mac nodded, saw Harp's face. 'I'd say the captains have three options. One – they decide one test's not enough and you're not ready. Two – they track the pirates and send you out when we get close. And three – they sneak up and launch *Raptor* early, before the pirates catch on to what we really are.'

'Wow.' Harp looked to Del for his opinion. 'Should we start…?'

'Nah, no orders yet. Finish your dinner.' Del's eyes glittered. 'Then I say we rest up, in case.' So that was what they did. Harp figured the last thing any of them felt like was sleep but Del was right, it was the only productive action they could take until someone said otherwise. Lying in his bunk, in his skintights just in case, Harp tried to feel a difference in *Defiant's* movement, or her engines, but being so far forward meant he never heard much anyway, or felt it. For him the only discernible shift was any passing footsteps sounded softer. 'Are people tiptoeing or what?'

'Nah.' Del spoke from the bunk behind. 'They're wearing softsoles. Sorry, kid, another thing we should have told you. Silly as it sounds, putting a few thousand crew – not the marines, mind – in slippers actually damps our scan if someone looks, though personally I think they just hope it does.'

Harp supposed it might, though he wasn't sure how either. He also recalled he had softsoles in his locker, so he'd better go and fetch them. This going dark was more complicated than he'd assumed; it was annoying to realise everyone else had known. Except the civs? Had no one thought of telling him because the people training him were almost all civilians? He could just see Simshaw plain ignoring anything he didn't know himself, or didn't value for his research. Crip. 'Is there anything else I should know?'

'Nah, you're good.' Swishing sounds suggested Del was getting comfortable. 'Outside of *Raptor* and here we don't have a duty station. Worst case, we get called as gophers for damage control.'

Like if *Defiant* saw action and called for her extra medics? It wouldn't be that bad. Would it?

'Del, how many pirates are we talking about?'

Yentl, coming from the shower, heard that as he

walked past. 'Who knows, they'll tell us if they need us to know.' He sank onto his bunk beyond Harp's feet. Harp heard him programming his wristcom – probably, on past experience, with soothing music. Maybe he should try that.

Everybody settled, more or less. Time dragged. Not literally but it felt like. Maybe the others were more used to this. Harp wasn't. Waiting for someone to assign him chores wasn't at all the same as waiting to go into a battle. How many ships had *Defiant*'s scan spotted? How big? The same number that caused so much carnage on Moon? But *Defiant* wasn't Moon. She could manoeuvre, she could surely handle pirates. It was why she now existed. Especially if they'd let him back into his turret.

His mind refused to sleep for once, fixated on the calc; how many guns a pirate ship might carry; how many incoming he might need to track. Replaying the test flight. And that single miss.

Mac's face appeared, upside down, above him. 'Harp, relax.' She must have heard him moving, and she needed to rest as well.

'Sorry.' He closed his eyes, deliberately loosened tensed muscles and tried to empty his head. He should have copied Yentl and used music.

+++

He was actually shocked he had to wake up when general com sounded. 'All crew, alert. Silent running applies. We've entered the Kraic sector in response to distress signals from Kraic IV, authorised by Kraic Prime. Third watch will stand down as relieved; off duty crews to standby. We estimate we'll be in range of the pirates' scans in approximately seven hours. Over.' The com clicked out.

Seven hours? That must mean *Defiant* was clear of Harpan space, and free to go to FTL. He wished he understood, but so far only knew it wouldn't work in-system; if they could have 'jumped', and bridged the yawning gap between at once, they might have caught the pirates over Moon and all this would be over. Moments later Ngow's voice replaced the general alarm. 'Flashback alert. Support teams report. Hawks and Falcons, briefing in thirty. Over.'

They were sending *Raptor* into battle.

'Maybe,' Yentl cautioned when Harp spoke out loud. 'Briefing only means they're prepping, just in case.' In case was still enough for Mac to have them up and dressed and packing in some serious protein in the time before the briefing.

+++

The meet was in K7, back in class except the medics got them for a while first and Harp, impatient, had to force himself to concentrate on wishing; the last thing he should do was to alarm a medic. The one he had was bad enough already. 'Your pulse rate's up, ser. Do you want a shot?'

'No.' Harp made himself sit still. 'I'll be fine once we move.'

'OK.' The medic made a note, presumably of his refusal. 'You remember your couch is stocked with both relaxants and stims?'

'Yes.'

'And you're clear on the dosage?'

'Yes, I'm clear. We done?'

The medic chuckled. 'Yes, we're done.' The man stepped back to let him rise. 'Good luck, ser.'

Suddenly the briefing didn't feel like 'maybe'. It felt even less so when the XO joined them. She looked pretty calm, but Ngow looked more grim than normal. The XO started things.

'As you can see, Kraic IV is at the extreme edge of Kraic space, nearer to us than their prime or their other planets. It was always considered a possible target, being so remote, but it's mainly agricultural, and the Kraic aren't that easy to snatch. Many of them still live in the trees they plant everywhere. Still, we've been in regular contact with them for about four years now, with Kraic Prime approval of course, just keeping a friendly link with a neighbour.' The XO sniffed. 'Off the record, we thought they were essentially a free early warning system; we were surprised the pirates hit us first.'

Because a traitor made it easy? But the XO wasn't saying, was she? 'So that caught us on the hop and the Family were not amused. This, gentlemen, is our chance to make good on that mistake. Colonel?'

The XO left, presumably back to the bridge, and it was Ngow's mission. 'The last signal from Kraic IV estimated eight enemy ships, pirates, each roughly equal in mass to our frigates or more. Normal procedure would be to send a flotilla against them; *Defiant* and at least three others. But... *Defiant*'s new silent running ability is superior to our other craft, which means *Defiant* can get closer before she's detected. Command feel that's a significant advantage at this time, given the addition of *Raptor* to her arsenal.' Ngow paused. Falcon team sat as still as Hawk. Maybe his gaze lingered just a moment on Harp. 'Our neighbours need us. We've not had as much time as I'd hoped, but it could be a while before we get this opportunity again, and I do believe we're ready.'

'Damn straight,' Del said curtly. Others murmured in agreement. Harp breathed deep, then nodded.

Ngow almost smiled. 'Kraic IV has stopped sending, so we are now operating off our own scan. *Raptor* is being armed. Hawk team will prep, Falcon will sit standby. Both teams will be patched into bridge com to keep abreast of developments. Questions?'

There were few, and none from Harp. He couldn't do much till he reached the turret and could see what he was facing. Till then everything was down to Del and Yentl. They dismissed. Yentl was quiet, of course. Del was bouncing on his toes. 'Well, friends, the bar just closed but–'

'No. No caffee,' Mac said firmly. 'Possibly a shower.' A look at Del. 'For some I'd say a cold one.'

Harp found a grin. No, Del was hyped enough already. A shower though, that sounded sensible. Space knew how long they'd be in *Raptor*. He didn't mind the glucose spigot, but he didn't think he'd ever love the sanitary hook-ups.

36

So they returned to J20, showered and replaced the skintights, with their shipsuits over, and the softsoles. They would change into their sealed shipboots prior to boarding *Raptor*. Boot soles went magnetic if one wanted, and of course they bonded to the skintights. The rebreathers – helmets now – would finish off the total-vacuum setup; backup air supply for Del and Yentl and the base requirement for Harp, who had to operate in vacuum to negate the static discharge. Yentl wasn't all that happy with skinsuits either but the thought of climbing into bulky armoured vac-suits onboard *Raptor* was too tortuous to think of. If the ship was ruptured they would have to take their chances in much lighter gear, praying for a speedy rescue.

They reported to *Raptor's* bubble. They should probably be nervous about now, but Del was bright eyed and Yentl looked as calm as ever. So did Mac, though maybe Oko looked a little panicked. That struck Harp as funny, then as touching.

Him? He felt... kind of removed. The voices in his com seemed distant, but he wished he could stop twitching.

Del was handed his rebreather. Techs checked out its functions though both his and Yentl's dangled round their necks now, only there if needed. Harp heard his tech copying the checks as well, though he still needed to adjust the bigger mask that he alone would need to wear inside the turret, with the extra tanks. The boots and sealed gloves that bonded to the skintights were already on, so that just left the sanitary hook-ups when they got onboard, cos *Raptor* had no head; they all had that delight in common.

'Ready, gentlemen?' said Ngow.

'Ser.' Del nodded, so did Harp and Yentl. Mac gave them a nod, the techs stood back; they headed for the airlock. *Raptor* waited.

It was only his second flight in her. What if... Harp

swam, manoeuvred to his turret, hearing Yentl's voice confirming Nav was now locked in 'behind' him. Then Del's voice announced their pilot 'locked and loaded', which Harp figured was a phrase that suited fighter pilots. Harp was last to call, still slower on the blasted hook-ups. Made it. 'Turret locked and ready.'

'OK, friends, time to tiptoe?' *Defiant* com would be listening but there'd be no exchanges this time; they would stick to their internal com if needed, till the pirates 'saw' them.

Déjà vu. *Defiant's* hull slid past. Harp watched the bubble close. Del wasn't rocketing away this time. He planned a speed, he'd said, the inertial sort of motion strays like asteroids, or wrecks, or simple rubbish might maintain till they hit gravity. *Defiant* would lag behind. To that end *Raptor's* bright new hull was dulled and camo-sprayed. If – when – a pirate did become aware of them a scan should pick up only a broken-looking sphere, hopefully signalling lumps of rock and metal. A pretty large amount of metal, but that wasn't so uncommon. They might even think it was a worthwhile prize on that account and head toward them. But that wouldn't be for hours yet; a blink in space time.

This sector of Kraic space had more stars than home; Harp's all-round view was all a-twinkle. He played with imaging controls till they were grey; it wouldn't do to mix them up with targets. Recalling last time out, he also set *Defiant's* com to quiet. Then he tried to relax. Del and Yentl talked a bit, between themselves; he didn't feel like he was with them any longer. No, he had this tiny universe all to himself.

It was so peaceful he dozed.

'Kraic IV colony in transmission range.' That was Yentl. Harp opened his eyes though even he knew transmission range was thousands of klicks short of any sighting, even here. He listened in though.

'I'm getting static, no trans.' Yentl was reassuringly calm.

'Jamming?'

'Almost certainly.'

Then for a long while, nothing, while they sidled closer.

'Crip.' Del's voice of course. 'Turret?

'Here.'

'You getting this?'

'Yeah.' Kraic IV was a small planet, no bigger than Moon and by what he'd heard no richer, other than in vegetation. Not much traffic. Which had to mean what he could see on *Raptor's* screens – his 'walls' – were either pirates or the luckless ships they'd ambushed. According to his walls nine tenths of what he saw were pirates.

On the good side, most of those weren't pointed *Raptor's* way, yet, either docked or in a stable orbit round the little planet. The initial attack phase had moved on into theft, perhaps abduction, though *Defiant* thought the latter was less likely this time. Apparently a human fetched a better price; who knew.

'Harp? You want to go live?'

'Not yet.' These guns woke up as fast as Harp did. 'Let's not make ourselves so obvious until we have to, eh?'

'OK by me. Creeping in, people. Hold on, I'll just wobble us a bit so we don't look too organised.' Harp's walls spun off then steadied; Harp, of course, stayed put but Yentl muttered something that ended, 'seasick'. Then he sounded brisker. 'Pilot, how close can we get before they'll pick up our internal com?'

'Panic not, I'm guessing they'll suss out our heat sig long before they hear us chatting, Nav. In fact my money's on them spotting *Defiant* first.' Which was the reason Del was on a course that ought to bypass Kraic IV by several thousand klicks; hey, asteroid, just passing through, no problem here. You just focus on the big bad Arc ship over that way. Yep, *Defiant*, all her size and power, made a pretty good diversion.

Closer. Closer. What had looked like lights on Kraic's surface could be fires. Their briefing said the docking station – not an orbital like theirs but smaller – was a sticklike structure rather than a ring. By this time Harp was close enough he could make out *two* sticks, one smaller than the other. They'd attacked there first, like Moon? His images were fuzzy; maybe distance or a haze of debris. He'd likely never know; they had strict orders not to dock, even afterwards; top secret and all that bull.

Yentl came on, extra deadpan. 'I'm getting faint transmissions. Still no sign they see us.'

'Not long now.' Del sounded eager. Harp's hands hovered, eyes on all his icons. Briefing had said eight, he made it nine. One red. Crip, destroyer size, how the hell did they get hold of that? Three purple; frigate strength. Four orange; cruisers, or outsystem shuttles. And one yellow; *Raptor* had that down as cruiser size but short on weapons, more an armed civilian than a fighting vessel.

There was some smaller stuff she wasn't sure about, coded murky brown, but only Kraic IV and portions of its broken docks showed green for friendlies. Plus a hulk that floated aimlessly, disabled, which she tagged as Kraic Security. He'd have to try to shoot around it.

Yentl came back. 'Pirate squawk, someone querying their scan. You won your bet, Del. It's *Defiant*.'

That's it, all look that way.

Defiant wasn't hiding any longer. A green dot on what was currently Harp's 'rear' wall showed *Defiant* becoming larger on *Raptor's* scan. From his position Kraic IV and pirates showed as hard-a-starboard; practically perfect placing. If *Defiant* had been any later joining the party *Raptor* would have been drifting past, too far to interfere. As it was Harp was as close as he could hope, so close right now that *Raptor* switched to showing tiny images instead of flatter, 2D icons.

And one pirate, a purple, had begun to roll, to come around to face *Defiant*. One at least wanted to look a threat in the eye. 'How long before they realise it's *Defiant*?'

Del chuckled. 'I'd say about now?'

The red, and the other three purples, already furthest out, were changing course too. Of course, they'd probably been too big for these docks. Those smaller browns in atmo could be shuttles, pirate-owned or 'commandeered' to transfer loot off planet. But the bigger four were definitely under way and heading for *Defiant*. All four together massed about the equal of the Arc ship. And could operate together, as a pack. It wouldn't be a pushover. The other question was what armament they had; enough to beat *Defiant*?

The rest of the pirate ships didn't seem to have changed their plans. At least one was still locked to the larger stick. Business as usual then, still loading? Confident their fellows would prevail? Still more interested in stealing?

'Turret? Ready on your go, OK?' That was Del, supportive of the rookie – but it wasn't his first fire fight, was it? Harp flashed on *Bounty's* hold, the kids. 'Crip, have they got Kraic kids on some of those ships?'

'Yeah.' Del sighed. 'Nothing we can do about that, kid. Gotta stick to the plan, right?'

'Maybe not.' The slipping-past had worked, the plan was now they'd go in from the rear, take out those orange, and the yellow. 'I think I can disable them instead.'

'Risky, Turret.' Del didn't sound approving; pilot-think was probably more hit or miss.

But Yentl, *Raptor's* voice of reason, didn't answer. Settled then? 'Right, turret arming... now.' His walls glowed brighter a moment then went back to normal. Or maybe that was him. His brain felt *Raptor* poised for orders. Harp didn't need to move since Del had pointed *Raptor's* nose toward an orange, with a second orange almost straight behind it on their current heading. Nice suggestion.

Breathe in. Breathe out. Relax and squeeze. The pirates could have made changes but his hours of navy training meant he knew what probably went where. They might have reconfigured holds and cabins but the engines? Not so likely, even if they'd added extra modules. And they wouldn't lock up any prisoners near engines, would they?

No, far too risky. He told *Raptor* to show him the targets' power sources, and their steering. Cripple but not kill would be the plan. It wouldn't take out all the guns, and he could still damage life support, but atmo would take time to fail, and it was the best he could do.

The first two targets were almost too easy but the explosions were dramatic; the element of surprise was gone but they had two down. After that, it got harder. While Del played dodgeball, taking care of *Raptor*, Harp rotated as *he* wanted. Target. Fire. Target. He wasn't seeing Del's and Yentl's worries any longer; *Raptor* showed him incoming as pale ghosts, only his targets were brighter. It didn't feel like Del was steering him at all, he was floating in his spinning world again, a galaxy of coloured blobs to aim at. He focussed in on engine rooms, and Del on dodging missiles. It seemed a fair division.

Raptor winced. He wouldn't call it a flinch, but he'd felt something. Yentl's voice, a little stuttered, reported minor hull damage. *Raptor* rerouted missiles away from one of her firing tubes. His wall showed him a white triangle, a small no-fire zone. Not a problem. Target. Fire.

Del swore. Another triangle. But all four orange dots had taken hits, one drifting, one rotating. Two still firing at them.

Good news; the yellow was making a run for it. Not so good; one of the purples had shied off the battle with *Defiant* and was coming round. But *Raptor* gave him minutes before it had them targeted; ample time to take the purple out, before it opened fire on them instead. The oranges had been way bigger. *Raptor*, after all, was smaller than a cruiser. He was going to be a giant killer if he pulled this off. This purple would have twice the mass of the oranges, but *Raptor* was telling him it had held back from *Defiant*, letting the other pirates make the running, so his newest enemy was coming in at near full strength, well armed and showing very little damage. And its engines were behind it, well concealed by its own, undamaged, splayed-out hull; not easy. 'Pilot, I don't have target, need you to go round.'

'Oh sure, why make it easy.' Del's voice sounded… busy. Kept forgetting his world was more peaceful.

'Can you do it?'

'Yours to command, kid.' Harp's walls spun wildly. The purple's flank, a mess of turrets, crept into sight and then a glimpse of what he thought were engine pods, slapped on as if they were an afterthought, protruding aft. He chose what armament he wanted, in a microsec, then hit the firing buttons. Amputated engines!

'Woah, right on target, kid. I always – Crip!'

'Del?'

Static

'Del?' Yentl sounded shaken too. 'Pilot, come in?'

No answer, but the purple's hull was opening; six, eight, nine dart-like craft erupting, heading straight for *Raptor*.

'Del?' Yentl's voice switched back to Yentl-normal; calm and steadfast. 'Turret, I've lost pilot. Do what you can.'

Harp *wasn't* calm. He could still fire but without evasive action from his pilot…and if they ran, that just put Yentl in the cross hairs.

Raptor twisted sideways, tilted, tore right through a non-existent gap between two darts and, naturally, fired at both in passing. Harp's walls flared to show him missiles he hadn't been aware of. Not exactly comforting, but *Raptor* seemed to have it covered, jinking right then dropping left, though now he felt the yawing movement in his stomach.

Between, Harp found more targets, pushed more buttons, vaguely hearing Yentl giving damage updates.

Time had slowed and in the zone was all. The only incoming missiles were farther away, no darts in range, so Harp wheeled to assess new threats. New missiles, from another purple trying to flee *Defiant*, still kept busy by that red. And look, the fourth purple was showing inactive and the last two oranges had given up and turned to flee as well. The fight was practically over.

But there were four missiles heading *Raptor's* way, someone's parting shot, and the number of white triangles had grown. No problem, she could handle four.

Cept one missile clipped the remnants of a dart, and detonated early. The shrapnel cloud pushed all the other three off course and Harp lost targeting – a fraction of a second, but too long. He managed two, the last veered wildly, hit more debris closer in and turned into a rain of fire and metal fragments twice as big as he was. Snarling, Harp threw *Raptor* backward, tossed her round so most of the explosions, and the impacts, hit her flank instead of bow or stern. Instead of Del or Yentl.

In his turret, it was like being bombarded by splinters of light, the least like silent fireworks. He almost moved enough, not quite. One half of his remaining walls went black. A crack appeared; an actual, solid splinter breached his hull and flew toward him, right on target.

Left leg; thigh. Felt cold, then hot. He had to set a patch. His hands fumbled, first time since he'd begun, but he found the medkit pod between his legs, happily still mostly whole, and slapped the biggest patch he had over the hole in his suit. Air in, vacuum out; thank space for all that training. Crip, but he was tired; his head was nodding. 'Note to tecs; could do with stronger stims, guys, maybe split the med pods into different places?'

'Harp?' Yentl sounded… '*Harp*?'

'Oh, hi Yentl… Just need a nap.'

+++

'Ser? Can you hear me? Crip, someone hold him down. Ser, you're back on *Defiant*. We just need you to relax and lie still. Ser, ser? Thank space for small mercies, let's get him sedated and prepped. Run tox and bloods while–'

Blood! Self preservation overrode the lassitude.

'Crip, grab him!' Pressure. Movement, then the sense the hands relaxed and then a high-pitched beeping and a lot of panicked voices.

37

'Emika my dear, how's navy life treating you?'

'Very well, Uncle Feldin.' Emika came to mental attention. There was a significant distance between Great Uncle Maxil's named heir – and her own Commander in Chief, who practically ran World and Moon, – and a lowly 'cousin' fifty years younger and at the start of what career she was allowed to follow. Emika's's brain made only one connection for an unexpected call; that 'lost' recruit again, the pretty Mooner she had tried, and failed, to uncover. Was she going to find out more? 'What can I do for you, ser?'

'You might recall Ms Chan enquiring about a young man I was trying to locate.'

'Yes, of course.' Best not to look too keen. 'I trust you found him?'

'Finally, yes.' On her screen, the older man's distinctive features seemed to freeze a moment, studying her. Uh-oh. 'You appear to be the only one of us who's had direct contact with him.'

What...?

'Yes, quite.' Her shock had obviously shown. 'I've reassigned you. You'll need to leave for *Defiant* as soon as possible. I've arranged a shuttle. Once there I'd like you to confirm his identity and possibly take up escort duty.' Orders, mitigated by a gentler smile. 'I hope you don't mind?'

The new *Defiant*? 'No of course not, sir.' Who cared what for, though she was dying to get some answers. 'Where is she?' Because according to a fast check, *Defiant* had been off scan for several days.

'I'll leave Jon to fill you in, if I may.'

'Yes sir, thank you.' Well at least she'd get to see the Arc, however briefly.

+++

Harp was still strapped in. Still onboard *Raptor*? Was *Defiant* still fighting that red? Were Del and Yentl OK? 'Yentl?'

'Ah, there you are. How're you feeling?' Not Yentl, female. 'Mac?'

The hand on his forehead made him jerk. Calm down, only brushing his hair back. He should probably open his eyes.

'Something for the pain?' Mac turned away, reaching.

'Nah.' Though it did hurt to talk.

Maybe it sounded like it cos the arm came back and offered him a beaker. 'Water?'

He couldn't lift his head, embarrassing, but she dealt – enough he could hit the spigot. Who knew drinking was so tiring. 'Thanks.'

'No problem. There's a queue of people. You up for visitors?'

'No.'

Maybe not the best response; Mac chuckled. 'Take it easy, there's plenty of time.'

Crip. 'How long…?'

'Since they got you out? Two days. You all caused quite a panic.'

'Del? Yentl?'

'Both OK. A bit battered, but you brought them home.'

He did? All right then, he could go back to sleep.

+++

The next time he woke Del was there instead. 'Hello, hero.'

Harp winced, but Del looked pretty good for someone with his arm strapped. Harp pushed up, a struggle but he got there. All right, Del helped him, raising up the Sick Bay cot behind him. 'Just the arm? Nothing else?' Some pilots had the luck of the devil. When he'd sworn on *Raptor's* com, then fallen silent…

'Yeah, pretty much, kid. Just enough I came out walking wounded, so the ladies love me even more now.'

Del settled back into the chair beside him.

'What exactly happened? You shouted.'

'Something shorted my main boards. Lucky for me I only had one hand on it at the time, eh?' Did he look paler for a moment? 'Burned the hell out of my arm, but the regen tank put everything back to rights. I'll be good as new once the new skin toughens up.' He shrugged. 'I guess I passed out, though. Sorry I left you to do all the work.'

Harp hitched the cover smoother. 'Nah, it was pretty much all over by then anyway.'

Del broke the silence. 'They tell me they're moving you, somewhere quieter.'

'Not J20?' Quieter would be nice – away from all the beeping – but Harp wasn't sure about the rest.

'No. This time they can admit you're a hero, even if they're not giving out details. There's orders to keep you safe, word is they came from World, so the top brass must have been briefed, and the marines have two guards outside round the clock'. Del grinned again. 'Protective custody's the only thing keeping the lines of wellwishers out of here. If I wasn't wounded I'd be jealous, but for now "wounded and available" is trumping "pretty boy banned visitors".'

'I'm not...' Harp stopped himself rising to the bait.

'And now I can tell the rest of the team you're back. Is there anything you want?' There wasn't. They shifted to talking about what music he had loaded, what manuals he was trying to stay awake for. Del programmed a selection of stuff he'd never learned into the screen above the bed, then stood.

'You're falling asleep so I'll be off. But thanks, kid, you brought us home, and almost in one piece. If they don't give you a medal this time, I'll eat *Raptor*.'

'Oh yeah, sure. Not happening.' He felt the faint twinge meant his bed was dosing him, again. Del's face grew fuzzy at the edges. Crip, he hated being helpless.

Still, the bastard with a medal, that was almost funny. Not that it would happen if the navy wanted him kept secret like the colonel reckoned, but he guessed it balanced…

+++

The next few days were still a bit of a blur, but this time when he woke they'd dimmed the lights so it was probably first watch. Not dim enough though he couldn't see he was in a single berth, not Sick Bay. Unless they had a lux version hidden away. This place was still stacked with med tech but it didn't look like it belonged. He recalled Del talking about them moving him somewhere quieter. And about being in protective custody, as if he needed that on *Defiant*. Hold on, was he still aboard *Defiant*? And what exactly did they mean by 'custody'? His brain woke up and started asking urgent questions.

Then he panicked anyway. There was a figure, female, in the fancy armchair by the fancy desk across the fancy cushioned flooring, and the screen was raised up from the desk, and in its glow he recognised some very telltale features. Crip, a real-Harpan, here?

He must have moved or something cos she turned her head then rose and walked toward him; several paces, cos this cabin was that big. 'Hello, Sergeant. How are you feeling?'

'Uh.' Harp could only stare.

'Want anything?'

Say something, fool. He pushed up. 'Er, water, please?' And time to think.

Water it was. She even raised the bed like in Sick Bay and let him hold the beaker once she knew he'd got a grip. It was all very polite, and embarrassing. Awkward as hell. And there was no way he was talking first. But she did. 'I'm Emika. You might not remember but we met once before. Back on World.'

That exact real-Harpan. When he was trying to find the way. She was in uniform again, the Hs marking her another captain. His superior in every way. Why was she here? Where *was* here? 'Ma'am, is this *Defiant*?'

Her mouth curved upward. 'Yes, Sergeant. You didn't know? You're in the VIP suite. Fleet ships keep one handy for visiting brass. They figured you deserved it.'

'Oh. That's... nice of them.' Whoever they were. He wasn't sure he liked it. 'Er, thankyou, Ma'am. When am I cleared to go back to J20?'

'Ah, I don't think you should expect that any time soon, though if you feel up to it you're invited to join the debriefing.'

Yes. Please. 'When, Ma'am?'

'I'll let them know you're available, shall I?'

'I guess.' Alarms were going off inside Harp's head. When he was "available"? And a real-Harpan acting like she had nothing better to do than organise him? 'Sorry, I mean thank you, Ma'am. I'm ready whenever.'

She tapped a pricey looking wristcom – not a navy issue? – exchanged some words then cut the call off. 'There. In case you're wondering it's the middle of first right now. Your team is back on their normal schedule so they'll be asleep, but we've set up the debrief for second watch.'

He'd been right about the time, and the rest of the Hawks had gone back to their old timetable now they were stood down. But he'd get to see them in a few more hours. 'Thank you, Ma'am.'

'Call me Emika.'

'Ma'am, that's not... You're...' Dodge the bigger truth. 'A captain, Ma'am.'

'We're not on duty, are we?'

Aren't you? 'No, Ma'am, but...'

'Hmm. OK, I'll let you off for now, though I don't think my rank will be a problem much longer. Now, how about something to eat?'

He *was* hungry. As Del said, it was his default. Mac reckoned he burned calories like no one she'd ever seen and he suspected he ate more the older he got. But it would give him something to do that wasn't talking. The idea of this woman getting him food didn't sit easy, but on the other hand she'd only need to give an order, while right now talking to her felt too big a challenge.

Once an orderly turned up with a tray she went to do whatever captains did and left him in peace. The same orderly came back for the dishes and stayed long enough to help him get dressed. Negotiating the head left him more drained than expected but the food, and a seriously decadent, very roomy shower, handily equipped with crash-bars, left him more awake than he had felt in days, and keen to see everyone. Maybe he'd been feeling left out. They'd all been back on duty, with things to do, he was idle.

He'd started to wonder if this protective custody thing had anything to do with their absence. He'd worried for a while, cos the folk he did see didn't talk much, but no one seemed to know he'd hijacked *Raptor*, and he really couldn't see a real-Harpan smiling at him if they did, so maybe, hopefully?

In navy pants and tee, he suffered being in a hoverchair down to K deck; getting dressed had proved how feeble he still was and while his leg was practically healed – regen? – it did ache some. Even if he wasn't going to admit it.

Two marines escorted him, not Ham, so the protective thing was still in force, though he'd got so used to having Ham around it felt quite normal for a moment. When he laughed the escorts' faces didn't alter and he wondered what outrageous thing he'd have to do to get a genuine reaction – till he warned himself he wasn't Del and should have better manners.

Early signs told him he'd been quartered on G deck, not far from the bridge. Definite officer country as Emika – the captain – had said. Thankfully there weren't any in sight right now and they dropped to K via a shiny service chute with a solid floor, presumably to coddle the invalid. Harp promised himself he'd start exercising as soon as this debrief was over. He'd never been ill for long before and he didn't like it.

K7. More marines, for once not asking for ID. The ones with him followed him inside. The classroom was pretty crowded today, both teams, a slew of techs and medics and a solid wall of officers-across-the-back, including one real-Harpan captain. And they'd all stopped talking when he entered. Crip.

Then they stood up, and nodded, very formal.

38

Embarrassing wasn't the word. Harp clutched the chair's arms. Mac came to his rescue, bless her. 'Let's get you over with the rest, eh?'

'Please. Hi guys.' A general meeting of palms – off-duty-welcome, hands not heads – as Hawks then Falcons met him, smiling; though perhaps the Falcons were a little cautious. Did they think he'd act big headed now or something? Grinning at them seemed to make things better so perhaps they were unsettled round the hover. Yeah, the sooner he got rid of that the better.

Ngow and the XO ran the debrief, which lasted two food deliveries. Next surprise, the XO congratulated him on his recovery, and called him captain.

'Your performance, before and under fire, has been exemplary, your crew confirmed your bravery. Your worlds are grateful, Captain.' Like she had rehearsed it, like the solemn nod was something special.

She obviously saw his shock. 'Your captaincy has of course been back-dated.' It had? And why "of course"? 'I'm told you're on leave once we reach World, but if there's anything you need onboard, ask.' There was a bit more stuff along the same lines. He had a physio schedule. His gear was being transferred.

That got through. 'I'm not going back to J20, at all?'

'No ser, that wouldn't be appropriate.'

'Ma'am.' He could hardly argue with his XO, but why the hell not?

Some of the debrief was solo, some as a team. Everyone was still extra polite, kept calling him "ser" like a real officer. Even Del's ribbing felt subdued, but that would be because of Ngow and the other highups.

In the solo time they took him through it all again, from launch to shutdown, trying to match his memories with *Raptor*'s. Most importantly they didn't argue when he said that it was Del who'd spun the ship so that the final blast had hit its flank. Far better if they thought so.

Besides, according to Harp's latest reading – being stuck on G with nothing but screen time had its benefits – people often couldn't recall moments before they lost consciousness, so even if Del said he hadn't there was still ample room for doubt. Wasn't there?

Evidently there was, cos they seemed to accept his version, listened to his praise of Del and Yentl, thanked him again for doing his job and finally let him go. This time real-Harpan Emika joined his marines for the walk back. The rest of his team had already been dismissed. He'd wanted downtime with the Hawks but no one had suggested it, and truth be told he was a little tired, again. A nuisance; maybe later.

The marines stopped outside his new door panel. Real-Harpan came in. 'Would you rather stay put or go back to bed?'

Did he look that bad? 'No, I'm OK, thank you, Ma'am.' Undressing was going to be a chore, one he wasn't suffering in front of her.

'It's Emika, remember? Now we're both off duty?' She did something to his chair; the whole thing sort of semi reclined. 'That better?' as she walked around to face him.

'Yeah. Yes. Look, I… it still wouldn't feel right, Ma'am, you being a Harpan and all.'

Her eyebrows rose. 'Me being… No one's told you?'

'Ma'am?'

'They ran the final tests while you were out.'

Harp's traitor-blood ran colder.

'I can get you the reports if you like. I haven't been up here till now so I assumed… OK.' She pulled the fancy armchair round to face him, sat and looked him in the eyes. 'This may come as a shock then, though it shouldn't.'

'Ma'am?' They'd found out he wasn't right. That explained the marine presence, the "custody". But not the captaincy, nor why she was in here with him, without protection.

'Harpan isn't your given name, it's your *House* name. You *are* a Harpan. Crip, are you all right?'

He must have heard wrong. 'But, the tests.'

'The tests just proved it. You're a perfect match.' She said the last part slower, like she thought he didn't understand it was important.

Which – obviously – it was. Cos... 'I have the same kind of blood as you?'

'A pure strain, I'm told. Direct line. We sometimes call that Inner Family.' She watched him swallow, looked more sympathetic. 'There's more, if you're ready to hear it, but if not it can wait.'

'No.' That took another swallow. 'I think I'd better hear whatever you have, if that's OK with you, Ma'am.'

'Try Emika, now you know we're cousins?'

Cousins. 'Emika, OK. You're sure?'

'That you should call me Emika, or you're a cousin? That's an affirmative on both counts, Captain.' She smiled sweetly. 'Need some caffee?'

When he nodded, words beyond him, she produced two steaming beakers from a tiny autochef he hadn't even spotted. 'Here, drink it. Ready for the rest? I don't know everything. I gather the reports were sealed for years, and I think the Family are still piecing some of it together. But I can give you the main points, OK?' She waited till he nodded. 'Your true identity is almost certainly Maxil Xen Harpan the Sixth. Bit of a mouthful? We tend to double names, like I'm really Emika Mai. With one to honour our beginnings. You're named after your Grandfather Maxil, and then back to the first Founder's second husband.'

'Not...?'

'Our current Founder is your grandfather. And I think maybe you'll do better with something stronger than caffee, before we go any further.' She strode across the cabin to the same dispenser. 'Mooner whiskey do you, it's the strongest thing on offer?'

'Yeah, whatever.' The liquor burned away some of the haze. 'You said *almost* certainly.'

'Yes, but that's Security, it doesn't look like there's any real doubt. I think Harpan DNA has always been unique, but you have to have known. How in all space did you manage to hide it so long?'

Unique. All the real-Harpans had whatever weirdness he did? If he hadn't wished it out of sight, for all these years… he'd still have ended up on Moon. 'So, I have Harpan blood, but not real, I mean, not legitimate.' Better to be honest.

'Not? Space, no, you're as Harpan as I am, maybe more.'

Harp was reeling, but. 'Then why send me to Moon?'

'We didn't.' She scowled, which didn't suit the heart-shaped face. 'It's a bit of Family history I've only just been told myself – one of ours being abducted as a child. I'm reading between the lines a bit here, but there was a ransom demand, and your grandfather was preparing payment, though that was kept quiet for obvious reasons, and knowing him I'm sure he was planning more than paying up. But then the final instructions never arrived, so the Family machine kicked into action, military and civilian, scouring World.'

Harp thought that through. 'They didn't search Moon?'

'For whatever reason they were convinced you were still on World. I think they closed the ports, searched outgoing ships and the like. Apparently they did flag any reference to incidents involving toddlers across both planets, probably more to avoid it looking strange than anything else, but if the crash was reported perhaps it wasn't flagged as relevant…'

Harp frowned. The crash. The fire. All the dead. 'But, if…'

'I'm afraid your great grandfather, the then-Founder, died about then too. I'm told the fanciful at the time put it down to losing you. Your grandfather succeeded at once, but between you and I, I suspect his predecessor wasn't entirely up to date, shall we say, toward the end, so Ser Maxil might have been a bit overworked. If word came of the crashed ship on Moon it would have said they found a very young body, badly burned, but Security was looking for a two year old and the only reported survivor was four, on record as Mooner, with parents. It's not that unreasonable everyone concerned thought the subject was closed. It probably never occurred to anyone that a Harpan-raised two year old might have looked like a Moon-raised four year old. Maybe you can find out more when you get home. But all that time.' Emika shook her head. 'We've always been careless where Moon was concerned. I suspect we didn't think their growing lack of proper records was important because the Family was never based there, and it was the Family's DNA we thought important. Now we're paying for it. Ser Maxil – senior – is having all their protocols reviewed as we speak, insisting on them being the same as World's. If we could lose one of our own to slipshod record keeping, who knows what else has gone awry. I'd no idea the other planet was so...' She stopped talking.

'Backward? You can say it.' OK, so Harp was reeling, but if ever it was time to speak out. 'Moon *isn't* World, but it's a good place. Or it was, before the drought. Now folks are starving.'

If he really was a real-Harpan, maybe somebody would listen?

An hour later Emika was still asking questions, and he'd caught on; she was recording every word. And gone from shocked to angry.

'I'm sure neither Ser Maxil nor Ser Feldin, that's your uncle, knew it was that bad, not till the pirate attack. Perhaps whoever reported didn't make the right connections; they're usually meticulous about being up to date so they'll be as shocked as I am. *I* hadn't heard anything, but that's probably because the navy who dock at that Orbital now don't normally visit the surface, and I'm sorry to say I doubt we mix much on the Orbital either. Oh, it's so stupid. If we weren't so big-headed about being Worlders – there should never have been a difference in the way we saw each other. I'd heard Uncle Feldin was looking at helping Mooners more lately, but I hadn't realised that wasn't just about the pirates. And you really need to rest, you look exhausted. I'll call the orderly, then I'm going to pass all this on to them, all right?'

Harp let it go. It sounded like she believed what she'd said, though he couldn't see it himself; how could these Harpans *not* get to hear what things were really like?

The panel slid aside a moment later on the first orderly. He'd acquired three, one for each watch. Emika – Cousin Emika – he was almost starting to believe, left them to it. The man helped him into bed, got him a water jug, dimmed the lights – and left him mulling over Harpan secrets that it looked like he was part of. Right there in the centre. Inner Family, she'd said. And real.

He tried to imagine. There'd have been no public announcement of his disappearance, nor assumed death, so no word would have been shared on Moon. No, the Founding Family wouldn't want it spread about, for fear of it repeating. They'd covered it up well enough even Emika hadn't known. Maybe his great grandfather, oh boy, had planned to track the kidnappers once the child – him – was found, but then he never had been. Instead the kidnappers had managed to evade the searches, space knew how or why, to crash onto a Mooner homestead. And he'd been the sole survivor. And he must be two years younger than he thought? That felt like the last straw.

Harp stared at the dim grey ceiling. The child he'd thought he was must have died in the crash. Was that homestead the kidnappers' destination, or had they been on the way to somewhere else? And if everyone else died that night, in the ship and on the ground, how the stars had *he* survived when no one else had? Would he ever know the answers to those questions? Maybe now it sounded like he had the Founding Family behind him. Only they might not find it as immediate as he did; more like dead and buried. Like that child. Best forgotten.

It was all brand new to him though. Maxil. Xen. Harpan. The sixth? Real-Harpan. And you're only twenty? Still nineteen? You don't even know your birthday. And the vaccing Founder is your grandfather? Nah, you'll wake up in a minute. But maybe it felt scary-good, for now, to think he had relations. Even if it wouldn't last long once they met him.

EPILOGUE

This was one dream he couldn't seem to wake from. There was some debate but he stayed a captain, even though officially he wasn't old enough to enlist. So his new ident said Captain Maxil Xen Harpan. With those all-important last two letters. He stayed in the VIP cabin, ate dinner with *Defiant*'s execs. And with Cousin Emika, who was trying to ease him into what being a Harpan was all about, and trying not to scare him. Fat chance.

The XO and the colonel had given him a private debrief on the pirate operation too. Him being Harpan now apparently entitled him to stuff like that, even to being cleared to see that old, damning report of the crash that changed his life. Him; not his superiors. If that didn't prove...

Said briefing had lasted several hours cos they'd gone right back to Worlds' early years, then fast-forwarded to the present. The good news: it looked like the pirates' incursion into this sector of space had been repulsed, or at least drastically reduced. So much so that neighbouring, more significant Kraic sectors were suddenly sending messages of friendship, even admiration. Ngow had looked understandably smug, and even Harp could see it was a political sort of coup.

The bad news: the pirate he'd named Throat, now identified as one Argon Zorr, might have escaped yet again. And so had Regis. Disappeared. Presumably he'd thrown in with the missing pirates. Space knew how Regis dodged surveillance. There was some suspicion he'd had help from Worlder relatives but not, as yet, the evidence to prove it.

Harp had supplied descriptions of the other pirates he'd seen, but Ngow had no further data there; they'd either been killed on *Bounty,* fried in the battle, or they'd escaped with Zorr. Ngow thought they'd fried. Harp hoped so, but this Zorr was clearly a survivor – hey, it took one to know one, right? He'd already dodged arrest on *Bounty.*

On the bright side, apparently the Harpan name was now exceedingly popular in those neighbour regions of space. There was talk that diplomatic ties were getting stronger, with resulting benefits for World – and Mooners too cos Moon was marginally closer to the Kraic – and the only jump-point out of 'local' space, producing credit that could help rebuild the pirate damage and adapt to what they said might stay a seriously hotter climate.

Cousin Emika said the Founder couldn't wait to meet his long-lost grandson.

Harp figured it was good one of them was eager, *Defiant* being on approach to World now, and him being 'fitted' for a brand new uniform for the occasion; specially tailored. Harpans didn't wear "off the rack". Harpans didn't often spend their off-hours drinking with lowlier ranks or medical orderlies either, except this one did, and had. He'd even spent an hour with Ham and Hendriks, catching up. He really hoped he wouldn't lose that friendship cos he had the sinking feeling he was going to have to adjust to a lot more than a new name. The thought of leaving the ship had become as daunting as once the thought of arriving was.

But then, that was about par for his whole existence so far, wasn't it? Every few years his life switched tracks on him. New places, new people. Even the new name fit that pattern. If that wasn't ironic nothing was. So he'd just have to man up and do it all again. He'd survived all his other lives. This one wouldn't be any worse, just different. OK, a lot different, but who knew, it might even be better.

Why did he not believe that?

Elsewhen Press

delivering outstanding new talents in speculative fiction

Visit the Elsewhen Press website at elsewhen.press for the latest information on all of our titles, authors and events; to read our blog; find out where to buy our books and ebooks; or to place an order.

Sign up for the Elsewhen Press InFlight Newsletter at
elsewhen.press/newsletter

UNDERSIDE series

Space opera meets gangland thriller

ZOË SUMRA

BOOK 1

SAILOR TO A SIREN

"If you like your space opera fast and violent, this book is for you"
– Jaine Fenn

When Connor and Logan Cardwain, a gangster's lieutenants, steal a shipment of high-grade narcotics on the orders of their boss, Connor dreams of diverting the profits and setting up in business for himself. His plans encounter a hurdle in the form of Éloise Falavière, Logan's former girlfriend, who has been hired by an interplanetary police force's vice squad.

Logan wants a family; Éloise wants to stop the drugs shipment from being sent to her home planet; Connor wants to gain independence without angering his boss. All of their plans are derailed, though, when they discover that the shipment was hiding a much deadlier secret – the prototype of a tiny superweapon powerful enough to destabilise galactic peace.

Crime lords, corrupt officials and interstellar magicians soon begin pursuing them, and Connor, Logan and Éloise realise they have to identify and confront the superweapon's smuggler in order to survive. But, when one by one their friends begin to betray them, their self-imposed mission transforms from difficult to near-impossible.

ISBN: 9781908168771 (epub, kindle) / 9781908168672 (288pp paperback)

BOOK 2

THE WAGES OF SIN

One young woman dies and another vanishes on the same chilly spring night. Connor Cardwain sees no reason to link his cleaner Merissa's murder to a mystery anchored within a high-end warship sales team, but reconsiders his position when he realises both women were connected to a foreign runaway.

Armed with an enterprising widow, an imperial spy and his own wits, Connor sets out to find the missing woman, in a city streaked with vice and a planet upturned by other ganglanders' ambition. If he fails to beat arms dealers, aristocrats, pirates and human traffickers at their own game, he and all his team will pay the price – and the wages of sin are death.

ISBN: 9781911409052 (epub, kindle) / 9781911409151 (312pp paperback)

Visit bit.ly/Underside

Gardens of Earth
Book I of The Sundering Chronicles

Mark Iles

Imagine an alien life force that knows your deepest fear, and can use that against you.

Corporate greed supported by incompetent surveyors leads to the colonisation of a distant world, ominously dubbed 'Halloween', that turns out not to be uninhabited after all. The aliens, soon called Spooks by military units deployed to protect the colonists, can adopt the physical form of an opponent's deepest fear and then use it to kill them. The colony is massacred and as retaliation the orbiting human navy nuke the planet. In revenge, the Spooks invade Earth.

In a last-minute attempt to avert the war, Seethan Bodell, a marine combat pilot sent home from the front with PTSD, is given a top-secret research spacecraft, and a mission to travel into the past along with his co-pilot and secret lover Rose, to prevent the original landing on Halloween and stop the war from ever happening. But the mission goes wrong, causing a tragedy later known as The Sundering, decimating the world and tearing reality, while Seethan's ship is flung into the future. The Spooks win the war and claim ownership of Earth. He wakes, alone, in his ejector seat with no sign of either Rose or his vessel. When he realises that his technology no longer works, his desperation to find Rose becomes all the more urgent – her android body won't survive long in this new Earth.

Gardens of Earth is the first book of *The Sundering Chronicles*. The story tackles alien war, a future that may be considered either dystopian or utopian, depending on who you ask, and a protagonist coping with his demons in an unfamiliar and stressful environment – not to mention immediate threats from a pathological serial killer, the remnants of Earth's inhabitants now living in a sparse pre-industrial society under the watchful eye of the Spooks, and returning human colonists intent on reclaiming Earth. Underlying all this are issues of social justice, human and android rights, and love that transcends difference. In many senses this is classic science fiction, but the abilities of the Spooks provide an environment, and archetypal creatures within it, that are reminiscent of myth and magic fantasy. Truly cross-genre, *Gardens of Earth* is an exciting adventure, a heart-rending quest, and an eye-opening insight into the coping strategies of a veteran.

ISBN: 9781911409953 (epub, kindle) / 9781911409854 (264pp paperback)

Visit bit.ly/GardensOfEarth

INTERFERENCE

Terry Grimwood

The grubby dance of politics didn't end when we left the solar system, it followed us to the stars

The god-like Iaens are infinitely more advanced than humankind, so why have they requested military assistance in a conflict they can surely win unaided?

Torstein Danielson, Secretary for Interplanetary Affairs, is on a fact-finding mission to their home planet and headed straight into the heart of a war-zone. With him, onboard the Starship *Kissinger*, is a detachment of marines for protection, an embedded pack of sycophantic journalists who are not expected to cause trouble, and reporter Katherina Molale, who most certainly will and is never afraid to dig for the truth.

Torstein wants this mission over as quickly as possible. His daughter is terminally ill, his marriage in tatters. But then the Iaens offer a gift in return for military intervention and suddenly the stakes, both for humanity as a race and for Torstein personally, are very high indeed.

Suffolk born and proud of it, Terry Grimwood is the author of a handful of novels and novellas, including *Deadside Revolution*, the science fiction-flavoured political thriller *Bloody War* and *Joe* which was inspired by true events. His short stories have appeared in numerous magazines and anthologies and have been gathered into three collections, *The Exaggerated Man*, *There Is A Way To Live Forever* and *Affairs of a Cardio-Vascular Nature*. Terry has also written and Directed three plays as well as co-written engineering textbooks for Pearson Educational Press. He plays the harmonica and with a little persuasion (not much persuasion, actually) will growl a song into a microphone. By day he teaches electrical installation at a further education college. He is married to Debra, the love of his life.

ISBN: 9781911409960 (epub, kindle) / 9781911409861 (96pp paperback)

Visit bit.ly/Interference-Grimwood

GALAXIES AND FANTASIES

A Collection of Rather Amazing and Wide-ranging Short Stories

ANDY MCKELL

Prepare for the unexpected

Galaxies and Fantasies is an eclectic collection of tales from master-storyteller Andy McKell, crossing genres from mythology to cosmology, fairytale to space opera, surrealism to hyper-reality. What they all have in common is a twist, a surprise, a revelation. Leave your pre-conceptions aside when you read these stories, prepare for the unexpected, the extraordinary, the unpredictable. Some are quite succinct and you'll be immediately wanting more; others are more elaborate, but deftly devised, and you'll be thinking about them long after you've finished reading. These are stories that will stay with you, not in a haunting way, but like a satisfying memory that often returns to encourage, enchant or enrich your life.

ISBN: 9781915304162 (epub, kindle) / 97819153041063 (186pp paperback)

Visit bit.ly/GalaxiesAndFantasies

Stray Pilot

Douglas Thompson

A passionate environmental allegory

Thomas Tellman, an RAF pilot who disappeared pursuing a UFO in 1948, unexpectedly returns entirely un-aged to a small town on Scotland's north-east coast. He finds that his 7-year-old daughter is now a bed-bound 87-year-old woman suffering from dementia. She greets him as her father but others assume she is deluded and that Thomas is an unhinged impostor or con man. While Thomas endeavours to blend in to an ordinary life, his presence gradually sets off unpredictable consequences, locally, nationally and globally. Members of the British Intelligence Services attempt to discredit Thomas in advance of what they anticipate will be his public disclosure of evidence of extra-terrestrial activity, but the local community protect him. Thomas, appalled by the increase in environmental damage that has occurred in his 80 year absence, appears to have returned with a mission: whose true nature he guards from everyone around him.

Douglas Thompson's thought-provoking novel is unashamedly science-fiction yet firmly in the tradition of literary explorations of the experience of the outsider. He weaves together themes of memory loss and dementia, alienation, and spiritual respect for the natural world; while at the same time counterposing the humanity inherent in close communities against the xenophobia and nihilistic materialism of contemporary urban society. Of all the book's vivid characters, the fictional village of Kinburgh itself is the stand-out star: an archetypal symbol of human community. In an age of growing despair in the face of climate crises, *Stray Pilot* offers a passionate environmental allegory with a positive message of constructive hope: a love song to all that is best in ordinary people.

ISBN: 9781915304131(epub, kindle) / 97819153041032 (264pp paperback)

Visit bit.ly/StrayPilot

GENESIS
GEOFFREY CARR

A conjunction of AI, the Cloud, & interplanetary ambition…

Hidden somewhere, deep in the Cloud, something is collating information. It reads everything, it learns, it watches. And it plans.

Around the world, researchers, engineers and entrepreneurs are being killed in a string of apparently unrelated accidents. But when intelligence-agency analysts spot a pattern they struggle to find the culprit, blocked at every step – by reluctant allies and scheming enemies.

Meanwhile a multi-billionaire inventor and forward-thinker is working hard to realise his dream, and trying to keep it hidden from everyone – one government investigating him, and another helping him. But deep in the Cloud something is watching him, too.

And deep in the Cloud, it plans.

What could possibly go wrong?

Geoff is the Science and Technology Editor of *The Economist*. His professional interests include evolutionary biology, genetic engineering, the fight against AIDS and other widespread infectious diseases, the development of new energy technologies, and planetology. His personal interests include using total eclipses of the sun as an excuse to visit weird parts of the world (Antarctica, Easter Island, Amasya, the Nullarbor Plain), and watching swifts hunting insects over his garden of a summer's evening, preferably with a glass of Cynar in hand.

As someone who loathed English lessons at school, he says he is frequently astonished that he now earns his living by writing. "That I have written a novel, albeit a technothriller rather than anything with fancy literary pretensions, astonishes me even more, since what drew me into writing in the first place was describing reality, not figments of the imagination. On the other hand, perhaps describing reality is what fiction is actually for."

ISBN: 9781911409519 (epub, kindle) / 9781911409410 (288pp paperback)

Visit bit.ly/GC_Genesis

ABOUT TERRY JACKMAN

Terry Jackman is a mild-mannered married lady who lives in a quiet corner of the northwest of England, a little south of Manchester. Well, that's one version.

The other one may be a surprise to those who only know the first. [She doesn't necessarily tell everything.] Apart from once being the most qualified professional picture framer in the world, which accounted for over ten years of articles, guest appearances, seminars, study guides and exam papers both written and marked, she chaired a national committee for the Fine Art Trade Guild, and read 'slush' for the *Albedo One* SF magazine in Ireland. Currently she is the coordinator of all the British Science Fiction Association's writers' groups, called Orbits, and a freelance editor. [She's also been living with cancer since 2011, and hasn't always shared that titbit either].

She knows she wrote her first story in infant school, but only remembers because of the harrowing experience of having to read it out to the class. Maybe that's why it took a considerable time and a lot of encouragement to get her to do anything like that again, not to mention choosing a nice, safe distance away in the USA, even if it did earn her five-star reviews. But now she's finally 'out' in the UK.

Printed in Great Britain
by Amazon

15732447R10185